NEW STORIES
FROM THE SOUTH

The Year's Best, 2004

The editor wishes to thank Kathy Pories, Brunson Hoole, Dana Stamey, and Anne Winslow, colleagues whose talent, skill, patience, and tact are essential to this anthology.

She is also most grateful to the many journals and magazines that, year after year, provide the anthology with complimentary subscriptions.

PUBLISHER'S NOTE
The stories reprinted in *New Stories from the South: The Year's Best, 2004* were selected from American short stories published in magazines issued between January and December 2003. Shannon Ravenel annually consults a list of about one hundred nationally distributed American periodicals and makes her choices for this anthology based on criteria that include original publication first-serially in magazine form and publication as short stories. Direct submissions are not considered.

Edited by
Shannon Ravenel

with a preface by Tim Gautreaux

NEW STORIES
FROM THE SOUTH

The Year's Best, 2004

Algonquin Books of Chapel Hill

Published by
ALGONQUIN BOOKS OF CHAPEL HILL
Post Office Box 2225
Chapel Hill, North Carolina 27515-2225

a division of
WORKMAN PUBLISHING
708 Broadway
New York, New York 10003

ISSN 0897-9073
ISBN 1-56512-432-4

CONTENTS

Tim Gautreaux

PREFACE:
WARTS AND ALL

I've been reading *New Stories from the South* for most of its nineteen years, and in the early days I expected the emergence of a nationally acclaimed competitor, perhaps a *New Stories from the West* series, or *New Stories from New England*. A wag friend suggested that such a Balkanization of the short story would eventually lead to the publication of something like *New Stories from the Amish,* but at any rate, no major regional rival ever came about, and I was left asking why *New Stories from the South* grew into the country's premiere showcase of short stories birthed in a particular area of the country. I also began to wonder why the American South is an important source of short fiction of distinctive literary quality.

Some people say it's because much of the region's population has been undereducated and poverty-stricken and thus the Southern writer's neighbors are always doing amusingly desperate, picturesque, and depraved things. Outlanders point out that many Southerners live isolated in tiny, inbred hamlets, and that the climate is also depraved. Nobody wants to admit the Civil War is over. Southern fictional characters supposedly live with odd religion, unhealthy food, ugly dogs, lots of guns, free-floating outrage, and cockleburs on their socks. But while this clichéd list of regional warts might explain a few interesting police reports in the local papers, nothing in the tally accounts for the imposing presence and popularity of Southern fiction.

There's an item that ought to be on the list that would explain everything: Southern storytellers seem to love where they are from, warts included. In even the saddest of stories I can sense this love in the spaces between the words. I can hear it in the telephoned voices of friends who have moved North or West. As of yet, I haven't met an expatriate Southern writer who doesn't daydream about moving back. I don't know what's missing, what loved thing can't be found in other parts. It might be the language, which is decidedly nonstandard, inventive, and ear-catching. For example, I walked into a grocery store in Ponchatoula, Louisiana, some time ago and saw a pyramid of Creole tomatoes standing next to the register. I asked if they had any taste to them, and the lady behind the counter said, "Oh, yeah, they *eat* real good." Or, it might be the religion, which is everywhere in the South from crucifixes in Bayou bar rooms, to Biblical exhortations painted on roadside boulders, religion hymning from televisions and radios, plentiful as tap water, soulful as the eyes of Mormon and Jehovah's Witness missionaries struggling up my driveway in the summer afternoons, half-crucified by the heat. It might be the awful weather which, though hot, will not blacken the skin like frostbite, and though miserably humid reminds us that not one Southerner to date has mildewed to death. It might be Carolina barbecue, Mississippi fried dill pickles, crawfish étouffée, Virginia ham, trays of hot, sweet cornbread ironed over with a block of butter.

And maybe some of that love is because of the meanness, too, because writers in the South have at least a bystander's notion of stolen rights, bad governance, and paternalistic manipulation by people with money or control of the land. In some of the darkest stories the writer understands the reasons behind the misery-inducing ignorance and violent natures of the characters, reasons political as well as spiritual, that go back historically to two things: that the South was founded on the notion that the man who owned the plantation was by blood better than the man, black or white, who grew his crops, the most un-American notion there is — and two, though it's easy for someone to be religious if he owns nothing to distract him from his beliefs, a life showing no profit for body or mind turns to vengeance more than it patiently endures wrongs. Such patience was for residents of the North, Midwest, and West, who could better afford to support their families and who endured wrongs of a smaller sort. Southern writers who know their history love to write about characters who suffer through, and they at least understand the mean ones wrecked by inherited or self-made misery.

Southern storytellers do love their cities, their places. Back through eighteen issues of *New Stories from the South* most tales begin with mention of Charlotte, New Orleans, the asylum at Dix Hill, a Biloxi supermarket, a beach in Texas, Grand Crapaud, Nickeltown, or places in the Everglades or along the Intracoastal Canal that never had a name, just a sprinkle of folks glad there's something good to eat and no snow on the ground at all. Whether a real place or made up, there seems to be a fine wry edge to locations where even the dark tales are lined with some unresurrected wit, where we find even O'Connor's murdering Misfit and Faulkner's Abner Snopes a little bit funny. I noticed the Southern writer's love of humor a long time ago when reading Sinclair Lewis and Erskine Caldwell at the same time. Gopher Prairie was plain depressing, merely ordinary, whereas one of Caldwell's murderous hamlets where the town butcher napped with a hunk of bloody roast under his head was nauseatingly hilarious. The scene smacked of life descended through a damned sordid history and reminded me of how many storytellers operating below the frost belt use humor as an anesthetic, or at least as a crazy distraction, sort of like refreshments served at an execution.

Southern writers love the short story form, too. Maybe this springs from the fact that Southerners like to talk so much and no two or three can sit at table long before some sort of liar's competition breaks out, generally involving animals or machinery. Talked-out tales are short, of course, self-contained, plotted even, like one I overheard in an airport where a Tennessee farmer was telling about how he took pictures of his cows' udders with his cell phone and e-mailed them to a veterinarian a thousand miles away who'd sold him a bag balm that wasn't clearing up an inflammation. Then there was the time I was sharing a meal with some writers from a very Northern state, my stomach comforted by the bland food, the folks at table intelligent and kind as could be, but there were actual silences in the conversation, kind of relaxing and respectful, really. The writers were talking about all sorts of things, how hard it was to teach writing, for example, but nobody told a story beginning "One time I taught this deaf student how to hear train whistles . . ." or "I had a great uncle who owned a Chihuahua that was an alcoholic . . ." I couldn't imagine a pause in conversation at a meal with Southern writers, who generally see storytelling as an Olympic competition, indeed life itself as a sequence of short narratives stitched together with the mantra "Hey, that reminds me of . . ."

Sometimes, Southern story writers reveal an embedded, complex need to communicate something they love, or something they wished they loved, or something they could've loved if they'd ever had it. Sometimes. You could read the stories in this book and find out for sure.

———————————

Tim Gautreaux is the author of two collections of stories, *Same Place, Same Things* and *Welding with Children*, and two novels, *The Next Step in the Dance* and, most recently, *The Clearing*. His short stories have appeared in many magazines and journals, including *The Atlantic Monthly*, *Harper's*, *GQ*, and *Zoetrope*. Just retired from thirty years teaching fiction writing at Southeastern Louisiana University, he lives in Hammond, Louisiana.

NEW STORIES
FROM THE SOUTH
The Year's Best, 2004

Edward P. Jones

A RICH MAN

(from *The New Yorker*)

Horace and Loneese Perkins—one child, one grandchild—lived most unhappily together for more than twelve years in Apartment 230 at Sunset House, a building for senior citizens at 1202 Thirteenth Street NW. They moved there in 1977, the year they celebrated forty years of marriage, the year they made love for the last time—Loneese kept a diary of sorts, and that fact was noted on one day of a week when she noted nothing else. "He touched me," she wrote, which had always been her diary euphemism for sex. That was also the year they retired, she as a pool secretary at the commerce department, where she had known one lover, and he as a civilian employee at the Pentagon, as the head of veteran records. He had been an army sergeant for ten years before becoming head of records; the secretary of defense gave him a plaque as big as his chest on the day he retired, and he and the secretary of defense and Loneese had their picture taken, a picture that hung for all those twelve years in the living room of Apartment 230, on the wall just to the right of the heating-and-air-conditioning unit.

A month before they moved in, they drove in their burgundy-and-gold Cadillac from their small house on Chesapeake Street in Southeast to a Union Station restaurant and promised each other that Sunset House would be a new beginning for them. Over blackened catfish and a peach cobbler that they both agreed could have been better, they vowed to devote themselves to each other and become even better grandparents. Horace had long known about the commerce department lover. Loneese had told him about the man two months after she had ended the relationship, in 1969. "He worked in the mail room," she told her husband over a spaghetti supper she had cooked in the Chesapeake Street home. "He touched me in the motel room," she wrote in her diary, "and after it was over he begged me to go away to Florida with him. All I could think about was that Florida was for old people."

At that spaghetti supper, Horace did not mention the dozens of lovers he had had in his time as her husband. She knew there had been many, knew it because they were written on his face in the early years of their marriage, and because he had never bothered to hide what he was doing in the later years. "I be back in a while. I got some business to do," he would say. He did not even mention the lover he had slept with just the day before the spaghetti supper, the one he bid good-bye to with a "Be good and be sweet" after telling her he planned to become a new man and respect his marriage vows. The woman, a thin school-bus driver with clanking bracelets up to her elbows on both arms, snorted a laugh, which made Horace want to slap her, because he was used to people taking him seriously. "Forget you, then," Horace said on the way out the door. "I was just tryin to let you down easy."

Over another spaghetti supper two weeks before moving, they reiterated what had been said at the blackened-catfish supper and did the dishes together and went to bed as man and wife, and over the next days sold almost all the Chesapeake Street furniture. What they kept belonged primarily to Horace, starting with a collection of six hundred and thirty-nine record albums, many of them his "sweet babies," the 78s. If a band worth anything had recorded between 1915 and 1950, he bragged, he had the record; after 1950, he said, the bands got sloppy and he had to back away. Horace also kept the Cadillac he had painted to honor a football team, paid to park the car in the underground garage. Sunset had once been intended as a luxury place, but the builders, two friends of the city commissioners, ran out of money in the middle and the commissioners had the city-government people buy it off them. The city-government people completed Sunset, with its tiny rooms, and then, after one commissioner gave a speech in Southwest about looking out for old people, some city-government people in Northeast came up with the idea that old people might like to live in Sunset, in Northwest.

Three weeks after Horace and Loneese moved in, Horace went down to the lobby one Saturday afternoon to get their mail and happened to see Clara Knightley getting her mail. She lived in Apartment 512. "You got this fixed up real nice," Horace said of Apartment 512 a little less than an hour after meeting her. "But I could see just in the way that you carry yourself that you got good taste. I could tell that about you right off." "You swellin my head with all that talk, Mr. Perkins," Clara said, offering him coffee, which he rejected, because such moments always called for something stronger. "Whas a woman's head for if a man can't swell it up from time to time. Huh? Answer me that, Clara. You just answer me that." Clara was fifty-five, a bit younger than most of the residents of Sunset House, though she was much older than all Horace's other lovers. She did not fit the city people's definition of a senior citizen, but she had a host of ailments, from high blood pressure to diabetes, and so the city people had let her in.

Despite the promises, the marriage, what little there had been of it, came to an end. "I will make myself happy," Loneese told the diary a month after he last touched her. Loneese and Horace had fixed up their apartment nicely, and neither of them wanted to give the place up to the other. She wanted to make a final stand with the man who had given her so much heartache, the man who had told her, six months after her confession, what a whore she had been to sleep with the commerce department mail-room man. Horace, at sixty, had never thought much of women over fifty, but Clara—and, after her, Willa, of Apartment 1001, and Miriam, of Apartment 109—had awakened something in him, and he began to think that women over fifty weren't such a bad deal after all. Sunset House had dozens of such women, many of them attractive widows, many of them eager for a kind word from a retired army sergeant who had so many medals and ribbons that his uniform could not carry them. As far as he could see, he was cock of the walk: many of the men in Sunset suffered from diseases that Horace had so far escaped, or they were not as good-looking or as thin, or they were encumbered by wives they loved. In Sunset House he was a rich man. So why move and give that whore the satisfaction?

They lived separate lives in a space that was only a fourth as large as the Chesapeake Street house. The building came to know them as the man and wife in 230 who couldn't stand each other. People talked about the Perkinses more than they did about anyone else, which was particularly upsetting to Loneese, who had been raised to believe family business should stay in the family. "Oh, Lord, what them two been up to now?" "Fight like cats and dogs, they do." "Who he seein now?" They each bought their own food from the Richfood on Eleventh Street or from the little store on Thirteenth Street, and they could be vile to each other if what one bought was disturbed or eaten by the other. Loneese stopped speaking to Horace for nine months in 1984 and 1985, when she saw that her pumpkin pie was a bit smaller than when she last cut a slice from it. "I ain't touch your damn pie, you crazy woman," he said when she accused him. "How long you been married to me? You know I've never been partial to pumpkin pie." "That's fine for you to say, Horace, but why is some missing? You might not be partial to it, but I know you. I know you'll eat anything in a pinch. That's just your dirty nature." "My nature ain't no more dirty than yours."

After that, she bought a small icebox for the bedroom where she slept, though she continued to keep the larger items in the kitchen refrigerator. He bought a separate telephone, because he complained that she wasn't giving him his messages from his "associates." "I have never been a secretary for whores," she said, watching him set up an answering machine next to the hide-a-bed couch where he slept. "Oh, don't get me started bout whores. I'd say you wrote the damn book." "It was dictated by you."

Their one child, Alonzo, lived with his wife and son in Balti-more. He had not been close to his parents for a long time, and he could not put the why of it into words for his wife. Their boy, Alonzo, Jr., who was twelve when his grandparents moved into Sunset, loved to visit them. Horace would unplug and put away his telephone when the boy visited. And Loneese and Horace would sleep together in the bedroom. She'd put a pillow between them in the double bed to remind herself not to roll toward him.

Their grandson visited less and less as he moved into his teen-age years, and then, after he went away to college, in Ohio, he just called them every few weeks, on the phone they had had installed in the name of Horace and Loneese Perkins.

In 1987, Loneese's heart began the countdown to its last beat and she started spending more time at George Washington University Hospital than she did in the apartment. Horace never visited her. She died two years later. She woke up that last night in the hospi-tal and went out into the hall and then to the nurses' station but could not find a nurse anywhere to tell her where she was or why she was there. "Why do the patients have to run this place alone?" she said to the walls. She returned to her room and it came to her why she was there. It was nearing three in the morning, but she called her own telephone first, then she dialed Horace's. He an-swered, but she never said a word. "Who's this playin on my phone?" Horace kept asking. "Who's this? I don't allow no playin on my phone." She hung up and lay down and said her prayers. After moving into Sunset, she had taken one more lover, a man at Ver-mont Avenue Baptist Church, where she went from time to time. He was retired, too. She wrote in her diary that he was not a big eater and that "down there, his vitals were missing."

Loneese Perkins was buried in a plot at Harmony Cemetery that she and Horace had bought when they were younger. There was a spot for Horace and there was one for their son, but Alonzo had long since made plans to be buried in a cemetery just outside Baltimore.

Horace kept the apartment more or less the way it was on the last day she was there. His son and daughter-in-law and grandson took some of her clothes to the Goodwill and the rest they gave to other women in the building. There were souvenirs from countries that Loneese and Horace had visited as man and wife—a Ghanaian carving of men surrounding a leopard they had killed, a brass menorah from Israel, a snow globe of Mt. Fuji with some of the snow stuck forever to the top of the globe. They were things that did not mean very much to Alonzo, but he knew his child, and he knew that one day Alonzo, Jr., would cherish them.

Horace tried sleeping in the bed, but he had been not unhappy in his twelve years on the hide-a-bed. He got rid of the bed and moved the couch into the bedroom and kept it open all the time.

He realized two things after Loneese's death: His own "vitals" had rejuvenated. He had never had the problems other men had, though he had failed a few times along the way, but that was to be expected. Now, as he moved closer to his seventy-third birthday, he felt himself becoming ever stronger, ever more potent. God is a strange one, he thought, sipping Chivas Regal one night before he went out: he takes a man's wife and gives him a new penis in her place.

The other thing he realized was that he was more and more attracted to younger women. When Loneese died, he had been keeping company with a woman of sixty-one, Sandy Carlin, in Apartment 907. One day in February, nine months after Loneese's death, one of Sandy's daughters, Jill, came to visit, along with one of Jill's friends, Elaine Cunningham. They were both twenty-five years old. From the moment they walked through Sandy's door, Horace began to compliment them—on their hair, the color of their fingernail polish, the sharp crease in Jill's pants ("You iron that yourself?"), even "that sophisticated way" Elaine crossed her legs. The young women giggled, which made him happy, pleased with himself, and Sandy sat in her place on the couch. As the ice in the Pepsi-Cola in her left hand melted, she realized all over again that God had never promised her a man until her dying day.

When the girls left, about three in the afternoon, Horace offered to accompany them downstairs, "to keep all them bad men away." In the lobby, as the security guard at her desk strained to hear, he made it known that he wouldn't mind if they came by to see him sometime. The women looked at each other and giggled some more. They had been planning to go to a club in Southwest that evening, but they were amused by the old man, by the way he had his rap together and put them on some sort of big pedestal and shit, as Jill would tell another friend weeks later. And when he saw how receptive they were he said why not come on up tonight, shucks, ain't no time like the present. Jill said he musta got that from a song, but he said no, he'd been sayin that since before they were born, and Elaine said thas the truth, and the women giggled again. He said I ain't gonna lie bout bein a seasoned man, and then he joined in the giggling. Jill looked at Elaine and said want to? And Elaine said what about your mom? And Jill shrugged her shoulders and Elaine said O.K. She had just broken up with a man she had met at another club and needed something to make the pain go away until there was another man, maybe from a better club.

At about eleven-thirty, Jill wandered off into the night, her head liquored up, and Elaine stayed and got weepy—about the man from the not-so-good club, about the two abortions, about running away from home at seventeen after a fight with her father. "I just left him nappin on the couch," she said, stretched out on Horace's new living-room couch, her shoes off and one of Loneese's throws over her feet. Horace was in the chair across from her. "For all I know, he's still on that couch." Even before she got to her father, even before the abortions, he knew that he would sleep with her that night. He did not even need to fill her glass a third time. "He was a fat man," she said of her father. "And there ain't a whole lot more I remember."

"Listen," he said as she talked about her father, "everything's gonna work out right for you." He knew that, at such times in a seduction, the more positive a man was the better things went. It would not have done to tell her to forget her daddy, that she had done the right thing by running out on that fat so-and-so; it was best to focus on tomorrow and tell her that the world would be brighter in the morning. He came over to the couch, and before he sat down on the edge of the coffee table he hiked up his pants just a bit with his fingertips, and seeing him do that reminded her vaguely of something wonderful. The boys in the club sure didn't do it that way. He took her hand and kissed her palm. "Everything's gonna work out to the good," he said.

Elaine Cunningham woke in the morning with Horace sleeping quietly beside her. She did not rebuke herself and did not look over at him with horror at what she had done. She sighed and laid her head back on the pillow and thought how much she still loved the man from the club, but there was nothing more she could do: not even the five-hundred-dollar leather jacket she had purchased for the man had brought him around. Two years after running away, she had gone back to where she had lived with her parents, but they had moved and no one in the building knew where they had gone. But everyone remembered her. "You sure done growed up, Elaine," one old woman said. "I wouldna knowed if you hadn't told me who you was." "Fuck em," Elaine said to the friends who had given her a ride there. "Fuck em all to hell." Then, in the car, heading out to Capitol Heights, where she was staying, "Well, maybe not fuck my mother. She was good." "Just fuck your daddy then?" the girl in the back seat said. Elaine thought about it as they went down Rhode Island Avenue, and just before they turned onto New Jersey Avenue she said, "Yes, just fuck my daddy. The fat fuck."

She got out of Horace's bed and tried to wet the desert in her mouth as she looked in his closet for a bathrobe. She rejected the blue and the paisley ones for a dark-green one that reminded her of something wonderful, just as Horace's hiking up his pants had. She smelled the sleeves once she had it on, but there was only the strong scent of detergent.

In the half room that passed for a kitchen, she stood and drank most of the orange juice in the gallon carton. "Now, that was stupid, girl," she said. "You know you shoulda drunk water. Better for the thirst." She returned the carton to the refrigerator and marveled at all the food. "Damn!" she said. With the refrigerator door still open, she stepped out into the living room and took note of all that Horace had, thinking, A girl could live large here if she did things right. She had been crashing at a friend's place in Northeast, and the friend's mother had begun to hint that it was time for her to move on. Even when she had a job, she rarely had a place of her own. "Hmm," she said, looking through the refrigerator for what she wanted to eat. "Boody for home and food. Food, home. Boody. You shoulda stayed in school, girl. They give courses on this. Food and Home the first semester. Boody Givin the second semester."

But, as she ate her eggs and bacon and Hungry Man biscuits, she knew that she did not want to sleep with Horace too many more times, even if he did have his little castle. He was too tall, and she had never been attracted to tall men, old or otherwise. "Damn! Why couldn't he be what I wanted and have a nice place, too?" Then, as she sopped up the last of the yolk with the last half of the last biscuit, she thought of her best friend, Catrina, the woman she was crashing with. Catrina Stockton was twenty-eight, and though she had once been a heroin addict, she was one year clean and had a face and a body that testified not to a woman who had lived a bad life on the streets but to a nice-looking Virginia woman who had married at seventeen, had had three children by a truck-driving husband, and had met a man in a Fredericksburg McDonald's who had said that women like her could be queens in D.C.

Yes, Elaine thought as she leaned over the couch and stared at the photograph of Horace and Loneese and the secretary of defense, Catrina was always saying how much she wanted love, how it didn't matter what a man looked like, as long as he was good to her and loved her morning, noon, and night. The secretary of defense was in the middle of the couple. She did not know who he was, just that she had seen him somewhere, maybe on the television. Horace was holding the plaque just to the left, away from the secretary. Elaine reached over and removed a spot of dust from the picture with her fingertip, and before she could flick it away a woman said her name and she looked around, chilled.

She went into the bedroom to make sure that the voice had not been death telling her to check on Horace. She found him sitting up in the bed, yawning and stretching. "You sleep good, honey bunch?" he said. "I sure did, sweetie pie," she said and bounded across the room to hug him. A breakfast like the one she'd had would cost at least four dollars anywhere in D.C. or Maryland. "Oh, but Papa likes that," Horace said. And even the cheapest motels out on New York Avenue, the ones catering to the junkies and prostitutes, charged at least twenty-five dollars a night. What's a hug compared with that? And, besides, she liked him more than she had thought, and the issue of Catrina and her moving in had to be done delicately. "Well, just let me give you a little bit mo, then."

Young stuff is young stuff, Horace thought the first time Elaine brought Catrina by and Catrina gave him a peck on the cheek and said, "I feel like I know you from all that Elaine told me." That was in early March.

In early April, Elaine met another man at a new club on F Street Northwest and fell in love, and so did Horace with Catrina, though Catrina, after several years on the street, knew what she was feeling might be in the neighborhood of love but it was nowhere near the right house. She and Elaine told Horace the saddest of stories about the man Elaine had met in the club, and before the end of April he was sleeping on Horace's living-room floor. It helped that the man, Darnell Mudd, knew the way to anyone's heart, man or woman, and that he claimed to have a father who had been a hero in the Korean War. He even knew the name of the secretary of defense in the photograph and how long he had served in the cabinet.

By the middle of May, there were as many as five other people, friends of the three young people, hanging out at any one time in Horace's place. He was giddy with Catrina, with the blunts, with the other women who snuck out with him to a room at the motel across Thirteenth Street. By early June, more than a hundred of his old records had been stolen and pawned. "Leave his stuff alone," Elaine said to Darnell and his friends as they were going out the door with ten records apiece. "Don't take his stuff. He loves that stuff." It was eleven in the morning and everyone else in the apartment, including Horace, was asleep. "Sh-h-h," Darnell said. "He got so many he won't notice." And that was true. Horace hadn't played records in many months. He had two swords that were originally on the wall opposite the heating-and-air-conditioning unit. Both had belonged to German officers killed in the Second World War. Horace, high on the blunts, liked to see the young men sword fight with them. But the next day, sober, he would hide them in the bottom of the closet, only to pull them out again when the partying started, at about four in the afternoon.

His neighbors, especially the neighbors who considered that Loneese had been the long-suffering one in the marriage, complained to the management about the noise, but the city-government people read in his rental record that he had lost his wife not long ago and told the neighbors that he was probably doing some kind of grieving. The city-government people never went above the first floor in Sunset. "He's a veteran who just lost his wife," they would say to those who came to the glass office on the first floor. "Why don't you cut him some slack?" But Horace tried to get a grip on things after a maintenance man told him to be careful. That was about the time one of the swords was broken and he could not for the life of him remember how it had happened. He just found it one afternoon in two pieces in the refrigerator's vegetable bin.

Things toned down a little, but the young women continued to come by and Horace went on being happy with them and with Catrina, who called him Papa and pretended to be upset when she saw him kissing another girl. "Papa, what am I gonna do with you and all your hussies?" "Papa, promise you'll only love me." "Papa, I need a new outfit. Help me out, willya please?"

Elaine had become pregnant not long after meeting Darnell, who told her to have the baby, that he had always wanted a son to carry on his name. "We can call him Junior," he said. "Or Little Darnell," she said. As she began showing, Horace and Catrina became increasingly concerned about her. Horace remembered how solicitous he had been when Loneese had been pregnant. He had not taken the first lover yet, had not even thought about anyone else as she grew and grew. He told Elaine no drugs or alcohol until the baby was born, and he tried to get her to go to bed at a decent hour, but that was often difficult with a small crowd in the living room.

Horace's grandson called in December, wanting to come by to see him, but Horace told him it would be best to meet someplace downtown, because his place was a mess. He didn't do much cleaning since Loneese died. "I don't care about that," Alonzo, Jr., said. "Well, I do," Horace said. "You know how I can be bout these things."

In late December, Elaine gave birth to a boy, several weeks early. They gave him the middle name Horace. "See," Darnell said one day, holding the baby on the couch. "Thas your grandpa. You don't mind me callin you his granddad, Mr. Perkins? You don't mind, do you?" The city-government people in the rental office, led by someone new, someone who took the rules seriously, took note that the old man in Apartment 230 had a baby and his mama and daddy in the place and not a single one of them was even related to him, though if one had been it still would have been against the rules as laid down in the rule book of apartment living.

By late February, an undercover policeman had bought two packets of crack from someone in the apartment. It was a woman, he told his superiors at first, and that's what he wrote in his report, but in a subsequent report he wrote that he had bought the rocks from a man. "Start over," said one of his superiors, who supped monthly with the new mayor, who lived for numbers, and in March the undercover man went back to buy more.

It was late on a warm Saturday night in April when Elaine woke to the crackle of walkie-talkies outside the door. She had not seen Darnell in more than a month, and something told her that she should get out of there because there might not be any more good times. She thought of Horace and Catrina asleep in the bedroom. Two men and two women she did not know very well were asleep in various places around the living room, but she had dated the brother of one of the women some three years ago. One of the men claimed to be Darnell's cousin, and, to prove it to her, when he knocked at the door that night he showed her a Polaroid of him and Darnell at a club, their arms around each other and their eyes red, because the camera had been cheap and the picture cost only two dollars.

She got up from the couch and looked into the crib. In the darkness she could make out that her son was awake, his little legs kicking and no sound from him but a happy gurgle. The sound of the walkie-talkie outside the door came and went. She could see it all on the television news—"Drug Dealing Mama in Jail. Baby Put in Foster Care." She stepped over the man who said he was Darnell's cousin and pushed the door to the bedroom all the way open. Catrina was getting out of bed. Horace was snoring. He had never snored before in his life, but the drugs and alcohol together had done bad things to his airway.

"You hear anything?" Elaine whispered as Catrina tiptoed to her.

"I sure did," Catrina said. Sleeping on the streets required keeping one eye and both ears open. "I don't wanna go back to jail."

"Shit. Me, neither," Elaine said. "What about the window?"

"Go out and down two floors? With a baby? Damn!"

"We can do it," Elaine said, looking over Catrina's shoulder to the dark lump that was Horace mumbling in his sleep. "What about him?"

Catrina turned her head. "He old. They ain't gonna do anything to him. I'm just worried bout makin it with that baby."

"Well, I sure as hell ain't gonna go without my child."

"I ain't said we was," Catrina hissed. "Down two floors just ain't gonna be easy, is all."

"We can do it," Elaine said.

"We can do it," Catrina said. She tiptoed to the chair at the foot of the bed and went through Horace's pants pockets. "Maybe fifty dollars here," she whispered after returning. "I already got about three hundred."

"You been stealin from him?" Elaine said. The lump in the bed turned over and moaned, then settled back to snoring.

"God helps them that helps themselves, Elaine. Les go." Catrina had her clothes in her hands and went on by Elaine, who watched as the lump in the bed turned again, snoring all the while. Bye, Horace. Bye. I be seein you.

The policeman in the unmarked car parked across Thirteenth Street watched as Elaine stood on the edge of the balcony and jumped. She passed for a second in front of the feeble light over the entrance and landed on the sloping entrance of the underground parking garage. The policeman was five years from retirement and he did not move, because he could see quite well from where he sat. His partner, only three years on the job, was asleep in the passenger seat. The veteran thought the woman jumping might have hurt herself, because he did not see her rise from the ground for several minutes. I wouldn't do it, the man thought, not for all a rich man's money. The woman did rise, but before she did he saw another woman lean over the balcony dangling a bundle. Drugs? he thought. Nah. Clothes? Yeah, clothes more like it. The bundle was on a long rope or string—it was too far for the man to make out. The woman on the balcony leaned over very far and the woman on the ground reached up as far as she could, but still the bundle was a good two feet from her hands.

Just let them clothes drop, the policeman thought. Then Catrina released the bundle and Elaine caught it. Good catch. I wonder what she looks like in the light. Catrina jumped, and the policeman watched her pass momentarily in front of the light, and then he looked over at his partner. He himself didn't mind filling out the forms so much, but his partner did, so he let him sleep on. I'll be on a lake fishin my behind off and you'll still be doin this. When he looked back, the first woman was coming up the slope of the entrance with the bundle in her arms and the second one was limping after her. I wonder what that one looks like in a good light. Once on the sidewalk, both women looked left, then right, and headed down Thirteenth Street. The policeman yawned and watched through his sideview mirror as the women crossed M Street. He yawned again. Even at three o'clock in the morning people still jaywalked.

The man who was a cousin of Darnell's was on his way back from the bathroom when the police broke through the door. He frightened easily, and though he had just emptied his bladder, he peed again as the door came open and the light of the hallway and the loud men came spilling in on him and his sleeping companions.

Horace began asking about Catrina and Elaine and the baby as soon as they put him in a cell. It took him that long to clear his head and understand what was happening to him. He pressed his face against the bars, trying to get his bearings and ignoring everything behind him in the cell. He stuck his mouth as far out of the bars as he could and shouted for someone to tell him whether they knew if the young women and the baby were all right. "They just women, y'all," he kept saying for some five minutes. "They wouldn't hurt a flea. Officers, please. Please, officers. What's done happened to them? And that baby . . . That baby is so innocent." It was a little after six in the morning, and men up and down the line started hollering for him to shut up or they would stick the biggest dick he ever saw in his mouth. Stunned, he did quiet down, because, while he was used to street language coming from the young men who came and went in his apartment, no bad words had ever been directed at him. They talked trash with the filthiest language he had ever heard but they always invited him to join in and "talk about how it really is," talk about his knowing the secretary of defense and the mayor. Usually, after the second blunt, he was floating along with them. Now someone had threatened to do to him what he and the young men said they would do to any woman that crossed them.

Then he turned from the bars and considered the three men he was sharing the two-man cell with. The city-jail people liked to make as little work for themselves as possible, and filling cells beyond their capacity meant having to deal with fewer locks. One man was cocooned in blankets on the floor beside the tiered metal beds. The man sleeping on the top bunk had a leg over the side, and because he was a tall man the leg came down to within six inches of the face of the man lying on the bottom bunk. That man was awake and on his back and picking his nose and staring at Horace. His other hand was under his blanket, in the crotch of his pants. What the man got out of his nose he would flick up at the bottom of the bunk above him. Watching him, Horace remembered that a very long time ago, even before the Chesapeake Street house, Loneese would iron his handkerchiefs and fold them into four perfect squares.

"Daddy," the man said, "you got my smokes?"

"What?" Horace said. He recalled doing it to Catrina about two or three in the morning and then rolling over and going to sleep. He also remembered slapping flies away in his dreams, flies that were as big as the hands of policemen.

The man seemed to have an infinite supply of boogers, and the more he picked the more Horace's stomach churned. He used to think it was such a shame to unfold the handkerchiefs, so wondrous were the squares. The man sighed at Horace's question and put something from his nose on the big toe of the sleeping man above him. "I said do you got my smokes?"

"I don't have my cigarettes with me," Horace said. He tried the best white man's English he knew, having been told by a friend who was serving with him in the army in Germany that it impressed not only white people but black people who weren't going anywhere in life. "I left my cigarettes at home." His legs were aching and he wanted to sit on the floor, but the only available space was in the general area of where he was standing and something adhered to his shoes every time he lifted his feet. "I wish I did have my cigarettes to give you."

"I didn't ask you bout *your* cigarettes. I don't wanna smoke them. I ask you bout *my* cigarettes. I wanna know if you brought *my* cigarettes."

Someone four cells down screamed and called out in his sleep: "Irene, why did you do this to me? Irene, ain't love worth a damn anymore?" Someone else told him to shut up or he would get a king-sized dick in his mouth.

"I told you I do not have any cigarettes," Horace said.

"You know, you ain't worth shit," the man said. "You take the cake and mess it all up. You really do. Now, you know you was comin to jail, so why didn't you bring my goddam smokes? What kinda fuckin consideration is that?"

Horace decided to say nothing. He raised first one leg and then the other and shook them, hoping that would relieve the aches. Slowly, he turned around to face the bars. No one had told him what was going to happen to him. He knew a lawyer, but he did not know if he was still practicing. He had friends, but he did not want any of them to see him in jail. He hoped the man would go to sleep.

"Don't turn your fuckin back on me after all we meant to each other," the man said. "We have this long relationship and you do this to me. Whas wrong with you, Daddy?"

"Look," Horace said, turning back to the man. "I done told you I ain't got no smokes. I ain't got your smokes. I ain't got my smokes. I ain't got nobody's smokes. Why can't you understand that?" He was aware that he was veering away from the white man's English, but he knew that his friend from Germany was probably home asleep safely in his bed. "I can't give you what I don't have." Men were murdered in the D.C. jail, or so the *Washington Post* told him. "Can't you understand what I'm sayin?" His back stayed as close to the bars as he could manage. Who was this Irene, he thought, and what had she done to steal into a man's dreams that way?

"So, Daddy, it's gonna be like that, huh?" the man said, raising his head and pushing the foot of the upper-bunk man out of the way so he could see Horace better. He took his hand out of his crotch and pointed at Horace. "You gon pull a Peter-and-Jesus thing on me and deny you ever knew me, huh? Thas your plan, Daddy?" He lowered his head back to the black-and-white striped pillow. "I've seen some low-down dirty shit in my day, but you the lowest. After our long relationship and everything."

"I never met you in my life," Horace said, grabbing the bars behind him with both hands, hoping, again, for relief.

"I won't forget this, and you know how long my memory is. First, you don't bring me my smokes, like you know you should. Then you deny all that we had. Don't go to sleep in here, Daddy, thas all I gotta say."

He thought of Reilly Johnson, a man he had worked with in the Pentagon. Reilly considered himself something of a photographer. He had taken the picture of Horace with the secretary of defense. What would the bail be? Would Reilly be at home to receive his call on a Sunday morning? Would they give him bail? The policemen who pulled him from his bed had tsk-tsked in his face. "Sellin drugs and corruptin young people like that?" "I didn't know nothin about that, officer. Please." "Tsk tsk. An old man like you."

"The world ain't big enough for you to hide from my righteous wrath, Daddy. And you know how righteous I can be when I get started. The world ain't big enough, so you know this jail ain't big enough."

Horace turned back to the bars. Was something in the back as painful as something in the stomach? He touched his face. Rarely, even in the lost months with Catrina, had he failed to shave each morning. A man's capable demeanor started with a shave each morning, his sergeant in boot camp had told him a thousand years ago.

The man down the way began calling for Irene again. Irene, Horace called in his mind. Irene, are you out there? No one told the man to be quiet. It was about seven and the whole building was waking up and the man calling Irene was not the loudest sound in the world anymore.

"Daddy, you got my smokes? Could use my smokes right about now."

Horace, unable to stand anymore, slowly sank to the floor. There he found some relief. The more he sat, the more he began to play over the arrest. He had had money in his pocket when he took off his pants the night before, but there was no money when they booked him. And where had Catrina and Elaine been when the police marched him out of the apartment and down to the paddy wagon, with the Sunset's female security guard standing behind her desk with an "Oh, yes, I told you so" look? Where had they been? He had not seen them. He stretched out his legs and they touched the feet of the sleeping man on the floor. The man roused. "Love don't mean shit anymore," the man on the lower bunk said. It was loud enough to wake the man on the floor all the way, and that man sat up and covered his chest with his blanket and looked at Horace, blinking and blinking and getting a clearer picture of Horace the more he blinked.

Reilly did not come for him until the middle of Monday afternoon. Somebody opened the cell door and at first Horace thought the policeman was coming to get one of his cellmates.

"Homer Parkins," the man with the keys said. The doors were supposed to open electronically, but that system had not worked in a long time.

"Thas me," Horace said and got to his feet. As he and the man with the keys walked past the other cells, someone said to Horace, "Hey, Pops, you ain't too old to learn to suck dick." "Keep moving," the man with the keys said. "Pops, I'll give you a lesson when you come back."

As they poured his things out of a large manila envelope, the two guards behind the desk whispered and laughed. "Everything there?" one of them asked Horace. "Yes." "Well, good," the guard said. "I guess we'll be seein you on your next trip here." "Oh, leave that old man alone. He's somebody's grandfather." "When they start that old," the first man said, "it gets in their system and they can't stop. Ain't that right, Pops?"

He and Reilly did not say very much after Reilly said he had been surprised to hear from Horace and that he had wondered what had happened to him since Loneese died. Horace said he was eternally grateful to Reilly for bailing him out and that it was all a mistake as well as a long story that he would soon share with him. At Sunset, Reilly offered to take him out for a meal, but Horace said he would have to take a rain check. "Rain check?" Reilly said, smiling. "I didn't think they said that anymore."

The key to the apartment worked the way it always had, but something was blocking the door, and he had to force it open. Inside, he found destruction everywhere. On top of the clothes and the mementos of his life, strewn across the table and the couch and the floor were hundreds and hundreds of broken records. He took three steps into the room and began to cry. He turned around and around, hoping for something that would tell him it was not as bad as his eyes first reported. But there was little hope — the salt and pepper shakers had not been touched, the curtains covering the glass door were intact. There was not much beyond that for him to cling to.

He thought immediately of Catrina and Elaine. What had he done to deserve this? Had he not always shown them a good and kind heart? He covered his eyes, but that seemed only to produce more tears, and when he lowered his hands the room danced before him through the tears. To steady himself, he put both hands on the table, which was covered in instant coffee and sugar. He brushed broken glass off the chair nearest him and sat down. He had not got it all off, and he felt what was left through his pants and underwear.

He tried to look around but got no farther than the picture with the secretary of defense. It had two cracks in it, one running north to south and the other going northwest to southeast. The photograph was tilting, too, and something told him that if he could straighten the picture it all might not be so bad. He reached out a hand, still crying, but he could not move from the chair.

He stayed as he was through the afternoon and late into the evening, not once moving from the chair, though the tears did stop around five o'clock. Night came and he still did not move. My name is Horace Perkins, he thought just as the sun set. My name is Horace Perkins and I worked many a year at the Pentagon. The apartment became dark, but he did not have it in him to turn on the lights.

The knocking had been going on for more than ten minutes when he finally heard it. He got up, stumbling over debris, and opened the door. Elaine stood there with Darnell, Jr., in her arms.

"Horace, you O.K.? I been comin by. I been worried about you, Horace."

He said nothing but opened the door enough for her and the baby to enter.

"It's dark, Horace. What about some light?"

He righted the lamp on the table and turned it on.

"Jesus in Heaven, Horace! What happened! My Lord Jesus! I can't believe this." The baby, startled by his mother's words, began to cry. "Its O.K.," she said to him, "It's O.K.," and gradually the baby calmed down. "Oh, Horace, I'm so sorry. I really am. This is the worst thing I've ever seen in my life." She touched his shoulder with her free hand, but he shrugged it off. "Oh, my dear God! Who could do this?"

She went to the couch and moved enough trash aside for the baby. She pulled a pacifier from her sweater pocket, put it momentarily in her mouth to remove the lint, then put it in the baby's mouth. He appeared satisfied and leaned back on the couch.

She went to Horace, and right away he grabbed her throat. "I'm gonna kill you tonight!" he shouted. "I just wish that bitch Catrina was here so I could kill her, too." Elaine struggled and sputtered out one "please" before he gripped her tighter. She beat his arms but that seemed to give him more strength. She began to cry. "I'm gonna kill you tonight, girl, if it's the last thing I do."

The baby began to cry, and she turned her head as much as she could to look at him. This made him slap her twice, and she started to fall, and he pulled her up and, as he did, went for a better grip, which was time enough for her to say, "Don't kill me in front of my son, Horace." He loosened his hands. "Don't kill me in front of my boy, Horace." Her tears ran down her face and over and into his hands. "He don't deserve to see me die. You know that, Horace."

"Where, then!"

"Anywhere but in front of him. He's innocent of everything."

He let her go and backed away.

"I did nothin, Horace," she whispered. "I give you my word, I did nothin." The baby screamed, and she went to him and took him in her arms.

Horace sat down in the same chair he had been in.

"I would not do this to you, Horace."

He looked at her and at the baby, who could not take his eyes off Horace, even through his tears.

One of the baby's cries seemed to get stuck in his throat, and to release it the baby raised a fist and punched the air, and finally the cry came free. How does a man start over with nothing? Horace thought. Elaine came near him, and the baby still watched him as his crying lessened. How does a man start from scratch?

He leaned down and picked up a few of the broken albums from the floor and read the labels. "I would not hurt you for anything in the world, Horace," Elaine said. Okeh Phonograph Corporation. Domino Record Co. RCA Victor. Darnell, Jr.,'s crying stopped, but he continued to look down at the top of Horace's head. Cameo Record Corporation, N.Y. "You been too good to me for me to hurt you like this, Horace." He dropped the records one at a time: "It Takes an Irishman to Make Love." "I'm Gonna Pin a Medal on the Girl I Left Behind." "Ragtime Soldier Man." "Whose Little Heart Are You Breaking Now." "The Syncopated Walk."

Edward P. Jones is the author of *Lost in the City,* a collection of stories, and the novel, *The Known World,* both of which were nominated for the National Book Award. The collection won the PEN/Hemingway Award for best first fiction. He is the recipient of a fellowship and an award from the Lannan Foundation. His story "Marie" appeared in *New Stories from the South: The Year's Best, 1993.*

JERRY BAUER

I am hoping to complete another collection of stories involving major and minor characters from Lost in the City. *In* Lost *there is a story, "A New Man," which has a teenager, Elaine Cunningham, who runs away from home and is never found. I believe I wanted to create something to show what had happened to Elaine, and thus "A Rich Man" was born. Elaine is still a minor character, but we know what happened to her, even though her parents may never know.*

Starkey Flythe, Jr.

A FAMILY OF
BREAST FEEDERS

(from *The Chattahoochee Review*)

W e're a family of breast feeders," Aunt Veronica tells me, age nine, apropos of nothing. Even as a child I find this odd, as we are mainly a family of old, single men, my mother included, some years dead.

Aunt Veronica identified, her brothers said, with Veronica Lake, the movie actress, during WWII. She wore her hair shoulder length, bleached blonde—"She looks ridiculous," my mother had said,— my aunt exaggerated the movie star's overhang, completely obscuring the left side of her face and her depth perception so that she failed her driver's license test three times until my mother had reached up in her own hair and pulled something out. "This is a bobby pin. You figure."

Factory managers, my bachelor uncles informed me, had asked Miss Lake to whack off her hair as so many young women imitated her famous do the girls' hair was getting caught in the machinery when women were aiding the war effort, or at least looking for men, the bottom of the male barrel having been scraped by the war, my uncles, too young for WWI, too old, physically defective—you should see their metatarsal arches—for WWII.

Aunt Veronica refused to comply—she refused to comply with any orders or suggestions—even my mother's about the driver's test; only passed, said her brother, by making out with the man who administered the test. Hard to believe, I thought, for even young, she couldn't have been what anybody would call pretty. At seventy something, still racily lemon headed, her thinning bangs more veiling her left eye than obscuring it, and still working at the factory which had once manufactured M-1 rifle barrels and was now turning out weed whackers, she was an old maid; her breasts, if indeed they existed within the chartreuse or day-glo orange acrylic skintight sweaters she favored—who her age hadn't had a mastectomy?—pointed outward, like Madonna's, sharp and searching as radar scanners, still combing the skies for the blips of Mr. Right.

"Ask your uncles," she said, "they know a bit more about it than I do. I'm not having some needle-toothed brat chomping down on these babies." She pointed them outwards, the horizon vibrating with the precision of her aim.

"Oh, you can read all about it," Uncle Sylvester said. "Ashley Montague. Dr. Spock. Rachel Carson. Warren Buffet. But reading about it isn't the same as experiencing it." I stared at him. Ninety-something—"Ninety-plenty," he referred to his age, or eighty, seventy-nine plus? nobody knew—he had, like most older men, the suggestion of breasts, never wore those knit polo shirts—"They're the Victoria's Secret of the golf set," he told me. "Doctors can tell up to the time you're a hundred which twin was breast fed. Higher I.Q. Lower incidence of uterine cancer," he stared at me—"in females, heart trouble, diverticulosis, diverticulitis—don't ask me what the difference is—prostatitis, myopia, dyspepsia. The baby sucks in the mommie's natural immunities." Like Aunt Veronica he thrust his chest forward, his suspenders rippling across his ruined pectorals.

"It's the only instinct humans possess," Uncle Rupert continued. Rupert was not—I never knew quite how—exactly my uncle. I called a plethora of men who either hung about Veronica or Rupert or Sylvester—Uncle. They stayed in the house, or left, in, or out, months, weeks, some, even years. Plenty of room. No such things as meals or rules. I loved that aspect, lived on cheese doodles and Diet Coke, wandered around where and when I wanted or where or when I wasn't wanted. "When the little babby's born—," he pronounced it to rhyme with *taxi-cabby*—he had found out his ancestors were Scots two hundred years before, had taken up the accent after seeing a Disney movie about a lost border collie and a whisky distiller—"she puts it to the booby"—pronounced like a London cop; "well, not right away, the colostrum comes in first— it's a different kind of milk, you know, not so strong, so milky. They live on that the first couple of days—the real stuff's indigestible at first, strong—well, if you touch the babby's mouth to the nipple it automatically turns to suck. You ever watch puppies, pigs, kittens? At their mother's teats?" He spoke as if we lived on an animal farm instead of a fifteen-room city Victorian salt shaker the yard of which had been sold off for a Washerteria and attendant parking. "The real stuff, well, nature knows what it's doing though you'd never guess it from looking at your Aunt Veronica; not too strong—the baby's intestinal tract—you know when you eat Roquefort cheese on top of raspberry-flavored Hawaiian punch?"

"God knows and He only, what this mite's been living on these years— months—seems like years, the lassies say," Sylvester put his hand on my head—"by the by they've changed the gestation period—used to be nine months, now forty weeks."

Rupert repeated this. "Farty weakes. The heads are getting too big to be born. Brains. But God knows they loses them, brains, soon as they hits the ground. And not running. Women I talk to— (did he ever?)—say it's too long, they should cut it, no, not the umbilical cord, the time in the oven, that thing sticking out in front of you. I don't know how they stand it.

"Well, when the babby's mouth—it can't find the nipple, you know, what does it know about culinary process?—babbies aren't born with place settings and etiquette books—so when the side of its lips touches the tip of the breast, ah, it instinctively turns to the source. Neat, huh?"

"What's 'instinctively'?" I ask. Why he's explaining these things to a nine-year-old I never question. I'm treated as an adult but not a very good one. They keep things from me like coffee, but point out condom racks in the drug store, and breast pumps, even asking the pharmacist to take one out of the display counter case and demonstrate its uses. "Nay, nay, no need to take off your shirt, man," my uncle says to the astonished druggist.

"You don't need to heat up formula or mix anything or buy anything or go into the kitchen, the refrigerator, the store, the elbow. All you do is slap the babby to the booby, boy. Any time, any place. A convenience store. One stop shop.

"The Nestlé people, the Carnation Evaporated canned-milk people, the new burpless, collapsible bottles, the coming, the advent—"

"—No, it was the Christmas," Sylvester, the Catholic laughed—

"—of plastic that suddenly and slowly made breast feeding a dirty dinner those years. La Leche and Princess Grace hadn't made their marks yet. People who saw a woman with her breast in a babby's mouth would say, 'Eeeuw.' Parents would point children away. 'Look! Look, over there! There's? There's Mickey, Pluto, Daffy Duck.'

"People's minds were focused on things like, 'My smoke detector's beeping,' and 'Isn't President Nixon's daughter bee-utiful? I hope she marries the Eisenhower boy. Wouldn't that be nice?' Life seemed inorganic."

Rupert or Sylvester's mother had studied art at Columbia University, and the graduate assistant who took the classes around to the museums had been Margaret Meade. "See how the Madonna's holding the child," Margaret would say, according to Rupert or Sylvester, the class breathless—"'breath,' not, 'breast,'"—in front of Belinni's Number Nine—there were that many. "See the baby's feet how they wriggle when he nurses. Sexual pleasure. For the baby. For the mother. In Samoa, they hang bells on the babies' toes. She holds the baby on her left hip so she can keep the right hand free for the frying pan."

They repeated this to me often, assuming I guess and rightly I would never get to Columbia or Margaret—Margaret by this time certainly not teaching school, maybe even dead. Had they known, I imagined, they would've gone to the funeral, embarrassed themselves, the family, me.

They assumed without ever thinking about it the world was theirs and they were the world's. They thought everything they did was interesting to everybody, and everybody and everything were interesting to them. "When I see the President, I'll let him know," they said, as if they would be dining at the White House tomorrow. "I'll tell the King. Queen Mary!" "What'll you tell them?" Aunt Veronica confronted.

My uncle and Rupert had loved this mother they spoke of "dangerously," Aunt Veronica said, "and there's nothing worse in this world. Why do you think none of us ever married?" Well, my parents had, or at least said they had, but had long ago split up, married again, split and died, not from marriages or divorces but from smoking, which was why I was here.

"Your daddy was a menopause baby," Veronica told me one day. She pronounced it "mental pause," actually paused between the two words. "Twenty years between him and the next youngest, Sylvester. I mean me. I'm closer in age to you than to your late father, a good deal younger than the others."

She then explained what "mental pause" was. "You see if women keep on having babies there'll be too many people in the world. The Creator wisely stops them around age forty, fifty. Puts a cork in it. I'm still considering whether I want to have a baby. I'm not altogether certain I want to bring a child into this whacked world. Still have a few years to decide. What do you think? They say it hurts like hell?"

She had had a bit part—as an extra in a movie—Jack Benny playing Hitler, or Hamlet—she forgot which though she admitted it may have been in the same movie. She never let you forget when she flipped her hair, the stiff, thin strands pretty much resistant to head tossing now. Her face was tightened by cosmetic surgery or alum—so she spent her money—a screw winch, or nut bolt on the back of her head seemed cranked tight enough to burst—"she makes Marlene Dietrich's face look like a shar-pei puppy's back-side," said Rupert, aside. Sylvester said Rupert and Aunt Veronica had been in love, once. He pronounced "love" as "louvre." And he winked. The only thing they taught me never to do. "Never fall in love. Never fall in anything. That's why they put lids on barrels and corks in bottles and handrails on stairs." "Like urinating in pub-lic," a year-long "uncle" told me.

"Go on with your uncles now," my aunt would say. "Not good for you to be with so many women." Was she a woman? Was she a "women"? Was that what women were like? "I've got to make up my face for this evening." Her face. If it had any more makeup on, the weight of the paint would've bent her over forward.

The walls in Uncle Sylvester's room were papered with brassiere ads from Sears' catalogues and Penney's newspaper inserts. Smil-ing, full-breasted women stared down at me with various con-structions across their chests. Some were flesh colored, some white, some black. Uncle Sylvester had grouped them according to color, in very strict blocks. Squinting a moment—would my mother have approved? Dead, what difference did it make?—they could almost have been flags, the tricolor symbol of that great nation, Under-wear Land. He had left the prices on the ads. "Why do the tops cost more than the bottoms?" I asked. "Engineering," he said. "Wires, plastic, reinforcements, cables—bras are like bridges, the Golden Gate, the Brooklyn. They're structures, the Eiffel Tower, the Empire State Building, the St. Louis Arch."

He had scrapbooks—the name struck me as wrong; the books were so carefully, neatly, laid out, measured, paged, running heads—of articles about how brassieres had aided the war effort by reduc-ing fatigue in women. About how new elastics and synthetic materials rather than imported rubber and latex had found their way into Allied vehicle tires and weapons systems. There were sur-gical illustrations of breast enlargement procedures, breast reduc-tion techniques, nipple reconstruction, mastectomies. Line drawings of falsies and prosthetics. Comic strip characters and actresses whose bosoms he had admired. They were not all young, pretty models. I remember gazing at a large *Life* magazine photo of Golda Meir in a sleeveless blouse.

"Are you a doctor?" I asked. He barely smiled. "No, no, though I've consulted on a number of procedures."

"You see, Sonny, there are two types of men. Those who spend their lives trying to take bras off, dangling with fasteners and hooks and desire and resistance; and those who try to put them back on, who see women in Africa and Southeast Asia and want to push their lives back inward, inside themselves so they exist for themselves, not *National Geographic*.

"See, these appendages are a relatively recent invention. Some time ago, well, about a million years ago, the breasts were behind us, I mean, women's buttocks—am I going too fast for you?. . ."

I must have stared at him. He went on more slowly.

". . . women's buttocks were like breasts, soft and round, pointy sometimes. The buttocks were the attraction. They were red and noisy, you know, like ape behinds. Macaques. Man, I mean, men and women, bred on the hoof. They never looked at each other. Never said, I love you, never looked into somebody's eyes and whispered anything like that. Understand?"

"I guess," I said, and nodded. What was he talking about? I think, like most children who listen to their elders talk or read stories, it was not so much the subject matter as it was the lull of the voice, their own interest in the subject, in passing something on to you, the act of generosity rather than the pure knowledge, that made it interesting.

"Women with three and four babbies were running after family units—that's what anthropologists call them—trying to keep up with their mates, men they'd never looked square in the eye before. Babbies was falling by the wayside and mommies was forgetting to pick them up. Something's got to be done, they announced, probably at a meeting of the women. So they started growing breasts, massaging their chests, rubbing attar of roses and other sweet oils into their fleshes. Slowly, we're talking about thousands of years, they budded and swelled and bloomed. The men said, *Vas is los?* They had to look into the women's eyes to ask."

"Ain't he in bed, yet?" Aunt Veronica demanded. She had a way of entering a room and then knocking after she got there. "Children need sleep. Has he done any homework? I can imagine how what you've been telling him will look on his test about *Silas Marner*. And I could think you'd take down some of those bloopers, it ain't like it's rose and treillage wallpaper."

There's other words for them, too," Uncle Sylvester said, paying no attention to his sister. "French, *soustien gorge,* German, *busten halter.* Remind me to find Italian for bra. Spanish? Arab? They probably don't have a word, don't have breasts. Those table cloths and veils they wear."

I went off to bed. I heard them still talking. "What in God's name is the point of your telling a nine-year-old about bras? A nine-year-old boy?" And my uncle's response, "Well, if I'd known something maybe I wouldn't still be here. In this old house. With this old sister, brothers, whatever you call us?" "One of each," Veronica said. "Oh, Veronica of the weeping handkerchief," Sylvester taunted.

That was the first I'd ever really thought or heard that they weren't happy. This was years before people studied serious unhappiness. Schools and parents didn't take children in groups out camping or to soccer or ballet. Most everybody was left to his or her own devices. You played, by yourself, with yourself, I guess, later, or with friends, imagined things. There was no standard for comparison. So far, no other kid at school or teacher had ever questioned my not having a regular set of parents. There were lots of kids from one-parent homes, homes where the grandparents were raising them. The wars had shaken up a lot of families and norms. No comparisons of money or residences or cars or clothes or parent sets. Sex had never been mentioned. Except, as Aunt Veronica stated, "a patriotic duty." I would've been hard put to grasp that what my relatives were talking about had anything to do with sex. The giggly things we whispered about in school during recess behind the boy's bathroom. Children accept things, it seemed. Whatever adults tell them, adults tell them.

But gradually I was beginning to learn the world was something that could roll over and squash you flat on the pavement. As it had done these. And that wouldn't put a Hollywood star in the sidewalk. I'd been bullied at school, and my "uncles" had cried when they heard about it. "Crying because I can't teach you how to defend yourself," Rupert said.

I would fall asleep at night and deep in my childish innocence see engineers hauling up women by their bras and laying them out across a pink river to make a bridge. A dog, a pretty cream colored spaniel stepped cautiously out onto the span after the ribbon had been cut by a big boxer dog mayor wearing a top hat. Immediately the bridge collapsed and the dog fell into a pink river of Double Bubble gum. You couldn't get candy or anything sweet during the war. Why I craved it, I guess. War meant you couldn't travel. Couldn't walk—no shoes. Anything that touched the ground, tires, soles, nylon stockings. Anything that touched a sweet tooth, sugar, wine—what did the war effort need sugar for?—whiskey, I guess.

Aunt Veronica was thoroughly democratic in her ideals and assessment of the opposite sex when she saw soldiers loitering around downtown.

"Just cause they got bars on their shoulders don't mean they got bars in their pants," she said to her brother when he urged her to make a match with an officer, and then glanced at me. They often talked as though time was not a qualifier that defined them or entered this childless but for me house. They mixed up wars, as time went by. Roosevelt for them was still alive. "I saw him," Uncle Sylvester said, "On the platform with Churchill. Or was it Mrs. Roosevelt? She looks a lot like Churchill." "Churchill's got on zipper bedroom slippers. You'd think they'd put him in something, lace ups or brogues, Prime Minister. He can't bend over, so fat. He don't look like he's rationing anything." Or, "I seen Franklin"—he would gargle his voice so he sounded like Mrs. Roosevelt, "Feranklin—" "and he's got something the matter with his legs. They're steel, like Frankenstein." "I think those Ruskies will help us win this man's war real quick." Viet Nam, Korea, that place in Central America where they had the medical school. Rupert said, "People get killed, wars, win or lose. Somebody makes a bundle. Somebody's able to say, 'I'm big, you're little.'"

Even I, by now, an untutored child, could observe how wrong they were about practically everything. That they learned nothing was a great source of pride to them. "Wise acre," was Uncle Sylvester's ultimate term of derision.

"Mr. ——?" the teller at the bank told him, "you know you could save a little if you changed your account to a senior citizen one." "Yes, well when I get to that age, you'll be the first to know," he replied. Everybody knew—you could tell by looking at him, that he was his age. And more.

"You might look softer—you know—Ms. ——, if you used a muted shade for your touch up and your lip gloss instead of such a strident red," said the woman at the cosmetics counter in the department store to Aunt Veronica who often spent hours there trying various perfumes, foundation shades, eye liner, rouge, blusher. "And you might look better without your commission, sister, if I ever decide to buy something in this store, again," Aunt Veronica replied. But their replies were simply part of their everyday repartee. They never changed banks— "they know me down there," or crimpers, "they can't get my shade anywhere else." "Except from a fire truck, or a school bus!" Rupert told her.

"Women these days don't seem to have enough, you know, lift," my uncle would say as if we hadn't exhausted the subject of support, and pushed up on his chest with his hands. When they talked about "price supports" for farmers on the radio, he would say, "What about urban women? Women in the city?" "Well, they can't get the rubber elastic because of some war." "They could use something else, yo-yo strings, little bitty elevators, bamboo scaffolding, kitchen twine?" "Or, you, you could just stand around holding them up since you don't have anything better to do," Aunt Veronica threw out. "Caryatid," she said. I wrote down the word, could figure out enough to find it in the dictionary, was disappointed it wasn't some secret, sexual thing. The picture of Uncle Sylvester, like Atlas, holding up the structure of womanhood was hard to get out of my head.

Our dog, not treated so well, left outside, even on the coldest nights, had puppies. Uncle Sylvester was wild to show me when I got home from school, Catholic school. "See, different mothers has different teats. Evolution, I guess. One for each puppy. If human women had three and seven babies, I guess they'd have nipples running up and down both sides of their ribs. You figure out the bra they'd have to invent to keep all that up. Like a Roman aqueduct. Cows, see they got one boob but it's got several spigots. Why I don't know. They only usually have one calf. You know they're breeding them so big—Herefords, for the meat—they can't get them passed through the birth canal. That's why they have all those Julius Caesar births."

I don't think, looking back, all these years later, there was anything remotely prurient in my uncles' thinking. They were as astonished to find they had nipples and breasts, that as they got older, their chests, except for the fur, seemed to resemble female chests more and more. They rejoiced in the renaissance of breast feeding. "See, I told you all along," they trumpeted in front of me. "The natural, golden vehicle."

Sadly I was with Uncle Sylvester in the train into New York City when he lost his ascendancy into women's anatomy. People had just started dressing up in the native outfits of their ancestors, and a couple got on in New Paltz who were decked out like Arabs. The woman's face was covered by her veil, and the man wore a burnoose. The woman nursed a baby. She held the child with every discretion. Her husband read a little book, murmured to himself as if memorizing. I went to the bathroom past their seats and saw it was in funny squiggles. "Most probably the Koran," my uncle said. "Like our Bible."

He gazed at them intently. Offensively, I thought. Smiling, nodding approval, he seemed transfixed. I sensed his staring must be rude. I pulled on his sleeve and shook my head, No. But he was beaming, hardly saw me, stared straight at the couple as if they were some part of our family in the old house.

"She's holding the baby all wrong," he said, and got up from his seat. He stumbled across the aisle and down to where they were sitting. "No, no," he said in a kindly voice as if he were Father Time or Santa Claus, "cradle the baby and urge him forward front ways. He'll choke the way you've got him. It'll get into his ear. Those ear infections babies get, it's from the milk dribbling into their Eustachian tubes."

My uncle leaned forward meaning, I believe, to take the baby gently from his mother and replace the infant correctly according to his lights, but just then the train lurched around a bend, and Uncle Sylvester fell forward, his hands landing on the woman's breasts.

The husband unfolded himself twice the size he had seemed in his djellabah, huge, a fierce hooked nose, and said in an accent closer to Queens than Morocco and perfectly audible in either place, "Get your f'ing hands off my wife, you f'ing pervert," and slammed Sylvester in the face. Again and again. I ran to him, tried to pull him away. He had lost his balance, though, his weight inadvertently bearing down on the woman. He couldn't right himself. The husband kept hitting him. "Stop it!" I yelled. "He's old. He can't get up." Calling him "old" was the worst thing I could've done, I realized as the man hit me. He had a gold ring on his fourth finger and it drew blood immediately. Uncle Sylvester turned to me, pleading, "They just don't know."

The conductor came, finally. Where do they go on trains after they punch your ticket? He shoved us into a forward car. We sat there staring at each other, Sylvester and me, our faces dripping blood. He looked terrible, destroyed. "I only wanted to show her," he said. "A lifetime of experience I've had. She didn't know. How could she? She was from where? They won't even let women drive cars over there, or vote, or drink." Did women, I wondered, know how to nurse their babies instinctively—that word—or, did they have to be taught? Not by an old man, a stranger on a train. Not by bra ads. By their mothers. And suddenly, well, slowly, but surely, I missed my mother, not so much her, but having a mother, somehow, in a different way, a worse way. I would've been different, maybe. Things would've been different. What was I going to grow up like? What had I learned from these old people? Something was running down my face, tears. Uncle Sylvester had said that was all right. I could see how pink they were, mixing with the blood. I hurt all over. Sylvester took my hand and looked at it. "Some people don't like to be told," he said. "Don't like to learn. See, he, that husband, thinks he owns her. People don't own people. People aren't things, like phonographs, or typewriters. Pound out letters on a Remington. Pound out babies on a woman. I should've led up to it gradually. Explained the Constitution, the Bill of Rights. Well, next time. Do you know baby whales drink a hundred fifty gallons of their mother's milk every day? Some countries do not have our technology. Their women may not even wear bras. I should have asked her. Whether she knew about them?" His hand was trembling violently. But he smiled. I think his tooth had broken off. Should I have gone back to look for it in the aisle? They can do wonderful things, they say, sticking them back on if you save them in damp cotton. I got up to go look, but Uncle Sylvester said, "No, sit here with me just a moment."

I looked out the train window. Little hills, like breasts, I imagined, wobbled away beyond the river that ran along the tracks. I thought of how we would get to the city and go where we were going, of how the Arab couple would get off the train and go wherever they were going, and of how they would tell somebody about what had happened to them, and of how we maybe wouldn't tell, or if we did, what we would say and how it would be different from what they'd say. Aunt Veronica would roll her eyes. "A nine-year-old," she'd say. "Or, are you ten?"

Starkey Flythe, Jr., served with the U.S. Army
in East Africa, clerked in a law office after
working as an editor for the Curtis Publishing
Company, and now earns his living repairing
old buildings. His stories have appeared in *The
Best American Short Stories* and *O. Henry Prize
Stories*. A collection, *Lent: The Slow Fast*, won the
Iowa Short Fiction Award in 1989, and he has
published two books of poetry. He lives in South
Carolina.

DAN TRAYLOR

*O*n the train, stuck in a snow storm coming back from two wonderful
weeks at Yaddo, in the round, domed room there they call "The Breast"
(Philip Roth wrote part of his novel The Breast *in that room), a Muslim
woman across the aisle was quietly nursing her baby. The anthropologist
Ashley Montague said he could distinguish, even in their nineties, persons
who'd been breast fed from bottle babies. In all the snow, everybody on the
train anxious about getting to New York City—it was New Year's Eve—the
conductors and engineers running back and forth to keep the diesel and
heaters going, this woman looked so peaceful and content. Her baby's future
and dreams seemed secure, and after a while, I guess, so did ours. Veronica
Lake was sitting in front of me.*

Chris Offutt

SECOND HAND

(from *The Iowa Review*)

M y prize possession is a pair of ostrich-skin cowboy boots standing by the bed. I never keep my boots in the closet because a part of me suspects that this house is haunted. There is one room in particular, the family room, that I stay out of. Maybe it is haunted by a failed marriage that is now interfering with me and my boyfriend.

He is talking to someone on the phone in another room. His voice lowers slightly, and I'm not sure if he has shifted his body, or doesn't want me to overhear. He says, "I don't know, I just don't know. Lately, she's just so, you know."

I'm still half asleep and wonder if he is talking about me or his eight-year-old daughter. She's a lonely kid, a little withdrawn, and very smart. She doesn't call me "Mommy" which is understandable, but sometimes I wish she did.

An acorn hits the roof. Our house is at the end of a country lane, surrounded by white oaks — not a bad house, but still a rental. People don't take care of rentals the way they do their own house and I am no exception. Eventually someone will buy this house after an advertisement says it's a fixer-upper. It's definitely not a starter home, nor a golden years home. It's a dump is what it is, and I decide to remain in bed the rest of the day and maybe my life. I'll tell my boyfriend it's cramps. I'll never own a house or be a real mother. I'll become a bed person.

Six months back, I moved here on a temporary basis for a secretarial job that went bad fast. I can't remember ever having a job that didn't go bad fast. I either get mad and quit or get mad and get fired. Most bosses think that having authority is a license to treat you poorly, and I won't let anyone do that to me.

Another acorn hits the roof. I used to like that tree until nuts covered the driveway, and last weekend I asked my boyfriend's daughter to dump them in a groundhog hole near the door. She did it for about ten minutes, then wanted to get paid.

"Paid," I said. "What about family chores?"

She held the bottom of her shirt high on her chest to make a pouch for the acorns. She didn't say anything but I knew what she was thinking—the same thing I was thinking—that filling a hole with acorns wasn't much of a family chore. Still it ticked me off because she didn't know the first thing about a mean boss or a bad job, or some guy brushing against your backside while you're leaning over the water fountain, or straining his neck to peek down your shirt when you bend forward. I wanted to tell her all this but I didn't. For one thing, she's in the third grade. For another, she already knows some things that aren't so hot. She's an only child to a single parent. Her mother is on parole in another state.

I am a new presence in this girl's life, one who made her fill a hole with nuts. I wondered if a real mother would do that. It occurred to me that she was probably wondering the same thing, and I told her to drop the acorns. She looked as close to happy as she'd been in months. Right then I knew things were not just going bad, they'd already got there.

Lying in bed bores me until I have no choice but to rise and dress. I can't even stick out staying in bed. I pull on the cowboy boots that were a gift from a man in Colorado with twins—one boot per kid is how I look at them. Payday just went by, and after the bills, I am sixty bucks to the good and there's a thousand things to do, chief among them taking that money to the beauty parlor and going for the makeover—haircut, manicure, mud wrap. Maybe buying my boyfriend a new belt buckle will make him feel better. On the other hand, maybe I shouldn't worry so much about making him feel better.

I fix coffee and the girl shuffles through the house, head down like a crippled dog. Her clothes fit loose. For a minute I consider moving on down the road until I find a new man's life to fit into. I've done it before. I don't need much of a push.

Every man I find seems like he needs more than one woman—one for money, one for sex, one to cook and clean and raise his kids, and one to make him feel better at all times. Each woman is supposed to wait at home while he stays out all night or serves jail time or goes fishing for a week. I'm good at picking the wrong man, or maybe they're good at picking me. One trick is to sit by the TV in a bar and they can't help but notice you. I know the right guy's out there, but then again, I thought my boyfriend was. He's a good man, just out of work, and his kid needs a mom. The problem is, I don't know if I'm fit for the job.

"Let's take a drive," I say to her.

"Where?"

"Anywhere. Just a drive. That's what living in the country means. Follow back roads and see where they lead."

"They don't lead anywhere."

"Maybe we'll find a road that leads to a new place."

"There's nothing new here. It's all just old."

"What I mean is a new place we haven't been to yet."

"I get car sick."

"On the school bus, you do. But we're not taking the bus today."

"I don't know."

"Tell your father."

She looks at me a long time, as if realizing I am truly serious, and that despite her overall mood, it might not be a bad idea to roam the land in my company. My boyfriend waves from the couch, an impatient kind of wave like someone warding off bugs at a picnic.

Outside, the day is full of autumn with a sky so blue and clear that it's not sky any more but water in a bowl. My old Chevy starts on the third try. The shocks are bad and the girl sits at the far edge of the bench seat. I ease down the road, hitting every pothole in sight. I tell the girl about hay stacks. I grew up in the country and it makes me feel good to let her know I have some knowledge that surprises her. I'm more than the newest woman to take up with her dad. I have worked on a farm. I own a car and can drive a tractor. I explain how hay is harvested in rounded rolls to shed water instead of the old-time square bales. Out West, I tell her, they still use square bales because it hardly ever rains and the sun is so clean you can see a bird a hundred miles away.

The girl looks out the window and says that she's car sick. She wants to go home and read a book in which magic works. She believes in magic and who am I to tell her she's wrong? People go to church, read the horoscope, and have lucky rocks. Sometimes I feel like I'm starving and everybody else has just finished a big meal and I'm still scratching holes in the dirt looking for a seed.

I park under a leafless willow beside a little dry creek bed that feeds into a bigger dry creek. I can't recall ever being alone with my own mother in a car. It must have happened, but it was either so long ago that I've forgotten, or nothing occurred that mattered. She never left the house until she left for good. I was seven years old.

I want to speak to the girl, but don't know how to pierce her misery, so I just shoot from the hip.

"Do you ever get scared of the family room?" I say.

"I'm scared of the whole house."

This surprises me. I don't know what to say because all I can think is how children are more sensitive than adults and if she's scared of the whole house, not only must it be haunted, but she is sure messed up.

"How come?" I say.

"Just am."

"What is it that scares you?"

"All of it."

"Like it's haunted or something?"

"Maybe," she says. "Do you think it is?"

"Of course not. There's no such things as ghosts."

"How do you know?"

I put the car in reverse and have to hold the brake and give it gas until it jerks into gear. We drive along the road. The transmission slips, and I remind myself not to get in a spot where I have to go backwards. Always forward is my motto.

The trees look like somebody dumped buckets of bright paint out of a helicopter and I start thinking how that would be a cool job, one you couldn't get fired from, then jerk the wheel hard to miss a dead raccoon. The girl makes a face. She is a city kid who likes bagels, video stores, and pizza delivery. There is no life outside this car for her and roadkill is living proof of this.

"What will make you happy?" I say.

She shrugs and shifts her body away, the same motion my boyfriend has used on me for two months.

"How about a bike?" I say.

"There's not any good places to ride."

"A mountain bike, then. It's perfect for the country. You know how to ride, right?"

She looks at me as if I've given her the worst insult possible, then rolls her eyes. She's only eight. I don't know how to talk to her. When her life doubles, she will drive a car. In thirty years she might be me—a woman trying to get by. The problem is, as I get older, the love gets harder to find. Sex used to be important but these days I just keep an eye out for somebody to team up with.

The girl turns her head to me.

"What," I say.

"What what?"

"What what what?"

"What what what what?"

A fragment of a smile flees across her face, and the rest of the drive goes smoothly. Town is town, full of people who went to town. I stop at a pawnshop, thinking that for sixty bucks, I can get a bike with three gears and tell her it's a mountain bike. The store smells like sweat and dust, which is really the smell of hope and loss. The small room is packed with guns, watches, video games, guitars, tools, stereo systems, fishing rods, cell phones, and radios. Cheap jewelry lies in a glass case with tape over the cracks. There is a row of leather jackets chained to each other through the sleeves, and if you wanted to steal one, you had to steal them all. This is a room of last resort, like a chapel before an execution. Everything in this place has been handled by people at the end of their rope, and that despair fills the air.

Against a wall are two big touring bicycles with ram's horn handles and tiny seats. Beside them is a little kid's bicycle with training wheels. In the corner stands a mountain bike with shock absorbers on the front tire, fifteen gears, and a water bottle. It has no bell, no streamers, and no fenders. It doesn't even have a kickstand. It looks like a bike that got stripped by a thief, and I wonder if the guy is going to try and sell me the rest in parts.

The girl goes right to that bike like a fly to sugar. Her entire posture is full of desire, a feeling I know well. My problem is I keep getting what I want—a new man, another job, a fresh start in a different place. As soon as I get it, I don't want it anymore. I stand in a room surrounded by all this stuff that people are supposed to have, and I have no desire for any of it. There's nothing in this store for me, nothing in any store. Six months ago I told myself that life with a new man would be different. It must be true, because this is the first time I've ever entered a pawnshop as a buyer. Usually I'm trying to raise money to leave town.

I ask if the girl can test ride the bicycle in the parking lot. He pushes the bike across the dark carpet. The girl follows and I watch through the plate glass window. She rides in a circle with a joyous look on her face.

"It's sold," I say. "How much?"

"Three hundred."

"New, sure. But what's the pawn price?"

"That is the pawn price. New is eight hundred."

"That's a lot of money."

"I can see it's been a while since you bought a new bike."

I don't say anything because it's been a while since I bought anything new. Somebody else's body has already filled all my clothes. Even my boyfriend was married before. I wish I had a career and the same man for a few years, but I'm stuck with this life. Every wrong decision I ever made has led me here, to this place at this moment—standing in a room full of things I don't want, facing a man alone.

"Let's talk turkey," I say. "You can see the jam I'm in. She wants that bike but three hundred's beyond reach. I don't have anywhere near that. I'm in a pickle and you can help. Let's work something out."

The pawnshop guy looks me up and down like I'm something pawnable that he doesn't really want, but might hold for a while. I know what's coming, too. He'll say something that hints at paying the other way, and if I pick up on it, he'll be more direct. Men are predictable. The key is to head them off early. This place is guaranteed to have two things hidden—a loaded pistol near the front, and a mattress in the back. I look at him and think about his body naked. I start taking off a cowboy boot. He is watching me carefully. He's probably seen people pull everything out of their boots— a wad of cash, a switchblade, a gun. All that comes out of my boot is a foot.

I lower my eyes to look at him through the lashes. I wet my lips and speak low.

"Ostrich," I say. "The toughest leather of all. Seven rows of stitching on the uppers. Heels are in good shape. These are thousand dollar boots."

He takes the boot and I remove the other. It gets hung because that foot is a little bit bigger than the other, which has always been a problem. Once I bought a pair of pumps that were a half-size apart. They fit well, and I worry about the poor woman who bought the other two shoes. The pawnshop guy looks the boots over. He is a lucky man. People walk in his store every day and place valuable things in his hands.

Outside, the girl rides back and forth across the lot. She is smiling and when a girl smiles that way, her whole body is happy and she can't remember when it wasn't. The bike swerves. She jerks the handlebars for balance, and glances through the window, and I do the right thing and pretend as if I didn't notice.

"Straight up swap," I say. "The boots for the bike."

"You wearing a belt?"

"No."

"Got anything in the car?"

"Like what?"

"CD player. Pistol. Different people carry different things. Maybe a coat. I had a man show up with forty car batteries once."

I follow him outside. The pavement hurts my feet and I am careful to avoid walking on broken glass. He looks in the car windows, checking for something to sweeten the deal. The back seat holds a grocery bag and a math book. There is nothing else in the car. It suddenly looks old and ratty, exactly what you'd expect to see parked in a pawnshop lot. I wonder if people driving by think I'm the kind of woman they'd expect to see standing here. My feet are cold. None of this is what I had in mind today.

The girl rides near. She's the most free creature in the world—a kid on a bike—and I envy her. She's only walked this earth for eight years. I've been here for thirty-eight and don't even have shoes to show for it. At this moment, to keep her happy, I will trade the whole car for the bike. I glance at the pawnshop guy to see if he can somehow read my mind and hold out for the Chevy, but he is looking in the trunk. The slot for the spare tire is empty. There is a dirty blanket and a jack. The pawnshop guy lifts the jack from the trunk. It is newish. It is the most newish part of my life.

"Your daughter," he says, "is very pretty. Just like her mother."

"Thank you. But she's not my daughter."

"I know," he said. "I was trying to be nice."

"How did you know?"

"Most people don't bring kids in here."

"I didn't have a lot of choice."

"Let me finish," he says. "Parents don't want their kids to see them in a tough spot. An aunt or a step-mom doesn't mind that much. Myself, I think it's good for children to see that grownups have it hard sometimes."

"Do you have kids?"

"Yes, but I don't live with them. I'm a good dad though. And I make sure they see me vulnerable."

"You don't seem like the usual pawnshop guy."

"It's just a job."

"Then how about leaving me that jack?"

"Can't," he says. "A deal's a deal."

He walks away and I realize that he didn't come on to me and I'm grateful for that. This surprises me because in my younger days I never thought I'd feel this way. Maybe I'm maturing. That strikes me as funny, because if it's true then I'm a mature woman with bare feet and no jack. I like to travel light.

I wave the girl over.

"Help me put it in the trunk," I say.

She says nothing.

"It's yours," I say.

She doesn't speak, and I wonder if she understands. The trunk won't close all the way. Driving will make the lid bang against the bike and I don't have any rope. I look at the pawnshop, but there's no way I will ask that man for help. I search the weeds at the edge of the lot and find nothing to tie the trunk with. The girl knows something is not right, but doesn't want to ask. I don't know what to say to make her feel better. A real mother would, but I can't think of anything. I just look at her and nod.

She watches me unsnap my bra under my sweater. I wriggle the strap off one shoulder, hook it past my elbow, and over my hand. The other side comes off easy. I pull the bra from my sleeve. As nonchalantly as possible I tie it to the inside of the trunk, and knot it around the bike like a bungee cord. The bra is ruined, but that doesn't matter since it was used to begin with.

We drive out of the lot and the girl never shifts her eyes away from me. This is the most she's ever looked at me. Her attention makes me nervous.

"Nice bike," I say.

She shrugs.

"It's yours," I say.

She stares at the dark trees flashing past in the dusk. I suddenly remember endless trips to town with my father, looking out the window, counting telephone poles and mail boxes, seeing the same houses and the same railroad tracks, all the time wishing I lived somewhere else. The memory is shocking because it runs dead against how I see my childhood now, one I hoped to give the girl, that of gathering wildflowers for a supper table and listening all day to the singing of birds. Instead, I hated where I grew up and resented my folks for living there. I was mad at God for having the gall to stick me in a world where I had no friends, nothing to do, and nowhere to go. It was a dead place. I left early.

I park near the house and get out of the car. The blacktop is broken into chunks like brownies. I untie my bra and remove the bike and place it on the road. The girl straddles the seat and pushes off. The bike wobbles until she gains speed, then she stops. She has to get off the bike to turn it around. Instead of riding, she pushes it back toward me. Her face is serious and I wonder if something is wrong—a broken spoke or a loose wheel. Maybe I got gypped on the deal. Somebody might already be wearing my boots and I am ready to get mad—at the girl, at the pawnshop guy, at myself. I didn't start going to pawnshops until I was an adult, but her whole life is secondhand, even me.

She looks at me and says, "Thanks, Lucy."

"You're welcome," I say.

She pushes hair from her face with shaking hands. I want to watch forever. It is the most beautiful sight I've ever seen, a child's hands trembling with delight. I can't remember my hands ever doing that. When mine shake, it is always with fear. She climbs on the bike and pedals away. I wonder if I'd have made the same trade for my own daughter.

———————

Chris Offutt grew up in Haldeman, Kentucky, a former mining community of two hundred people. He graduated from Morehead State University and is the author of *No Heroes*, *The Same River Twice*, *Kentucky Straight*, *Out of the Woods*, and *The Good Brother*. His writing has received many honors, including Lannan, Whiting, and American Academy of Arts and Letters awards; the Prix Coindreau in France; and fellowships from the Guggenheim Foundation and the NEA. He is currently a visiting professor at the Iowa Writers' Workshop.

My stories often bog down in the writing process. Many times I have reread the first draft to try and understand what I thought I was up to initially. I wrote the first draft of "Second Hand" in October 1998 while living in my home county in Kentucky. Written in first person from the point of view of a man with a son, the story's original title was "Boots for Bike." I believed it to be about the difficulties of moving to Kentucky.

A year later, I drafted the story again, changing the point of view to second person, an experiment I was running on several stories. (Only a couple survived.) A year later, I began revising the story once more. The title had changed to "Real Ghosts," and it was back in the first person. It was also twice as long. I realized the story was about my son, but I needed distance from the events, so I changed the genders of everyone. Finally, at draft eight, two years after the first draft, the story became narrated by a woman.

I began submitting the story to magazines in May 2000. It was rejected by the New Yorker, O, The Oprah Magazine, *the* Atlantic Monthly, Paris Review, Harper's, Open City, *and* Tin House. *In the spring of 2003, it was published in the* Iowa Review, *my first publication with that magazine.*

*The early versions of "Second Hand" were based on my strained relation-
ship with my eight-year-old son. He was miserable in the Kentucky school
system. He understood that we were living in Kentucky because I had wanted
to go home, and he quite openly and correctly blamed me for his unhappiness.
I thought buying him a bicycle might help him feel better. It didn't. I
thought writing this story might make me feel better. It didn't. The only solution, sadly, was to leave Kentucky once more forever.*

*My son is now in eighth grade. He uses his bike to travel between his
mother's house and mine. When I look at this story today, examining all the
drafts, I realize it was not about Kentucky at all, nor is it about my son.*

*Naturally, I am engaged in writing other stories now. I try to revise them
based on what I suspect they are trying to be about. But I know that it may
take another five years before I understand what the stories are really about.
Trusting this process allows me the freedom I need to make art.*

Ingrid Hill

VALOR

(from *Image*)

The sight of her just took my breath away. On the edge of the veranda, three feet above the fringe-silky pale green lawn, tiny Colby Anne Mouton perched barefoot and heaved a huge perfect round sun of a bright navel orange out toward a pile of branches and brush I was told was a woodchuck's nest. I recall laying my hand (I want to say my *little* hand) diagonally across my sternum, passionate in my astonishment. Colby Anne Mouton was six, and the child of someone who seemed to live here in this grand house in Jackson where three of my friends and I had been sent for the warm December weekend.

Colby Anne was a beautiful child with soulful brown eyes and springy pale hair, a strange contrast. I was smitten with her, in that electrical-storm-somewhere-exotic way that little girls have of falling in love with one another. I was four years older. My legs were too long, my waist was too high. I was on the awkward verge of a growth spurt.

Just last night my husband Will protested effusively that I *put to shame the pale fire of the moon.* He had had a glass of retsina on an empty stomach, and he was quoting someone in his faux-professorial way, a joke that wasn't a joke. I know that he meant it. But I surely never was beautiful as a child like little Colby Anne.

Colby Anne heaved one more orange with her pretty little arm, and it fell near the first one. One by one, she heaved all of the oranges in the brown bowl, quite a few, until a bright orange W lay in the grass, the spread-out shape of the constellation Cassiopeia.

The previous week, a woman named Rosa Parks, pale brown as the coffee with too much cream that I liked for my breakfast and that was forbidden to me at school, had, in Montgomery, declined to defer to a bus driver when he suggested she give up her seat to a white man.

She had been arrested. She had said that her feet were tired, that was all. This news was in the paper, along with a photo of Rosa Parks next to a somewhat vain-looking policeman who seemed, judging from the expression on his face, to believe that as the fruit of this publicity he might become the next Tyrone Power. Mrs. Rosa Parks was having her fingerprints taken. Her face retained a great dignity in the event. My understanding of all of the issues involved was a limited one, but I liked the way Rosa Parks's eyes in the newspaper photograph held a kind, sparkly wisdom.

Friday afternoon we were to be picked up in the courtyard of Saint Pet's by the aunt of a classmate of mine, Garnet Blevins, and taken for the weekend to the estate of their Jackson relations. The Academy of Saints Perpetua and Felicitas sat cozily back off Freret Street in the Garden District, on a one-block dead end called Narcissus Street. Its courtyard was paved with slate tiles that looked ancient, and bordered by palms and magnolia trees, which at this time of the year looked, according to Sister John Marie, "peaked." Sister John Marie had quite a number of words that intrigued me. I wrote them down, looked them up, made them mine.

In spring in the courtyard there were grand displays of purplish azaleas and buttery, creamy camellias, but now the area had a sparse, wasting-away look to it. The statue at the heart of the courtyard was covered with dried vines that obscured what was beneath. Sister Thomas Aquinas was shepherding us at the moment. She was in charge of the upper school and thus somewhat formidable to me, but I turned and asked her what the statue looked like underneath that. She screwed up her brow and said, as if to an unseen audience, "What a curious child." I looked straight back at her. Adults had a way of trying to intimidate children with that sort of move, I thought. When I didn't look away she said, "Do you have to know *everything?*"

I said, "I guess that means you don't know.

She looked shocked and disgusted.

I said, looking off at the wan winter palms, "Maybe there isn't a statue in there at all. Maybe it's only a pile of dead vines."

She rustled her hands in the sleeves of her robe, grabbing each ghost-pale forearm with the other. This move, I later learned, was called "custody of the hands." She turned and marched muscularly indoors on her flat black priestlike oxfords. A smell of ironing wafted off her enormous black veil, which billowed jubilantly like the sail of a ship heading off to the Indies in our new geography books. That ironing smell was intoxicating to me. It beat out the power of intimidation. It was said that Sister Tommy could hit a softball quite a distance. I was told by a classmate that when spring came we'd see the odd spectacle of her, a dozen or so steel butterfly clips holding her skirts and veil and coif and wimple out of the way, rounding the bases maniacally. I could not imagine that.

We four girls stood in our burgundy-colored wool school blazers with their gold crests and our matching pleated skirts, with our little valises, inside the arched gate awaiting the aunt in her Cadillac. Garnet said we would love the smell of the car's leather seats, and when the aunt arrived, yes, we did. Those seats smelled edible.

The aunt's name was Adele. Garnet introduced her to us as Aunt Adele. We were hardly out of the city onto the flat pale road skirting the lake before the woman, a tidy brunette in her thirties with very red lipstick, craned her head around at us, seeming not to need to watch the road. This alarmed me, the super-responsible one. She told us, "You can all call me Quillie." Her smile was brilliant, a Pepsodent smile.

Garnet looked at me oddly, surprised, as if to confirm that she'd heard this. She turned back toward her aunt, who was once more facing forward, and said, "Even me?"

"Yes," said her aunt. "Even you."

I sat in the back seat with Garnet and Katya Nuryeva, and up in the front, next to Quillie, sat little dark-eyed Sonia Villanueve, whose father worked at the consulate downtown, and who spoke little English. I had gone to the consulate with her on the streetcar one day, to a building that smelled of damp marble and had polished brass cuspidors in the halls. The elevator buttons lit up from inside.

Her father had a mustache like a matinee idol from decades before. I expected him to pick up a rose, place it between his teeth, and dance with crisp, pointy-toed steps past the cuspidors, clicking his heels. He did not. He simply bowed slightly to me, ushered us into his office, and finished some papers while Sonia and I ate little pale bricks of nougat in cellophane from a cut-glass bowl. His secretary gave us each a pen with a picture of a cathedral in Barcelona on it and complimented us on our pretty uniforms.

Katya Nuryeva had been born in Russia but come to America by way of some other country. Her father, it was said, had been beheaded in some revolution, and her mother was in a hospital in New York State for rich people who had nervous breakdowns.

"Now then," I said to Katya, "is your mother really really crazy? Or just sort of?" She frowned at me, a little bit cross-eyed. One of her eyes was slightly off, amblyopic. She seemed to be seeing someone spooky over my shoulder.

"She only have tuberculosis," said Katya. "But not any more."

I didn't ask about her father because I thought perhaps the story was just a rumor, and I did not want to be disabused of the image of that silver blade, razor-sharp, coming down on his neck. It was so very gallant. Saint Paul had died that way, and so many other saints too. I admired beheadings. I read about Anne Boleyn, and Mary Queen of Scots, and I thought I might like to die that way. My own patron saint, Joan of Arc, had been burned at the stake, and that just sounded messy. I had heard that burnt flesh smelled atrocious.

The saints after whom our school was named, Perpetua and

Felicitas, had been martyred at Carthage. Felicitas had had seven sons, all of whom were killed by vicious Romans before her eyes, one by one. The other had a baby at the breast: because it was phrased this way, I pictured the child hanging there, on a dug, swinging monkeylike, sucking so noisily that people up in the very back rows could hear, *squuck squuck,* as the veiled prisoners were disgorged into the arena. The women had been released from their cells to be gored by a heifer, but the heifer would not gore, and simply stood there pawing. In consequence they too went under the axe.

It was all quite delicious to me. I wondered whether underneath all that tangle of ivy in the courtyard there was a recalcitrant heifer, or the seven sons of Felicitas clinging to her skirts, or a pile of severed heads, or what. The columnar clump of ivy was substantial.

Katya Nuryeva got carsick just outside of Hammond. Quillie said she was allergic to throw-up and asked me to clean it up because I was the tallest. The seats wiped up easily, and I didn't mind because the vomit was purple and interesting. We had eaten berry cobbler for lunch at school.

At a little gas station with ancient pumps, just before Tickfaw, Quillie and Sonia and Garnet stood in a row like see-no-evil hear-no-evil speak-no-evil monkeys, a good ways away from the Cadillac, holding their noses while I mopped up the back seat and then mopped it again. The wife of the gas station owner held a little plaid ice bag to Katya Nuryeva's forehead on the steps to the little store and murmured consolingly. She gave Katya a bottle of 7-Up and then looked over at me mopping the seats and gave me one, too.

Garnet made a sound that was a lot like whining, so the woman brought out three more 7-Ups from the ice chest outside the front door. She dragged each drink bottle noisily along its little track, through the chipped ice and water, and hauled it out in triumph, as if it were a fish she had caught.

We were ready to leave, and Quillie had not even thanked the lady but rather took it all as her due, seeming to be one of the children rather than the one in charge. I went inside to the station owner's wife, who seemed to me a little uncomfortable at this, and I whispered into her ear, "That was good that you did that. Katya's father—that little wall-eyed girl's father—was beheaded in Russia." I made a sad face and she looked alarmed, then we got back on the road.

We passed signs for Roseland, and Fluker, and Tangipahoa, and then we were in Mississippi. We went through McComb and Brookhaven. Katya slept leaning against the door, and Garnet slept leaning against Katya, and I worked a crossword puzzle whose clues I recall thinking seemed to have been made up by someone who was really crabby and thought he was hot stuff.

Quillie tried to get a conversation going with Sonia several times, but Sonia was quiet and shy, and her Castilian accent was impenetrable to Quillie, so mostly we drove in silence. Several miles past Hazlehurst I leaned forward and asked Quillie if she knew a five-letter word for mother-of-pearl that began with an *n* and ended with an *e*.

She said, "Honey, you cannot be serious!" and laughed uproariously. "Is that your idea of *fun?*" she said. "I'd rather get my eye-teeth drilled!" She laughed again.

Then we were there. The Blevinses who lived in Jackson were Garnet's father's cousins. Their estate had a crushed-stone drive as long as a city block, with a wrought-iron gate. Quillie got out to open it and then had me get out to go back and close it.

The house, built of dark stone at the turn of the century, had long high strange windows, which at certain hours of the day let in full light but mostly seemed only to gather the shadows. There were few trees but the ones that there were rose stately and tall from the lawn. As we drove into the grounds I saw birdbaths with putti that peed ostentatiously, flagstone walks circling and twining through shrubbery, a central fountain with three tiers of scallop-shaped basins and miniature waterfalls. We pulled up to the house and got out. The house loomed.

A stout older gentleman in a white suit with pale, near-invisible stripes clunked his way down the stairs with a cane. "Hallelujah," he grumbled. "You're here. I was ready to call out the state police, Quillie." He looked at us. "Who are these . . . ?" he didn't know what to call us. Strangers. Casket girls. Orphans.

"Oh, Aunt Oney knows about it," Quillie said dismissively. "Girls, this is Uncle Governor." For a moment, given that Jackson was the capital of the state, I wondered if he were *the* governor, whose name I already knew from school was James Coleman. Later on, she explained: that was not a title, it was his name, Governor Blevins. He had a white Vandyke beard and round tortoise-shell glasses.

"Uncle Governor knows everything." Then she laughed. "Except who *you* are." Behind Uncle Governor was a slight, aristocratically bored-looking boy of eighteen or nineteen. His forelock flopped across his forehead in a way I would later identify as Edwardian, Rupert Brooke-ish. "And this is Garnet's second cousin Carlyle." I was trying to figure out how everyone was related, and I had lost my way already.

"That would be once removed," said the young man diffidently.

"Get on inside, y'all," said Uncle Governor. "I swear, you make me break out in goddamn hives, Adele, when I know you're on the road."

"I have *never* had an accident," Quillie said.

"Unless you count the time that you went off that bridge," Uncle Governor said.

"What bridge," said Quillie. No question mark. Stoppage. A sealed gate.

"Oh, get those girls upstairs and show them their rooms," Uncle Governor said, waving impatiently at the French doors on the veranda with his cane. "If Oneida knows, I suppose there must be rooms prepared." I watched his beard waggle as he spoke, in fascination. His face was bright pink and his eyebrows resembled an Eskimo dog's I had seen being walked by a maid on Freret Street.

We were two to a room, Katya with me and Sonia with Garnet. The windows in our room looked straight out into a tree, thick and dark with leaves. The colored maid who had brought us upstairs said we should have a bath before dinner and that we should give her our dresses to iron. Katya looked over at me, and also, with her errant eve, slightly behind me. "It's okay," I said. I unpacked my pale green polished cotton with smocking and handed it over.

The maid flared her nostrils. "I ain't got time to wash it besides," she said. She held it out to show me the clump of egg yolk on the front of the sash.

"Oops," I said. The hard, nasty yellow-brown crust looked permanent.

"You can wear one of mine," Katya said. She took out two dresses, both rich-colored and enviable, and handed them to the maid.

At dinner there were other grown-ups we had not seen before and did not see afterward. Uncle Governor held forth on the subject of tung oil prices and other topics of no interest whatsoever. Little Colby Anne played with her big heavy butter knife, tipping her plate and sending her kaiser roll flying into Cousin Carlyle's finger bowl. Great peals of laughter. I watched everyone closely and ate without looking at anything on my plate.

I remember thinking that food in Mississippi was blander than what we had at home, even at school. I supposed that was true even in the governor's mansion. Colby Anne slid under the table and disappeared. I felt her crawl across the toes of my Vaselined-to-a-high-shine Mary Janes. I saw Carlyle roll his eyes as she crawled over him and then the white linen cutwork tablecloth rippled and pulled imperceptibly as she passed the rest of the unoccupied places on her little knees then popped out for a moment at the far end. Quillie shot her a glance so quick it was almost not there. Sonia looked over at me with a quiet smile of delight, wishing that she too could crawl away.

When the little squares of moist dark cake, the only part of the dinner to hold interest for me, had all been consumed, except by a few grown-ups—Uncle Governor had snatched Aunt Oney's and she had laughed in feeble protest—we retired to a grand room with long plum-colored damask drapes, in which Cousin Carlyle was asked to sit at the piano and play, for what seemed hours, piece after piece of Brahms and Liszt.

Two or three times, little Colby Anne wandered in and out of the room snapping a pale wooden paddle-and-ball in deep concentration. Quillie watched me watching Colby Anne with an odd look on her face, which I caught when I turned my head quickly. When she looked away, I studied her. She seemed younger than I had thought at first, perhaps in her late twenties. Her lipstick had worn off except for a hard line around the edges. She chewed at her bottom lip nervously, or perhaps thoughtfully.

The next morning there was breakfast in the big dining room, and then people dispersed. We seemed to be free to wander. Quillie drove into town and Aunt Oney took Garnet and the other two girls shopping with her, just for the ride. They were going to look for a grass-catcher for the lawnmower, because it seemed the gardener had threatened to go on strike if he had to rake any more, and he was required to mow even in winter.

Out on the veranda, Uncle Governor was tutoring Carlyle in his studies. I sidled out and pretended to be playing with a calico cat that had just appeared out of nowhere. The cat was the sort that had little interest in being stroked. It tired quickly of my half-hearted cajoling. I was at loose ends.

"Get over here, then, child," called Uncle Governor, as if I had said something. "Put your mind to something other than that foolish cat of Oney's."

"The cat hissed at him once and he wanted to have it put to sleep," said Carlyle in his languid way.

"Sleep!" Uncle Governor said. "Be precise, nephew. Death!" He turned to me. "I am trying to preserve for generations to come the irreproducible joys of the classics." He and Carlyle had open across their respective laps heavy identical gray-covered textbooks.

"We have studied today lesson twenty-three of Latin II, entitled 'Rome Sweet Home,' by some silly constructor of textbooks," said Carlyle.

"Sacred geese sat upon the walls. Lo, when the Gauls approached, climbing like vermin on ladders to enter the city, one Manlius, our hero, woke at the squawking and — oh my!! — the city was saved. Sacred geese!" Carlyle seemed simultaneously contemptuous and enamored of the idea. I found that complex and attractive. No one at home talked to me this way.

"Sit down, girl," said Uncle Governor enthusiastically. "Learn something!"

I sat down excitedly, glad I had not gone to shop for a grass-catcher.

Uncle Governor began reading as if he were addressing a crowd, *"Anseres non fefellerunt, quos sacros Iunoni in summa inopia. . . ."*

Lobelia interrupted, "Mister Governor."

"Tsk! Belia! Let me finish my sentence!" he chided her. *"Romani tamen non occiderant.* Now. What."

"How anybody ever gone know when you finish, way beyond me," said Lobelia, eyes to the sky. I marveled at her gorgeous spunk. I had never heard household help talk this way. "Neetsie want to know you gone to give her them shoes you was talking about to polish or what," Lobelia said.

"I am *wearing* the shoes in question," Uncle Governor said.

"Then you got a choice," said Lobelia. "Neetsie say she going home after lunch and not coming back till Tuesday. Sunday her day off and Monday Miss Oney say she don't have to come because they got a funeral in Paspagoula for her uncle Lucretius that have three strokes and die last night." She paused. "He the one own that nigger motel."

Uncle Governor stared at her in perplexity. Then he said in a bewildered tone, stopping dead on each word, "There is no nigger motel in Pascagoula." He emphasized the hard *c,* to correct the maid's country pronunciation.

"You mean you ain't seen one," Lobelia said. "Lawd." She rolled her eyes.

Uncle Governor continued to stare, his eyebrows up in astonishment.

"Y'all get to choose, said Lobelia, clear and patient. "Y'all dignity or them shoes polish."

Uncle Governor sighed in disbelief and leaned over his vest-encased belly to untie his shoes.

Lobelia turned to me. "Mister Governor be choosing to give up he dignity," she said. A flicker of mischief rolled like a wave across her brow. He handed her the shoes and she waved away the sock-sour, Ben-Gay-laced smell of Uncle Governor's feet. "Mister Governor got *two* degrees from Ole Miss, I believe." She was not really looking at me, but she seemed to be announcing it for my information. "Ain't that right, Mister Governor?"

"Thank you, Belia," Uncle Governor said, scowling and motioning her indoors. "That will be all."

Lobelia held the shoes out away from her and made as if her eyes were beginning to water. I laughed. Carlyle seemed intrigued at my laughing.

"Now, Carlyle," said Uncle Governor. You will recall in the previous lesson we talked about the notion of the genitive of the whole. As in *nihil imperi,* no power. As in *plurimum terroris,* a great deal of terror. Do you see any examples of that construction in the passage at hand?" His feet, thin and flat for so large a man, wiggled in his black silk socks on the flagstones.

"*No power,*" Lobelia said musingly. "*A great deal of terror.* I never." She headed indoors with his shoes held out as if they might snap at her. As she walked away I heard her mutter under her breath, "*sacred geese,*" as if that were the silliest thing she had heard in a good long time.

Uncle Governor cleared his throat as if to erase the memory of Lobelia's momentary incursion. "Excuse me, Carlyle," he said. "A bit of review. The two verbs from yesterday's lesson: kindly decline them for me."

Carlyle said, like a machine, but a languid aristocratic machine, "*diripio, diripere, diripui, direptus,* to plunder." Uncle Governor nodded: check.

"*Parco, parcere, peperci, parsurus,*" to spare. Another nod: check.

Uncle Governor turned to me. "I imagine this must all seem rather unusual to you," he said. "Ancient Rome! Indeed!" He laughed, loving his possession of the Empire.

"Not at all," I said, lifting the phrase and inflection from some movie I'd seen in which Grace Kelly had said that so easily, seeming to take the high ground.

"In fact," I said, "the two saints our academy's named after were of that era."

Uncle Governor and Carlyle looked at me as if I had stepped off a saucer from Mars.

"*That era!*" Uncle Governor echoed.

"Sister Thomas Aquinas said they died in Carthage," I said. "In the arena, but not in Rome."

Uncle Governor stared at me again in disbelief. Carlyle stared at *him,* bemused.

"Who would those saints be, and who are you young ladies, and why the pernicious dickens are you *here* for the weekend *anyway?*" Uncle Governor said. He seemed to have been holding back this outburst ever since we arrived.

"Saints Perpetua and Felicitas," I said. "We board at the Academy of Saints Perpetua and Felicitas, on Narcissus Street, in the Garden District of New Orleans, and I have no idea why we're here except that none of us has parents in town at the moment. My parents are in imports and last thing I heard they were in Portugal buying mosaics and holy-water fonts for their store. We were told we were being shipped to Garnet's relations for the weekend, and then Quillie came and picked us up."

Again, that stare. I intuited that I needed to sound more my age. "Katya vomited just outside Tickfaw," I said. That seemed to normalize me a bit. "It was purple," I said. "We'd had blackberry cobbler for lunch at school." There, I had done it all the way. I was a regular child once again, and appropriate.

Carlyle burst out guffawing and laughed until he began choking. He staggered toward the French doors, croaking, "*Aqua, aqua,* Lobelia." Uncle Governor stared me down, white eyebrows meeting above his pink nose. "Saints Perpetua and Felicitas?" Uncle Governor said. "On Narcissus Street?"

"They were martyrs," I said.

"I believe I know that," Uncle Governor said, seeming affronted.

"They were martyred at Carthage," I said.

"Such a little fountain of knowledge," marveled Carlyle, staggering back, seemingly recovered. Lobelia had paid no attention to his little drama.

"Pipe down, Carlyle," said Uncle Governor, as if to a terrier. "Give the little lady some room. She is, what, eleven years old?"

"Ten," I said. "I'm just a little tall." I felt compelled to tell all that I knew. "Felicitas had seven sons. Perpetua had a baby at the breast." I looked brazenly into Uncle Governor's eyes, clenching my teeth slightly, when I said *breast*. "We have a statue of them in the courtyard at school but there's ivy over it. I don't know whether all seven of her sons are there."

"Well," Uncle Governor drawled, "in point of fact, that was another Felicitas, one who died in the arena at Rome, half a century earlier, before the persecutions had spread to the provinces, who had the seven sons." Carlyle stared at him. So did I. "The sons' names were Philip, Felix, Alexander . . ."

"*A different Felicitas?*" Carlyle said. "And what do you know about saints, Uncle Governor, you atheist?" He scoffed.

"What indeed do I know about the Roman Empire, and the Roman language, and Roman martyrology? Carlyle, some deference." Uncle Governor puffed out his chest. "The rest of the sons of Felicitas," he announced. "Martial. Vitalis. Silvanus. And—last but not least—Januarius."

I sat in silence considering what it might take to know so many facts about which no one else gave a hoot. I thought of Quillie in the car mocking my passion for crosswords. In the space of a split second, there on the veranda, with a damp coolish wind lifting off the lawn, I considered the complex question of whether indeed, as Sister Tommy had said, I did need to know everything, how futile facts were, and finally, that the accretion of all the facts in the world would never add up to wisdom.

Immediately I said anyway, unable to stop myself, "Well, if Carthage is in Africa, were the saints my school is named after colored?" That had never occurred to me. I thought that if it was true it was wonderful.

The wind suddenly dropped away, and the branches stopped waving, the leaves hushed themselves. Uncle Governor seemed to inspect his feet in his black silk socks on the flagstones of the terrace; he wiggled his toes. Carlyle looked up at the suddenly still branches and tossed his rust-colored Rupert Brooke forelock up out of his eyes. The sky, which had passed quickly from pale blue to overcast, opened and dumped rain in big drops, like summer's. We hurried in from the veranda to the dining room.

Above an ornate mahogany sideboard hung an oversized portrait of a woman with soft features, sweet-faced, in gray-blue silk. The backs of her hands looked as if I could touch them and feel their delicately pulsing veins and their living warmth. In the portrait she stood with her back to a mirror, which reflected the back of her warm brown hair, braided and intricately pinned up. An asymmetrical cherry-red bow in her hair mirrored the red of small flowers behind her, reflected again in the mirror. She seemed to be of a time long past.

"Is this somebody's grandmother when she was young?" I said.

"I would *imagine* so," Carlyle said, as if I ought to know everything.

Uncle Governor made a spitting sound. "Don't tease the young lady," he said. "That is a fine Ingres reproduction," he said. "The lady is one Madame d'Haussonville. No one we know. But one would assume she had offspring. Unless she did not." He looked over at Carlyle and said, before Carlyle could offer a witty or lame retort, "Shut up, Carlyle."

He turned to me then and said, "So, miss. Narcissus Street, did you say? It so happens that Carlyle's lesson today is the myth of Echo and Narcissus. Would you care to sit in?"

He ushered me into a small study, dark with the gray of the stormy midday. He switched on a light atop the desk. It oozed thick yellow light into a small confined cloud on the leather-colored blotter. I was placed in a small velvet chair next to Carlyle's bigger cane-bottomed chair so that I could see the text he was working from.

Uncle Governor walked around us like a ringmaster, tapping a stick as he talked. "Here, Carlyle, we see Juno punishing the nymph Echo for her talkativeness by curtailing her power of speech." Carlyle cast a sidewise glance at Uncle Governor. Was Uncle Governor trying to tell him something? "Here we see Echo falling in love with Narcissus, that cold bastard—excuse me, missy—and finally, after she echoes Narcissus' voice, falling away herself to nothing *but* a voice. Carlyle?" he said, like a master of ceremonies, his voice seeming to usher Carlyle onto the stage.

Carlyle began reading aloud. The drone of his voice, intensified by the sound of the rain sheeting down, summer-like, on the tall windows, mesmerized me. I nearly slipped off to sleep. Then Carlyle began almost shouting, *"Spreta!"* he shouted. *"Latet! Silvis! Pudibundaque! Frondibus ora!"*

From the next room, where he had apparently migrated while I was nodding off, Uncle Governor shouted in to him, "Carlyle! That will be enough!"

I pulled myself up in my chair. Uncle Governor came in and snatched Carlyle's book from him and slammed it shut. "In the name of all. . . ." Uncle Governor muttered. He stormed out. I sat mystified.

He returned carrying something I thought at first was a gun— all the shouting had set my nerves on edge—but which turned out to be a stapler. "Bring this to Oney," he instructed Carlyle through clenched teeth.

He glanced over at me with a look that seemed an apology. I could make no sense of that. I knew no one who would apologize to a ten-year-old. My parents were wrapped up in their business, which gave me the luxury of a cocoon for my feelings: I dealt with them all inside me, insulating whatever I felt from whatever had caused it. I re-call a badly tinted photo in my science book of a cocoon hanging on a dried branch by a thread, obviously quite strong but mysterious; I recall thinking at that moment, *That's me*. I felt an urgent need just then to leave the room or the planet, go somewhere and cry, which was something I never did. Where was my cocoon? I was off my branch, here at the Blevinses'. I needed to cry now. I felt an enormous grief. I didn't know why. None of these people had anything to do with me. Why should my heart wring this way?

I wanted to know why Carlyle was so snappish, besides the ob-vious fact that he was still probably a teenager. I wanted to know what the stapler was for, and I wanted to know in particular why he made fun of me when I asked about the soft-skinned woman with the intricately braided hair with its cherry-red ribbons.

I wanted to know why Quillie seemed like at least two differ-ent people, and who she was anyway, really. I wanted to know about that "nigger motel" in Pascagoula, where it was, what it looked like, whether there was a sign in the front of it that said *col-ored* or whether that fact was clear to anyone looking at it. I wanted to know how Colby Anne Mouton fit into this family. I wanted to know who was whose grandfather, cousin, aunt, random visitor.

I went further, the little cart in my mind careening over the edge and forcing me to catch my breath in mid-air as I plummeted to-ward a glittering river so far below. I wanted to know how Sister Tommy got to be a nun, and whether she ever had been as sweetly feminine as Madame d'Haussonville. I wanted to know which Felicitas really was under the dried ivy clump in the courtyard at Saint Pet's. I wanted to know how Lobelia, and Rosa Parks, and the Carthaginian martyrs, and anyone else who had ever been brave got to be that way. I decided that Quillie was not brave at all, and with equal speed that I myself was. I decided that, in fact, I my-self was a good candidate for martyrdom. I reflected, however, that one moment of high-quality sacrificial courage—the rack, the stake, the noose, the pawing heifer—might be easier than a long life of small pilgrim braveries.

At that moment, through the high proscenium-style archway at the far end of the room, in the interior shadows, I saw Colby Anne Mouton. She was playing dress-up. She had draped herself in soft mauve dotted-swiss curtains sashed with a man's tie. She was wearing a slightly crushed straw summer hat, a man's, with a silk flower poked into its band. She looked straight ahead, not at any of us, concentrating on something that she was pretending inside herself. Yes, I was in love with Colby Anne Mouton.

The group who had gone into town shopping for a grass-catcher returned.

The day felt wildly empty. Sonia and Garnet and Katya and I were sent up to our guest-beds to take a nap so we would be rested for the ride back to New Orleans. We tossed, of course, and did not sleep. And then we drove back to New Orleans, Quillie in the driver's seat seeming peckish and saying not much at all.

A full decade later, when I was in Northampton in my third year at Smith, I got a letter from Sonia, who was engaged to a junior diplomat in Barcelona, and with whom in her dark-eyed peacefulness—hoping perhaps to absorb some of that—I had kept up a sporadic correspondence.

In the same week, a postcard arrived from Katya, whose mother as it turned out had never been in the rumored hospital, but worked as a translator. Katya's postcard, in a tiny neat hand, said, "Do you remember that strange trip to Jackson? I dreamed about it. What was that all about, anyway?" Garnet no longer kept in touch with any of us and no one had any idea where or how or even who she was.

I thought about Katya's question. I constructed alternative answers. I settled on one that said Quillie had had a black boyfriend who played tenor sax, in a time when that kind of thing could not be spoken or thought of, much less dovetailed into one's life, and that this was the root of some of Uncle Governor's peevishness.

I decided that Colby Anne Mouton was the child of that unspeakable union, that Oney and Governor had promised Quillie they'd raise her if she would just stay the hell out of it and shut up.

I figured Carlyle was just Carlyle. I bet myself that he had become an attorney, and piled his earned wealth on top of what he had been born to.

Several years later I was in New Orleans for Christmas vacation. My parents' business plans had changed—they owned seven stores now, all across the South—and so I wound up in their big house alone for a week, wondering why I had come. I saw the name Colby Anne Mouton in the society pages. The young woman in the picture above the brief article bore a great deal of resemblance to the little girl throwing oranges off the veranda. She had a kind of delicate beauty. She was marrying someone from Gramercy whose family was in sugar.

During that visit, one evening I found myself in the French Quarter, where my parents' first store was still located, doing some errands involving huge boxes of lace table-scarves from Belgium and tiny boxes with porcelain figurines from Japan packed in excelsior.

I passed a bar whose door was wide open. I could see a smoky interior, walls red as Pompeii's, long shadows from flickering electric torch lights along the walls. I smelled liquor, a deep marination. There were only a few customers. It was early yet. I walked through the door and sat down at a table. I ordered a Scotch and Drambuie, because it was the only thing I could think of. I'd tasted one once, and I wasn't much of a drinker. I let the ice cubes melt and watched the sky darken outside the door. The old buildings of the Quarter seemed to lean together over the street trying to block out the sky.

I could not remember the last time I'd done a crossword puzzle, but I looked down at the checks of the tablecloth and suddenly I began thinking about crossword puzzles. A word I had encountered only once came to mind: *nene,* a Hawaiian goose. I remembered the geese in Carlyle's Latin text, on the city wall, squawking to keep out invaders.

The band shuffled in. A rosy-faced trumpeter licked his lips and sputtered into his mouthpiece. The bass player leaned like a willow branch over his instrument, waiting. The pianist counted off, snapping his small chubby fingers expertly into the air, and a black tenor saxophonist launched into the first notes of "Mood Indigo," slower than I'd ever heard it.

A strange little liquorish leap hit my heart. I was certain as I could be that this man, with his graceful elongated notes and his grizzled, wise look, was the father of Colby Anne Mouton. I felt surely I must have been sent to tell him that beautiful girl in the *Times-Picayune*'s engagement announcements the previous weekend was his daughter, of whose existence he surely must be unaware. I looked forward with joy to the wedding where he would step out of his smoky life into the real world, where he would walk Colby Anne, pillowing a huge bouquet of gardenias in the crook of her left arm, down the aisle to meet her pale but well-mannered Gramercy sugar heir, but with another quick flicker, I reminded myself that I had made all of that up.

I wondered where Miss Rosa Parks was now, and what each day of her life looked like, and whether that silly Tyrone Power policeman fingerprinting her had had any idea who he was, or who she was, or how ignominious had been his moment of fame. Outside the door, above the three-storied galleried buildings, rising into the purple sky and strung out like a broken decade or two of the rosary, geese flew south. I could not hear their squawks for the metronome-regular, tapping, funereal sounds of the music.

Ingrid Hill has published stories in many literary magazines, including the *Southern Review,* the *Michigan Quarterly Review, Shenandoah, Louisiana Literature,* and *Image,* and a collection of fiction, *Dixie Church Interstate Blues.* She has held fellowships from Yaddo and MacDowell and is a two-time NEA Fellowship recipient. She grew up in New Orleans and is the mother of twelve children, including two sets of twins. Her first novel, *Ursula, Under,* will be published in June 2004.

ANDREW SCHMIDT

A few years ago my daughter Maria, then the size of Colby Anne
Mouton, gave me the tiny gold key to this story. I had set some fat
navel oranges in a bowl in sunlight on the dining room table. They looked so
beautiful as a still life that no one wanted to eat them. Bye-any-bye, it was
time to bid them adieu. Maria suggested that we feed them to the woodchuck
who lived at the back of our property under a brush pile by the creek that ran
through. I said sure, that was a lovely idea.

What Maria did next astonished me: she carried the bowl out onto the
deck and one by one pitched the oranges out toward the woodchuck's home.
They landed about halfway, in the shape of a W. A poet might have used this
snapshot moment intact and unembellished to good effect, but for me such
images gather momentum over time like a pole-vaulter running: they fling
themselves forward, up, over the bar, into story.

After a midwinter trip to Jackson, Mississippi, a couple of years later, that
image came back to my mind's eye on a day when I'd heard Rosa Parks's
name spoken. As dry leaves before the wild hurricane fly, a number of
elements whiled into place as if on cue: the boarding school, its denizens,
several irresistible Roman martyrs, the smell of the leather seats in my New
Orleans grandmother's Cadillac, the trip to buy the grass-catcher, lines from
my second-year high school Latin text, the Ingres portrait, the "n—— motel,"
the geese: all of it, right down to "Mood Indigo."

Tayari Jones

BEST COUSIN

(from *Sou'wester*)

When my cousin, Vanessa, was thirteen I had been only eleven. I was flat chested and bony, a whole season away from puberty while she was leggy and curvy enough to be mistaken for a real teenager. This was the last summer we spent in Oakdale visiting our grandmother, who had no interest in children. This didn't bother me at all; I had no interest in stooped old ladies.

Every year, Mom and I would hit the road, three days after school let out for summer. Fourteen hours from Chicago to Oakdale, where my grandmother lived. Just the two of us, like the song said. Riding with my mother on these road trips helped me forget that my dad was on his way to Alabama so he could visit his mother, whom I'd never met. He was also visiting his first wife and their daughter, Sandria, who was grown and had a little baby of her own. This meant that I was an aunt, but I didn't think it counted at all if you'd never seen the people.

Mom and I listened to the music she liked, old Motown, especially Smokey Robinson. The radio blared, infusing the very air of the car with her personality. I sang loud while we drove down the dark highway. I wanted her to hear that I knew all the words to her favorite songs.

"What does it mean, you better shop around?" I asked.

"Depends on who's doing the talking."

I sang until I fell asleep, crossing the Mississippi with my face pressed against the car window.

Vanessa and Uncle Chet arrived three long days after we did. Mom, M'dear, and I sat on the sloped porch of the house, watching the heat squiggle up from the asphalt road. Across the street, a bunch of boys wrestled. I knew them from last summer and the summers before but I didn't say hello to them.

"What time is it?"

"Two o'clock," Mom said. "They might be here after a while."

They came at five.

"Wouldn't you know, Chet'd get here just in time to eat," Mom said.

I sprang up from the porch step, bouncing slightly on bent legs.

This year, Uncle Chet arrived in a black Lincoln Continental. The year before it had been a navy blue Thunderbird with a beige T-top. In my opinion, the Lincoln was the best car yet. Even better than the red Cadillac two years back. He stopped the car in front of M'dear's house but didn't get out immediately. He gave us a few moments of stand-and-admire.

I pulled my mother's arm. "Look at that."

She whispered. "Calm down and stand still. Don't act like you never seen a nice car before."

I stood still and took deep breaths like when I was in the choir. I wiggled my fingers at my side, hoping that Vanessa would see them through the gray tinted window. I think she did see, because she let down the glass with one smooth electric motion. Even from the porch I could see that she had changed since last summer.

Uncle Chet climbed out the car and sauntered over the passenger side to unlock Vanessa's door.

"Jesus," my mother said. "Does he have to go through the whole Queen of Sheba routine every year?"

Vanessa got out of the car like a movie star, all legs at first until she showed us her new self, busty and tall. She stood for a second, beside the open door, letting us take in her clothes, all red and white, even white sandals with a red loop holding the big toe in place. Her hair was spiraled into ringlets that landed at the top of her shoulders. She stood stock-still, posing for an invisible camera, Uncle Chet shutting her door like a limo driver.

"Shit Chet," my mother called from the porch. "Are you going to stand out there until we ask for your autographs? Come give your sister a hug."

Uncle Chet was tanned deep brown and bulky. He broke into a smile, a real smile, not just a rehearsed showing of teeth to go along with his fancy car and Vanessa, light-skinned and long-haired by nature. Even after living in the Arizona desert, she was only the pale color of a brown egg.

Uncle Chet took Vanessa's hand and helped her step across the canal that ran across the side of the street. I thought about my own father, in Alabama with his other family. Why didn't he ever take my hand like a suitor? What exactly was he doing with those other people? His other daughter and her daughter too.

When they finally made it to the porch, Mom wiped her wet hands on her thighs and then wrapped Uncle Chet in a sweaty hug. "You looking good," she said. Then she took both of Vanessa's hands and held her at arm's length. "And you are growing into quite a young lady."

Vanessa smiled and I noticed that she was wearing pink lip gloss.

"Hey Vanessa," I almost whispered, wanting someone to notice that I was there.

"Hey Shelly," she said back just as quietly.

We were always careful with each other when our parents were around.

"That's all you got to say?" Mom said shoving me my cousin's direction. "When we were driving down here it was all Vanessa this and Vanessa that. In her letter Vanessa said such and such. Now you act like you scared of her."

Embarrassment was hot in my stomach and spread upwards to my face.

Uncle Chet laughed. He roared and I felt more ashamed.

I looked down at my plastic thongs, feeling foolish and child-like. My fingernails were crusted with calamine lotion I had scratched off my mosquito bites. A scrape on my thigh was bleeding a little bit. I was ashamed of myself and angry with my cousin. She had changed over the last year, but hadn't mentioned these alterations in her letters. She'd sent me pages of stationery filled with details about her school, the new wallpaper and furniture in her bedroom. But there hadn't been any hint about her new figure, or her new clothes, dresses with darts to make them fit better. There I was wholly unready in my tube top of gathered cotton with elastic, tied behind my head in a girlish bow. No one had told me. And even had I known, what could I have done?

We stayed this way, Vanessa and me, nearly strangers, speaking softly to each other at meals. It was always this way at first. It took some time for us to warm up, to remember the rhythm of communication we enjoyed in our letters. But this time, I worried that there might not be a seam in the silence. That this distance that separated us might be permanent and unbreachable.

I scooted close to her at dinner, moving my chair to the right so that my leg touched the crisp fabric of her seersucker dress. Vanessa shifted slightly away from me. I was crushed and didn't eat the spaghetti on my fork, wound tight.

At night, Mom and I stayed at M'dear's, asleep with spines touching, on the too-soft mattress in the middle room. The fan in the window swirled hot humid air around us. I wondered about Vanessa as I listened to my mother's muted snoring. I imagined her asleep with her hair twined around plastic curlers, resting on a cool firm motel bed.

Finally, our parents left. My mother put gas in our Buick, checked her own oil, and hit the road. She played "Going to Chicago," on the tape deck because that's what she sang when she left here twenty years ago on a segregated greyhound. "Love you," she said out of the window, her words mixing with the dust. Uncle Chet climbed into the Lincoln and let the window down with an electric whirring.

"Bye Mother," he said to M'Dear. "I'll be back to get this girl in a month." M'Dear nodded. To Vanessa he said, "Take care of yourself, Baby. Call me if you need me. And don't forget what I told you." Vanessa gave a nod of her head so slight that it didn't move her now-frizzy curls. He stayed there with his face framed by the open window. Vanessa waited for a few moments; I watched yellowjackets circle her calves. Then she left the porch and stuck her face into the open car window and kissed Uncle Chet fast on the lips. He smiled and then let up the smoky gray car window. I waved as Uncle Chet started the car and left without saying anything to me.

When my own daddy had left to go to Alabama, he'd kissed my jaw, said "Later, Gator," before pulling slowly out of the driveway. The scrape of his tailpipe had brought water to my eyes.

"Cheer up," Mom had said. "He'll be back."

"Why does he have to go in the first place?"

"Because he's a good man."

I'd given a firm nod and tried hard to understand.

With our parents on the highway, Vanessa and I sat together on the ugly concrete porch. My grandfather built it with his own hands and he was a preacher, not a carpenter. As a result, it's a sort of unimaginative structure, gray siding, square, without arched doorways or window seats. The only flourish is a latticed trellis that supported an ungainly, creepy, rose bush. Vanessa and I watched the bees push their way into the blossoms and fly out again.

M'dear came out and handed each of us a Styrofoam cup half-filled with frozen Kool-Aid. We peeled away most of the Styrofoam and sucked the purple ice. The only sounds were the bees and our lips.

Vanessa spoke first. "I wrote you a bunch of letters."

"I wrote you back. I wrote back every time. I bought a whole book of stamps. You didn't get them?"

"I got them," she said. She sucked a white spot on her frozen-cup. "You look the same as last summer."

I picked at the scab on my knee. "I know. I can't help it."

"I can't help it either."

I squeezed the sides of my cup; the ice jumped out and landed in the crabgrass. "Maybe I can pick it up and wash it off at the hose."

"That's nasty," Vanessa said. "Have some of mine."

Her nails against the white Styrofoam were painted shell pink. I took it from her fast, not wanting her to look at my fingernails, chewed and ragged. I hesitated before putting it to my mouth.

"Don't be scared," she said. "We're family. We got the same germs. Unless." She looked at me sideways and I noticed a thin line of black kohl on her eyelids. "Unless you've been kissing boys. That's how you get new germs."

I shook my head hard. The beads on my braids slapped my cheeks. "I didn't kiss any."

"Me either," she said. "Not yet. He tried but I didn't let him put his tongue in my mouth."

"That's nasty," I said. "That's worse than eating something that you dropped on the ground."

"I'm saying I didn't do it."

"Yes you did," I said. "I can tell from the way you looked at me."

"No I didn't. If you think I'm lying then don't be my friend. I thought we were best cousins. Almost sisters."

"We are," I blurted. "I believe you." To show her I fastened my mouth to the white spot where she had sucked all the color from the frozencup. My cheeks sunk in as I pulled hard on the ice. I knew there were boy germs on there, nasty boy germs, but I sank my teeth into the frozencup, pulled out a chunk and chewed, sending electric bolts of pain from my molars through my entire head.

In the afternoons, we took walks. Mondays to the corner store to buy hot tamales from the Hot Tamale Man who sold them out of the back of a blue El Camino. To go almost anywhere, we had to pass the plaster-front funeral home where Granddaddy had lain before his funeral, three years before. It wasn't that I missed him;

my mother's parents lived too far away for me to really bond with them. But I knew that when M'dear died, she'd be there too, with her clothes stuffed with Spanish moss so no one could see how much she'd shrunk before she died. This is what they did with Granddaddy. At the funeral, I saw spidery green fronds poking out at his collar. When my mother dies, she will be brought here too.

But Vanessa didn't mind walking that route. She never paused to look at the funeral home. Once we passed it, she rolled up her shorts until most of her thighs showed. My thighs were already exposed, and M'dear didn't care. But Vanessa had to be covered.

"You're getting too old to be walking around half-naked," she said to Vanessa. "People get to wondering about what's at the top of those thighs."

On Wednesdays, we walked to town to check the mail. M'dear had the same post office box since 1956. Back then, the postman would bring the mail to white people's doors, but black folks had to get theirs at the curb. Granddaddy said he didn't want his mail delivered unless it was delivered to his door. By the time such things were made illegal, the postmaster said that all new addresses would have their mail delivered to the curb. So my grandparents kept the P.O. Box.

And Fridays, Vanessa liked to go to the park to see the boys. They played basketball with their shirts off in front of a goal that used chains for nets. We walked the mile to the park licking Popsicles and laughing, pretending that we were going to ride the swings, like we told M'dear. On these days, Vanessa rolled her shorts a little higher. The curls she'd worn the first day were long gone and her hair hung in a wild disorderly ponytail that I tried to style with a strange round brush she'd brought with her from Arizona.

By the time we arrived at the park, sweat wormed down our faces and down our necks. We sat on metal swings near the basketball court and wiggled our legs enough to make ourselves sway. There were other girls at the park, girls that lived in Oakdale. They hated us and called us bitches.

We had known these girls from summers before. Our parents

had gone to high school together. We had never been inside their houses, but we knew each other, in a way. Before this summer we'd smiled hello across the aisles of the corner stores.

"How come those girls can't stand us?"

"Because the boys like us."

"Us?" I said. "It's you. Nobody's looking at me."

"Both of us," she said.

I swatted a mosquito on my leg; it left a bloody print. "Not me."

She laughed. "It's like how you hate the white girls at school. Because all the boys like them."

"We don't have white girls at my school."

She laughed. "That's all we have at mine."

The boys played rough that day, shoving and jabbing with their elbows. I didn't like to watch, but Vanessa looked toward the court, moving her swing with legs locked at the ankle. The basketball thwacked against the concrete court.

Bam Bam threw the ball toward the goal and missed badly, not even smacking the rim. The worn basketball bounced off the court and landed near us. He wiped his face with the bottom of his over-sized T-shirt. It was blue and the sleeves had been cut off. Vanessa pointed her toe like a ballerina and flicked the ball in his direction with the tip of her canvas sneaker. She wasn't wearing socks.

"Y'all Miss Lucy Mae grandkids?"

"Yeah," I said.

"I thought that was y'all. But y'all look different from last year. At least she does." He turned his head toward Vanessa.

"Well you look the same," I said. "Your friends are waiting on you to bring the ball back."

"I ain't studying them fools," he said. "I'm trying to handle my business."

I looked over at Vanessa. She pulled one of her knees to her chin and rested her face against it. She didn't seem to be aware of the angry girls watching us from across the court, or the sweating boys pretending not to watch from beneath the basketball goal. But I knew that she felt the scrutiny and I felt a little mad at her for pretending that she didn't.

"You don't have any business with us," I said. "You need to go back over there where you were."

"I didn't come over here to talk to you."

Now Vanessa lifted her head from her knee. She smiled with lips shiny from Vaseline.

"You need me to walk you back over to your grandmama house after we get through playing?" Bam Bam asked.

"I don't care," Vanessa said.

He walked back to the basketball court with his slightly lopsided walk.

When he was playing again, Vanessa started swinging for real, not this lazy rocking we'd been doing before. She pumped her legs hard and leaned back, going so high that the chains jerked each time she sailed out. I copied her movements. This was the way I liked to play. I swung high enough to see the blue green water tower at the edge of town. The dirty words spray painted there were just purple and orange blurs, but I knew what they said.

When I noticed that Vanessa had stopped swinging, I slowed down, dragging my feet in the dust; the leather strap on my sandals gave with a pop.

"Go on back," she said to me.

"What?"

"Go on back to M'dear's house. I'm going to walk back with Bam Bam."

"You want me to go back by myself? What if those girls try to jump me?"

"You'll be all right. Leave now. They're going to stay to watch the game."

I stood up from the swing with legs wobbly from all the exercise. My broken sandal flapped against my heel. With my head tucked to my chin, I left feeling like all the other kids were laughing at me, having been sent away with dirty clothes and broken shoe. Insects buzzed around my face, trying to drink my sweat. I slapped at the halo of gnats overhead as I made my way back down the road.

Bam Bam's sister, Angie, caught up with me just before I got to the funeral home. I knew her name and she knew mine, but we had never talked to each other.

"Wait up," she called.

I waited because I didn't know what else to do. She was a big girl, thick and robust. She wasn't shapely like Vanessa, but she wasn't little-girl skinny like me. Her hair was combed into a single stubby plait jutting from the back of her head.

"You the one they call Shelly, right?"

I nodded.

"That light-skinned one is your cousin?"

I nodded again.

"Where y'all from?"

"I'm from Chicago. She's from Phoenix."

Angle said, "You talk proper. Both of y'all talk proper. But she talk white. You just talk proper."

I shrugged one shoulder. We passed the funeral home and I made an effort to keep my eyes on my feet.

"How old are you?"

"Eleven."

"What about her?"

"Thirteen."

"She look older than that."

I shrugged again.

"She like Bam Bam?"

"I don't know."

"He like her."

"I know," I said. And for some reason I felt suddenly sorry for him. His tricks this afternoon, deliberately throwing the ball at her feet and his offer to walk her home seemed sad and pitiful.

"You like any of the boys around here?"

I shook my head. "I don't like boys."

"That's good," Angie said. "I'm just telling you this because me and you been knowing each other a long time. I seen you every summer. So I'm just telling you what's up. You and your cousin better not mess with none of the boys around here. Dionne say if she catch her with Bam Bam she going to snatch her ball headed. You tell her I told you that."

"Which one is Dionne?"

"You know Dionne. She always be with me."

"Oh," I said. "I know who you're talking about." But this was a lie. I remembered a clutch of girls with Angie, but I couldn't sort out their features, remember one from another.

"She wanted to follow you from the park but I told her to stay back. That I was going to talk to you."

"Thank you."

"And you tell this to your cousin, all right."

I nodded. We were in front of the house. M'dear stood on the porch in a blue cotton shift, her legs done up in beige support hose.

"Hello Miss Lucy Mae," Angie called.

"Hello there, Angie," M'dear said. "How's your mother?"

"She's doing better," Angie said. "She's walking around more."

"You tell her I said hello."

"Yes ma'am," Angie said and walked away in the direction of the park.

"Where's your cousin?" M'dear followed me into the dark living room.

"I don't know," I said and flopped down on the tweed couch.

She stood over me, old and lean like the sick-looking pine trees in the park. "What do you mean you don't know where she is? You left here together."

There was a sharp pain at the top of my head. A stinging I would come to know well over the next few years. Maybe I'd even known it before, but this is the first time I remember.

"Gray hair is luck," she said. "You'll get a good husband."

I opened my hand and she laid the strand, kinky and white across the lines of my palm.

"I hope Vanessa gets herself back here soon. I don't want to have to call her daddy. Chet never did have good sense when it comes to that girl."

Vanessa didn't make it home before dinner. I sat by myself at the large oval table, with my fork twined through a plate of spaghetti stained orange with just a dollop of canned sauce. M'dear used a battered tin ladle to serve Kool-Aid from a glass punch bowl.

"She'll be back before the street lights come on," I said. "Bam Bam said he was going to walk her home."

"Who you say she was with?"

"Bam Bam?"

"Who?"

"Bam Bam."

"Child, what's his given name?"

"I don't know." I turned my fork the other way to unwrap the pasta. "His sister was the one who walked back with me."

"Oh, Little Herman," she said. "He's a nice one. But Vanessa's getting to the age where she needs to learn that nice ain't everything. It's a good place to start, but it's not nearly enough."

"It's because he doesn't have money," I said. "My daddy didn't have money when he married Mama. He only had one pair of pants. And just two shirts; he had to wash them in the sink every night."

M'dear stood over me and snatched another white hair from my head. "All this gray hair don't make you grown."

"There's nothing wrong with my daddy," I said, rubbing the sore spot. Tears pricked the corners of my eyes. "He's a good daddy."

"Didn't nobody say he wasn't."

The phone rang as I ate the mound of bland noodles. As I buttered Wonder bread, I listened to M'dear speak to Uncle Chet: she didn't know where Vanessa was at the moment. She didn't know she was supposed to spend her whole day chasing half-grown children all around town. There was no reason for him to get all bent out of shape. Vanessa was with Herman Jr. It wasn't even dark yet.

M'dear put the phone on the hook and looked over at me. "Chet never did have good sense."

"You're not my real grandmother," I said. "He's not my real uncle."

M'dear waved my words away with her bent fingers. "You just like your mama. When Ruthie was your age she used to say the same thing when she got mad with us. *Y'all not my real family.* And I used to say to her, *We put that real plate of beans in front of you. We gave you a real bed to sleep in.* And she would just sit and pout because she knew it was the truth. The mother that birthed her used to live right next door at the time and we used to hear her hollering and carrying on. We'd see her running around with this man and that one. Until she finally got herself killed. That was a relief, really. Ruthie hushed up all that 'real mama' talk after that."

"She got hit by a car," I said. "My real grandmama. A red speeder."

M'dear took the empty plate from in front of me. "That's what Ruthie told you? Mattie Lee got hit by a car, but it was her man that done it to her. His name was LaFoy Floyd. Run her over like a dog. Right out here." M'dear pointed to the narrow road just beyond the front porch.

"Did my mom see? I hope she didn't see." I thought of my mother and I saw her being my own age, wearing my clothes, her hair in my braids. "I hope she covered her face."

"She was at school. She saw the mark on the road and that's all. Everybody told her what happened and I just told her that this is why you got to make sure you get yourself a good husband. A decent man that won't leave you with fifty-eleven babies and then run you down on the street."

"Was that my granddaddy?"

"No," M'dear said. "I'm not quite sure who Ruthie's daddy was. But it wasn't LaFoy Floyd. He didn't come to Oakdale until Ruthie was in first grade. She had been with us two years by then."

• • •

Vanessa made it back just before the street lamps buzzed on. M'dear didn't rise from the lopsided recliner to let her in. Vanessa rapped against the door frame with her fist.

I opened the door and it smacked shut behind her.

"Call your father," M'dear said to Vanessa. "He's waiting to hear from you."

To me, she said, "Go on in the back, hear?"

On my way, I heard the scratch and snap of the rotary phone.

The back room was cold. Frosty air erupted from the wall unit in opaque gusts. I huddled under the covers in my clothes. Pulling my knees up to my flat chest, I wished for socks. I whispered Vanessa's name, hoping that she would hear me and come back here, maybe pretending to go to the bathroom, but really she'd want to check on me. Lying in the freezing dark, I listened to the scrape of fork against plate as M'dear prepared Vanessa's dinner. I waited until I heard the splash of dishwater.

"Vanessa," I said louder this time, in my normal voice. "Vanessa."

She didn't answer. I lay in the quiet of the back room, sealed in to keep the cold air from escaping into the warm house. I lay there until I slept.

"Shelly," Vanessa shook me. "You better get out of the bed with your clothes on. M'dear is going to have a hissy fit."

"She made me come in here."

"It's freezing," Vanessa said. "Why don't you turn off the air?"

I shrugged, embarrassed for not thinking of such a simple and obvious solution.

She pulled the string above the bed and the bulb provided a murky yolk of light. She then went to the window and pressed a red button. The air conditioner went silent. "Holy cats."

"What happened?" I said to her.

"Nothing," she said with an elegant toss of her hair. "M'dear called Daddy and told him I walked home with a boy and he hit the roof."

"I know that," I said. "But before then. What happened when you was with Bam Bam? You didn't kiss him did you? Angie told me to tell you that Dionne said you better not mess with him. She was going to jump on us."

"I didn't kiss him," she said. "You are as bad as my daddy. I wouldn't kiss a boy like him."

"It's nothing wrong with him," I said. "He can't help who his parents are."

Vanessa took off her T-shirt and sat on the edge of the bed in her pale blue bra. "I can't help who my parents are either."

"You're not my real cousin," I told her.

She didn't answer me. Instead she fiddled with the yellow rose sewn between the cups of her bra. It seemed boastful and I wished she would be kind and cover herself.

"I already know who I'm going to marry," she said. "And I'm not going to kiss anybody but him. Tongue kissing I mean. The other kind of kissing is different."

"Who?"

"Kyle Robertson," she said.

"A white person? That sounds like a white-boy name."

She swatted at me with her soft hand. "Whatever. He's black. Well, half. He's the only black boy at my school."

"He's light-skinned?"

"Not really. He's in-between you and me. His mother is white but it really didn't take."

"Oh," I said. "Aren't you cold?"

She shook her head and took off her shorts, showing her brown-egg thighs. Her legs were smooth and unscarred. Mine were spotted with constellations of mosquito bites, scratched until they became sores and left scars. "You're going to be my maid of honor. You're my best cousin."

My breath increased with a little jolt of excitement. "For real?"

"I have it all planned out. The date and everything. June 12, 1991. I'll be twenty-two. That's the best time to get married, while you still look good. My mother told me that. She says you get prettier every day until you're twenty-five and then it's all down hill. I want to be a beautiful bride," she said. "My colors are going to be rum pink and lilac. You'll get to wear rum pink with lilac trim. For the other maids, it will be the other way around."

She reached into the basket of clean laundry and pulled out her sleeveless gown. She sniffed it before pulling it over her head and then wiggled inside until she pulled her bra out from under her armpit. She smiled at me. "White girls at school taught me that. They showed me how to shave my legs too." She took my hand and ran it up her sturdy calf. "See how smooth it is? My mother says I'm too young to shave so I hid my razor from her."

I pulled my hand away and touched my own leg. It was covered with gentle peach fuzz.

"I'll teach you next summer," she said. "Do you want to hear more about my wedding? Kyle has a sister so she is going to have to be a bridesmaid. I can't stand her."

"What does a maid of honor have to do?"

"You just have to be there for me," she said. "Keep my train from getting twisted up. Hold my bouquet so Kyle can put the ring on my finger. It's so everyone can see you're my favorite cousin and everything."

"I'm not your real cousin," I said. My lips wobbled as I said the words. I didn't know what was wrong with me. I had known this for as long as I had known what family was.

Vanessa crawled across the bed to where I lay facing the wall. Fat stupid tears rolled down my cheeks and under my chin. She fitted her body around me and held me close with one arm.

"That's all right," she said with warm breath on my neck. "Nobody cares about that."

Tayari Jones's first novel, *Leaving Atlanta,*
received the Hurston/Wright Legacy Award for
Debut Fiction and was named Best Novel of
the Year by *Atlanta* magazine. She has won
fellowships from the Bread Loaf Writers'
Conference, Arizona Commission on the Arts,
and the LEF Foundation. Recently, she served as
Geier Writer in Residence at East Tennessee State
University.

CRAIG WELLS

*B*est Cousin" *grew from my strong interest in the evolving South and all
of its conflicts. As a girl, I would spend the entire month of June with
my grandmother in Oakdale, Louisiana, my father's hometown. During
those humid weeks, my girl cousins and I straddled the boundaries between
rural and urban, Northern and Southern, middle and working class, and of
course, the line between girlhood and womanhood. I have not returned to
Oakdale since my grandmother died a decade ago. I have not seen many of
my cousins since I graduated from high school. My mother provides regular
reports culled from Christmas letters, but I feel as though I don't quite know
what has become of my cousins and me, so I busy myself by writing stories to
help me recall how we were.*

George Singleton

RAISE CHILDREN HERE

(from *The Georgia Review*)

Whenever I retreat to wonderment at how my life turned to one of hoardment and obsession, I stop at the memory of a muggy June night, inside a smoke- and curse-filled beer joint on Highway 301 near the Fruitcake Capital of the World. I see myself bending over to pick up a fallen blue, blue cube of Silver Cup cue-stick chalk, reaching over to set it on one of two pool tables, then hearing an overall-wearing mountain man—gray beard as windblown as John Brown's—yell at me, point toward my hand, ask if I got Stonewall Jackson or John the Baptist. That night, not two weeks after I'd graduated from high school, I ran through every reason to answer either one man of history or the other.

"Don't rub it up, goddamn. *Look* at it. Whichen is it?" the man said. He leaned on a house cue stick so warped it could've been used as a bow. I saw a knife blade *spack* glare from his other hand.

I said, "I don't know." I looked down to see a perfectly carved visage on one side of the chalk. "Yeah, it's one or the other. I'm not so sure I'd know Stonewall Jackson or John the Baptist if they both walked in the door."

The old man jerked his head once, and held out the hand with his knife. I handed over the chalk. Two men from the fruitcake company—they wore work shirts with various candied ingredients sewed above their pockets—started a game of eight ball. The one

87

who broke barely made the rack move, as if he was challenging Newton's action and reaction theory.

"Its one or the other, I believe, but I can't remember. And I carved the son-bitch," the man said. "Goddamn it to hell, I'mo have to get my book out again and see who this looks like. I got a book I keep at home. It's got famous people's pictures in it. Everything I carve ends up looking like somebody, somewhere." He handed the miniature near-bust back. "You figure it out and tell me."

And then he walked out. When he got to the door, without turning around, he yelled out, "If Stonewall Jackson and John the Baptist came in this bar alive and you couldn't tell the difference, I feel sorry for you, boy. One would be a-rolling and one would be a-strolling.

I had my back to the two pool players. One of them said, "I bet Brother Macon's on his way to the schoolhouse. They already told him he couldn't steal they chalk no more."

I went over to the four-stool bar and ordered a beer from a woman whose face held an expression of a rose of Sharon bud about to blossom. "You a buyer?" she asked me.

I said, "No, ma'am. My last name's Dawes."

"Huh," she said. "That's not what I ast you, but that's aw-ight."

My new boss, Marcel Parsell, suggested that I start in Claxton, move my way north to Tallulah Falls, Georgia, then drive east to Chimney Rock, North Carolina, south to Denmark, South Carolina, then back west. He said I could then go inward, always traveling clockwise in a smaller and smaller square. This was my first real, not-gotten-by-my-father job—working for a disgruntled ex-editor of Fodor's travel guides who wanted to put out a book about places in the United States to *avoid* completely. From what I had gathered, from this year onward he would hire fifty or sixty new high school graduates every June to write sarcastic thousand-words-or-less articles about towns that offered no real cultural, artistic, or dining experiences. It was supposed to look like we got a scholarship, I guess. "A book like this will make everyone in bigger cities feel better about themselves and their lives. Plus, this idea has trade paperback bestseller written all over it, from here on out."

I had answered an ad that read, "Like to travel for money?" Imagine that. How come my high school counselor never veered me toward a class in economics or ethics or logic, or never took one herself?

I said to the bartendress, "I'm here because I'm writing a book on little-known places you might want to visit," for two reasons. First off, I figured that if I told the truth then I'd end up being lynched for making fun of whatever slight populace inhabited places like Claxton, Georgia. Second, since I didn't take that ethics course at Forty-Five High I felt no remorse about lying outright.

Marcel Parsell—who had studied both geography and culinary arts—told my new colleagues and me that, just as it was okay to exaggerate how wonderful a city might appear, so was it all right to exaggerate its limitations. "A local roadside diner that brags on its pork-flavored ice cream isn't a bad thing for our purposes," he said. I took notes.

"That man gave you piece a chalk ain't like our regular people around here," the barmaid said. "Don't judge Claxton or its peoples from crazy Brother Macon. He says God told him to carve what he could into people God blessed before. He chose chalk 'cause it's made over in Macon. He seen a reason and connection."

I said, "I won't judge y'all by one man's vision."

"Hey!" she yelled. "This boy here's writing a book about us!"

At first I thought I'd've been better off only skimming the town limits of all my tiny prearranged choices, that I should've been objective while detailing odd Catfish or Bucktooth festivals. Marcel Parsell handed all of us a ten-point Do's and Don'ts bulletin that included not falling in love with a local and not believing mayors.

I got paid $50 for every article that made it into a book that ended up being called *Wish You Weren't Here.* I got paid five bucks for towns Marcel Parsell decided against. This was 1976. I had no clue about money, and just saw myself getting about three grand over a two-month period, then moving on to work for the South

American, European, and Australian versions of the same book, working college summers. It didn't occur to me that if fifty travel writers each got fifty-thousand-word essays published, the book might be a little on the thick side. I didn't realize that staying in twelve-dollar-a-night motels went way beyond extravagant, that maybe I should've considered KOA campgrounds, or the back seat of my old Jeep at roadside rest areas.

I never got the chance. What I learned immediately in the Fruit-cake Capital of the World was that there were citizens who would pay decent money to have their borders made to sound utopian, and just as many people who would offer favors to keep strangers away.

"Oh, I'll tell you all you fucking want to know about a place people elsewhere think we make fruitcakes for doorstops," one of the pool players said.

"No, no," said his opponent. "This is a good place to raise children. Come talk to me about here."

Not that this has anything to do with my story, but over the years I've learned that any human who brags about his or her town being a good place to raise kids only says so because that particular town has no art museum that kids might beg their parents to visit. There's no theater without the word *Little* on the sign. The horrendous school system doesn't offer afterschool field trips and activities outside of dollar admission sporting events. Nothing dangerous exists that might cause parents to *think* and *act* in these places. I was brought up in the town of Forty-Five, South Carolina, by God—the Raise Children Here Capital of the World.

Maybe my future background in anthropology was jading me, though.

I stood in the Rack Me roadhouse bar and fingered my carved cube of chalk. I didn't mention how I wasn't really writing a book solely on the Fruitcake Capital, but tried to emit an air that, at any moment, I might change my mind and load up the Jeep, find some people to talk to at the Pecan Roll Capital of the World.

The barmaid opened a drawer beneath the cash register and

handed me a dozen carved blue pieces of Brother Macon's chalk. The best one looked like Mount Rushmore, on all sides and the bottom. The worst might've been one of those famous pirates, or Cyclops, or James Joyce.

Lookit: the ad went, "Do you want to make money and travel?" and then there was a non-1-800 number to call for a preliminary interview. For all I know *everyone* who called made it over the first hurdle. I was asked to send a biographical essay, a descriptive essay about my hometown, an argumentative essay concerning my views on cats versus dogs, and a comparison/contrast essay about any two fast-food chains. I almost told the truth about myself, Forty-Five, and dogs because I was kind of tired of the whole process. My final essay went, "I only know diners and home-cooked meals built over a fire out back. I'm from a town called Forty-Five, named after a piece of vinyl that turns second fastest."

The stuff about my place of training wasn't all true, of course, but I feel certain now that it got me the job. In reality, Forty-Five got its name from an old Indian princess who jumped forty-five creeks in order to warn townspeople of advancing British soldiers. Or: it got its name from a man who showed up with forty-five head of cattle to his name. Or: Forty-Five got named for a wealthy Englishman who wasn't but forty-five inches tall.

I didn't tell Marcel Parsell any of the other theories, of course. He called me, went over the payment situation, and said I could start immediately. He sent his ten Do's and Don'ts—my favorite, Rule No. 9, went, "Never let them see you spit out food"—and I drove to Claxton with a suitcase, some Mead composition notebooks, a cheap hand-held tape recorder, and a camera.

I returned from Rack Me to my motel outside town, a little L-shaped place called the Fall Inn. It advertised free TV, radio, and telephone. The dozen doors to the place were each painted a different pastel shade, which I learned later was symbolic of the various colored candies in a five-pound fruitcake.

I wasn't in the room five minutes on my first night when the

phone rang. I expected my dad, or my imaginary girlfriend checking up on me, or Marcel Parsell wanting to offer congratulations
on my first day at *Wish You Weren't Here*. I cleared my throat and
said, "Mendal Dawes," all professional, like I had seen Frank Sinatra
do in a 1950s movie that showed up at the Forty-Five drive-in theater in 1972 or thereabouts.

It was the desk clerk. She said, "I'm calling to see if there's anything you need, hon."

When I checked in she'd not spoken at all, just taken my cash
money and handed me a crude flier explaining checkout time and
how I shouldn't leave lights or the TV on unnecessarily. The woman
looked to be my age, and held her face in a way that told me how
she didn't hold fruitcake-working people in highest regard. I said,
"I'm fine."

"This is Callie at the front desk."

I said, "Yeah."

"You sure you don't need anything? It's free. Soap, towels, a big
old bucket of ice." She paused and lowered her voice. "You know.
Anything you want."

It's hard to be a man and admit that I didn't recognize nuance,
temptation, or outright blatant sexual advances at the age of eighteen. I said, "I wouldn't mind a beer, I guess, but y'all don't sell
them in the Coke machine and the only store I've seen out this way
won't open until morning." I took all of Brother Macon's carved
billiard chalks out of my pants pockets and lined them around the
rotary telephone. One of them looked exactly like Callie—at least
how I remembered her all slack-jawed and blank-faced at check-in
time. It might not have been carved at all, I thought. Or maybe
Brother Macon carved a *Night of the Living Dead* character, I don't
know.

Callie said in a drawl that could come only out of a Southern,
Southern woman with a mouth full of honey, "Beer. Well, at least
that's a start," and hung up.

The television received two channels. One showed the local
news. Before I finished watching a piece on Claxton's mayor ex-

plaining why the jail needed two more cells added on, Callie let
herself in with a passkey. She carried two quart bottles of Schlitz
under one arm, and held an ice bucket. I said, "Okay. All right.
Come on in. Make yourself at home and tell me all about your
lovely hometown."

She set everything down on a chair. "So word is you're the famous man come down here to write about all us. Call me patriotic,
but I want you to know what a friendly place we got." She took out
a church key and opened one bottle. "Don't think we're only fruitcakes here. They's much more to offer for fun."

I got off the bed and found two wax-paper-wrapped drinking
glasses from the bathroom. I called out, "Oh, I know that. I'm only
supposed to find places like this that're misunderstood."

I don't want to come across as crude or insensitive—and I need
to make a point that I didn't instigate what occurred soon there-
after—but the only thing else I remember about my first night in
Claxton, Georgia, was when Callie pulled her head away from my
crotch in order to say, "We have field days all the time down at the
rec center. It's a great place to raise children. I won the sack race
one time."

I'm pretty sure that's what she announced. I wanted to call up
my father and tell him what I went through on my first real job. I
wanted to say a bunch of things concerning the life of an artiste.

I focused on the television, though. The local weatherman said
it would be another hot and humid day.

Maybe 1976 Claxton ran similarly to those backwards Southern
TV sitcom towns where everyone eavesdrops on party lines, I don't
know. But on my second day of full-time work I drove into town
and hadn't come close to the Chamber of Commerce before being
stopped by people from all walks of life eager to exaggerate their
hometown's worth or drawbacks. I could only figure that Callie left
my motel room by midnight, called her best friend or mother, and
had her information stolen by half of the population. A woman
at the drugstore, where I went to buy batteries for the tape recorder

and headache powders for my hangover, said, "I can tell you that we have the clearest water between the Mississippi River and Richmond, Virginia, at least."

Out on the sidewalk, a Lion's Club member selling straw brooms said, "I've lived all over the place: Savannah, Atlanta, Chattanooga, Talladega. Not one of my neighbors in any of those cities ever asked me and the wife over for a barbecue supper. Here in Claxton, it happens almost every night. You got any children, son?"

I smiled and shook hands with complete strangers and nodded. A woman from Claxton Flowers ran out of her shop and gave me a boutonniere. A man from Claxton Gulf went out of his way to offer a free oil change and tire rotation. A cop came out of nowhere and handed me two complimentary tickets to the Claxton Policemen's Ball, which—he explained—was really a square dance held at the VFW.

I got stopped by a man and woman in front of what appeared to be a vacant theater of sorts. Both of them wore Bobby Jones alpaca golf sweaters, and they shifted their weights from leg to leg. I slowed down. "We want you to know that people have come out of here and done good for themselves," the woman said.

"Grainger Koon's in the movies. He's got a list of credits longer than our telephone directory. He played Crazy Customer in one movie," the woman said. "He's played Man at Bar, Man on Bench, Man without Glasses, and Man with Goat—all in the same year. I forget what movies, though. What were some of the titles, LaFoy?"

"I don't recall either," LaFoy said to me. "But you'd know him if you saw him. He's got a good face. He played Man Who Falls Off Dock in one of those teen movies. Me and Peggy here, we both taught him singing and dancing lessons. At the rec center. Grainger was in a *Munsters* episode, too."

"It's a good place to raise children," Peggy said.

"That's what I understand," I said, but didn't go into my theory about people who make such claims.

I walked and waved like a returning hero, or at least like a celebrity who returned home after appearing as Scary Man in Park. I picked litter off the sidewalk and carried it down short Main Street until finding a receptacle. The hardware store man came outside and handed me two complimentary yardsticks, and a beautician offered me a haircut. I could only think, I wonder what these people would do should a rock star or visiting dignitary happen by. I kind of stood in front of the local bank, waiting for a teller to come out with a bag of unmarked currency.

And it was in front of the bank that a woman pulled her 1976 Pinto into a parking space and wiggled her finger for me to heed. I leaned down to the closed passenger window and barely heard her say, "Get in."

I did. What the hell.

Her name was Lulinda. She worked at the fruitcake factory, but her husband drove an eighteen-wheeler coast-to-coast. "I heard that you were in town, and I thought you might want to know what most people down here won't offer up."

I said, "Okay. I appreciate that." What could I say? She wore a polka-dotted cotton dress, the hem of which might've come down to her knees had she not hiked it up past midthigh.

She introduced herself and drove in the direction of my motel room. That's where I figured we were going. I kind of wished that I had more than one old high school friend to tell all of these stories about Claxton women.

"We won't keep you long, but we wanted to make sure you knew why no one should visit here, among other things."

I caught the "we." I tried to remember if, in the movies, hostages opened a moving vehicle's passenger door and tried to run, or if they covered their heads and rolled like crazy. I said, "I can't be gone too long. The mayor's expecting me. And the police chief," which wasn't true. I wondered what I should do with the yardsticks I kept, leaning against my right side.

I glanced over at Lulinda's panties more than once.

We passed the Fall Inn, and ended up at Rack Me. The parking lot was full. Lulinda said, "They ain't nothing to worry about. You ain't gone get hurt none," and smiled. She parked a distance from any of the pickup trucks and said, "I don't want anyone backing up into my car and exploding it."

I carried the yardsticks inside, but left the boutonniere on Lulinda's cracked dashboard. I went over kung-fu moves in my mind, how to deflect pool cues with my own two weapons. When we opened the door to Rack Me, though, the only thing I thought about was how difficult it might be to keep my "Claxton, Georgia—Fruitcake Capital of the World" essay down to a thousand words.

Brother Macon stood at the bar, across from the barmaid I'd met the night before. The two pool players stood there, too, along with a group of a half-dozen men wearing blue-jean jackets. Brother Macon tossed me a cue-stick chalk and said, "This is for you, son. It's Marco Polo. He traveled around writing about places, too."

"It ain't too early for you to join us in a beer, is it?" one man said. He reached over the counter and pulled a can of PBR from the cooler. "My name's Gerald. Just like our president."

I said, "No, sir."

Lulinda went back to the door and locked it. I could feel my knees shaking, just like any other normal cartoon character's. My palms sweat so badly I went ahead and leaned the yardsticks against a barstool.

"You can't write no story about us, saying how Claxton would be a perfect place to bring the family on summertime vacations," another man said. He took the can of beer, opened the pop-top, and handed it to me. "We'd rather not go into detail, so let's just leave it at that."

Lulinda said, "It has to do with things changing, and things staying the same, and things changing. And then staying the same."

I put Marco Polo in my shirt pocket. Brother Macon said, "To be honest, I want people showing up to buy my carved works of God. But these old boys talked me out of it. I got to go with the flow, you know. Its a democracy."

"Here." Gerald reached back in the cooler and pulled out a grocery bag. "You take this as a gift from us, and go off to somewhere else, and forget that you ever come here." Gerald's hair stood up two perfect inches. One of his eyes seemed misplaced.

"Oh, you'll forget," someone said, and everyone started laughing.

I opened the top of the bag to find a good four or five pounds of the kind of thick buds I'd only seen on the national news. Brother Macon, already carving another piece of blue chalk, said, "They's certain parks and public properties we don't need people discovering, or trampling all over, you know what I mean. The way things are now, we ain't got nobody bothering us. Everybody thinks we just simple fruitcake-baking peoples. And they can keep that thought."

"It's not easy paying bills on what the fruitcake company pays out. All of us had to find other measures," Gerald said. "Now, if you'd prefer not to drive around with an illegal substance in your Jeep, Lulinda here has permission from her husband to buy it all back. We normally get thirty dollars an ounce for this stuff. Shit, it's so good we got people down in Mexico and South America buying from *us*."

I'd never heard of marijuana going for more than five dollars a nickel bag. This was a time before sensemilla, or whatever cross-pollinations got developed out in northern California. I said, "Well. Hmm. Is there any way I could maybe keep a couple ounces, you know, and sell some of this back to y'all?"

The barmaid—she had a bowling shirt on this morning, but I doubted that her name was Cecil—said, "Let me tell him about the fingers, let me tell him about the fingers."

Gerald said, "I'm figuring there's two grand in that bag. You keep you a handful, and we'll still give you two grand. And then you leave us alone. Leave us out of the book. We'll run you down and find you, otherwise." He got off his barstool, pulled out his thick wallet, and extracted twenty one-hundred-dollar bills.

"Hey," Cecil yelled from her spot behind the bar. "Somewhere in America they's fruitcakes on the shelf with human fingers stuck inside from when LeRoy McDowell had his accident."

"There's worse than fingers," someone else said. "Don't forget about when Lulinda's brother's sister-in-law took that knife to her sleeping husband. Oh, she went into work that next morning and they never did find that old boy's manhood."

The jukebox came on without anyone putting in a quarter that I saw. Merle Haggard sang. I yelled out the only thing which seemed proper at the time, namely, "Drinks on me!" like a pardoned fool.

To be honest I don't remember my return to the Fall Inn. I awoke in darkness, though, because Callie banged on my door. I looked through the peephole to see her sporting a tiara and sash that read "Little Miss Fruitcake 1970." She held a baton.

I opened the door and said, "Hey," wondering if she could smell what pot still hung in my clothes.

"It's your lucky day!" she singsonged out in a drawl. "You're officially our only lodger left. Are you hungry?"

I stepped back to let her in. "It looks like I won't be staying here much longer, either. I might be leaving in the morning."

Callie didn't enter. She looked to the side, waved her arm, and the same woman who offered me a free haircut pushed a handtruck of boxed fruitcakes my way. "Mendal's cool," Callie said.

The beautician said, "I still owe you the haircut if you want one and got the time. Or a full-body massage."

I had put my hush money in every single page of Revelations in the Gideon's Bible. I remembered that much. Callie said, "Open up your fruitcakes, open up your fruitcakes. My talent's baton-twirling, but I can't do much with a low ceiling."

I said, "Oh your talent might be something else," all wink-wink, as if the beautician weren't present.

"I'm Frankie," said the other woman. "Like in the song."

"Hey, Frankie," I said. "I remember you."

"Open the fruitcake like Callie said." Callie walked toward the sink and shimmied up on it. "Its from the Small Business Owners Association. I'm part of them."

I had no option but to believe in a God who looked down upon and cared about me. I pulled open the first box to find a fifty-dollar bill sitting atop it. Subsequent boxes held twenties, tens, more fifties, and a roll of silver dollars. "What're you people doing?" I asked. This was a half town of people willing to bribe me to leave them alone, and another half town bribing me to exaggerate their wonderful environs.

"You the money man," Frankie said. "The Christmas dessert and money man." She walked past me and stretched out on the bed. "I wish they was a good movie on tonight. Anyway, the association only asks that you let the world know how great Claxton is. Then people will indeed come visit. And it'll be nothing but an economic boom for the community as a whole."

All told I got forty-eight free fruitcakes and another thousand-plus dollars. "Well y'all might win Friendliest Town in the South," I said. I foresaw a fine life of driving from one small forgotten place to the next, each town's populace evenly divided between hopeful do-gooders and ne'er-do-well outlaws, garnering illicit payoffs. I said, "Do y'all want any of this money from the shopkeepers? I mean, did y'all come here to trade off some work, or what?"

Callie said, "I got to get back to the front desk."

Frankie got up off the bed, looked at herself in the mirror, and fingered her hair upwards. She squeegeed her teeth and popped gum I'd not noticed before. "I hope you're not talking about what I think you're talking about, as cool as you are or not. Anyway. If the mayor or anybody comes by and asks tomorrow, don't forget to tell them we brought over the gifts."

That night I didn't call Marcel Parsell to tell him I'd be mailing Claxton in presently before moving on to Egypt, or Canoochee, or Kibbee, or Emmalane. I didn't call my father to say how I'd succeeded in finding a satisfying job, regardless of what I might go on to study. I thought about calling Shirley Ebo, my imaginary black girlfriend who worked the summer as a counselor at a camp for children with missing extremities. Shirley taught knitting, somehow.

I didn't telephone my lost and wayward mother in St. Louis, Nashville, New Orleans, or Las Vegas. Compton Lane—my best friend since birth—didn't get a call.

I had three thousand dollars in my room, in a town of a thousand people, during an economic recession.

I took my leftover marijuana and pressed it in the Bible, like an autumn leaf. Don't think I left money in there stupidly so the chambermaid could change her station in life. Then I called Rack Me. When Cecil answered I announced myself and asked if anyone played pool, then told her I'd come bring tip money in the morning if she directed the receiver toward the table. I said something about how I needed to hear the crack of one sphere hitting the other, unexpectedly, that I needed to prove to myself that at least one law of physics worked somewhere. She covered the mouthpiece, but I heard her laugh right before she hung up altogether.

I packed and made a point to fold my sparse collection of clean clothes neatly. It seemed important to place my money everywhere possible—in my shoes, glove compartment, between two opened fruitcakes shoved together. It would take another twenty years for me to understand what little value all of these bribes held, and how fortunate I was—even if it was only a joke at the time—to stick a carved cue chalk of either Henry Ford or William Tecumseh Sherman on my dashboard as I left for another hopeless group of citizens two hours away. My remaining collection of Brother Macon miniatures vibrated atop the passenger seat in an awkward and mysterious historical orgy that would one day attract both friends and strangers to my door. Everyone in my later life would remark how great it was that I could line up these chalk busts and offer little lectures at tiny libraries to kids wishing a place worthy of their rearing.

George Singleton has published two collections of stories, *These People Are Us* and *The Half-Mammals of Dixie*. His next collection of stories, *Why Dogs Chase Cars*, is scheduled for publication in fall 2004. His stories have appeared in a number of magazines and journals, including the *Georgia Review*, the *Atlantic Monthly*, *Harper's*, *Zoetrope*, the *North American Review*, and *Shenandoah*.

GLENDA GUION

I've always been enamored of and puzzled by small towns whose citizens cherish their locale's one special feature. My own hometown had two: World's Widest Main Street! and Second Largest Population of Albino Squirrels in America! It didn't seem to help me get into colleges when I put that down on the applications, but what the heck.

Anyway, I had been writing a slew of linked stories told from the point of view of young Mendal Dawes, here at my current home in Dacusville, South Carolina—Home of the Largest Antique Farm Implement and Tractor Pull Celebration in the South Every Labor Day Weekend!—and wondered what kind of first "real" job I could give the poor fool. Already he'd worked in a nursing home, done clandestine vandalism for his father's best friend, and what not.

For some unknown reason a man from Dallas called me up and asked if I would speak to a conference for travel writers. He said, "I know that you don't write travel writing per se, but we'd still like to have you say some things about Place."

I said, of course, "No," because it was a writers' conference and I'm of the firm belief that one should write, not spend all of one's time talking about writing. If one wants to build a house, one should not merely watch Bob Vila and never learn the nuances of a miter box. If one wishes to bake bread, one shouldn't only watch one of those religious channels and how the host makes a mean Jesus Crust on her rye.

I could go on and on. So I hung up the telephone and thought, Hey, maybe I can't be a travel writer, but I bet Mendal Dawes could. "Raise Children Here" is what came out.

Rick Bass

PAGANS

(from *The Idaho Review*)

There once were two boys, best friends, who loved the same girl, and, in a less-common variation on that ancient story, she chose neither one of them, but went on to meet and choose a third, and lived happily ever after.

One of the boys, Richard, nearly gambled his life on her—poured everything he had into the pursuit of her, Annie—while the other boy, Kirby, was attracted to her, intrigued by her, but not to the point where he would risk his life, or his heart, or anything else. It could have been said at the time that all three of them were fools, though no one who observed their strange courtship thought so, or said so; and even now, thirty years later, with the three of them as adrift and asunder from one another as any scattering of dust or wind, there are surely no regrets, no notions of failure or success or what-if: though among the three of them, it is perhaps Richard alone who sometimes considers the past, and imagines how easily things might have been different. How much labor went into the pursuit, and how close they all three passed to different worlds, different histories.

Richard and Kirby were seniors in high school, while Annie was yet a junior, and as such, they were able to get out of class easier than she was—they were both good students—and because Kirby had a car, an old Mercury with an engine like a locomotive, he and Richard would sometimes spend their skip days traveling down to the coast, forty miles southeast of Houston, drawn by some force they neither understood nor questioned, traveling all the way to the water's edge.

The boys traveled by themselves at night, too, always exploring, and on one of their trips they had found a rusting old crane half-sunk near the estuary of the Sabine River, salt-bound, a derelict from gravel quarry days. They had climbed up into the crane (feeling like children playing in a sandbox) and had found that they could manually unspool the loopy wire cable, and with great effort, crank it back in. When they did so, the rusting, giant gear teeth gave such a clacking roar that the nightbirds roosting down in the graystick spars of dead and dying trees on the other shore took flight, egrets and kingbirds and herons, the latter rising to fly long and slow and gangly across the moon; and as the flecks and flakes of salt rust chipped from each gear tooth during that groaning resurrection, the flakes drifted down toward the river in glittering red columns, sifting fine as sand, orange wisps and strands of rust like magic dust being cast onto the river by the conjurings of some midnight sorcerer. Was I falling in love with her, Richard wonders now, or the world, or both?

With such power at their fingertips, there was no way not to exercise it. Richard climbed down from the crane, and muck-waded out into the gray slime salt-rimed shallows. Poisoned frogs yelped and skittered from his approach, and the orange sky-dancing flames of the nearby refineries wavered and belched, as if noticing his approach and beckoning him closer; as if desiring to stoke their own ceaseless burning with his own bellyfire. As if knowing they might be able to capture him, if not the slightly more cautious other one.

That first night at the crane, Richard grabbed the massive hook of the cable's end and hauled it back to shore and fastened it to the undercarriage of Kirby's car, then raised his hand over his head and gave a twirling motion.

Kirby began cranking, and the car began to ascend in a levitation, rising slowly, easily, vertical into the air. Loose coins, pencils, and Coke cans tumbled from the windows at first, but then all was silent save for the steady ratchet of slow gears, cranking one at a time, and the boys howled with pleasure, and more birds lifted from their rookeries and flew off uneasily into the night.

It was only when the car was some twenty feet into the air—dangling and spinning—that Richard thought to ask if the down-gears worked—imagining what a long walk home it would be if they did not—and imagining, too, what the result might be if one of the old iron teeth failed, plummeting the Detroit beast into the mud below.

The gears held. Slowly, a foot at a time in its release, the crane let the car back down toward the road.

The boom would not pivot—had long ago been petrified into its one position, arching out toward the river, like some tired monument facing the direction of a long ago, all-but-forgotten war—but there were hundreds of feet of cable, so that they were able to give each other rides in the rocket car now, one of them lifting it with the crane while the other gripped the steering wheel and held on for dear life, aiming straight for the moon, and praying that the cable would hold.

They soon discovered that by twisting and jouncing around in the passenger seat, the car could be induced to sway further, and to even spin, as it was raised—the Coriolis effect swirling below like an unseen, unmapped river—and it took all of an evening (the spinning headlights on high beam, strafing the mercury-green bilious cloudbank above, where refinery steam crept through the tops of the trees) before they tired of that game (startled birds flying right past the sky driver's windows, occasionally).

They began hooking onto other objects, attaching the Great Claw of Hunger, as they called it, to anything substantial they could find: pulling half-submerged railroad ties from out of the sandbank, the old bumpers of junked cars, twisted steel scrap, rusting slag-heaped refrigerators, washers and dryers.

As if in a game of crude pinball, or some remote-controlled claw-clutch game at an arcade, they were able to lurch their attachments out into the center of the river; and with a little practice, they learned how to disengage the hook midair, which led to satisfying results—dropping junked cars into the river from forty feet up, landing them sometimes back on the road with a grinding clump of sparks, though other times in the river's center amidst a great whale-plume of splash.

A sculpture soon appeared in the river's middle: a testament to machines that had been hard-used and burned out early, spring-busted not even halfway through the great century: the steel wheels of trains, cogs and pulleys, transmissions leaking rainbow sheens into the night water, iridescent sentences trailing slowly downstream in perhaps the same manner in which shamans once tossed entrails to determine or sense the world's flow and coming events.

Within a few nights the boys had created an island in the slow current's middle, an island of steel and chrome that gathered the bask of reptiles on the hot days, and into the evenings—turtles, little alligators, snakes, and bullfrogs.

Nights were the best. There were still fireflies back then, along the Sabine, and the fireflies would cruise along the river and across the toxic fields, swirling around the angel-ascending car, the joy ride: and the riders, the journeyers, would imagine that they were astronauts, voyaging through the stars, cast already out into some distant future.

In September the river was too low for barges to use, though when the rains of winter returned the river would rise quickly (flooding the banks and filling the cab of the crane), and the riverboat captains working at night would have to contend with the new obstacle of the junk slag-island, not previously charted on their maps, and they might or might not marvel at the origin or genesis of the structure, but would merely tug at the brim of their cap, note the obstacle in the logbook, and pass on, undreaming, laboring toward the lure of the ragged refineries, ferrying more oil and chemicals, hundreds of barrels of toxins sloshing quietly in the rusty steel drums stacked atop their barges, and never imagining they were passing the fields of love . . .

Richard and Kirby bought an old diving bell in an army-navy surplus store for fifty dollars—they had to cut a new rubber gasket for the hatch's seal—and after that, they were able to give each other crane rides into the poison river.

For each of them it was the same, whether lowering or being lowered: the crane's operator swinging the globe out over moon-lit water the color of mercury, then lowering the globe, with his friend in it, into that netherworld—the passenger possessing only a flashlight, which dimmed quickly upon submersion, and then disappeared—the globe tumbling downcurrent then, and the passenger within not knowing whether the cable was still attached or not, bumping and tumbling, spotlight probing the black depths thinly, with bright brief glimpses of fish eyes, gold-rimmed and wild in fright, and the pale turning-away bellies of wallowing things flashing past, darting left and right to get out of the way of the tumbling iron ball of the bathysphere.

The cable stretching taut, then, and shuddering against the relentless current: swaying and shimmering in place, but traveling no more.

Then the emergence, back up out of total darkness and into the night. The gas flares still flickering all around them. Why, again, was the rest of the world asleep? The boys took comfort in the knowledge that they would never sleep: never.

On their afternoon school-skip trips together, the three of them traveling to the Gulf Coast, they would wander the beaches barefooted, walking beneath the strand line, studying the gulf as if yearning to travel still farther—as if believing that, were they to catch it just right, the tide might one day pull back so far as to reveal the entire buried slope, entirely new territory—though this was not a clamant yearning, for already, so much else was just as new. It was more like a consideration.

Beyond the smokestack flares of the refineries, there was an abandoned lighthouse, its base barnacle-encrusted, out on a windy jetty, that they enjoyed ascending, on some such trips, and once up into the glassed-in cupola, they would drink hot chocolate from a thermos they had brought, sharing the one cup, and would play the board game of Risk, to which they were addicted.

And slowly, within Annie, a little green fire began to burn, as she spent more and more time with the two older boys; and more quickly, an orange fire began to flicker, then burn, within Richard, as he began to desire to spend more and more time in her company.

Only Kirby seemed immune, his own light within cool and blue. They played on.

By mid-September Kirby and Richard were bringing Annie out to play the bathysphere game, and to view their slag island. They would come out on lunch break, and would skip a class before and sometimes after, to buy them the time they needed. There was a bohemian French-African oceanography teacher who was retiring that year, and who could see plainly what Richard, if not Kirby, was trying to do, chasing the heart of the young girl—the junior. The teacher—Miss Countée, who wore a beret—would write hall passes for all three of them, knowing full well they would be leaving campus, issuing the passes under the stipulation that they bring back specimens for her oceanography lab.

They drove through the early autumn heat with the windows down and an old green canoe on top of their car. They paddled out to the new slag island and had picnics of French bread and green apples and cheese.

They piled lawn chairs atop the edifice. And even though the water was poisoned, the sound of it, as they lay there in the sun with their sleeves rolled up, and their shoes and socks off, eyes closed, was the same as would be the sound of waves in the Bahamas, or a clear cold stream high in the mountains. Just because the water was ugly did not mean it had to sound ugly.

Richard knew that to the rest of the world Annie might have appeared slightly gangly, even awkward; but that had nothing to do with how his heart was leaping now, each time he saw her—and after they began traveling to the river, he started to notice new things about her. Her feet pale in the sun, her shoulders rounding, her breasts lifting. A softening in her eyes, as the beauty in her heart began to rise out of her. And many years later, after their lives separated, he would believe there was something about the sound, the harmonics, of that ravaged river, and her ability to love it, and take pleasure in it, that released something from within her: transforming in ancient alchemy the beautiful unseen into the beautifully tangible. And Kirby would agree with him: that there had been alchemy, in those days, even amidst so much poison.

The water lapping lightly against the edges of the green canoe, tethered to one of the steel spars mid-pile. Umbrellas for parasols: crackers and cheese. Annie's pale feet browning in the sun. Perspiration at their temples, under their arms, in the small of their backs. Richard felt himself descending, sinking deeper into love, or what he supposed was love. How many years, he wondered, before the two were married and they would browse upon one another, in similar sunlight, in another country, another life? He was content to wait forever.

It was, however, as if Annie's own fire, the quiet green one, would not or could not quite merge with his leaping, dancing orange one. As if the two fires (or three fires) needed to be in each other's company, and were supported, even fed, by each other's warmth—but they could not, or would not yet, combine.

Without true heat of conviction, Annie would sometimes try to view the two boys separately, and would even, in her girl's way, play or pretend at imagining a future. Kirby, she told herself, was more mature, more responsible—he could run an old crane! As well, there was an instinct that seemed to counsel her to both be drawn toward, yet also move away from, Richard's own more exposed fires and energies . . .

It was too much work to consider, it was all pretend anyway, or almost pretend. They had found a lazy place, a sweet place, to hang out, in the eddy between childhood and whatever came next. She told herself she would be happy to wait there forever: and for a while, she believed that.

Occasionally, the befouled river would ignite spontaneously; other times, they found that they could light it themselves by tossing matches, or flaming oily rags, out onto its oil- and chemical-slicks. None of the three of them were churchgoers, though Annie, a voracious reader, had been carrying around a Bible that autumn, reading it silently on their picnics, while crunching an apple. The bayou-breeze, river-breeze, stirring her strawberry hair.

"I want to give the river a blessing," she said, the first time she saw the river ignite. The snaky, wandering river fires, in various bright petrochemical colors, seemed more like a celebration than harbinger of death or poison, and they told themselves too that they were doing the river a favor, helping to rid it of excess toxins, through such incinerations.

They loaded their green canoe with gallon jugs of water the next day, tap water straight from their Houston faucets and hoses.

The canoe rode low in the poisoned water on their short trip out to the iron-and-chrome island, carrying the load of the three of them as well as their jugs of water. The gunwales of their green boat were no more than an inch above the vile murk of the river, and they sat in the canoe as still as perched birds to avoid capsizing, and let the current carry them to the island of trash.

Once there, they spent nearly the rest of the afternoon scrubbing with steel wool, and pouring the clean bright water over the crusted, rusted, mud-slimed ornamenture of bumpers and freezers, boat hulls and car bodies. They polished the chrome appurtenances and rinsed the mountain anew. They waded around its edges, oblivious to the sponges of their own pure skin taking in the river's, and the world's, poison.

When they had it sparkling, Annie climbed barefooted to the top and read a quote from Jeremiah: "And I brought you into the plentiful country, to eat the fruit thereof and the goodness thereof; but when ye entered, ye defiled my land and made mine heritage an abomination."

On her climb up to the top, she had gashed her foot on the rusted corner of one sharp piece or another. She paid it no mind as she stood up there in her overalls, her red-brown hair stirring in the wind, a startlingly bright trickle of blood leaking from her pale bare foot, and Richard had the uneasy feeling that something whole and vital and time-crafted, rare and pure in the world, was leaking out of her through that wound, and that he—with his strange vision of the world, and his half-assed, dreamy shenanigans—was partly responsible: if not for leading her directly astray, then at least leading her down the path to the flimsy or even unlatched gate, and showing her a view beyond.

And Kirby, too, viewing her blood, felt an almost overpowering wave of tenderness, and with his bare hand quickly wiped the blood from her foot, then put his arm around her as if to comfort her, though she did not feel discomforted: and now the two of them sank a bit deeper into the fields of love, like twin pistons dropping a little deeper, leaving Richard off-balance for a moment, for a day, poised above, distanced now . . .

There was no clean water left with which to rinse or purify themselves, after the ceremony. Instead, they burned handfuls of green Johnson grass, wands of slow-swirling blue smoke. Like pagans, they paddled back to shore, mucked across the oily sandbar, and while Richard and Kirby were loading the canoe back onto the car, Annie went off into the tall waving grass to pee, and when she came back she was carrying a dead white egret: not one of the splendid but common yellow-legged cattle egrets, but a larger and much rarer snowy egret (within their lifetime it would go extinct), whiter than even the clouds—so white that as Annie carried it, it seemed to glow—and it had died so recently that it was still limp.

She laid it down in the grass for them to examine. They stroked its head, and the long crested plumes flowing from the head. Perhaps it was only sleeping. Perhaps they could resuscitate it. Kirby stretched the wings out into a flying position, then folded them back in tight against its body. Nothing. Annie's eyes watered, and again Kirby felt the overpowering wave of tenderness that was not brotherly, but stronger, wilder, fiercer: as if it came from the river itself.

It seemed that the obvious thing to do would be to bury the egret, but they couldn't bring themselves to give such beauty back to the earth, much less to such an oily, drippy, poisoned earth, and so they took the canoe and paddled back out to the island, and laid the bird—fierce-eyed and thick-beaked—to rest in the crown of the island, staring downriver like a gunner in his turret, with the breeze stirring his elegant plumage, and a wreath of green grass in a garland around his snowy neck.

This time on the way out they remembered their oceanography assignment, and scooped up a mayonnaise jar full of water and sediment that was the approximate color and consistency of watery diarrhea, and swabbed a dip net through the grass shallows, coming up with a quick catch of crabs and bent-backed, betumored mullet minnows, and then they loaded the canoe and drove back to school, through the brilliant heat, the brilliant light, the three of them riding in the front seat together.

When they got back to school—a feeling like checking back into a jail—they hurried up the stairwell with their fetid bounty, late to class as usual, and placed their murky-watered bottles on the cool marble lab table at the front of the room for the rest of the class to see.

Miss Countée made alternating clucking sounds of pleasure and then dismay as she examined the macroinvertebrates as well as the crippled vertebrates, murmuring their names in genus and species, not as if naming them but as if greeting old acquaintances, old warriors perhaps from another time and place—and the other students got up from their seats and crowded around the jars and bottles as if to be closer to the presence of magic.

Richard and Annie and Kirby would still have the marsh scent of the river upon them, and the blue smoke odor of burnt Johnson grass, and sometimes, for a moment, Miss Countée and the students would get the strange feeling that the truly wild catch that had been brought in resided not in the mayonnaise jars, but in the catchers themselves.

Miss Countée took an eyedropper and snorted up a shot of dead Sabine; dripped it onto a slide, slid it under a microscope, and then crooned at all the violent erratica dashing about beneath her: the athleticism and diversity, the starts and stops and lunges; the silky passages, the creepings and slitherings, the throbbings and pulsings.

The river was dying, but it was still alive.

By October the leaves on the wounded trees at water's edge were turning yellow, and Annie was riding in the bathysphere.

It was different, in the daytime. As the sphere tumbled, she could orient herself to the surface by the bright glare above—the bouncy, jarring ride to the bottom, the tumultuous drift downstream, and then the shuddering tautness when the cable reached full draw. Usually she was busy laughing or praying for her life, but sometimes, at full stretch, she considered sex.

It was different, in the daytime, when the crane lifted the sphere free and clear of the river: different, in the birth back into that bright light, water cascading off the bathysphere and glittering in sheets and torrents of sun diamonds—the awful river transformed, in that moment, into something briefly beautiful.

Sometimes, to tease her, the boys would let her remain down there just a beat or two longer, each time: just long enough for the precursor of a thought to begin to enter her mind, the image that—despite their obvious love for her—something had snapped within them. Not quite the thought, but the advancing shadow of the thought—the chemical synapses stirring and shifting, rearranging themselves to accommodate the approaching, imagined conception—of the boys, her friends, climbing down from the crane and getting in the car and driving off. Not *abandoning* her,

but going off for a burger and fries. And then forgetting her, perhaps, or getting in a wreck. Something. Anything.

Not quite loneliness, and not quite desperation. But not quite
the old security she'd known all her life, either. She loved it, and
was terrified by it.

Always, the boys pulled her up and reeled her back in, before the
thought of abandonment came, and the thought beyond that—the
terror of utter loneliness, utter emptiness.

None of them questioned the fact that the crane was there for
them, a relic still operating for them. They didn't question that it
was tucked out of the way below a series of dunes and bluffs, away
from the prying, curious eyes of man, and didn't question the
grace, the luck, that allowed them to run it, day or night, unob-
served. They didn't question that the world, the whole world, belonged to them.

There were still a million, or maybe a hundred thousand, or at
least ten thousand, such places left in the world, back then. Soft
seams of possibility, places where no boundaries had been claimed—
places where reservoirs of infinite possibility lay exposed and waiting for the claimant, the discoverer, the laborer, the imaginer.
Places of richness and health, even in the midst of heart-rotting,
gut-eating poisons.

For the first time, Richard and Kirby began to view each other
as competitors. It was never a thought that lasted—always, they
were ashamed of it, and able to banish it at will—but for the first
time, it was there.

The egret fell to pieces slowly. Sunbaked, rained-upon, wind-
ruffled, ant-eaten, it deflated as if only now was its life leaving it;
and then it disintegrated further, until soon there were only piles
of sun-bleached feathers lying in the cracks and crevices of the junk-
slag island below, and feathers loose too within the ghost-frame of
its own skeleton, still up there at the top of the machines.

As the egret decomposed, so too was revealed the quarry within—
the last meal upon which the egret had gorged—and they could

see within the bone-basket of its ribcage all the tiny fish skeletons, with their piles of scaleglitter lying around like bright sand. There were bumps and tumors, misshapen bends in the fishes' skeletons, and as they rotted (flies feasting on them within that ventilated ribcage, as if trapped in a bottle, but free, also, to come and go) the toxic sludge of their lives melted to leave a bright metallic residue on the island, stained here and there like stripes of silver paint.

Sometimes they would be too restless to fool with even the magnificence of the crane. Bored with the familiar, the three of them would walk down the abandoned railroad tracks, gathering plump late-season dewberries, staining their hands with the juice until they were as black as if they had been working with oil. Kirby or Richard would take off his shirt and make a sling out of it in which to gather the berries. Their mouths, their lips, would be black-ringed, like clowns.

She beheld their bodies. They filled her dreams—first one boy, then the other—as did dreams of ghost ships, and underworld rides. Dreams of a world surely different from this one—a fleshing, a stripping back to reveal the bones and flesh, the red muscle, of a world not at all like the image of the one we believe we have crafted above.

Unsettling dreams, to be shaken off by her, with difficulty, upon awakening. Surely all below is only imagined, she tried to tell herself, only fantasy. Surely there is only one world.

The berries they brought home were sweet and delicious, ripe and plump. The dreams of gas flares, simmering underworld fires, only an image, possessed nothing of the berries' reality. Only one world, she told herself. There is nothing to be frightened of, no need to be cautious about anything.

The cracks and fissures of chance, the ruptures at the earth's surface claiming the three of them, then, as surely as all must be claimed—those crevasses manifesting or masquerading as random occurrence rather than design and pattern, but operating surely, just beneath the surface, in intricate balancings of need-and-desire, cost-and-recompense— an alignment of fates as crafted and organic, al-most always, as the movements of the tides themselves. There was a school Halloween dance that autumn, a party, which Kirby was unable to attend, due to some family matter that had arisen just that week. The crack or crevice, seemingly without meaning.

It was a low-key evening, filled with chaperones, and with the elementary and middle schools combining, that evening, with the high schoolers. The party was filled with Twister and pin-the-tail-on-the-donkey and bingo and bobbing-for-apples. There was a haunted house, and masked children of all ages in all manners of costumes ran laughing and shouting through the school hallways, and the high schoolers hung back for a while, but then gave them-selves over to the fun.

There was dancing in the basketball gym, with some of the chil-dren and adults still wearing their masks and costumes, though many of the teenagers had taken off their masks and were now only half-animal— tiger, bear, lion, gorilla. Their faces were flushed, and the discrepancy between what their hormones were telling them— *destroy, rebel*— and what the rigid bars of their culture were telling them, *no, no, no,* was for the most lively of them like a pressure cooker.

Annie was dressed as a princess, and Richard a red devil. They sat for a while and watched the other children dance. Annie waited, and was aware of no pressure. It's possible she could afford to step aside of the drumming, mounting pressure her peers were feeling because she had Richard and Kirby in her life, and Richard at her side, much as a young girl might have a pet bear or lion in her back-yard. She turned and smiled at Richard, serene, while the records played and the little monsters ran shrieking, bumping against their legs. The scent of sugar in the air. The aura dense around them of all the other itchy, troubled, angst-bound teenagers, wanting sex, wanting power, wanting God, wanting salvation—wanting home and hearth, wanting the open road.

There was no need yet for Annie to participate in any of that confusion. Everything else around her was swirling and tattering, but she was grounded and centered, and she was loved deeply and seemingly without reason. She smiled, watching Richard watch the dancers. She reached over and took his hand in the darkness and held it, while they watched the dancers, and while they felt the palpable fretting and shifting of their peers. It was lonely, being sunk down to the bottom of the world, she thought, but comfortable, even wonderful, to have each other.

"What do you think Kirby's doing right now?" she asked, twisting his hand in hers.

They left the party and went out for an ice cream sundae, and enjoyed it leisurely, watching the rest of the city zoom by out on the neon strip of Westheimer Road, a busy Friday night, hearing dimly even in the restaurant the whooping and shouting from open car windows, and the screeching of tires, and gears accelerating.

They enjoyed the meal with no conscious forethought of where they were going next—though if anyone had asked them, they would have been able to answer immediately—and after a little while, Kirby drove past, finished with his family engagement, saw Richard's car, and he pulled in and joined them.

With Richard and Annie still wearing their costumes, they journeyed to the east, riding with the windows down as ever, and with the radio playing, but with a seriousness, a quietness, the three of them knowing with the somehow-heavy knowledge of adults that they were ascending now into the world ahead, as if to some upper level, a level which would sometimes be exciting, but where more frequent work would be the order of the day: less dreaming, and more awareness and consciousness. Carve-and-scribe, hammer-and-haul. Almost like a war. As if this unasked-for war must be, and was, the price of all their earlier peace, and all their peace-to-come.

Richard and Annie held hands again in the car on the way east, and the three of them knew by the way the allure for the crane was dying within them as they drew nearer to that sulfurous, wavering glow on the horizon that they would soon be moving on to other things, and in other directions. It was almost for them then—for the first time—as if they were pushing into a heavy headwind.

It was getting late. The city's children had finished their trick-or-treating, and as they passed through a small wooded suburb sandwiched between shopping malls, they stopped and went up and gathered several gutterstubbed candle remnants from the scorched mouths of sagging, sinking, barely glimmering pumpkins.

One pumpkin had already been taken out to the sidewalk for the garbage men to pick up the next morning, and they resurrected that one, placed it on the front seat between Annie and Kirby, and fed it a new candle, coaxed it back to brightness as one might offer a cigarette to an injured or dying man.

They rode through the city and then east toward the refineries, with their runty candles wax-welded all over the front and back dashboards, with the windows rolled almost all the way up now, to keep from extinguishing the little flames—the light on their faces wavering, as they passed through the night (to the passengers in the cars and trucks they passed, it seemed strangely as if Kirby and Richard and Annie were floating, so disorienting was the sight of the big car filled with all those candles)—and they kept heading east, toward the flutterings and spumes of the refineries' chemical fires, toward that strange glow that was like daytime-at-night.

It was the night that Annie and Richard went down into the bathysphere, and into the river, together, with Kirby above them, working the manual crank on the crane like a puppeteer. They were still wearing their costumes—there was barely room for them to squeeze in together, and Annie's satin dress spread across the whole bench, and Richard's devil's tail got folded beneath them—he rode with his arm around her, and hers around him, for stability as well as courage, as the globe was lifted swaying from the earth—that first familiar and sickening feeling of powerlessness, as the ground fell away below them—and they rode with an array of candles in front of them.

Their faces were almost touching. *This,* Richard was thinking, *this is how I want it always to be.*

They glimpsed the stars, swinging, as Kirby levered them out over the river, and then there was the thrill of free fall—"Hold on!" Richard shouted, covering her with both arms and shielding her head—and the concussion of iron meeting water, the great splash—candles went everywhere, spilling warm wax on their hands and wrists, their faces—one landed on Annie's dress and burned a small hole in the silk—and then, once underwater, the globe righted itself and settled in for the brief ride downstream; and with the candles that were still burning they relit the scattered ones, and leaned forward, and cheek to cheek studied the interior of the foul river as they tumbled slowly through its center.

"What if the cable snapped loose?" Richard asked, "when we hit the water so hard?"

Not to be outdone, Annie said, "What if some old bum, as a Halloween joke, sawed the cable down to its last fiber, so that when we reach the end, it will snap?"

There was a long silence as Richard's imagination seized and worked with that one for a while, until it became too-true.

"What if we were stranded on a desert island?" Richard asked.

"How about a forested island?"

"Right," Richard said. "What if? And what if we had only a little while to live?"

"The last man and woman on earth," Annie said.

"Right." *Man and woman.* The phrase sounded so foreign and distant: light years away, still.

"Well," said Annie, "let's wait and see." But her arm tightened around his significantly, and Richard found himself urging the cable to *break, break, break.*

The cable reached full stretch; there was a bumping, and then the globe was swept up and out, tumbling them onto their backs—as if a carpet had been pulled from beneath their feet—and again the candles fell over on them, as did the hot wax, and this time no candles stayed lit, so that they shuddered in darkness, and felt the waves, the intimate urgings of the injured river, washing over and around their tiny iron shell.

The force of the current made eerie sounds, murmurings and chatterings against their craft, as if it, that sick river, had been wait-ing to speak to them for all their lives and had only now gained that opportunity—and they lay there, reclining in each other's arms, safe from the eyes of the world and its demands, its appetites for paradox and choices; and just as the air was beginning to get stuffy and they were beginning to get a little light-headed, they felt the surge begin: the magnificent power, the brute imprecision of gears and cogs hauling them back upstream, just when they would have imagined (convinced by those fast murmurings and chatterings) that there could be no force stronger or greater than that of the river.

Gradually they broke the surface—through their portal, still lying on their backs, and arm in arm, but relaxed now, they could see the plumes and spray of water as they were birthed back to the surface; they could see the crooked, jarring skyline of the refinery fires, and farther above, the dim stars just beyond the reach of the gold-green luminous puffs of steam that marked the factories.

There was not much time now. Soon they would be up and free of the river, swinging, and then Kirby would land them on the beach. They were hot now, sweating, and there was barely any air left. Annie leaned over and found Richard's face with her hands, and kissed him slowly, with both hands still on his face. He kissed her back—took her face in his hands and tried to shift, in order to cover her with his body, but there was no room—for a moment, they became tangled, cross-elbowed and leg-locked like some human Rubik's cube—they broke off the kiss quickly, and now there was no air at all—as if they had each sucked the last of it from out of the other—but they could feel the craft settling onto the sand beach now, and knew that in scant moments Kirby would be climbing down and coming toward them; that there would be the rap of his knuckles on the iron door, and then the creak of the hatch being opened.

Time for one more kiss, demure and tender now, and then the gritty rasp of the hatch: the counterclockwise twist, and then the lid being lifted, and Kirby's anxious face appearing before them, and beyond him, those dim stars, almost like the echoes or spent husks of stars. Cool October night sliding in over their sweaty faces.

Richard helped Annie out—her dress was a charred mess—and then climbed out behind her, marveling at how delicious even the foul refinery-air tasted, in their freedom. Kirby looked at them both curiously, and started to speak, but then could think of nothing to say: and he felt a strange and great sorrow.

They left the bathysphere as it was, sitting hatch-opened and still attached to the crane with its steel umbilicus; for any number of reasons, none of them would ever go back, would never see how the crane would eventually tip over on its side, half-buried in silt; nor how the bathysphere would become buried too.

They rode back into the city, still in costume and with the pumpkin and candles glimmering once more, silent and strangely serious, reflective, on the trip home: Annie and Richard holding hands again. The candle wax was still on their faces, and it looked molten upon them in the candlelight.

On the drive home Annie peeled the candle wax from her face and then peeled off Richard's as well, and held the pressings carefully in one hand.

When Kirby pulled up in front of her house—the living room lights still on, and one of them, mother or father, waiting up, and glancing at the clock (ten minutes past eleven, but no matter; they trusted her)—Annie leaned over and gave Richard a quick peck, and gave Kirby a look of almost sultry forgiveness, then climbed out of the big old car (they had extinguished their candles upon entering the neighborhood) and hurried up the walkway to her house, holding her long silk skirt bunched up in one hand and the candle wax pressings in another.

"Well, *fuck*," said Kirby, quietly, unsure of whether he was more upset about what seemed like to him Annie's sudden choice, or about the fracturing that now existed between him and his friend. The imbalance, after so long a run, an all-but-promised run, of security.

"Shit," said Richard, "I'm sorry." He lifted his hands helplessly. "Can we . . . can it . . ?" *Stay the same,* he wanted to say, but didn't.

They both sat there, feeling poisoned, even as the other half of Richard's heart—as if hidden behind a mask—was leaping with electric joy.

"I'm sorry," Richard said again.

"The two of you deserve each other," Kirby said. "It's just that, I hate it that—" But the words failed him, there were none, only the bad-burning feeling within: and after sitting there a while longer, they pulled away from her house and drove for a while through the night, as they used to do, back before she had begun riding with them. And for a little while, they were foolish enough, and hopeful enough, to believe that it would not matter, that they could get back to that old place again, and even that that old place would be finer than any new places lying ahead of them.

The romance lasted little longer than did the carcass of the egret. The three of them continued to try to do new things together, though Richard and Annie went places by themselves, too, and explored, tentatively, those new territories. Always between or beneath them, however, there seemed to be a bur: not that she had made the wrong choice, but rather, that some choice had been required—that she had had to turn away from one thing, even in the turning-toward another—and that summer, even before the two boys, two young men, prepared to go off to college, while Annie readied herself to return for her senior year of high school, she informed Richard that she thought she would like a couple of weeks apart, to think things over, and to prepare for the pain of his departure. To prepare both of them.

"My God," Richard said, "*two* weeks?" They had been seeing each other almost every day. Their bodies had changed, their voices had changed, as had their patterns and gestures, and even the shapes of their faces, becoming leaner and more adultlike, so that now, when Annie placed the old wax pressings to her face, they no longer fit.

"I want to see what it's like," she said. "Maybe everything will be just fine. Maybe we'll find out we can't live without each other, and we'll end up married and child-raising and happy-ever-after. But I just want to know."

"All right," he said, far more frightened than he'd ever been, dangling from the crane. "All right," he said, and it seemed to him that it was as if she was climbing into the bathysphere alone, and he marveled at her bravery and curiosity, her adventurousness, and even her wisdom.

There is still a sweetness in all three of their lives, now: Kirby, with his wife and four children, in a small town north of Houston; Richard, with his wife and two children; and Annie, with her husband and five children, and, already, her first grandchild. A reservoir of sweetness, a vast subterranean vault of it, like the treasure-lair of savages—the past, hidden far away in their hearts, and held, and treasured, mythic and powerful, even now.

It was exactly like the treasure-trove of wild savages, they each realize now, and for some reason—grace? simple luck?—they were able to dip down into it back then, were able to scrape out handfuls of it, gobs of it, like sugar or honey.

As if, still, it—the discovery of that reservoir—remains with them, a power and a strength, so many years later.

And yet—they had all once been together. How can they now be apart, particularly if that reservoir remains intact, buried, and ever-replenishing?

Even now, Richard thinks they missed each other by a hair's breadth: that some sort of fate was deflected—though how or why or what, he cannot say. He thinks it might have been one of the closest misses in the history of the world. He has no regrets, only marvels. He wonders sometimes if there are not the ghosts or husks of their other lives, living still, far back in the past, or far below, or even farther out into the future, still together, still consorting: other lives, birthed from that strange reservoir of joy and sweetness, and utter newness.

And if there are, how does he access that? Through memory? Through imagination?

Even now, he marvels at how wise they were, then, and at all the paths they did not take.

Rick Bass, born in Fort Worth, has worked as a biologist in Arkansas and a geologist in Mississippi and now lives in northwest Montana's Yaak Valley. He is the author of eighteen books of fiction and nonfiction, including, most recently, a fiction collection, *The Hermit's Story*, and editor of an anthology, *The Roadless Yaak*. He is active with a number of local and regional environmental organizations, seeking to gain wilderness designation for the last roadless areas in the Yaak Valley.

NICOLE BLAISDELL

I have trouble remembering whether much in my life was fact or imagined. It's true that in high school I ran around with a couple of friends like Kirby and Annie, and true enough that more was true than in this story. Not to bend "Pagans" more toward the realm of essay or memoir than short story, but it's a fact also that I think Kirby and I either saw, or believed we saw, an old diving bell at an army-navy surplus store, and then we either did, or did not, purchase it. From this imagining or near-memory, it appears to me that I have followed themes of exploration and boundaries, as well as notions of What is vital? and What is pure?

But now I'm moving toward a kind of talk that I dislike, with regard to short stories—not even so much a deconstruction as a neutering of the generative forces and mysteries that attend the curious and shifting intersections of imagination and memory—and so shall close by saying I'm grateful to the editors and staff of the Idaho Review *for working with and publishing this story, and for its use here as well.*

K. A. Longstreet

THE JUDGEMENT OF PARIS

(from *The Virginia Quarterly Review*)

From where Charles Graves sat, several rows back and to the left among the other fourth year cadets in Stonewall Jackson Memorial Hall, Colonel Jefferson Randolph Kean's uniform, as he walked to the podium, seemed to have been fitted before its owner lost an amount of flesh. His dark hair was tamed across his skull with pomade while his bush of a beard remained long and unkempt. Charles wondered if the cadets, sitting row after row under the dark-beamed roof and hanging blossom-shaped lamps, had any individuality for the speaker at all. Putting himself in Colonel Kean's shoes, he could not imagine discerning any feature that would have set any one of them apart, so similar did they appear with their identical haircuts and fitted gray jackets. Yet Colonel Kean's face conveyed a sure sense of personal character while his declarative voice carried through the auditorium without a tremor.

"In undertaking to talk to you this afternoon, in this year of our Lord 1912, on the subject of personal hygiene, which your superintendent has selected for me, it is with full knowledge of the risk of appearing to you as just another one of those signposts which appear from time to time in your path with the tedious refrain, 'Stop! Look! Listen!'"

The wood floor, which Charles suddenly found himself staring at, was damp from snow melting off boots, the eternal winter slush that gave the boards a soft dull sound when trod upon. He was relieved to see that his boots, which he had noticed that morning were beginning to crack, still appeared intact from the present short distance. He raised his head and saw that the scene was a series of grays, the image of winter through which one searched for something of color and warmth, indoors or out, but found only the light of arctic skies, a constant subterranean glow in the long Valley of Virginia. The massive United States and Virginia flags draped behind the podium seemed ashen as if with frost, the high Gothic windows a stern device for framing sky now absent.

Yet in spite of the bleak scene, Charles liked being there, for it gave him a free hour to arrange his thoughts, to apply his usual methodical approach to both the future and the past, the same satisfaction he felt in composing lines and interspaces and conjunctions to form the structure of a building in architectural drawing class. He had been accused by his maiden sister, Adelaide, of putting a grid to nature, a bird crank, Adelaide called him in jesting affection, for he recorded the date of every feather he picked from the ground, every bird's nest he clambered up a tree for, every clutch of eggs he retrieved from the nest and blew out to set upon his display shelves at home, as well as every bird his father had taught him to stuff and mount. He recorded the arrival dates in spring of each species from the ruby-throated hummingbird to the song sparrow and their departure dates in the fall.

"Personal hygiene," Colonel Kean said, "is a story of an old and well-trodden path, but withal a difficult one, along which even knowledge herself can make but poor progress unless her older sister, Wisdom, take her by the hand."

At Charles's right, Ned McAlister, phlegmatic and long-lashed and sloe-eyed, who had not had a bath for a week, for his turn was coming up on Monday, leaned towards Charles, while his eyes, in pretext, looked straight at the speaker.

"You bet I'll take her, but not by the hand," he whispered.

Charles felt a great discrepancy between himself and Ned McAlister, not only in the bath department—for Charles had just had his turn the night before—but in other areas as well, what Adelaide would have referred to as social deportment, a quality she had taught him to raise above all others.

He reckoned there were a number of things he ought to be using the time to think about, though certainly the disposition of the mourning dove—which was difficult to hide—stood out as most immediate. It would be a sore tribulation, indeed, if the bird caused him to be confined to barracks so that he would not be able to go to town to pursue his social interests.

"Tennyson is, I think, getting to be an out of fashion poet, but I can recommend to those of you who are not familiar with it, his poem, "Oenone." The goddess of discord, you will remember, cast one day upon the banquet table of the gods a golden apple inscribed, 'To the most fair.' It was at once claimed by the three goddesses, Hera, queen of heaven, Pallas Athena, the goddess of wisdom, and Aphrodite, the goddess of love."

Willie Swann, to Charles's left, with a constant look of reproach that he often used to place himself above fault, gave a sigh of profound disrespect and indifference. He nudged Charles and formed, in imitation, a circle with his thumb and forefinger the size of a silver dollar. From his face, that reminded Charles of cold porridge, a sober wink escaped. In his usual, pedantic way, he said under his breath,

"Ah, Pallas Athena, of course. I have always preferred the more classical term Cyprian—the place of the goddess's birth—to the rather unsavory term *soiled dove*."

Charles shot him a delaying look.

The problem was whether to let the bird go free now that its leg and wing were mended or keep him sheltered in barracks until the snows had melted. The Blue Book specified that no dogs or horses were to be kept in barracks, but didn't mention birds. But then, the Blue Book could not always be trusted, for it also specified no waiters in barracks, and every waiter the school had did cooking and cleaning and boot polishing on the side in barracks. A coal-black waiter named Jesse had asked to look in Charles's ornithology books in order to identify a bird that came to the back door of the kitchen after cracked corn. It was decided that the bird was a willet, *Catoptrophrus semipalmatus,* blown off course, the waiter having described the bird's distinctive black-and-white wing pattern and call, *pill-will-willet, pill-will-willet,* as it flew off. In his white serving jacket, his face polished and oiled from the kitchen, the waiter brought scraps of bread and suet for the mourning dove, and once an unusually knotted wing bone from a snow goose, the result of a healed fracture. He always asked for payment, of course, just something small, but Charles told him the truth, his father was only a pharmacist, not a lawyer or doctor or first family planter, and he didn't have it.

"Must carried that bird ten thousand mile and now to get shot," the waiter said. "Just like the Negro. Work his self hell and gone and high water beside to end a server for the white after all. Me and this snow goose done discovered. He in a pot and me with no gratuity."

Charles thought the analogy far-fetched.

"Why don't you go with the railroad? They get tips," he said, but the waiter only looked at him solemnly and left.

On the whole, when he thought about it, items even remotely scientific were almost always accepted in barracks. His collection of eggs and nests, for example. The white-eyed vireo nest in perfect condition, which, on close inspection, revealed not only leaf skeletons and snake skins, but fine grasses, horsehair and scraps of cloth, down, moss, bark fiber and weed stems, spider webs, bits of string and paper. Or the small, compact nest of a hummingbird which had been camouflaged with the same wrinkled gray lichen as its forked branch. As well as a two-headed blacksnake, the greatest nest robber of them all, that Charles had found flat and dry on the road the past summer.

"Paris, the son of Priam, King of Troy," Colonel Kean said in a voice that lost neither inflection nor syllable as it carried through the auditorium, "was selected to be the arbiter of the dispute. Before him appeared the three disrobed Goddesses, each making offers to win his vote."

Willie Swann sighed morosely, and said, "Paris was consort to Oenone at the time. He was not *entirely* innocent. One can trust no one to take the time to get history—let alone literature—right."

Perhaps the dove would make a fitting gift for Adelaide, who turned back toward home when she reached Pearce Avenue, the western demarcation of her own neighborhood. For when Charles opened its cage, the dove was now able to fly to the ceiling then down the walls and around the table and wash stand and slop bucket, leaving small crusty droppings on the wardrobe and gun rack—but never flying out the window—as if it knew, like Adelaide, exactly how far it was allowed to go. At any rate, the dove had been quite a hit in barracks, a mascot of sorts given the moniker Buff after mathematics professor Dr. Hiram Buff, who enjoyed tending chickens behind the officers' quarters and sometimes came to class wearing a feather or two on the cuffs of his trousers.

"First Hera, queen of heaven, offered him wealth and worldly power. The splendor of her bribe so tempted him that he had already raised his arms to hand her the golden apple when Pallas spoke:

> Self reverence, self knowledge, self control,
> These three alone lead men to sovereign power.
> Yet not for power alone, power of herself
> Would come uncalled for, but to live by law,
> Acting the law we live by without fear,
> And because right is right to follow right,
> Were wisdom in the scorn of consequence."

"That's rich," whispered Ned McAlister. "It doesn't make a doodle of sense."

One more gift to Adelaide, he thought sentimentally, who had been both mother and sister since the day of their mother's death, for he had never once seen his mother, unless, as he sometimes thought, the veil of birth that covers an infant's eyes—not a caul but something less physical having to do with the transposition of the spirit—had lifted and he had truly glimpsed his mother's form lying on her bed at the moment of his birth. Yes, Adelaide had been the best of substitutes. For a moment he wondered if Mary could ever replace her, though he supposed one looked for different qualities in a wife than in a sister or a mother. For one thing, Mary seemed to know nothing of birds or nature. This past Sunday she had worn a hat like a little flat plate tilted over her forehead, a fan of plover feathers fastened onto the brim. He had tried to explain the danger of this, the killing of rare species for the millinery trade, the exportation of game birds simply for the unbridled profit of the Northern markets. She had colored and looked suddenly abashed.

"Well I never intended to hurt any one of God's creatures," she said.

"No, no of course not," he had answered, "but they're disappearing so fast what with forest fires that no one can seem to put out and the game laws that are never enforced. Then there's the Negro problem. They won't do a lick of work, but they're never too lazy to hunt no matter what time of day or season. And they don't give a hoot whether they've trespassed or not with their sickly, half-starved dogs—I tell you the lower the Negro, the more dogs he owns, you can be sure of it—scouring the fields and woods breaking up nests, destroying the young."

"I'm so sorry," she said with feeling. "I simply had no idea. Is there anything I can do?"

He had to admit her concern seemed genuine enough and she could certainly be taught. Add to that a streak of impropriety that did not disturb him in the least. When they danced, she shot him cunning, fragile looks. When she held his hand walking home under the stiff black locusts in the dark, she held it tightly as if she might suddenly float up and away from the earth. He kissed her goodnight, and it seemed to him that she herself had instigated and was in charge of the kiss, so prolonged did she insist its duration be, so cunningly did she hold his head between her two gloved hands. Yet it had not occurred to him to want more, for he was taken care of elsewhere.

Colonel Kean continued to quote Tennyson.

                                            "Yet indeed,
        If gazing on divinity disrobed,
        Thy mortal eyes are frail to judge of fair
        Unbias'd by self profit, oh, rest thee sure
        That I shall love thee well and cleave to thee
        So that my vigour wedded to thy blood
        Shall strike within thy pulses, like a God's."

He had been offered a teaching job at the manual high school in Staunton which would allow him to marry as well as repay his father for his tuition. And why wouldn't Mary make a fine wife? He could not think of one reason why she wouldn't be the most dutiful and reverent and organized queen of any man's castle. And she would not refuse him, he was certain. After all, he was liked by everyone, an expression of esteem usually reserved for the deceased, he suddenly realized thinking of his mother's headstone. He was serious, studied hard, and did not mind discipline, the formations in barracks always indicated by the time on the tower clock. Life came to him by instinct in the same way that he knew without thinking that the signal for full dress was three taps on the drum after the first call, that for overcoats it was a roll, for raincoats a roll followed by two taps, and fatigue coats a single. But he was not without a sense of fun, he told himself. If there was ice on the river, he was always the first to suggest a skate; if the spring thaws had come and cracked the ice into thin, melting sheets, he was the first to suggest a naked dip. Yet he was never blamed when ladies of the town complained of the nudity in a letter to both Superintendent Nichols as well as the editor of the Lexington *Gazette*. In short, he was as accomplished and as well liked as any cadet could be who played neither football nor baseball.

"Again the decision trembled in the balance, when Aphrodite, the beautiful goddess of love, stepped forward.

        She with a subtle smile in her mild eyes,
        The herald of her triumph, drawing nigh
        Half-whisper'd in his ear, 'I promise thee
        The fairest and most loving wife in Greece.'"

His appraisal of Mary's abilities was, in part, based on the discerning and competent behavior of her mother, the gleaming floors and unworn carpets, the shining brass knocker on the door, the small pecan cakes that flaked apart in his hand, the older woman's look of utter calm and magnificence when she saw Charles and her daughter together. And yes, he felt for certain that Mary was strong enough to withstand the discomforts of love and dangers of childbirth.

"Her beauty and her promise together won her the prize. Under her guidance, Paris sailed away to Greece, where, in violation of the law of hospitality, he seduced and carried off Helen, the wife of Menelaus, King of Sparta. The result of this crime was the Trojan war and the destruction of Paris, his family, and his native city."

Charles received two hard pokes in his back, and a "Psssst!" under the breath. His hand moved from his lap and slid behind his chair, then made as if to flick the voice away when he felt a crisp new bill placed in his palm. His fingers closed around it, then his hand slid back to his side as he raised one hip in order to slip the bill into his pocket.

"One pack," a voice behind him whispered. "You hear me? One pack of five."

Charles nodded once.

Another immediate problem was his inability to finish the concluding paragraph of an essay entitled "Nature" that he had promised to write for the *Cadet,* the school's monthly magazine of science, literature, and art. He'd put his mind to it the evening before with no results.

Gazing in thought toward the nearest high Gothic window, he saw a mockingbird flit beyond the glass, and his mind went blank. What had he been thinking of, he wondered? Ah yes, his essay for the *Cadet.* But the mockingbird brought up another question that he'd often pondered. Why did some species winter over, while others left? Why did some birds of the same species, such as the kingfisher, decide to stay while his fellows migrated south? It would be plain impossible to suffer a winter without birds, he thought, impossible to march from one bleak crenulated building to the next without hearing the occasional whistle of partridge, not seeing the ring-necked pheasant foraging in the hedgerows, the red-winged blackbird, song sparrow, or meadowlark waiting for spring. Pine creeper or wood robin. And bluebird.

His company had been the first to disturb the white snow of the parade ground as they marched towards Jackson Hall. The sun had come out for a brief interval of time and he had seen the shadows of buzzards, gliding diffuse and listless as shades across the wide and unblemished expanse of snow.

Now, sitting in Jackson Hall, he extricated a small notebook from his pocket and wrote with a slow, cumbersome hand upon his knee. *If it were not for the sun delivering her light, the atmosphere of the earth would quickly become infected with poisonous matters which would spread disease and death to all parts of the earth.* He thought a moment and added, *The earth would abhor these impurities caused by the breath of the animal kingdom, and refuse to purify the air for their use.* In order not to waste another page, he turned the notebook ninety degrees and wrote along the edge of the paper, *Indeed, everything that grows would lose its green color, become limp, then withered and yellow, no longer impart fragrance, refuse to bud and flower, and finally perish.* He looked up from the paper and noticed that Harper Stringfellow, sitting in front of him, had a fiery boil on the back of his neck half-hidden by the black braid on his collar.

"To each of you, when you go out into the world, will come the three goddesses. One with promises of worldly success and the power of money, another promising intellectual excellence and moral force, and the third with allurements of sensual pleasure. It is my intention to speak of the decision of Paris and the widespread ruin that comes to those who, like him, turn their backs on the good things and the noble things of life for the gratification of the lusts of the flesh."

Someone made a softly lewd and liquid sound, and Ned McAlister whispered, "The old goat. He condemns it because he's not up to it, I'll bet."

"The training and cultivation of the body so as to bring it to its highest perfection of vigor and beauty was to the Greek a duty both to himself and to the state, and was on an equal footing with the education of the mind."

"Oh, educate me, please," Ned McAlister whispered.

"The Greeks well understood the athletic value of temperance and chastity. They had learned that the sexual impulse is a dynamic force which if controlled and turned into other channels of wholesome activity carries men far."

"Oh darling girl, carry me far to heaven," came from Ned McAlister.

"At the same time, they knew the precious value of physical exercise in subduing and controlling these desires which nature, in her care for the preservation of the race, has made the most imperious of brute and human passions."

From down the row, a small folded paper was passed. It reached Charles and he read, *I, Harold G. Jenkins, do promise to remit to Charles H. Graves the sum of $10 dollars on receipt of two packages of ladies household stockings.* Charles retrieved his pencil and wrote across the note which he had spread upon his knee, *All goods paid at time of order. No exceptions. Sorry, Harold. I can not afford it.*

"A recent editorial," Colonel Kean said, in the *Journal of the American Medical Association* states: 'For a long time the outwardly predominating factor of asceticism has conspired with a host of shadowy, undefined motives to keep all enlightenment of the subject from the young with the same fearful zeal that guards a powder magazine from sparks. The ban of silence has been lifted, and organized effort has set unflinchingly about the task of revealing the consequences, frightful or loathsome though they may be, of transgressions against the hygiene and ethics of sex. Not all the organs of the body require constant use, and the reproductive organs can go for long periods of disuse without atrophy just as a man can go years without weeping and not lose the capacity to shed tears. The natural secretion of the testicles where it accumulates, is discharged either during sleep or little by little with the urine. This is normal and is no cause for uneasiness unless it should become unduly frequent in which case there is usually some undue stimulation, either by thought or local irritation, which should be removed.'"

"Oh mother, mother bring that irritation on!" Ned McAlister whispered.

"A good doctor should be consulted without shame or hesitation for any apparent disorder of these important organs, and one should avoid the quacks who make their living by preying upon the ignorance and fears of men. You may be sure that any doctor who advertises to cure impotence, gleet, venereal diseases, and lost manhood is a fraud and a robber."

The gray interior of the auditorium was suddenly stilled, as if each of them had been reminded of Hiram Stokes, a third year cadet sent to the infirmary, then finally sent home to Culpeper. It was said—but how the information was originally obtained no one knew, because Hiram had not been allowed visitors—that his legs had turned to boils and pus, that a wooden frame had been made to support the sheet and blanket, that a specialist from Washington had come to photograph his legs and chest and arms and face and returned to Washington shaking his head, that Doctor Meadows had sprinkled morphine powder into the boils, but it had not helped, that chloride of zinc had been injected into his arteries and veins. Charles looked at the neck in front of him, the boil he had assumed was due to acne, and wondered if it were not something else.

"It used to be a common saying among men about town that a clap was no worse than a bad cold, and many cases do apparently recover without serious consequences. It was not then known that the infection is apt to linger for months and years in tissues to reappear after marriage and doom the pure and innocent bride to a life of suffering invalidism and sterility."

Charles remembered Hiram Stokes's bravado as a "rat" or first year cadet, his unwillingness to get up at reveille and shut the light off at taps, his procrastination when it came to going to the dentist, his refusal to protect himself from the ailments of Venus. Charles had gone out of his way to caution Ned more than once. He hoped to serve as an example of safety and discipline, to instill in his friends his own form of higher ground.

"I won't have anything to do with the skins of an animal," Hiram had said. "They're not clean, and besides, they reduce the experience by half."

"I tell you," Charles had said, "they're constructed of the finest India rubber. My father gets them straight from New York."

How many lives have I saved, he asked himself with pleasure as he sat in Jackson Hall, thinking of those who had not refused his offer. How many Cyprians, the lowest form of our race, have my endeavors afforded a meal, or a blanket, a bottle of cod liver oil for the woman's sick child.

"One-fourth of all the blindness in this country," Colonel Kean said, "is caused by the injection of the eyes of the infant during birth. The ravages of syphilis are not confined to the dissolute and depraved, but fall heavily upon infants and wives. Among the saddest tragedies of life is to see mature men of high standing and ability, respected fathers of happy families suddenly smitten with the insanity of paresis or the helplessness of syphilis, and to know that this is the long deferred penalty of some forgotten sin of heedless youth. These diseases are not reported in the vital statistics and usually appear under the cloak of other diagnoses in the death certificates."

If he could have looked into the mind of every cadet sitting there, now so reserved and still, Charles was certain that each would be searching for remembrance of those who had died by natural causes, those whose symptoms might be recognizable. He turned his head to glance down the row, and was suddenly not sure of this at all, not certain of the thoughts of any of them. Perhaps they had decided long ago, generations ago—when one thought of it—that the subject, as presented, had nothing to do with their own lives or motives. Yet every month before his father and Adelaide came to visit, he took many orders. Perhaps men can be of two minds, he thought. Perhaps men can accept and resist at the same time.

Perhaps it is right and natural for them to do so. A soft, deep blue, a depth of dusk and falling snow, reflected through the high arched windows.

"In the United States Army, soldiers who expose themselves to the risk of contracting these diseases are required, before returning to their barracks, to report to the hospital where they are made to thoroughly wash themselves and use certain disinfectant preparations which have been demonstrated to be protective. Those who fail to take these simple precautions and develop a venereal disease are punished for failure to obey orders."

His uncle James had developed a nervous palsy in his later years. His aunt had been sickly, after his uncle James returned from the war, with arthritis in her knees which were always sore. How was one to know? It seemed to him that life was like a women's garments, always one more layer under which the truth of things was said to repose. He could remove them all, every skirt and blouse and slip and chemise, the bustier, stockings, and underdrawers. One entered and what was found? What was found that lasted more than a few minutes at the most? What was found that might satisfy longer? Longer than those few moments that seemed, at the moment of climax, to hold all truth and beauty in their midst. And the mystery of a woman's sex? But that was just darkness. No different than the mystery of the speckled egret's egg that rested on his bookshelf.

"Temptation can be conquered by keeping a pure mind and a trained and vigorous body, by exercise, cold baths, a hard bed and, above all, the avoidance of alcohol."

But alcohol was simply a question of economy. He couldn't afford to take Mary to hops and sleigh rides and minstrels, buy pipe tobacco, visit Mrs. Bristow, and then on top of it buy liquor.

"If I have brought to any of you a new and broader point of view, so that when the goddesses make their appeal to you, you will choose Pallas, it will be a pleasure even above that of visiting this beautiful town and this historic institution rich in glorious memories."

Colonel Jefferson Randolph Kean stepped back from the podium and looked about him as if he wasn't quite sure where he was. The cadets rose and clapped as he removed his wire-rimmed spectacles and rubbed his eyes with his thumb and forefinger. His spectacles slipped from his hand and fell to the floor. He took a step back attempting to find them, and a cadet quickly came to his rescue, but not before Colonel Kean had stepped on the spectacles and they had shattered. He took the broken spectacles from the cadet, shook his head, then stared with perfect blind confidence over the heads of the clapping audience and bowed.

As he filed out of the building with the others, Charles tallied in his mind how many men had placed orders, how many sheaths his father would have to bring when he and Adelaide came to visit. Over the last two weeks, he had received requests from twenty-three men which was a total of $165.

His boots sank into the soft ground, his hands, though gloved, were stiff and cold. When they had first left the auditorium, the flakes had melted on his eyelashes, now they stayed on his face, not melting at all. Those marching in front of him carried large white flakes on their shoulders and caps. Falling snow hid the crenellated buildings, the black limbs of trees, the bronze statue of Virginia mourning her dead surrounded by cannon, the roofs and steeples of the town in the distance below Institute Hill. The weather seemed given by authority. Yet surely, he thought, even this snow drifting softly down, surely even this snow was a layer of sorts hiding something else. And she too, was probably diseased, he thought. He heard the squawk of a cranky in the distance and said, "They ought to be gone south, bitter cold as it is."

The image of the heron was clear in his mind, the yellow bill pointed as a dirk, the long, curving neck, the massive gray wings in flight. He felt a sense of happy satisfaction imagining it. Life, as it had been given to him, was remarkably suited to his needs, remarkably sufficient, he decided. He was going to give the dove to Adelaide, he had finished his essay for the *Cadet,* and he had collected the last of the payments to give his father. There was to be a hop that night and he was to be at Mary's at eight o'clock. Perhaps he would even broach the subject of marriage. He looked up at the clock tower and saw that it was almost five. Three hours before he had to pick Mary up. He knew that in this snow her father would insist he borrow the carriage. As his company broke formation, he calculated that he could dress and shave in half an hour. True to form, twenty-five minutes later he walked through Limit Gates.

A wagon became visible in the falling snow, the horse walking with some difficulty in the soft road, the driver huddled under a blanket thrown over his coat, the sound of the wagon, muffled. The streets, the intersections, the frame houses and ragged picket fences, the yards and sheds and bare trees were barely visible. Yet his sense of the distance was innately remembered. No one passed to nod hello to, no one would have known him if they had. Occasionally, as he walked, he saw a rectangle of vague lamplight held in place by curtains in a vague window, a dusky hidden glow. He imagined her opening the door and then imagined the act. As he thought about it, the intricacies of it enlarged in his mind so that he began to feel its pleasure even there in the snow two blocks from her house. Yet there was always the problem of appointments, for she hardly kept track. Ned McAlister, for one, would visit on the spur of the moment. Once Charles had been upstairs with her and just beginning when Ned had come pounding on the front door. Her child had opened it and the little girl's voice had carried through the walls thin as paper.

"Please to tell you, mother is occupied with a gentleman upstairs."

Charles had heard Ned say, "Well then, I'll wait my turn."

"I don't know how long they will be," the child had said.

And Ned had apparently placed something on the table, for the child had asked,

"Oh Ned, what's in it, Ned? Tell me what it is. Is it a present for me?"

And Ned answered, "It's candy for your beautiful mother, but if you're a good girl you can have some too."

"My mother is not beautiful," the child said. "None of us Bristows is beautiful."

"That's what you think," Ned said.

Charles and Mrs. Bristow had dressed and gone downstairs, and discovered Ned playing marbles with the child. He had even gone so far as to bring in a stack of wood. He had stoked the stove, washed the plates and glasses in the sink, and placed them in a pile on the table.

Now lost in snow, Charles barely discerned the ramshackle house and its chimney, black with soot, the chinks between the rocks where mortar had fallen out. The door shook gently with each knock, but no one answered, though he was certain he could hear the sound of her footsteps. He knocked again, he stamped the snow off his boots. He took a glove off so that the sound of his knock would be louder, then blew on his bare hand cupped against his mouth. He suddenly became concerned that he might be late picking Mary up.

"Mrs. Bristow? Are you at home?" he said loudly, though his voice seemed lost.

Then the knob turned, the latch clicked, the door scraped open, and there she was. She had put on her coat for warmth, though it hardly protected her from the cold, for her nose and eyes were flaming red. The child looked eagerly from behind her mother's skirts.

"Have you brought me something, Charlie?" the child asked, and he saw that she too was wearing a coat.

"Katie? Don't you move away from that stove while Mamma and her gentleman are upstairs. You hear me?" the mother asked.

"I've brought you a jaybird feather. Don't you see?" he said to the child.

The child took the gray-blue feather with its slight black markings.

"I can wear it in my hair," she said.

"It's for your collection," Charles answered. "You must put it up with the others and add it to your list. You must write in the little book I gave you, 'Jaybird, *Cyanocitta cristata,* January 21, 1912.' I'll help you to do it when I come back downstairs with your mother."

"You hear me, Missy?" her mother said. "You are not to come bothering us."

The child settled down to play with her rag doll, teaching it to spell by the hot stove. He didn't mind her being there. She was part of what warmth there was. Neither did he mind the sloping floor, the narrow, worn stairs as he followed the woman, the one room at the top with its damp wallpaper that she always led him into, the spavined iron bedstead. These were all things now connected in his mind with the feeling and the act.

Mrs. Bristow closed the bedroom door and began to unbutton her skirts.

"Here, let me do that," he said.

Her expression did not change, placid and immovable as if she had heard the words a thousand times before, her dark hair, beginning to show gray, was pinned tightly against her neck, the skin of her face was soft and sallow, her eyes as deep and black as the snow falling softly outside the window.

He lowered himself to his knees and his fingers went for the buttons of her skirts. He could feel her hands on the top of his head, as if to say that she was present, as if to say that she remembered what he was about. Her dank wool skirts smelled of wood smoke and bacon fat as they fell to the floor. She shivered in the cold and he remembered the weather, then he forgot about it. He felt her waist, then stood up and put his hands under her chemise and felt her breasts, soft and slack.

It was she who took the envelope from him after he had undressed and stretched out upon the cold bed. It was she who removed the sheath from the envelope, put it perfectly in place, then unrolled it upon him. She said nothing, made not a whimper of pleasure, only stood shivering as she dressed when it was over, then hurried down to tend the fire. It was the child, Katie, who waved good-bye after he had paid and stepped out into the cold.

The air was clear and vigorous. He looked up into the sky and saw the stars, brittle and distinct, each in their expected place. This is a moment of perfection, he thought. Nothing can harm it. This moment of perfect release, this interval of time, this moment just after the snow has fallen and before its first blemish appears. He sighed deeply, then inhaled a confident breath of air and set off toward Mary's house.

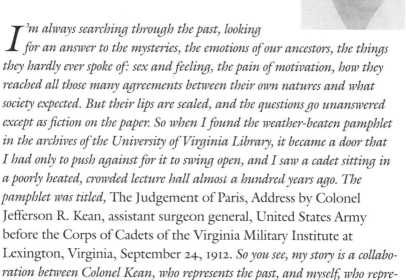

K. A. Longstreet's stories have appeared in numerous magazines, including the *Georgia Review*, the *Southern Review*, the *Sewanee Review*, and *New England Review*. Her collection of stories, *Night-Blooming Cereus*, was published in 2002 by the University of Missouri Press. She lives in Orange, Virginia.

I'm always searching through the past, looking for an answer to the mysteries, the emotions of our ancestors, the things they hardly ever spoke of: sex and feeling, the pain of motivation, how they reached all those many agreements between their own natures and what society expected. But their lips are sealed, and the questions go unanswered except as fiction on the paper. So when I found the weather-beaten pamphlet in the archives of the University of Virginia Library, it became a door that I had only to push against for it to swing open, and I saw a cadet sitting in a poorly heated, crowded lecture hall almost a hundred years ago. The pamphlet was titled, The Judgement of Paris, Address by Colonel Jefferson R. Kean, assistant surgeon general, United States Army before the Corps of Cadets of the Virginia Military Institute at Lexington, Virginia, September 24, 1912. *So you see, my story is a collaboration between Colonel Kean, who represents the past, and myself, who represents the present and the need to know.*

Brock Clarke

THE LOLITA SCHOOL

(from *StoryQuarterly*)

Another semester at the Lolita School. The students begin the first day of class by straddling their chairs. The chairs are white wicker, lined up in a row against an exposed brick wall. We encourage the girls to sit in whatever way they please, just as long as they straddle their chairs and wear seductive outfits. Our definition of seductive is generous, although we do suggest, in our catalogue, that each student wear a dress, something loose and red and short, so as to accentuate their thin, ghostly legs. In our catalogue, we state clearly in bold print: Do Not Bring Lollipops to the First Day of Class, but a few girls always do. We tell them that they are hopeless and send them home immediately. This expulsion makes some of the remaining girls quite bold. They take it upon themselves to hook their ankles around the wicker chair legs and lick their lips lasciviously. When they do this, we ask rhetorically, "What is gained by being so obvious?" The girls are cowed. They retract their legs and nervously hide their lips and their shoulders wilt. For the moment, they look exactly like fourteen-year-old girls straddling wicker chairs, which is what we want.

The Lolita School was founded by Vladimir Nabokov's widow, Vera, in 1978. Its mission: to instruct and assist young girls in their quest to emulate the heroine of Mr. Nabokov's magnificent novel,

Lolita. There are now eighteen Lolita Schools nationwide. Ours is on the outskirts of Charleston, South Carolina.

Once the girls are properly positioned in their chairs, we, the teachers at the Lolita School, take our places. We ask the students not to tell us their names, and we don't teach them ours. There is intimacy in anonymity. This is what we tell them. Not all of the teachers are men, but we all dress like we are. We wear crewneck sweaters and khaki pants and worn penny loafers and baseball hats with long bills and large, billowing barn jackets. When the girls are ready, we wheel out a long hedge of artificial forsythia bushes, behind which we hide and stare at the girls. The forsythia bushes are scraggly, and the girls can see our eyes, bulging out at them.

We who teach at the Lolita School are not pedophiles, as some newspaper accounts have suggested, but we do cultivate an ambiance of pedophilia. During the more advanced role-playing exercises, we turn the heat up high. We have installed misting machines, which kick in automatically. We have placed a rusted swingset in the corner of the room. Primal music is piped in through hidden speakers. At crucial moments, all the teachers don thick glasses, to give the impression of leering.

But in the first hour of the first day of the semester none of this comes into play. We give the girls no instructions at all. This is part of our pedagogy. We simply ogle them from behind the bushes and wait to see what happens. The girls' mothers, who are encouraged to attend the first day of class, stand off to the side and shift awkwardly from one foot to the other. They rummage around their purses for gum and hope their daughters don't do something embarrassing. I can tell this from their pinched faces. They are ready to be mortified.

Mothers enroll their daughters at the Lolita School for a number of reasons. For some, they feel their daughters are simply too innocent to survive in this bold, modern world. Others recognize that their daughters are inclined toward sluttishness and want to cultivate that talent. Then there are those mothers who are entirely confused about the mission of the Lolita School. Either these women don't read our catalogue carefully, or they don't know a thing about Mr. Nabokov's novel. All these mothers know is that they've been told by the public schools that their daughters aren't traditional learners. These particular mothers, on the whole, think that the Lolita School is an alternative country day school of some sort.

Be difficult whenever possible. If asked, insist that you loathe your parents, even if you do not. Do not make yourself useful. Lolita did not use any bad words. Money is funny, but the flesh is serious business. These are just some of the things we teach our students at the Lolita School.

There is one girl who is especially impressive. She doesn't know a thing about our mission, I am sure of it; I can see her mother off to the side, looking panicked, furiously flipping through our catalogue. The girl probably has attention-span problems and probably has performed miserably on all the standardized tests at her middle school, etc. But here, she is a wonder. First, she stares directly at us and looks perfectly bored: she smacks her chewing gum loudly and scratches at a scab on her left arm. Then, after a moment, something catches her attention outside the window—a bird, maybe, or a strangely shaped cloud. The girl's top lip curls slightly upward and her deep black eyes squint and her right leg moves absently from side to side, the unmuscled, translucent skin slicing the air. Some of the teachers murmur and nudge each other and take agitated, copious notes. The girl hears our noise and stares back at us again, bored. A few of us grow even more excited. But some of the other teachers, some of the more traditional teachers, make disappointing clucking sounds. Some of them write angry comments in their notebooks like: "Apathy is Not Sex!!!" and "Subtlety *Qua* Subtlety?" There is a great deal of hushed arguing back and forth. The girl who sparked this debate is almost entirely forgotten.

It should be said that there is a schism at the Lolita School. It began a few years ago, when we were faced with an identity crisis of sorts. The church groups hadn't protested outside our building in years; the girls were the same age as always, and yet we found that they seemed much older, much more vulgar, much less artful. There was talk of the Lolita School's irrelevance. And so we conducted a thorough self-evaluation. *What do we want from ourselves?* we asked each other. *And what do we want from our students?* Unfortunately, this self-interrogation produced a more severe identity crisis. Some of the teachers championed the Lolita of Mr. Nabokov's novel, while others preferred the less cerebral 1962 movie version Lolita. At first, we did not try to hide our differences. At first, we spoke a great deal of our theoretical diversity. One day, we had the movie Lolita, Sue Lyon, come speak to the class; on another day, we welcomed a Nabokov scholar from Duke. To the engaged mind, it was all very useful, very interesting. But in the end, it did no good. The girls could not see the fifty-year-old Ms. Lyon in themselves; and they were unsure whether they were supposed to seduce or repel the scholar from Duke. The faculty saw in the speakers what they wanted to see. The schism remains to this day.

We do not train our students to be prostitutes, but a number have been arrested for prostitution. This hasn't happened in years, but it was a regular occurrence in the early days. Mostly, the girls were arrested for standing on Meeting Street, waiting for a bus, and looking vaguely seductive. Once when this happened, I answered the phone when the police called the school, asking one of us to come down to the station immediately. When I got to the station, the student was sitting demurely on a wooden bench, her straight blonde hair in a limp ponytail, her hands folded meekly in her lap, her legs crossed at the ankles. "She's just a student," I told the desk sergeant.

The sergeant glanced over at the girl, who did indeed, at that moment, look exactly like a student. "She does look like a student," the sergeant said. "But the officers who arrested her said she's a hooker. There was something about her. They couldn't put their finger on it."

The girl and I smiled knowingly at each other. I remember that moment wistfully. It was wonderful to be so completely misunderstood, so utterly confusing.

The rest of the opening lesson is a disaster. The girls must sense our dissatisfaction. They grow desperate. A very thin girl with long, straw-like red hair and mottled cheeks takes off her leather sandals and faded red underwear and flings them in the direction of the bushes; a few other girls slowly run their index fingers along the frame of their wicker chairs. This produces loud, theatrical yawns from some of the faculty. One of the newest, most arrogant teachers breaks his pencil in half and throws the pieces to the floor. It is all very unprofessional. One of the students—a sickly looking towheaded girl in an absurdly low-cut polka-dotted dress— starts crying. Great, embarrassed, heaving sobs. It is the only shocking thing that has happened thus far. The mothers look at each other out of the corners of their eyes. The school's policy is to refund your tuition at any point during the first week of classes. The school's director stands up and suggests that we break early for lunch.

Our school is on the second floor of a defunct wooden crate factory from whose windows one can see the oil tankers creep into Charleston Harbor. It is the fifth busiest harbor in the United States. This is a known fact, we tell the girls, but it is not interesting in-and-of-itself. *What is interesting?* we ask our students. It is a provocative question. The girls seem provoked by it. During the break, we arrange the crates in a circle and the girls sit on the crates and eat vanilla wafers. We read to them from Mr. Nabokov's novel:

> She was Lo, plain Lo, in the morning standing four feet ten in one sock. She was Lola in slacks. She was Dolly at school. She was Dolores on the dotted line. But in my arms she was always Lolita.

Everyone is much inspired. The girls nibble determinedly on their wafers. We, the faculty, remember what we're here for, and nod apologies to each other.

There is a story about Mr. Nabokov. When writing *Lolita,* he refused to look to other human beings for beauty, or for love. When his own wife made sexual overtures, he fled to his butterflies. Mr. Nabokov was an avid butterfly collector. He found arousal in his dead butterflies: when he would pin them to a piece of wax paper, first delicately through the wings and then savagely through the thorax; when he would insert the butterflies into a slide and sandwich them between the two pieces of glass; when the butterflies gave up their secrets—with great resistance, and only under a microscope.

After lunch, we conduct voice lessons. We lecture our students on the importance of lilt and inflection. Many of the girls are recent transplants from the North. We teach them to speak more like Southerners. As for the native Southerners, we teach them to speak a little less like themselves. The girls are competent; by the end of the voice lesson, they all sound exactly the same. We all wanted to teach at the Lolita School because we were desperate to shock and to be shocked. But this lesson is standard procedure at the Lolita School and we do it without questioning its logic.

It was Mrs. Nabokov herself who told us the story about her husband and the butterflies. It was 1988, the Lolita School's tenth anniversary, and Mrs. Nabokov was touring the school's various campuses. She was wearing a black shawl and her gray hair was arranged in misshapen piles on top of her head. Her face was bright red, and divided into sections by deep, dramatic wrinkles. There was something about Mrs. Nabokov's story that disturbed us. Its profundity. Its abstractness.

"The butterflies were preferable," Mrs. Nabokov said. "My husband preferred them to me." One of the school's original teachers— a man of great sensitivity—was especially horrified by her story. "That's awful," the teacher said. "How did that make you feel?"

"Feel is not important," Mrs. Nabokov said. "The butterflies were surprising. I was not."

The rest of the afternoon is a familiar blur. We send the girls through their basic role-playing exercises. There is no schism evident between us teachers, but there is no sense of community, either. We are merely doing a job, and play our parts without noticeable passion. Some of the girls talk to a stranger on a park bench; some of them sit at their table desks, staying after school and flirting with the math teacher; some girls wear bikinis, hug potted palmetto trees, and chat up the lifeguards. I watch the girl who some of us found so extraordinary earlier in the day. She is standing in a line for the Ferris wheel, sweet-talking the carny. I am playing the role of carny today, and I watch her closely for a long time: the way she stands on one leg and twirls her hair, the way her mouth hangs open like a sack. I stare in her face, gaze into her eyes—black surrounded by brown surrounded by white—and find nothing arousing, nothing remarkable at all. There is a lesson to be learned here about the dangers of being a teacher at the Lolita School. I don't think you can stare at a person for too long a time without finding them horribly ordinary.

A memo from the Lolita School's Office of Teaching Innovation and Effectiveness: "Please attend our seminar on: 'Losing the Sense of Menace in Your Classroom, and How You Can Get it Back!'" For years, I thought my life would be unbearably boring without the Lolita School, but now, at times, I simply want it to go away.

The students zip their backpacks. We have gathered them into a circle to give them final instructions. Whether they're listening or not, it is impossible to tell. *Zip.* There has been no mention yet of dismissal. *Zip.* We pass around photocopies of Mr. Nabokov's early sketch of Lolita, how he envisioned her. The assignment: to study the drawing. What in this drawing is worth emulating and what is not? This is what we want them to think about. There is a powerfully built redheaded girl sitting Indian style in front of me. Her arms are muscular and short. Her backpack has many compartments, many zippers. She appears determined to zip all of them. I ask her if she understands the assignment. "I got it," she says. *Zip. Zip.* The girl stands up and shoulders her backpack. I ask her if she has somewhere more important to be. "Yes," she says, truthfully, without hesitation.

Finally, class is dismissed. The mothers gather up their daughters and whisper in their ears. The girls seem no different, no more dangerous or subtle or mysterious than when they began the class. What have you learned? the mothers ask their daughters. And how does it apply to real life?

After class, a few of us stand around and talk about our options for professional stimulation. It seems undeniable that the Lolita School has outlived its usefulness. But we are not entirely without prospects. For instance, after a request from various men's groups, the school has begun offering a night class for Lolitos. The night class staff lights up the room like a pool hall. The boys are told to wear cutoff jeans shorts with tins of chewing tobacco in their back pockets. They are taught to curse amateurishly and to cock their hips suggestively while speaking to their teachers. The teachers, who to this point are only women, are costumed in brightly colored, clingy T-shirt dresses and calf-high leather boots. Their hair is flecked with gray and has been styled into loose curls. The teachers smoke Virginia Slims, circle the boys like sharks, and speak only in obvious double entendres. All of this has upset the more traditionally minded teachers at the Lolita School. But still, a few of us are considering asking for a transfer to the Lolito class. Perhaps something shocking will happen there.

Brock Clarke was raised in upstate New York and now lives in Cincinnati, Ohio, where he teaches creative writing at the University of Cincinnati. His novel, *The Ordinary White Boy*, was published in 2001, and his short story collection, *What We Won't Do*, which won the Mary McCarthy Prize in Short Fiction, in 2000. His fiction and nonfiction have appeared in many magazines and anthologies, including *New England Review*, the *Southern Review*, *Mississippi Review*, the *Georgia Review*, *StoryQuarterly*, the *Believer*, and *New Stories from the South: The Year's Best, 2003*. "The Lolita School" is from

his just-finished collection, *Carrying the Torch*, and he's currently finishing a novel called *An Arsonist's Guide to Writers' Homes in New England*.

I used to teach at Clemson University, in Clemson, South Carolina, and one warm spring day a friend of mine (Catherine Paul) and I walked past a group of young girls—probably high school freshmen or sophomores—who were wearing far too little clothing and doing some outrageously awkward flirting with boys who were significantly older than they were. It was embarrassing to watch even though Catherine and I spent a long time watching it, and finally Catherine said, "Those girls need to go to Lolita School."

She was right, and it seemed a shame that there was no such institute of higher (lower?) learning (at least not that I know of) and so I wrote this story.

COAL SMOKE

(from *The Louisville Review*)

Lynn is in the bedroom getting ready while her boyfriend, Gary Dean, cuts them a line of coke.

She glances at her hair one last time, dabs her eyeliner with her little finger, and purses her lips. She perches her cigarette in a small ashtray that is shaped like an open palm and puts on more lipstick without blinking her eyes. She considers herself in the mirror for a long time and wonders what her brother will see in her tonight. He is at the foot of the mountain, visiting with their mother while he waits on them. What will he think of the way she looks now, the way she carries herself with her head held high and her jacket hung over her arm, the way she only has to raise her hand so the waitress will scurry over to see what it is she wants? She loves nights like these, when Gary Dean sits in there waiting for her, sipping water-backed bourbon and smoking Winstons. Lynn loves being dressed up and having somewhere to go.

She has put on a Bob Seger album and "Betty Lou's Getting Out Tonight" comes on just in time for her to dance in front of the floor-length mirror. She always dances in her bedroom before going out so she can see how her outfit will move when they get to the honky-tonk. The green velvet dress is short and high-waisted. It sways about her long legs.

Lynn twirls around the room, moving her hips, snapping her

fingers. She holds her lips firmly together and catches a glimpse of herself as she turns around. She knows every word of this song and sings under her breath. She grabs up her bottle of Beautiful while she dances and sprays it on her neck and her wrists. She directs a squirt towards her open door so the scent will travel to Gary Dean.

"You 'bout ready, baby?" Gary Dean hollers.

Lynn goes to the bedroom door and poses with one black-hosed leg forward, hands on her hips. She cocks her head. "Do I look ready?"

Gary Dean answers by smiling and putting out his big hand as she walks towards him. He cups his hand on her ass and gives it a hard squeeze. His hands are the very reason Lynn first took to him. They are strong and dark-skinned, the veins round and wide. He has hands like her father's: long fingers that move while he talks, palms criss-crossed with love lines. They look like hands that ought to pick a banjo, but Gary Dean doesn't know how to play any instrument at all. Her father played the banjo. She always loved the way he would lean into the song, moving back and forth as his fingers danced across the strings. He used to put a tambourine under his foot and stomp on it to punctuate the banjo's throaty song. But now he's dead and that music died with him.

It is nearly Christmas and she has had her father on her mind ever since they put up the tree a week ago. She thinks of him all the time, of course, but her memories of him are more vivid during the holidays. Every night since she untangled the lights and hung the ornaments from the fake, wiry branches she has dreamt of his hands. She awoke not knowing how to feel.

"Damn, you look good," Gary Dean says.

"What's this?" Lynn asks and nods to the table, where two lines of cocaine are laid out on the plastic place mats.

"I chopped us up a line," he says and hands her a tightly rolled dollar bill. The money is new and feels slick in her fingers.

Lynn takes both lines in two quick snorts, then wets the tip of her finger. She gets the granules she has left behind and swipes them on her tongue to sizzle. She imagines she can hear the grains popping and fizzing, like that Pop Rocks candy she and her brother used to beg for when their father took them to the store.

Gary Dean spreads out three more lines. He makes a big commotion, pinching his nostrils and snorting good and loud, which is the one thing about him that annoys Lynn the most. He has told her that he once had nosebleeds all the time on account of cocaine, so now he only partakes on occasion. This is all part of being a good businessman: Gary Dean says that the only smart drug dealer is one that only touches the stuff every once in a while. If you get hooked, then you've lost your business to yourself.

When they get outside, Lynn is surprised at how cold it is. The black night sky is moving quick and low. Lynn feels like she can reach up and touch the jagged clouds. There is a wet, spitting snow and the wind blows down the holler. Naked tree limbs scratch across the top of their trailer.

"Week before Christmas, and already snowing," Lynn says. "I never seen the beat."

"It won't amount to nothing," Gary Dean says without turning to face her.

They walk on down the mountainside. Gary Dean never did get around to sowing grass after they moved the trailer in last summer, so it's muddy where the dozers worked to straighten up the steep yard. Gary Dean has laid wide planks down the mountainside as a makeshift sidewalk, and Lynn holds her arms out to her sides to balance herself in places. The mud has been beat into uneven lines by the autumn rains and stands like rows in a plowed garden. Lynn thinks that the mud is probably frozen; snow is beginning to stick to it. Below them, the windows of all the little houses along Free Creek are lit with Christmas lights. Her mother's house is decorated more than any of the others—she is famous for this, and people sometimes drive up the road just to see all of her blinking decorations.

Lynn smells coal smoke, and she stops for a minute to breathe in its good scent. It reminds her of when she was little. She stands there on the plank, arms straight out, her drawstring purse dangling from one finger. She closes her eyes and breathes in as much of this smell as she can.

"What the hell are you doing?" Gary Dean says. He thrusts his hands out to his sides to emphasize the question and his car keys click together like wind chimes.

When they get to the foot of the mountain, Gary Dean goes on ahead to warm up the Z-28. Lynn opens the back door of her mother's house and steps into the kitchen. It smells warm and close with the scent of coffee and bacon grease. Her brother, Dooley, is sitting at the little formica table with their mother and his girlfriend, whose name is something from *Gone With the Wind,* but Lynn can't remember what exactly. They are all bathed in a peach light that Lynn remembers from childhood. It seemed this room always glowed at night. Her mother barely glances her way when Lynn shuts the door behind her. She is sitting at the head of the table, her hand curled around a coffee cup. Even though the furnace is roaring, she is still wearing a sweater, with the top button latched. Dooley looks up and smiles, same big blue eyes and wavy black hair. "Hey, sis," he says.

"You all ready?" Lynn asks.

Before anyone can reply, Dooley's girlfriend—Lynn thinks maybe her name is Melanie or Scarlett or Butterfly—stands up and touches Lynn's mother on the shoulder. "Dinner was wonderful," she says. It is strange to hear such a word—"wonderful"—spoken here. Lynn bets herself that this has never before been said in her mother's kitchen. She also wants to tell the girl that in this part of the state, dinner is served at lunchtime, and that she has just had supper. But she doesn't.

"Lynn, you ought not be taking your brother to no honky-tonk and him visiting," her mother says. "Why don't you all take them over to the steakhouse?"

"It's all right," Dooley says and kisses their mother on the cheek. "We'll have a good time."

Lynn backs out the door and calls, "Love you, Mommy" before her mother can say anything else.

Down in the narrow holler, between the two mountains, the night is so black Lynn can't even see the wide creek, which is rushing along on the other side of the road. All she can see is the column of white twirling up from the exhaust of Gary Dean's car.

She reaches her hand out until she has secured the crook of Dooley's arm and pulls herself up close to him while they walk. "What about Mommy acting goody-goody in front of your woman?" Lynn says, and lets out a high, single laugh. "Her and Daddy used to stay at the clubs."

"You'd never get her to admit that," Dooley says.

Lynn climbs into the back seat and waits impatiently while Dooley's girlfriend takes forever to get in the back with her. Dooley holds the door open even after the girl has gotten in. "Hurry up and get in, brother. I'm frostbit," Lynn says. Dooley gets in and slams the door. The car has heated up but the leather seat is still cold to the backs of her legs.

Gary Dean doesn't back out right away. He rummages around in the console looking for a tape. His face looks rough and older in the dim glow of the dome light.

"Well, I ain't even introduced you all to Gary Dean," Lynn says. "He was at work yesterday when you all got in."

"Good to meet you, buddy," Gary Dean says and shakes Dooley's hand. Lynn watches them—Dooley's thin white hand swallowed up by Gary Dean's dark-skinned paw. Gary Dean seems even bigger up there in the smallness of the front seat. She's not embarrassed of him, though. She kind of likes his big belly. He looks through the rearview mirror and waits for Lynn to tell him the girl's name, but Lynn shoots him a look to let him know she is clueless. "Hidy," Gary Dean says, turning his eyes to Dooley's girlfriend. He nods. His eyes, seen alone in the mirror, suddenly strike Lynn as black and scary, somehow. She has never thought of his eyes in any particular way before.

"Hi, I'm Tara," the girl says. Lynn knew it was something like that. While the dome light is still on, Lynn sizes up Tara's outfit. She is wearing a print dress with a collar on it. Flats and brown hose. Hair pulled up in combs on the sides. She looks like she's going to church instead of a honky-tonk. She will be laughed out of the Hilltop Club.

"Why do you call him Dooley?" Tara asks, just as Gary Dean finds the tape he is looking for and turns off the light. He backs out onto the road slowly.

"After that old song," Lynn says. "You know. It just suited him somehow. Better than Douglas, that's for sure."

"What song?" Tara says. They are bouncing down the rough road.

Gary Dean is easing over the mud holes, but still the back seat hops and screeches.

"That old bluegrass song," Lynn says, trying to sound friendly. She puts a little laugh into her voice. "Where are you from?"

"Louisville."

"Oh," Lynn says. She already knew this by the way Tara talked, by the way she pronounced "Why?" so curved and drawn-out. "You ever been out in this part of the world before?"

"No," Tara says. "But I wasn't actually raised in the city. We had a farm outside Louisville. In the country."

"Country up there ain't like country here," Lynn says.

Gary Dean pulls out of the holler and onto the main road. As an oncoming car approaches, Lynn sees that Tara is smiling at her without showing her teeth. Her lips are tightly set. Lynn doesn't trust people who smile this way.

"Well, there are no mountains at home, you're right. Douglas stays homesick for these hills. It's a shame they don't have a good college closer," Tara says. Lynn knows the girl is not trying to sound snooty, but it still comes out that way. Lynn watches Tara smile in that closed-mouth way and thinks that she could be a pretty girl if she knew how to fix herself up.

Lynn scoots to the edge of her seat and puts her arms around

Dooley's neck. She sticks her hands down into the top of his shirt. His chest is warm and her hands are ice-cold. When he shivers, she laughs like she did when they were little. She remembers the way his shoulders looked then, wet and shining when he climbed out of the creek when they would go swimming. They were always together as children.

"Can't believe we're finally partying together!" Lynn hollers. Gary Dean has put in a good tape, but he turns it down when he sees she wants to talk to her brother. "It's been three year since I seen you drunk, Dooley."

"That was probably the last time I was drunk," Dooley says.

"Lord God," Lynn says and turns her head to glance back at Tara, who looks terrified. Her hands clench the edges of the seat. Lynn figures she is probably not used to these curvy mountain roads. There is a wall of snowflakes in front of them. It glows in the headlights. Gary Dean is flying up Buffalo Mountain, even though Lynn can't see a thing but whiteness, like curtains lit from behind by summer sunshine. She remembers when they were little. She and Dooley would stay out in the snow all day. When they finally went in, their mother let them drink coffee in front of the stove. They huddled together under a quilt, trying to thaw their hands and feet.

"Dooley used to be the awfullest sot that ever lived," Lynn tells Tara.

"He was?" Tara asks, sounding surprised, as if Dooley has told her nothing of his past.

"He was a pure drunk. He got knee-walking drunk one time and grabbed a fifth of Jim Beam and drunk half of that whole bottle in one lick. That about got him," Lynn says. She cackles out and throws her head back. "I had to hold a washrag to his forehead all night long." Lynn punches the back of Dooley's seat with her knee. "Remember that?"

"Speaking of Jim Beam," Gary Dean says and snickers, low and sneaky. He holds up a pint he has fished from the inside pocket of his blazer. He shakes it in front of Dooley's face. "Drink the neck and shoulders out of that. Warm you up right quick."

"Shew. I ain't drunk no liquor in ages," Dooley says and shivers. Lynn hits Dooley's seat with her open hand. The cold leather rings out like a man's face being slapped. "Hell-fire, Dooley," she says. "You've went to college and turned into a pure pussy."

Tara laughs nervously.

"Come on," Lynn says, grabbing the half-pint from Gary Dean. She unscrews the top just enough to break the seal and hands it to Dooley. "For old times sake," she says. "For your old sis."

Dooley lets two good shots bubble into his mouth, then wipes his lips on his sleeve. He exhales a stream of hot breath and whistles. "That brings back the old times all right," he says.

Lynn takes a long drink, then offers it to Tara.

"No, thanks," Tara says. She won't even take the bottle.

Lynn smiles. "Hey, you ever drunk any moonshine?"

"No," Tara says, "but I've—"

"I bet everybody in Louisville thinks we just sit around and drink moonshine all day," Lynn says, talking close to Tara's face, which suddenly seems very wide and pale. Lynn can feel the cocaine sizzling up to her brain. "It's rare you get it any more, ain't it, Gary Dean? And it's higher than hell! How much did you pay for that last gallon we got, baby?"

"Forty dollars," Gary Dean says.

"Higher than a cat's back," she says, and shakes her head. "And we knowed that old boy good."

Dooley takes another drink of the bourbon. Lynn watches him to make sure he's not putting on to humor her. Gary Dean takes it and drains the last two drinks before tossing the empty bottle onto the floorboard between Dooley's feet.

Lynn feels as if the car is floating above the white ground as Gary Dean drives them off the exit ramp and down the Daniel Boone Parkway. They speed by a rumbling salt truck with a scraper on its front bumper. The blade sends white sparks along the top of the road, and Lynn turns to watch them. Lynn thinks they look like cigarettes being thrown onto the highway, and she is mesmerized by this. She keeps looking back, long after the truck and its sparks have gone out of sight.

She puts one finger on Tara's leg. "Hey, you ever been clubbing before?"

"Douglas and I go to a couple bars up in Richmond, once in a while."

"Shit," Lynn says. Gary Dean and Dooley have been talking, but apparently they overhear this and giggle loudly. Lynn guffaws. "People nowhere don't party like we do. We're taking you honky-tonking, girl. Loosen up and have a good time. I'll get you a screwdriver when we get up to the Hilltop."

"About the only thing I drink are wine coolers," Tara says. "I love wine coolers."

"Lord, I can't drink nothing sweet," Lynn says. She lays her head back against the car seat. She feels good. She's ready to party. One of her favorite songs is playing—"All She Wants to Do Is Dance," by Don Henley. Lynn thinks to herself that this ought to be her theme song. It's not loud enough, but she still moves in her seat to the rhythm. She smells pot and realizes Gary Dean has rolled up some homegrown. She stretches her arm up between the seats and Dooley puts the joint between her fingers.

Tara leans forward a little, suddenly aware of what they are doing. Lynn waits for her to say something like, "Douglas? Do you think you should?" If Tara says something like this, Lynn will absolutely die laughing. She won't be able to contain herself. She has been around girls like this before. What Tara finally says is: "How are we getting home?"

Lynn holds the smoke in as long as she can before answering. "Gary Dean'll drive us," she says. "He don't never get drunk."

Tara's face is flat and serious. "He's drinking right now."

The boys laugh maniacally. They are feeling no pain, Lynn thinks.

"Gary Dean would have to drink a half-gallon of liquor to even feel it. I ain't never seen that man drunk."

Gary Dean pulls into the Hilltop's lot and parks the car and Lynn can see the Christmas lights running down the eaves of the club. When he turns off the car, she can feel the beat of the music from the band playing inside.

"I'm ready to dance!" Lynn yells and puts both hands on Dooley's seat and shakes it wildly. When they get out, the snow falls down around them like damp feathers. Lynn throws her head back and catches some flakes on her tongue, but when she looks at Dooley, the smile fades from her face. He looks stoned. For the past three years she has imagined him at a desk, in a dorm room, hunched over a book in the library. Now he looks like the boy she always knew. She had wanted to party with him, to get high, but now she is not so sure. She wishes that he had never come home from college. Everything would be easier if she never saw him again.

Lynn loves walking into the Hilltop and having everybody look at her, call to her by name. They all know her. Men watch her and take long drinks of beer, tapping their blunt-tipped fingers on the table. Women pay attention when Lynn Biggerstaff comes in, too. Three times last month she wore something and then the next weekend, several women had on the same thing. She never was a trendsetter in high school, but she sure is now. People wave, clap big hands on Gary Dean's shoulder, stop Lynn to tell her gossip as she makes her way toward their table.

She can tell Dooley is impressed by all the friends she has here at the club. She doesn't hear what they are saying when they flutter around her like bluebirds, like cardinals and sparrows. But she nods and laughs when she thinks she is supposed to. *Can't they see I'm stoned out of my fucking mind?* she thinks.

The Hilltop is packed. People are celebrating Christmas a week early. The honky-tonk is decked out in garland and lights. There are three trees—one right in the middle of the dance floor. The base has been bolted to the floor so drunks won't knock it down or grab it up to throw at an enemy. A girl in a leather miniskirt and a low-cut blouse is walking around with a basket, selling plastic mistletoe. Red-faced men buy it and hold it over women's heads so they can kiss them. Everybody laughs like this is funny.

Lynn thinks how it is almost sacrilegious, having Christmas decorations in a club like this. There are even some Jesus ornaments on one of the trees, and this makes her nearly sick to her stomach. Despite her partying, she has always respected the church. Before her father died, he got saved. The car wreck had paralyzed him and had torn him up so bad that his insides could only survive two months before he passed away. But during that time, he insisted on going home. He didn't want to die in a hospital. He made his brothers pack him into the church and he laid on a mattress in the floor, listening to the preaching. The congregation gathered around him and anointed him with oil and spoke in tongues. Lynn had cowered into the corner of the pew, watching all of this. She was seventeen, and her mother only sat there and heaved with tears. She never tried to console Lynn. Dooley was the only one who did this. The church people shouted and kneeled down to lay hands on her father. Lynn had thought he would be healed, but he hadn't been, despite her faith. When he died, she couldn't even look at those people—the women with their wigged-up hair, the men in their pressed white shirts, their devout determination stamped flat across their foreheads. She refused to speak to them at the funeral, the way her mother refused to speak to her. Every time her mother looked at her, her eyes were saying *It's your fault. Out running wild. And him out looking for you.*

She is thinking of all this while she dances, but she knows people think she is having a good time. She shakes her ass and snaps her fingers, closes her eyes and acts as if the music is taking her, lifting her. Lynn and Gary Dean have danced for two solid hours. That is the other thing that got Lynn about Gary Dean. Most men won't dance to save their lives once they've got a woman, but Gary Dean is always the first to jump up. Gary Dean might be big and fat, and he may not be much to look at, but he is a good dancer. And there's just something about him that's cool. She likes a man that's in control of the situation.

Tara and Dooley have only danced to the slow songs. They sit at the table, all hugged up and smiling at Lynn and Gary Dean while they watch them dance. Tara claims she can't fast-dance, and Lynn has tired of begging the girl. She hates people that won't try something new. Lynn can tell that it is killing Dooley to sit there and not dance, so when the next fast song comes on, she pulls him onto the dance floor.

People move back to watch Lynn and Dooley. He is an even better dancer than Gary Dean. She taught him all the moves. She showed him how to hold his face high and serious, to only smile every once in a while. Attitude is what makes a good dancer. If you laugh and go on the whole time, it ruins the effect. No one watches you dance when you act like you're having a big time. Dooley moves his hips, steps back and forth, throws his hands out while his elbows jut at the air, keeping time. He looks no one in the eye. Lynn looks out and sees all the girls lusting after him. She loves having everyone watching them.

When the loud music dies, a two-stepping song comes on. Dooley has already turned around and started walking back toward the table, but Lynn grabs his hand. "Let's two step," she says.

"I better get back," Dooley says. The pot has worn off and his eyes look tired. He is still a little drunk, though. She can tell. "Tara ain't never been in a place like this before."

Lynn puts her hand in the small of his back. "God almighty, Dooley. She'll be all right."

They begin to dance, their feet matching steps perfectly. It is as if he never left at all. He smells the same, like Coast soap. She closes her eyes and takes a deep breath of him. It makes her dizzy to have her eyes shut.

"I've missed you a sight," she says. She hears herself as if from very far away. "I can't wait till you come home, after you graduate."

"I doubt I'll come back, Lynn," he says. "I want to teach at the college. I want more than what this place can offer me."

"How can you stand it, away from this place?" she asks. "Away from us?"

"It's hard," he says. His breath is hot and tangy with bourbon. "I have a different life now, though. I won't go too far away, but I can't come back."

Suddenly she feels tears at the corners of her eyes. His scent seems to seep into her own skin. "You're my best friend, Dooley. I can't stand it, you being gone. Mommy treats me like a stranger."

"That's not true," he says and laughs at her a little. "I swear, you're drunk as a monkey."

"I'm not," she says, but she knows it is true. She wonders if it is the coke or the pot or the Mezcal that is affecting her. She has been taking shots of the tequila ever since they walked in.

He twirls her around and doesn't say anything else. Every once in a while a couple brushes up against them, couples directed by the women who want to get Dooley's attention. It was always like this, girls wanting to be friends with Lynn because he was her brother. Everybody worshipped him in high school, even when Lynn was a senior and he was just a sophomore.

In the dim light of the dance floor, Dooley looks just like their father. Catching a glimpse of him as she spins around, it takes her breath for a minute. It is like seeing a ghost, like dancing with a ghost. She wants to stop and put her hand up to his face. *Daddy,* she thinks, and even in her mind the sound of this word is spoken in hushed awe. But then Dooley smiles at her, and she knows it is just him. He is not a ghost at all. She is thinking of how her father's death caused her to never change one thing about herself, and how it made Dooley want to run away. And her mother, who is bitter and barely leaves the house. Barely leaves that seat at the kitchen table, always a cup of coffee in hand. "When he died, our family did, too," Lynn says. "I don't feel like I'm part of anybody no more."

Dooley never wants to talk about this. "Gary Dean acts like he's crazy over you," he says.

She knows that he is humoring her, just trying to talk her through this little sad spell that she always gets into when she has drunk too much. Usually, the coke lifts this grief. Not tonight. But before long, this feeling will pass and she will be laughing again. She will be leaning over to grab Gary Dean's rough hand and telling him that she can't wait to get home so they can stay up all night, messing around in the bed. She will put her hand on his crotch for emphasis. She will be running from table to table, talking to all the friends she has made since she and Gary Dean became regulars up here. She will throw back a couple more shots of tequila—eventually swallowing the worm to everyone's delight—and then she will get up and dance by herself when they play a good clogging song. Everybody will clap for her and there will be Dooley, smiling when he looks at her. Finally he will be there to watch her.

After a long time, she says, "It was my fault Daddy died. If I hadn't snuck out that night, he never would have been out on the road. Mommy's done everything but come right out and say that to my face."

"Don't be stupid, Lynn."

She turns her face up to Dooley's and tries to kiss him on the jaw. Her eyes are closed tight and everything is spinning. She just wants to kiss his cheek, but suddenly her mouth is so close to his that she can feel his hot breath right on her teeth. She realizes that she is about to kiss him on the mouth when he pushes her away. He looks back quickly to see if Tara and Gary Dean have seen this.

"Jesus Christ, Lynn," he says in a rough whisper. His eyes dart around to the people dancing close to them. "Why'd you do that? Shit, man. Every time you get drunk, you do that. It's not right to act thataway, drunk or not."

His hands are barely touching her now. He seems to be holding them out from her sides, so he will not actually have to feel her.

"I was just trying to. I just wanted. I'm sorry, Dooley." She is trying to not cry. "I didn't mean to do. God Lord I'm drunk. Please."

"It's all right," he says, but she knows that it is not all right. Lynn realizes that something has ended between them. The music begins to fade away as the song goes off and he seems glad; he simply walks away from her, but then waits for her to catch up. He grabs her arm tightly. "Let's just forget it," he says. "Let's try to have a good time."

When they get back to the table, Lynn sees that Gary Dean has moved over to the seat beside Tara. He is leaning over and talking to her and she is laughing. She is the kind of girl who covers her mouth when she laughs. Lynn has never done this. She has always spread her mouth wide, proud of her straight white teeth, proud of the clear high laughter she has not lost since childhood. She wonders how she held onto it.

"Hey," Gary Dean says. "Did you all finally make it back?"

Tara is still laughing. Apparently she is drunk and doesn't know how to act. Lynn feels like smacking her face. Dooley sits down and kisses Tara on the cheek, and then on the top of her hand. "What's so funny?" He smiles, as if nothing is wrong. Tara leans over to tell him the joke Gary Dean has shared with her.

"You all right, baby?" Gary Dean squeezes Lynn high up on her thigh. He always plays with her legs while they sit at the table, sometimes running his long fingers up under the edges of her panties. "You're pale as a ghost."

"I'm all right," she says and lights a Virginia Slim. She makes herself smile through the smoke escaping her lips. In a few minutes she will get herself back together and everything will be all right. She'll forget her Daddy's big hands and the way she used to help him stack up their coal next to the back porch and the sound of Dooley's laughter before Daddy died. She won't think of the way her mother used to paint her fingernails red and dance around the kitchen when Waylon Jennings came on the radio. She would hold her hands straight out at her sides, so the nail polish wouldn't get on her clothes, and float about the room, singing along to "Good Hearted Woman." Sometimes, she even danced with Lynn.

"Aye, Dooley," Gary Dean hollers over the music. "Go piss?"

Dooley nods and they make their way through the churning crowd. Lynn watches them until they are out of sight. She can't think of anything to say to Tara, so she asks her if she wants to go to the bathroom, too.

"I better not," Tara says. "The waitress is supposed to bring me a 7 Up. I've got to sober up."

"Well, I'll be right back," Lynn says.

Instead of going to the bathroom, she walks on outside. About an inch of snow has fallen since they arrived at the Hilltop, and it's messy with a thousand footprints from people traipsing across the parking lot.

The snow falls impossibly slow, as if it is so light that it will never reach the ground. Lynn puts her hand out flat in front of her and waits for the flakes to touch her skin. She wishes that she wasn't so drunk so she could wake up feeling good tomorrow. She likes to get up early and sit at the kitchen table with her coffee and look out the window to see Free Creek sprawled out below her. This is the first snow that has come since they perched their trailer on the mountainside, and now she will not get to see it. By the time she wakes up, the snow will be melted. It will be nothing more than thin white stripes lying across the most shaded ridges.

The whole world spins for a moment but finally sways to normal, like curtains coming to rest after an unexpected breeze. She walks slowly across the parking lot, letting the cold air rush down into her lungs. She remembers this sensation from the day they buried her father. There was a snowstorm the night he died. The ground was so frozen that they had to wait four days to bury him. Standing there, watching his casket go down, the air had been so cold in her mouth she feared it might eat away the skin inside her throat. The graveyard was on top of the mountain and looking out over the valley she had seen a hundred columns of smoke, pumping towards the sky.

She is not really aware of where she is headed until she arrives at Gary Dean's Z-28. The light is on inside the car, the snow-covered windshield glows bright. When she pulls open the door, Dooley jerks his head up from the line of cocaine Gary Dean has prepared for them. The powder is caked around his nostrils to suggest he is not used to doing this. His eyes are large, full of questions. She wonders what her face looks like. She wonders what he sees. In a gray blur behind him she makes out the shape of Gary Dean, smiling. It looks like he is about to laugh.

She slams the door and walks away. She realizes how cold the air is on her bare arms and hugs herself as she walks back to the honky-tonk. She doesn't know how the car will ever make it back home, over that great black mountain, in this snow. The ground is so cold that her feet numb as soon as they touch it, but she doesn't care. There is a long tear in her hose, running up from one heel. She has walked out here barefoot. She remembers kicking her shoes off on the dance floor.

Once inside, someone hollers at her to come talk to them. She ignores them and looks at the floor as she makes her way back toward her own table. She is trying to figure out where she will go when she quits Gary Dean. This is all she can think about now. Even that is too much. She walks into a man's back and when he turns to smile at her, she says "Get me out of this place," but he can't hear her over the music and the noise. He leans down so she can repeat herself, but she can't make her voice work, so he shrugs and walks away. She finds herself in the middle of the dance floor. She just stands there, trying to find her table, but she can't remember where it is. She is swallowed up by the loudness of the place, overtaken. There is a good song on, so there are a lot of people out there, dancing. But she doesn't join them.

Silas House is the author of *Clay's Quilt, A Parchment of Leaves,* and *The Coal Tattoo,* forthcoming in fall 2004. He is the recipient of the Kentucky Book of the Year Award, the James Still Award from the Fellowship of Southern Writers, and many other awards. His short fiction has appeared in numerous magazines and anthologies, including the *Beloit Fiction Journal, Night Train,* and *Bayou.* A graduate of the MFA

TESS GAMBREL

in Writing at Spalding University, House lives in Eastern Kentucky with his wife and two daughters.

*N*ot *too many years ago, every Saturday night found me and my wild cousins out at honky-tonks like the one in this story. One of those nights we all took note of a beautiful young woman who came in on the arm of burly man she didn't match. She laughed and spoke to everyone and immediately started dancing. We couldn't take our eyes off her, because of her joy as much as her beauty. Over the course of the night, however, she deteriorated before our eyes. She threw back shots of tequila and made a fool out of herself, dancing out of time and staggering about. By night's end she was standing in the middle of the dance floor, looking completely forlorn. There was something in her face that struck me very hard. I could see in her eyes that this was a pivotal point in her life, maybe her "rock bottom" that people often have to hit before they turn their lives around. I began to wonder what events led to that moment in her life. I thought about her the rest of the night, even after we all went back to my cousin's house to party until daylight. I slept a couple of hours and then got up and wrote this entire story over the course of a hungover Sunday. A few people have told me that the ending is too sad, but I disagree. I think leaving Lynn on that dance floor is a hopeful image. I believe she gets someone to take her home and the next day she breaks up with Gary Dean and talks to her mother about how she feels and tries to get her life straightened out. I hope this for her.*

Ann Pancake

DOG SONG

(from *Shenandoah*)

Him. Helling up a hillside in a thin snow won't melt, rock-broke, brush-broke, crust-cracking snow throat felt, the winter a cold one, but a dry one, kind of winter makes them tell about the old ones, and him helling up that hill towards her. To where he sees her tree-tied, black trunk piercing snow hide, and the dog, roped, leashed, chained, he can't tell which, but something not right about the dog he can tell, but he can't see, can't see quite feel, and him helling. Him helling. His eyes knocking in his head, breath punching out of him in a hole, hah. Hah. Hah. Hah, and the dog, her haunch-sat ear-cocked waiting for him, and him helling. And him helling. And him helling. But he does not ever reach her.

This is his dream.

His dogs started disappearing around the fifteenth of July, near as he could pinpoint it looking back, because it wasn't until a week after that and he recognized it as a pattern that he started marking when they went. Parchy vanished first. The ugliest dog he ever owned, coated in this close-napped pink-brown hair, his outsides colored like the insides of his mouth, and at first, Matley just figured he'd run off. Matley always had a few who'd run off because he couldn't bear to keep them tied, but then Buck followed Parchy a week later. But he'd only had Buck a few months, so he figured maybe he'd headed back to where he'd come from, at times they did that, too. Until Missy went because Matley knew Missy would never stray. She was one of the six dogs he camper-kept, lovely mutt Missy, beautiful patches of twenty different dogs, no, Missy'd been with him seven years and was not one to travel. So on July 22, when Missy didn't show up for supper, Matley saw a pattern and started keeping track on his funeral-home calendar. Randolph went on August 1. Yeah, Matley'd always lost a few dogs. But this was different.

He'd heard what they said down in town, how he had seventy-five dogs back in there, but they did not know. Dog Man, they called him. Beagle Boy. Muttie. Mr. Hound. A few called him Cat. Stayed in a Winnebago camper beside a househole that had been his family homeplace before it was carried off in the '85 flood, an identical Winnebago behind the lived-in one so he could take from the second one parts and pieces as they broke in the first, him economical, savvy, keen, no, Matley was not dumb. He lived off a check he got for something nobody knew what, the youngest of four boys fathered by an old landowner back in farm times, and the other three left out and sold off their inheritance in nibbles and crumbs, acre, lot, gate and tree, leaving only Matley anchored in there with the dogs and the househole along the tracks. Where a tourist train passed four times a day on summer weekends, and even more days a week during leaf colors in fall, the cars bellied full of outsiders come to see the mountain sights—"farm children playing in the fields," the brochure said, "A land that time forgot"— and there sits Matley on a lawn chair between Winnebagos and househole. He knew what they said in town, the only person they talked about near as often as Muttie was ole Johnby, and Johnby they discussed only half as much. They said Mr. Hound had seventy-five dogs back in there, nobody had ever seen anything like it, half of them living outside in barrels, the other half right there in the camper with him. It was surely a health hazard, but what could you do about it? that's what they said.

But Matley never had seventy-five dogs. Before they started disappearing, he had twenty-two, and only six he kept in the camper,
and one of those six was Guinea who fit in his sweatshirt pocket, so
didn't hardly count. And he looked after them well, wasn't like that
one woman kept six Pomeranians in a Jayco pop-up while she stayed
in her house and they all got burned up in a camper fire. Space heater.
The outside dogs he built shelters for, terraced the houses up the side
of the hill, and, yes, some of them were barrels on their sides braced
with two-by-four struts, but others he fashioned out of scrap lum-
ber, plenty of that on the place, and depending on what mood took
him, sometimes he'd build them square and sometimes he'd build
them like those lean-to teepees where people keep fighting cocks.
Some dogs, like Parchy, slept in cable spools, a cable spool was the
only structure in which Parchy would sleep. Matley could find cable
spools and other almost doghouses along the river after the spring
floods. And he never had seventy-five dogs.

Parchy, Buck, Missy, Randolph, Ghostdog, Blackie, Ed. Those
went first. That left Tick, Hickory, Cese, Muddy Gut, Carmel, Big
Girl, Leesburg, Honey, Smartie, Ray Junior, Junior Junior, Louise,
Fella, Meredith, and Guinea. Junior Junior was only a pup at the
time, Smartie was just a part-time dog, stayed two or three nights
a week across the river with his Rottweiler girlfriend, and Meredith was pregnant. Guinea was at the end of the list because Guinea
was barely dog at all.

They could tell you in town that Matley was born old, born with
the past squeezing on him, and he was supposed to grow up in
that? How? There was no place to go but backwards. His parents
were old by the time he came, his brothers gone by the time he
could remember, his father dead by the time he was eight. Then
the flood, on his twenty-third birthday. In town they might spot
Matley in his '86 Chevette loaded from floorboards to dome light
with twenty-five pound bags of Joy Dog food, and one ole boy
would say, "Well, there he goes. That ruint runt of Revie's four
boys. End piece didn't come right."

Another: "I heard he was kinda retarded."

"No, not retarded exactly . . . but he wasn't born until Revie was close to fifty. And that explains a few things. Far as I'm concerned. Old egg, old sperm, old baby."

"Hell, weren't none of them right," observed a third.

"There's something about those hills back in there. You know Johnby's from up there, too."

"Well." Said the last. "People are different."

Matley. His ageless, colorless, changeless self. Dressed always in baggy river-colored pants and a selection of pocketed sweatshirts he collected at yard sales. His bill-busted sweat-mapped river-colored cap, and the face between sweatshirt and cap as common and unmemorable as the pattern on a sofa. Matley had to have such a face, given what went on under and behind it. The bland face, the constant clothes, they had to balance out what rode behind them or Matley might be so loose as to fall. Because Matley had inherited from his parents not just the oldness, and not just the past (that gaping loss) and not just the irrational stick to the land—even land that you hated—and not just scraps of the land itself, and the collapsed buildings, and the househole, but also the loose part, he knew. Worst of all, he'd inherited the loose part inside (you got to hold on tight).

Now it was a couple years before the dogs started disappearing that things had gotten interesting from the point of view of them in town. They told. Matley's brother Charles sold off yet another plat on the ridge above the househole, there on what had always been called High Boy until the developers got to it, renamed it Oaken Acre Estates, and the out-of-staters who moved in there started complaining about the barking and the odor, and then the story got even better. One of Dog Man's Beagle Boy's Cat's mixed breed who-knows-what got up in there and impregnated some purebred something-or-other one of the imports owned, "and I heard they had ever last one of them pups put to sleep. That's the kind of people they are, now," taking Matley's side for once. Insider vs. outsider, even Muttie didn't look too bad that way.

Matley knew. At first those pureblood dog old people at Oaken Acre Estates on High Boy appeared only on an occasional weekend, but then they returned to live there all the time, which was when the trouble started. They sent down a delegation of two women one summer, and when that didn't work, they sent two men. Matley could tell they were away from here from a distance, could tell from how they carried themselves before they even got close and confirmed it with their clothes. "This county has no leash ordinance," he told that second bunch, because by that time he had checked, learned the lingo, but they went on to tell him how they'd paid money to mate this pureblood dog of some type Matley'd never heard of to another of its kind, but a mongrel got to her before the stud, and they were blaming it on one of his. Said it wasn't the first time, either. "How many unneutered dogs do you have down here?" they asked, and, well, Matley never could stand to have them cut. So. But it wasn't until a whole year after that encounter that his dogs started disappearing, and Matley, of course, had been raised to respect the old.

The calendar was a free one from Berger's Funeral Home, kind of calendar has just one picture to cover all the months, usually a picture of a blonde child in a nightgown praying beside a bed, and this calendar had that picture, too. Blonde curls praying over lost dog marks, Matley almost made them crosses, but he changed them to question marks, and he kept every calendar page he tore off. He kept track, and for each one, he carried a half eulogy/half epitaph in his head:

Ed. Kind of dog you looked at and knew he was a boy, didn't have to glimpse his privates. You knew from the jog-prance of those stumpy legs, cock-of-the-walk strut, all the time swinging his head from side to side so as not to miss anything, tongue flopping out and a big grin in his eyes. Essence of little boy, he was, core, heart, whatever you want to call it. There it sat in a dog. Ed would try anything once and had to get hurt pretty bad before he'd give up, and he'd eat anything twice. That one time, cold night, Matley let him in the camper, and Ed gagged and puked up a deer liver on Matley's carpet remnant, the liver intact, though a little rotty. There it came. Out. Ed's equipment was hung too close to the ground, that's how Mr. Mitchell explained it, "his dick's hung too close to the ground, way it almost scrapes stuff, would make you crazy or stupid, and he's stupid," Mr. Mitchell'd say. Ed went on August 10.

Ghostdog. The most mysterious of the lot, even more so than Guinea, Ghostdog never made a sound—not a whimper, not a grunt, not a snore. A whitish ripple, Ghostdog was steam moving in skin, the way she'd ghost-coast around the place, a glow-in-the-dark angel cast to her, so that to sit by the househole of a summer night and watch that dog move across the field, a luminous padding, it was to learn how a nocturnal animal sees. Ghostdog'd give Matley that vision, she would make him understand, raccoon eyes, cat eyes, deer. And not only did Ghostdog show Matley night sight, through Ghostdog he could also see smells. He learned to see the shape of a smell, watching her with her head tilted, an odor entering nostrils on breeze, he could see the smell shape, "shape" being the only word he had for how the odors were, but "shape" not it at all. Still. She showed him. Ghostdog went on August 19.

Blackie was the only one who ever came home. He returned a strange and horrid sick, raspy purr to his breath like a locust. Kept crawling places to die, but Matley, for a while, just couldn't let him go, even though he knew it was terribly selfish. Blackie'd crawl in a place, and Matley'd pull him back out, gentle, until Matley finally fell asleep despite himself, which gave Blackie time to get under the bed and pass on. September 2. But Blackie was the only one who came home like that. The others just went away.

Before Mom Revie died, he could only keep one dog at a time. She was too cheap to feed more, and she wouldn't let a dog inside the house until the late 1970s; she was country people and that was how they did their dogs, left them outside like pigs or sheep. For many years, Matley made do with his collection, dogs of ceramic and pewter, plastic and fake fur, and when he was little, Revie's rules didn't matter so much, because if he shone on the little dogs his heart and mind, Matley made them live. Then he grew up and couldn't do that anymore.

When he first started collecting live dogs after Mom Revie was gone, he got them out of the paper, and if pickings there were slim, he drove around and scooped up strays. Pretty soon, people caught on, and he didn't have to go anywhere for them, folks just started dumping unwanteds along the road above his place. Not usually pups, no, they were mostly dogs who'd hit that ornery stage between cooey-cute puppyhood and mellow you-don't-have-to-pay-them-much-mind adult. That in-between stage was the dumping stage. The only humans Matley talked to much were the Mitchells, and more than once, before the dogs started disappearing, Mrs. Mitchell would gentle say to Matley, "Now, you know, Matley, I like dogs myself. But I never did want to have more than two or three at a time." And Matley, maybe him sitting across the table from her with a cup of instant coffee, maybe them in the yard down at his place with a couple of dogs nosing her legs, a couple peeing on her tires, Matley'd nod, he'd hear the question in what she said, but he does not, could not, never out loud say. . . .

How he was always a little loose inside, but looser always in the nights. The daylight makes it scurry down, but come darkness, nothing tamps it, you never know (hold on tight). So even before Matley lost a single dog, many nights he'd wake, not out of nightmare, but worse. Out of nothing. Matley would wake, a hard sock in his chest, his lungs aflutter, his body not knowing where it was, it not knowing, and Matley's eyes'd ball open in the dark, and behind the eyes: a galaxy of empty. Matley would gasp. *Why be alive?* This was what it told him. *Why be alive?*

There Matley would lie in peril. The loose part in him. Matley opened to emptiness, that bottomless gasp. Matley falling, Matley down-swirling (you got to hold), Matley understanding how the loose part had give, and if he wasn't to drop all the way out, he'd have to find something to hold on tight (Yeah, boy. Tight. Tight. Tighty tight tight). Matley on the all-out plummet, Matley tumbling head over butt down, Matley going almost gone, his arms outspread, him reaching, flailing, whopping. . . . Until, finally. Matley hits dog. Matley's arms drop over the bunk side and hit dog. And right there Matley stops, he grabs holt and Matley . . . stroke. Stroke, stroke. There, Matley. There.

Yeah, the loose part Matley held with dog. He packed the emptiness with pup. Took comfort in their scents, nose-buried in their coats, he inhaled their different smells, corn chips, chicken stock, meekish skunk. He'd listen to their breathing, march his breath in step with theirs, he'd hear them live, alive, their sleeping songs, them lapping themselves and recurling themselves, snoring and dreaming, settle and sigh. The dogs a soft putty, the loose part, sticking. There, Matley. There. He'd stroke their stomachs, finger-comb their flanks, knead their chests, Matley would hold on, and finally he'd get to the only true pleasure he'd ever known that wasn't also a sin. Rubbing the deep velvet of a dog's underthroat.

By late August, Matley had broke down and paid for ads in the paper, and he got calls, most of the calls from people trying to give him dogs they wanted to get rid of, but some from people thinking they'd found dogs he'd lost. Matley'd get in his car and run out to wherever the caller said the dog was, but it was never his dog. And, yeah, he had his local suspicions, but soft old people like the ones on the ridge, it was hard to believe they'd do such a thing. So first he just ran the road. Matley beetling his rain-colored Chevette up and down the twelve-mile-long road that connected the highway and his once-was farm. Holding the wheels to the road entirely through habit, wasn't no sight to it, sight he couldn't spare, Matley squinting into trees, fields, brush, until he'd enter the realm of dog mirage. Every rock, dirt mound, deer, piece of trash, he'd see it at first and think "Dog!" his heart bulging big with the hope. Crushed like an egg when he recognized the mistake. And all the while, the little dog haunts scampered the corners of his eyes, dissolving as soon as he turned to see. Every now and then he'd slam out and yell, try Revie's different calling songs, call, "Here, Ghostdog, here! Come, girl, come!" Call "Yah, Ed, yah! Yah! Yah! Yah!" Whistle and clap, cluck and whoop. But the only live thing he'd see besides groundhogs and deer, was that ole boy Johnby, hulking along.

Matley didn't usually pay Johnby much mind, he was used to him, had gone to school with him even though Johnby was a good bit older. Johnby was one of those kids who comes every year but don't graduate until they're so old the board gives them a certificate and throws them out. But today he watched ole Johnby lurching along, pretend-hunting, the gun, everyone had to assume, unloaded, and why the family let him out with guns, knives, Matley wasn't sure, but figured it was just nobody wanted to watch him. Throughout late summer, Mrs. Mitchell'd bring Matley deer parts from the ones they'd shot with crop-damage permits; oh, how the dogs loved those deer legs, and the ribcages, and the hearts. One day she'd brought Johnby along—Johnby'd catch a ride anywhere you'd take him—and Matley'd looked at Johnby, how his face'd gone old while the mind behind it never would, Johnby flipping through his wallet scraps, what he did when he got nervous. He flipped through the wallet while he stared gape-jawed at the dogs, gnawing those deer legs from hipbone to hoof. "I'm just as sorry as I can be," Mrs. Mitchell was saying, talking about the loss of the dogs. "Just as sorry as I can be." "If there's *any*thing," Mrs. Mitchell would say, "*Any*thing we can do. And you know I always keep an eye out."

Matley fondled Guinea in his pocket, felt her quiver and live. You got to keep everything else in you soldered tight to make stay in place the loose part that wasn't. You got to grip. Matley looked at Johnby, shuffling through his wallet scraps, and Matley said to him, "You got a dog, Johnby?" and Johnby said, "I got a dog," he said. "I got a dog with a white eye turns red when you shine a flashlight in it," Johnby said. "You ever hearda that kinda dog?"

• • •

What made it so awful, if awfuller it could be, was Matley never got a chance to heal. Dogs just kept going, so right about the time the wound scabbed a little, he'd get another slash. He'd scab a little, then it would get knocked off, the deep gash deeper, while the eulogies piled higher in his head:

Cese. Something got hold his head when he was wee little, Matley never knew if it was a big dog or a bear or a panther or what it was, but it happened. Didn't kill him, but left him forever after wobbling around like a stroke victim with a stiff right front leg and the eye on the same side wouldn't open all the way, matter always crusted in that eye, although he didn't drool. Cese'd only eat soft food, canned, favored Luck's pinto beans when he could get them, yeah, Matley gave him the deluxe treatment, fed him on top of an old chest of drawers against the propane tank so nobody could steal his supper. Cese went on September 9.

Leesburg. Called so because Matley found him dumped on a Virginia map that must have fallen out of the car by accident. Two pups on a map of Virginia and a crushed McDonald's bag, one pup dead, the other live, still teeny enough to suck Matley's little finger, and he decided on the name Leesburg over Big Mac, more dignity there. When that train first started running, Leesburg would storm the wheels, never fooled with the chickenfeed freight train, he knew where the trouble was. Fire himself at the wheels, snarling and barking, chasing and snap, and he scared some of the sightseers, who slammed their windows shut. Although a few threw food at him from the dining coach. Then one afternoon Matley was coming down the tracks after scavenging spikes, and he spotted a big wad of fur between two ties and thought, "That Missy's really shedding," because Missy was the longest-haired dog he had at the time, and this was a sizeable hair hunk. But when he got home, here came Leesburg wagging a piece of bloody bone sheathed in a shredded tail. Train'd took it, bone sticking out that bloody hair like a half-shucked ear of corn, and Matley had to haul him off to Dr. Simmons, who'd docked it down like a Doberman. Leesburg went on the thirtieth of September.

That sweet, sweet Carmel. Bless her heart. Sure, most of them, you tender them and they'll tender you back, but Carmel, she'd not just reciprocate, she'd soak up the littlest love piece you gave her and return it tenfold power. She would. Swan her neck back and around, reach to Matley's ear with her tiny front teeth and air-nibble as for fleas. Love solidified in a dog suit. Sometimes Matley'd break down and buy her a little bacon, feed it to her with one hand while he rump-scratched with his other, oh, Carmel curling into U-shaped bliss. That was what happiness looked like, purity, good. Matley knew. Carmel disappeared five days after Cese.

Guinea he held even closer, that Guinea a solder, a plug, a glue. Guinea he could not lose. Now Guinea wasn't one he found, she came from up at Mitchell's, he got her as a pup. Her mother was a slick-skinned beaglish creature, a real nervous little dog, Matley saw the whole litter. Two pups came out normal, two did not, seemed the genes leaked around in the mother's belly and swapped birthbags, ended up making one enormous lumbery retarded pup, twice the size the normal ones, and then, like an afterbirth with fur and feet, came Guinea. A scrap of leftover animal material, looked more like a possum than a dog, and more like a guinea pig than either one, the scrap as bright as the big pup was dumb, yes, she was a genius if you factored in her being a dog, but Matley was the only one who'd take her. "Nobody else even believes what she is!" Mrs. Mitchell said. From the start, Guinea craved pockets, and that was when Matley started going about in sweatshirts with big mufflike pockets in front, cut-off sleeves for the heat, and little Guinea with him always, in the pocket sling, like a baby possum or a baby 'roo or, hell, like a baby baby. Guinea luxuring in those pockets. Pretending it was back before she was born and came out to realize wasn't another creature like her on earth. Matley understood. Guinea he kept close.

Columbus Day weekend. Nine dogs down. Matley collapsed in his lawn chair by the househole. Matley spent quite a bit of time in his lawn chair by the househole, didn't own a TV and didn't read much besides *Coonhound Bloodlines* and *Better Beagling* magazines; Matley would sit there and knuckle little Guinea's head. Fifteen years it had been since the house swam off, the househole now slow-filling with the hardy plants, locust and cockleburs and briar, the old coal furnace a-crawl with poison ivy. Fifteen years, and across the tracks, what had been the most fertile piece of bottom in the valley, now smothered with the every-year-denser ragweed and stickweed and mock orange and puny too-many sycamore saplings. Matley could feel the loose part slipping, the emptiness pitting, he held Guinea close in his pocket. Way up the tracks, the tourist train, mumbling. Matley shifted a little and gritted his teeth.

The Mitchells had ridden the train once when they had a special price for locals, they said the train people told a story for every sight. Seemed if there wasn't something real to tell, they made something up, and if there was something to tell, but it wasn't good enough, they stretched it. Said they told that the goats that had run off from Revie decades ago and gone feral up in the Trough were wild mountain goats, like you'd see out West. Said they told how George Washington's brother had stayed at the Puffinburger place and choked to death on a country-ham sandwich. Said they pointed to this tree in Malcolms's yard and told how a Confederate spy had been hanged from it, and Mr. Mitchell said, "That oak tree's old, but even if it was around a hundred and forty years ago, wasn't big enough to hang a spy. Not to mention around here they'd be more likely to hang a Yankee." Matley couldn't help wondering what they told on him, but he didn't ask. He'd never thought much about how his place looked until he had these train people looking at him all the time. He was afraid to ask. And he considered those mutt puppies, sleeping forever.

By that time, he'd made more than a few trips to Oaken Acre Estates despite himself (how old soft people could do such a thing). He'd sneak up in there and spy around, never following the new road on top of the ridge, but by another way he knew. A path you picked up behind where the sheep barn used to be, the barn now collapsed into a quarter-acre sprawl of buckled rusty tin, but if you skirted it careful, leery of the snakes, there was a game path above the kudzu patch. He usually took four or five dogs, Hickory and Tick—they liked to travel—and Guinea in his pocket, of course Guinea went. They'd scramble up into the stand of woods between househole and subdivision, Matley scuttling the path on the edges of his feet, steep in there, his one leg higher than the other, steadying Guinea with one hand. Matley tended towards clumsy and worried about falling and squashing Guinea dead. This little piece of woods was still Matley's piece of woods, had been deeded to him, and Matley, when he moved on that little land, could feel beyond him, on his bare shoulders and arms, how far the land went before. Matley angled along, keen for any dog sign, dog sound, dog sight, yeah, even dead-dog odor. But there was nothing to see, hear, stink.

Then they'd come out of the woods to the bottoms of the slopey backyards, shaley and dry with the struggling grass where the outsiders played at recreating those Washington suburbs they'd so desperately fled. Gated-off, security-systemed, empty yard after empty yard after empty, everything stripped down past stump, no sign of a living thing up in there, nor even a once live thing dead. Hickory and Tick and whoever else had come would sniff, then piss, the lawns, been here, yeah, me, while Matley kept to the woods edge, kept to shelter, kept to shade. Guinea breathing under his chest. He had no idea where the pureblood-dog people lived, and they left no sign—no dogs, no pens, no fences—and although the ridge was full of look-alike houses, garages, gazebos, utility sheds, a swimming pool, it was the emptiest place he'd ever felt. How you could kill a piece of ground without moving it anywhere. And Matley'd watch, he'd listen, he'd sniff best he could. But no dog sights, no dog sounds, no smells, and nothing to feel but his own sticky sweat. Matley'd never discover a thing.

Matley tensed in his lawn chair, nine dogs gone, Guinea in his pocket, Junior Junior cranky in his lap. He listened to that train creak and come, the train was coming and coming—it was always coming and you would never get away. The train slunk around the turn and into sight, its bad music an earbeat, a gutbeat, ta TA ta TA ta TA, locomotive slow-pulling for the sightseers to better see the sights, and how did they explain Matley? Plopped between Winnebagos and household with some eighteen doghouses up his yard. How did he fit into this land that time forgot? ta TA ta TA ta TA, the beat when it passed the joints in the rails, and the screee sound over the rail beat, and even over top that, a squealing, that ear-twisting song, a sorry mean ear-paining song. Starers shouldered up in open cars with cameras bouncing off golf-shirted bellies, and from the enclosed cars, some would wave. They would only wave if they were behind glass. And Matley would never wave back.

He comes to know. In the dream, he is a younger man than young he ever was, younger than he was born, and the hillside he hell-heaves, it's hill without end. The leaves loud under snow crust, his boots busting, ground cracking, the whole earth moanering, and him, him helling. Snow lying in dapples, mottles, over hillside, ridgeside, dog-marked like that, saddles, white snow saddles, see, his side seizing, breath in a blade, and the dog. Who he dream-knows is a girl dog, he knows that, the dog haunch-sat waiting pant, pant, pant. His hill pant, her dog pant, the blade in his ribs, who pants? say good dog "good dog" good, him helling and the dog roped leashed tethered to a cat-faced red oak black against the snow blank, dog a darker white than the snow white and. He cannot ever reach her.

Eventually it trickled down to them in town. A few had seen. The fuel oil man. The UPS. Gilbert who drove the school bus to the turnaround where the road went from gravel to dirt. Dog Man blundering in bushes, whistling and yodeling some chint-chant dog-call, when few people besides the Mitchells had ever heard Muttie speak beyond shopping grunts. Of course, there were the lost ads, too, and although Matley wouldn't spend the extra dollar to print his name, just put a phone number there, well, the swifter ones put it together for those who were slow. Then somebody cornered Mr. Mitchell in the Super Fresh, and he confirmed it, yeah, they were vanishing off, and right away the story went around that Muttie was down twenty-seven dogs to a lean forty-eight. The UPS driver said he didn't think those old people out in Oaken Acre Estates were hard enough for such a slaughter, but then somebody pointed out the possibilities of poison, "people like that, scared of guns, they'll just use poison," a quiet violence you didn't have to see or touch. Yeah. A few speculated that the dogs just wised up, figured out Cat was crazy and left, and others blamed it on out-of-work chicken catchers from Hardy County. One (it was Mr. Puffinburger, he didn't appreciate the ham sandwich story) suspected the train people. Who knew to what lengths they'd go, Mr. Puffinburger said, the househole, the campers, the doghouses and Mr. Hound, that scenery so out of line with the presentation, so far from the scheme of decoration. Who knew how they might fix ole Beagle Boy and his colony of dog. He'd heard they tried to organize the 4-H'ers for a big trash clean-up. Then a sizeable and committed contingent swore Matley had done it himself and ate 'em, and afterwards either forgot about it or was trying to trick people into pity, "I wouldn't put anything past that boy."

"I wouldn't, either, now. He's right, buddy. Buddy, he. Is. Right."

"Hell, they were all of them crazy, you could see it in their eyes."

"And I heard Charles lives out in Washington State now, but he won't work. Say he sits around all day in a toolshed reading up on the Indians."

"Well," the last one said. "People are different."

Matley standing at his little sink washing up supper dishes, skillet-sized pancakes and gravy from a can. His dogs have took up a dusk-time song. An I'm gonna bark because I just want to song, a song different from an I'm barking at something I wanna catch song or I'm barking at somebody trying to sneak up song or I'm howling because I catch a contagion of the volunteer fire department siren-wailing different from I'm barking at a train full of gawkers song.

A sad sad song. The loose parts in him. Daylight puts a little hold down on it, but with the dark, nothing tamps it, you never know. You got to hold tight. He'd seen Johnby again that morning, humping along through the ditch by the road, and now, behind his eyes, crept Johnby, hulking and hunching to the time of the song. Dogs sought Johnby because Johnby wasn't one to bathe much and dogs liked to pull in his scents, Johnby could no doubt bait dogs to him, Matley is thinking. The way Johnby's lip would lift and twitch. Muscles in a dead snake moving. Tic.

Matley stepped out, pulled Guinea from his pocket and took a look. As sometimes happened, for a second he was surprised to see her tail. The dog song made a fog around them, from sad to eerie, Matley heard the music go, while Matley counted those dog voices, one two three to twelve. Matley hollowing under his heart (the part slipping), the fear pimpling his skin, and then he called, moany, a whisper in his head: *come out come out come out come out.*

He breathed the odor the place made of an evening, a brew of dropping temperature, darkness and household seep. A familiar odor. The odor of how things fail. Odor of ruin in progress, of must and stale hay, spoiling silage, familiar, and mildew and rotting wood and flaked paint; twenty-year-old manure, stagnant water, decaying animal hides, odor of the household and what falls in it, the loss smell, familiar, the odor of the inside of his head. And Matley stroked little Guinea, in full dark now, the dog song dimming, and he heard Mrs. Mitchell again ("but I never did want to have more than two or three"), the not-question she used to ask, him not thinking directly on it, but thinking under thinking's place, and he knows if you get a good one, you can feel their spirits in them from several feet away, right under their fur, glassy and clear and dew-grass smelling. If you get a good one. You can feel it. No blurriness to the spirit of a dog, no haze, they're unpolluted by the thinking, by memories, by motives, you can feel that spirit raw, naked bare against your own. And dogs are themselves and aren't nothing else, just there they are, full in their skins and moving on the world. Like they came right out of it, which they did, which people did, too, but then people forget, while dogs never do. And when Matley was very young he used to think, if you love them hard enough, they might turn into people, but then he grew up a little and knew, what good would that be? So then he started wishing, if you loved one hard enough, it might speak to you. But then he grew up even more and knew that wasn't good, either, unless they spoke dog, and not just dog language, but dog ideas, things people'd never thought before in sounds people'd never heard, Matley knew. And Matley had studied the way a dog loved, the ones that had it in them to love right, it was true, not every one did, but the ones that loved right, Matley stroking, cup, cradle and hold, gaze in dog eyes, the gentle passing. Back and forth, enter and return, the gentle passing, passing between them, and Matley saw that love surpass what they preached at church, surpass any romance he'd heard of or seen, surpass motherlove loverlove babylove, he saw that doglove simple. Solid. And absolutely clear. Good dog. Good dog, now. Good. Good.

Meredith. Was just a couple weeks shy of dropping her pups, no mystery there, she was puffed out like a nail keg, and who in their right mind would steal a pregnant Lab/Dalmatian mix? it could only be because they were killing them, if Matley'd ever doubted that, which he had. Which he'd had to. Meredith'd been a little on the unbrightish side, it was true, had fallen into the househole more than once in broad day, the spots on her head had soaked through and affected her brain, but still. And it was her first litter, might have made some nice pups, further you got from the purebloods, Matley had learned, better off you'll be. Meredith went on October 17.

Muddy Gut. A black boy with a soft gold belly, and gold hair sprouting around his ears like broom sedge, soft grasses like that, he had the heaviest and most beautiful coat on the place, but the coat's beauty the world constantly marred, in envy or spite. Muddy Gut drew burrs, beggar's lice, devil's pitchforks, ticks, and Matley'd work tirelessly at the clobbed-up fur, using an old currycomb, his own hairbrush, a fork. Muddy Gut patient and sad, aware of his glory he could not keep, while Matley held a match to a tick's behind until it pulled out its head to see what was wrong. A constant grooming Matley lavished over Muddy Gut, Matley forever untangling that lovely spoiled fur, oh sad sullied Muddy, dog tears bright in his deep gold eyes. Muddy Gut went on October 21.

Junior Junior. Matley'd known it was bound to happen, Ray Junior or Junior Junior one. Although they were both a bit ill-tempered, they were different from the rest, they were Raymond descendants several generations down. Junior Junior was Ray Junior's son, and Ray Junior was mothered by a dog across the river called Ray Ray, and Ray Ray, Mr. Mitchell swore, was fathered by the original Raymond. In Junior Junior there was Raymond resemblance, well, a little anyway, in temperament for sure, and Matley didn't stop to think too hard about how a dog as inert as Raymond might swim the river to sow his oats. Raymond was the dog who came when Matley could no longer make the toy dogs live and who stayed until after the flood, and for a long time, he was the only dog Matley had to love. They'd found Raymond during a Sunday dinner at Mrs. Fox's Homestead Restaurant when Matley had stretched out his leg and hit something soft under the table, which surprised him. Was a big black dog, bloodied around his head, and come to find out it was a stray Mrs. Fox had been keeping for a few weeks, he'd been hit out on 50 that very morning and had holed up under the table to heal himself. Later, Revie liked to tell, "Well, you started begging and carrying on about this hit dog, and Mrs. Fox gave him up fast—I don't believe she much wanted to fool with him anyway—and here he's laid ever since, hateful and stubborn and foul-smelling. Then after we got done eating, Mrs. Fox came out of the kitchen, and she looked at our plates, and she said, 'You would've thought finding that hit dog under your table would've put a damper on your appetites. But I see it didn't!' It was a compliment to her cooking, you see." Junior Junior was Raymond's great-great grandson, and he disappeared on Halloween.

Matley in the bunk at night. He'd wake without the knowledge. He'd lose the loss in his sleep, and the moments right after waking were the worst he'd ever have: finding the loss again and freshly knowing. The black surge over his head, hot wash of sawsided pain, then the bottom'd drop out. Raw socket. Through the weeks, the loss rolling, compounding, just when he'd think it couldn't get worse, think a body couldn't hold more hurt, another dog would go, the loss an infinity inside him. Like how many times you can bisect a line. They call it heartbreak, but not Matley, Matley learned it was not that clean, nowhere near that quick, he learned it was a heartgrating, this forever loss in slow motion, forever loss without diminishment of loss, without recession, without ease, the grating. And Matley having had in him always the love, it pulsing, his whole life, reaching, for a big enough object to hold this love, back long before this crippling mess, he reached, and, now, the only end for that love he'd ever found being taken from him, too, and what to do with this love? Pummelling at air. Reaching, where to put this throat-stobbing surge, where, what? the beloved grating away. His spirit in his chest a single wing that opens and folds, opens and folds. Closing on nothing. Nothing there. And no, he says, no, he says, no, he says, no.

Come November, Matley was still running his ads, and he got a call from a woman out at Shanks, and though he doubted a dog of his would travel that far, he went anyway. The month was overly warm, seasons misplaced like they'd got in recent years, and coming home right around dusk, he crested High Boy with his windows half-down. At first, he wasn't paying much mind to anything except rattling the Chevette over that rutty road, only certain ways you could take the road without tearing off the muffler. But suddenly it came to him he didn't see no dogs. No dogs lounging around their houses, and no dogs prancing out to meet him. No dogs squirting out the far corners of the clearings at the sound of the car, even though it was dog-feeding time. No Guinea under the camper, no Hickory and Tick fighting over stripped-down deer legs, no welcome-home dog bustle. Not a dog on the place. None.

A panic began in the back of Matley's belly. Fizzing. He pushed it down by holding his breath. He parked the car, swung out slow, and when he stood up (hold on tight) there between the car seat and door, he felt his parts loosen. A rush of opening inside. He panic-scanned Winnebago and househole, sunken barns and swaying sheds, his head cocked to listen. Doghouses, tracks, bottom and trees, his eyes spinning, a vacuum coring his chest, and then he heard himself holler. He hollered "Here!" and he hollered "Come!" and he hollered "Yah! Yah! Yah!" still swivelling his head to take in every place. Him hollering "Here, Fella! Tick, C'mon now! Yah, Big Girl, Yah," his voice squawling higher while the loose part slipped. Matley hollered, and then he screamed, he clapped and hooed, he whistled until his mouth dried up. And then, from the direction of the sheep barn, way up the hill, he spied the shape of Guinea.

Little Guinea, gusting over the ground like a blown plastic bag. Matley ran to meet her. Guinea, talking and crying in her little Guinea voice, shuttling hysterical around his shins and trying to jump, and Matley scooped her up and into his pocket, stroking and trembling, and there, Guinea. There. And once she stilled, and he stilled, Matley heard the other.

Dog cries at a distance. Not steady, not belling or chopping, not like something trailed or treed. No, this song was a dissonant song. Off beat and out of tune. A snarling brutal song.

Matley wheeled. He charged up the pasture to the sheep barn there, grass tearing under his boots. He leaned into the path towards the subdivision, despite dark was fast dropping, and he hadn't any light. He pounded that game path crazy, land tilted under his feet, his sight swinging in the unfocus of darkened trees, and the one hand held Guinea while the dead leaves roared. He was slipping and catching his balance, he was leaping logs when he had to, his legs bendy and the pinwheel of his head, and the parts inside him, unsoldering fast, he could feel his insides spilling out of him, Matley could no longer grip, he was falling. This land, this land under him, you got to grip, tight, Guinea crying, and now, over top the dry leaves' shout, he heard not only yelping, but nipping and growling and brush cracking, and Matley was close.

It was then that it came to him. He dreamed the dream end awake. Him helling up that endless hillslope, but the slope finally ends, and he sees the white dog tree-tied ear-cocked patient waiting, but still, Matley knows, something not right he can't tell. Black trees unplummetting out of white snow skiff, and Matley helling. Him helling. Him. Helling. He reaches, at last he reaches her, a nightmare rainbow's end, and he's known all along what he has to do, he thrusts his hand behind her to unleash her, free her, and then he understands, sees: behind the live dog front, she is bone. Her front part, her skin and face, a dog mask, body mask, and behind that, the not right he's always sensed but could not see, bone, and not even skeleton bone, but chunky bone, crumbled and granular and fragrant, the blood globbed up in chunks and clots, dry like snow cold day skiff and Matley moaning, he'd broke free of the woods and into a little clearing below the subdivision, ground rampant with sumac and dormant honeysuckle and grape and briar. It truly darkening now, and the way it's harder to see in near dark than it is in full dark, how your eyes don't know what to do with it, and Matley was stopped, trembling, loose, but he could hear. A house-sized mass of brush, a huge tangle of it making like a hill itself, dense looped and layered, crowned with the burgundy sumac spears. That whole clump asound with dog, and Matley felt himself tore raw inside, the flesh strips in him, and Matley started to yell.

He stood at a short distance and yelled at them to come out, come out of there, he knew inside himself not to dare go in, he knew before seeing what he couldn't bear to see. But nary a dog so much as poked its head out and looked at Matley, he could hear them snarling, hear bones cracking, see the brush rattle and sway, but to the dogs Matley wasn't there, and then he smelled it. Now, the smell of it curled to him on that weird warm wind, as it had no doubt curled down to the househole and lured the dogs up, and he was screaming now, his voice scraping skin off his throat, ripping, and Matley, with the single ounce of gentle still left in his hand, pulled out Guinea and set her down. Then he stooped and plunged in.

Now he was with them, blundering through this confusion of plant, and he could see his dogs, saw them down through vine branch and briar. Louise, the biggest, hunkered over and tearing at it, growling if another dog got close, she held her ground, and Ray Junior writhing in it on her back, and Honey layering his neck in dried guts. Big Girl drawn off to the side crunching spine, while Hickory and Tick battled over a big chunk, rared up on their hind legs and wrestling with their fronts, and Matley pitched deeper, thorns tearing his hands. Matley tangled in vine and slim trunk, the sumac tips, that odor gusting all over his head, and he reached for Tick's tail to break up the fight. But when he touched Tick, Tick turned on him. Tick spun around gone in his eyes, and he drew back his lips on Matley and he bared his teeth to bite, and Matley, his heart cleaved in half, dropped the tail and sprung back. And the moment he did, he saw what he'd been terrified he'd see all along. Or did he see? A sodden collar still buckled around a rotting neck, did he? The live dogs eating the dead dogs there, what he'd suspected horrified all along, did he? And then Matley was whacking, flailing, windmilling looney, beating with his hands and arms and feet and legs the live dogs off the dead things because he had nothing else to beat with, he was not even screaming any longer, he was beyond sound, Matley beyond himself, Matley reeling, dropping dropped down until Guinea was there. Against him. Hurtling up to be held. And Matley took her, did hold her. He stroked her long guinea hair, whispering, good girl, Guinea. Good.

Matley stood in the midst of the slaughter, shaking and panting, palming little Guinea's head. Most of the beat dogs had slunk off aways to wait, but the bolder ones were already sneaking back. And finally Matley slowed enough, he was spent enough, to squint again through the dim and gradual understand.

There were no collars there.

Slowly.

These colors of fur, these shapes and sizes of bones. Were not dogs. No.

Groundhogs, squirrels, possums, deer.

Then he felt something and turned and saw: Johnby crouched in the dead grass, rifle stock stabbed in the ground and the barrel grooving his cheek. Johnby was watching.

Somehow it got going around in town that it had been a pile of dead dogs, and some said it served Muttie right, that many dogs should be illegal anyway. But others felt sad. Still other people had heard it was just a bunch of dead animals that ole Johnby had collected, Lord knows if he'd even shot them, was the gun loaded? his family said not; could have been roadkill. Then there were the poison believers, claimed it was wild animals and dogs both, poisoned by the retirees in Oaken Acre Estates, and Bill Bates swore his brother-in-law'd been hired by the imports to gather a mess of carcasses and burn 'em up in a brush pile, he just hadn't got to the fire yet. Mr. Puffinburger held his ground, he felt vindicated, at least to himself, because this here was the lengths to which those train people would go, this here was how far they'd alter the landscape to suit themselves. What no one was ever certain about was just how many'd been lost. Were they all gone? had any come back? was he finding new ones? how many were out there now? Fred at the feed store reported that Muttie wasn't buying any dog food, but the UPS truck driver had spied him along a creek bed with a dog galloping to him in some hillbilly Lassie-come-home.

Despite all the rumors, it must be said that after that, they didn't talk about Dog Man much anymore. Even for the skeptics and the critics, the subject of Matley lost its fun. And they still saw Muttie, although he came into town less often now, and when they did see him, they looked more closely, and a few even sidled up to him in the store in case he would speak. But the dogless Matley, to all appearances, was exactly like the dogful one.

• • •

These days, some mornings, in the lost-dog aftermath, Matley wakes in his camper having forgot the place, the year, his age. He's always had such spells occasionally, losses of space and time, but now it's more than ever. Even though when he was a kid, Mom Revie'd only allow one live dog at a time and never inside, they did have for some years a real dog named Blanchey, some kind of wiener-beagle mix. And now, these mornings, when Matley wakes, believing himself eight in the flood-gone house, he hears Mom Revie's dog-calling song.

Oh, the way that woman could call a dog, it was bluegrass operatic. "Heeeeeere, Blanchey! Heeeeeeere, Blanchey, Blanchey, Blanchey," she'd yodel off the back porch, the "here" pulled taut to eight solid seconds, the "Blanchey" a squeaky two-beat yip. Then "You, Blanchey! C'mere, girl! 'mon!" fall from high-octave "here's" to a businesslike burr, and when Blanchey'd still not come, Revie'd switch from cajole to command. "Yah, Blanchey, Yah! Yah! Yah! Yah!" a bellydeep bass; while the "Here's" seduced, the "Yah's" insist, oh, it plunged down your ear and shivered your blood, ole Mom Revie's dog-calling song. And for some minutes, Matley lets himself hover in that time, he just lies abed and pleasures in the tones. Until she cuts loose in frustration with a two-string riff— "comeoutcomeoutcomeoutcomeout"—rapid banjo plinkplunk wild, and Matley wakes enough to know ain't no dogs coming. To remember all the dogs are gone but one.

He crawls out of the bunk and hobbles outside. Guinea pokes her head from his pocket, doesn't like what she sniffs, pulls back in. It is March, the train season is long over, but Matley hears it anyway. Hears it coming closer, moaning and sagging like it's about to split. Hears the haunty music that train plays, haunty like a tawdry carnival ride. Train moving slow and overfull, passing the joints in the rails, beat beat, and the scree sound over the railbeat, he hears it shriek-squeal over steel. And Matley stands there between househole and Winnebago, the morning without fog and the air like glass, and he understands he is blighted landscape now.

He is disruption of scenery. Understands he is the last one left, and nothing but a sight. A sight. Sight, wheel on rail click it on home, Sight. Sight. Sight. Then Matley does not hear a thing.

Ann Pancake is a native of West Virginia. Her collection of short stories, *Given Ground*, won the 2000 Bakeless Prize. She has also received a 2003 Whiting Award, an NEA grant, a Pennsylvania Council on the Arts grant, and the Glasgow Prize. Her fiction and essays have appeared in journals like *Glimmer Train*, the *Virginia Quarterly Review*, *Shenandoah*, and *Five Points*. She now lives in Seattle.

JERRY BAUER

*D*og Song" was born from a confluence of vivid images, painful emotions, and old failed drafts. A dream I had about climbing the mountain behind the house where I grew up and finding my dog bloodied and tied short to a tree. A novel I tried to write about an eccentric old woman and her equally eccentric son trying to save their house and dog from a flood. The time my dog ran away and we found her in a clump of brush pushing her muzzle into a decaying dog corpse. The story finally came together for me during a period when I was suffering the greatest loss of my life, including the loss of my dog. I have to add that almost all the dog biographies, including Guinea's, are true.

Drew Perry

LOVE IS GNATS TODAY

(from *The Nebraska Review*)

I got fired from BBQs Etcetera two weeks ago. This was back
when the heat was still going strong and it wasn't raining all
that much. Mr. Albergotteson fired me. He's the store manager
and also a Norwegian. You know he's Norwegian because he finds
some way to work this fact into damn near any conversation you
have with him. "It was never this hot growing up in Norway," he'll
say. "No sir." Always with that "No sir" in there, like you're some
kind of diplomat or celebrity or something and he's just pleased
as hell to be talking to you. Only you can tell he's not. Pleased to
be talking to you, I mean. I'm not sure he cares one way or the
other if he's talking to you. I think he probably just tells the Norway stories to fill up space in his head.

Mr. Albergotteson the goddamned Norwegian fired me from
BBQs Etcetera two weeks ago because I told him there was absolutely no fucking way I was going out into the parking lot in the
middle of the hot of the goddamn day to change his bitch of a sign
around. Those were pretty much my words. A little coarse, maybe,
but I did it for emphasis. Sometimes you want emphasis. BBQs
Etcetera has one of those signs with the white rows that hold the
letters so you can make it say whatever you want. That's the bottom of the sign. The top is this red square with black cursive letters that say BBQs Etcetera.

I mean, I was in my rights, I think. The man after all wanted me to go out there at noon, or close to it, right in the hot of the day, to change the sign. And the thing is something like ten feet off the ground, so it's not like you can just walk out there and do it. You have to get the telescoping pole with the suction cup on it and stand out there forever taking one letter down, and then another, and then putting up the new letters one at a damn time, too. It's hard enough if it's not hot, if you're not sweating right into your goddamn eyes. Plus he wanted me to go out there to change the sign over from saying GAS GRILLS $129.99 to COOK UP SOME DOGS FOR THE DOG DAYS OF SUMMER. The man is an idiot. There he's got a sign up that makes sense, a perfectly good sign already up there that tells people what they need to know, which is that we have gas grills and that they cost what they cost, and instead of that, he wants me out there laying out some half-assed pun. Straight and simple, I said. People just want to be told things straight out. None of this dog days shit. He said I was to go out and change the sign. Crossed his arms at me. I said if he wanted it changed so badly then he could take his pasty white Norwegian ass outside into the 95 degree heat and damn well do it himself.

Then Mr. Albergotteson got this sort of Viking look on his face, this kind of scowl you could tell he practiced at home in front of a mirror and was proud of, and he very quietly handed me the box of letters and the telescoping pole, and he told me that I had better reconsider myself. That's what he said. Reconsider myself. The man's English could be a little better, if you want to know the truth. He told me to go out there and start changing the sign and reconsider myself, and that if I didn't like it I could stop coming to work altogether. He said I should consider my job history, mister. He called me mister. Like the next thing he was gonna do was either pull a quarter out of my ear or call my mother. He was talking in this very serious tone, hissing a little, even. Here's what he also said: He said that he was the manager, and that managers got to think up the signs, that that was one of his very important duties, and that one of my duties was to put up the signs when I was told to. And he said I had better not question his managerness. Like that.

I remember a couple customers in the store were sort of half-watching our argument. I remember looking outside, too, out into the hot. It was one of those days Savannah gets where you think things might just sort of cook off to cinders and blow away. The kind of day where you can see the hot coming up off the asphalt in these little jumpy pools. There was a guy out in the parking lot looking at this display of gas grills we had set up, four or five of them in a row, in formation like jet fighters. The guy was like every other customer we got in BBQs Etcetera, one of these older guys. You know the kind. Bermuda shorts and some golf shirt with a corporate logo he got from some client or some buddy at the office. He looked like he might have fallen out of a catalog for old people. People who are interested in denture toothpaste commercials. Hair not gray enough, kind of a dead yellow instead, socks and sandals. That kind. He was looking way down into one of the grills, not one of the sale grills, but one of those huge fucking monster outdoor kitchen deals. At one point he had his head all the way down in it. Then he stood back up and started playing with the knobs. He'd twist one, look inside, twist another one, look inside again. Like he was waiting for the flames to come on. He was playing with the damn thing like we'd have it hooked up or something, like we'd have the damn grills hooked up to propane tanks right out there in the parking lot. Like we're asking for lawsuits and trips to the burn unit. He was trying to figure out why he couldn't make the fire come on. You could tell. I goddamned hate the people who come in the store thinking the gas grills are hooked up. Idiots. For Christ's sake.

I decided right there standing in the store with Mr. Albergotteson holding the box of letters out to me, right there watching that man try like hell outside to get the little blue flames to come on, that I'd had about enough of working at BBQs Etcetera. It wasn't worth it. I'd never really liked it, anyway. For one thing, they had their abbreviations backwards on the sign. Who the hell spells out *etcetera?* They should have flipped it around, or at least abbreviated them both. That should have been an indication right from the start. Add about forty-eight other things about working there that made me want to shoot myself in the head and that about did it.

So I told Mr. Albergotteson to go fuck himself. Just like that. I shoved the box of letters and the pole back at him and I told him in this very calm voice to go fuck himself. I have a calm voice that is just right for occasions like that. It seemed the simplest way of doing things. He didn't take it all that well, and he started in yelling at me right there in the store about insubordination and how it was the employee's responsibility to respect the manager and that he was the manager and I was supposed to respect him. Said he'd already given me enough chances, mister, called me mister again, but I was already going for the door. I figured whether I was quitting or getting fired, whichever came first, I didn't really have to stand there and listen to too much of what he had to say. He yelled at me that I was fired and I yelled right back that that was goddamn fine with me anyway and walked right out the door into the middle of one of the hottest days of the year. The heat just sucks it out of you. I walked right past the old man and didn't even tell him the grills weren't hooked up. Wasn't my job anymore.

You get right down to it, and I hated that job. It was all the time things like some asshole standing there in front of the woodchips asking me did I think applewood or hickory would be better for his salmon, and I could tell just from looking at his seventy-five dollar shirt and fancy-ass woven leather shoes and nice clean hands that it didn't matter what he bought. He'd burn whatever he was cooking anyway. His wife would be the sort of person to get her hair done once a week. I didn't even bother telling people like that you have to soak the chips down first so they'll smoke instead of burn. Some people, it just doesn't matter. I usually just pulled whatever was closest off the shelf and handed it to them and walked away.

You just don't want to work somewhere if you're all the time having to deal with fools. It wears you down.

• • •

Jeannie wanted to know what I was doing home in the middle of the afternoon. I told her I quit my job, which I figured was mostly true. True enough to go on. Jesus H. Christ in a stainless steel bucket was she pissed off. She got more dialed up than she's normally good for, which is saying something. I guess she had something of a right. We had just bought the minivan about a month earlier, and she wanted to know how I thought we were going to make the payments. She wanted to know how we'd pay for groceries next week. I told her I had one more check coming. That information didn't really do much for my side of things. She was all over me yelling at me about how I knew how much we needed that job and so naturally I was yelling back about how I had to keep my dignity or some shit like that. I was also trying to explain how it was to have to work at BBQs Etcetera, but she didn't want to talk about anything except how I'd managed to blow another job. We went around like that for a while, neither of us listening all that closely to the other.

An important fact: Jeannie throws things when she's mad. After an hour or so it came out that I'd quit over the sign, and then she really blew a gasket. She picked up the television, our goddamned nice television, a little picture-in-picture gig that I loved for football Saturdays, and threw it out the door. She got her arms wrapped all the way around it and threw it right out through the sliding glass door and onto the back porch. One minute we were yelling at each other and the next she had just tossed it out through the door like it was nothing. It made a really serious noise. There was glass everywhere. Then we were both quiet. A thing like that will quiet you. Neither of us talked a while. We just stood there looking at the hole in the door and the cable running out from the wall, out onto the back porch, and into the busted TV.

And it would have been OK, I guess. I mean, everything might have simmered back down, except for us being out a TV, but Arton, her kid—my kid now, too, really—Arton came running out from his room to see what the noise was, saw the TV, and went running outside after it hollering something like, "Big Bird is broken." He's only five. He couldn't really know. He was past us before either of us could move. Then he got his arm hung up on the glass door on his way out, and naturally that gave him a pretty good cut. It was a bad scene. The cut wasn't all that deep, but Jeannie damn near had a seizure over the whole thing, running all over the house and coming back with one of my good white shirts to use as a tourniquet or something. I told her not to tie it too tight, that it was just a little cut, and then she was back at me twice as angry as ever wanting to know if that's what I thought a little cut was.

Little kids will bleed some. I will say that right fucking here. There was a pretty fair amount of blood. But she used one of my good shirts to clean him up. I was standing there thinking, why not a T-shirt? She was screaming. Arton was crying. The whole thing was an absolute royal fuckup. Finally I just took a seat on the couch. She decided to take the kid to the hospital and said no, she didn't want me to come, that I'd done enough for one day. Told me I should clean up the goddamn mess I'd made. I wanted to point out that it wasn't really me who'd made the mess, but I decided against that, because with Jeannie, sometimes there's not much explaining to be done.

It wasn't that bad a cut. Probably everything would have been fine with a few Band-Aids, a little cleanup and maybe some gauze and tape at the most, but she took him to the hospital anyway. She called me later that night from the hospital to tell me they'd given him three stitches. I have a feeling they did that just to make her feel better or calm her down or something. She told me on the phone that she wasn't coming home that night, that she was going to go out to her parents' place. I can't say I was all that surprised. Upset, but not all that surprised. We move out on each other every now and then. Somehow Arton cutting his arm on the door had gotten to be my fault.

So I sat there in the house a good long time that night after she said she wasn't coming home and after we hung up and looked at the walls. Finally I decided I had to do something, what with her gone. Something to even up the score with the universe. I like to keep tabs that way. It had been a bad goddamned day. I think it's fair to say that. I sat there in my red BBQs Etcetera shirt, which I had kept, drank a few beers, and got myself good and pissed off. After a while I decided I should go back to the store. It was at least midnight, but I still had my key on my keychain, so I drove over there and let myself in. Maybe this wasn't all that smart, looking back on it. But still. I was pissed. I got the pole and the box of letters out of the back office, and I went outside and took down the damn message, which sure as hell he'd changed over to COOK UP SOME DOGS FOR THE DOG DAYS OF SUMMER. Idiot. I put up my own message instead. I figured I was probably even doing them a favor, since some ASPCA quack would have mistaken the sign for grilling actual canine dogs, and there would have been protests and some kind of crazy uproar about the whole thing. So I made things simpler for Mr. Albergotteson. Keep things straight and simple, I say. It didn't take me all that long to do it. I just put up there WE SELL SHIT.

Jeannie called me the next morning. Woke me up. "Was that you?" she asked.

"Was what me?"

"With the sign. Did you do that?"

"Yeah. I did."

"What the hell's the matter with you?"

"What do you care?" I said.

"The police called over here, you know."

"What? What for?"

"They wanted to know if you had anything to do with it. Said they were looking for you. Said your phone's off the hook. But it rang when I called."

"I left it off overnight," I said.

"They said Mr. Albergotti—"

"Albergotteson."

"Whatever. They said you were supposed to call them. They said he might press charges."

"Charges for what?"

"Vandalism. Breaking and entering."

"I didn't break anything."

"I'm telling you what they said."

"What did you tell them?"

"I told them you were sleeping. That you'd been at the hospital with me. I said you'd call them today."

Jeannie loves me. This is one of the ways I know. "Thanks," I said.

"Don't thank me yet, you dumb shit. They said they were going to come see you today. I told them you'd be there."

"But you told them I was with you, you said."

"I'm just telling you what they said they'd do."

"OK," I said. "Thanks."

"Why don't you ask me how Arton is," she said.

"How's Arton?"

"He's fine. Mom's making a big fuss over him."

"Good," I said. "When are you coming home?"

"Shut up," she said.

I didn't say anything.

"I've got to go," she said.

"I love you," I said.

"You found a job yet?"

"It hasn't even been a day," I said.

She hung up on me.

So the damn police did come over to the house. I sat on my front porch with my coffee, even though it was hot as hell. I was not all that interested in having the police in the den to ask questions about the broken door. They stood in the yard and I sat on the porch and I told them I'd been at the hospital and I told them I didn't even have a key to BBQs Etcetera, told them Mr. Albergotteson had taken it away from me a while back after one of my incidents. An argument about stocking shelves full of spatulas or something. I told them he was Norwegian. I told them he took the key as punishment. I told them he thought it would teach me something. All that was true enough, because Mr. Albergotteson had taken the key from me, made a big show of it, like I'd care about that kind of thing. It didn't matter to me. I'd had a copy made before I gave it back.

I wasn't all that worried about getting caught for the WE SELL SHIT. I figured the case probably wasn't big enough to get the kind of investigation you see on TV dramas. No one was going to interview all the key guys in town. And I was right. The police just ended up basically saying OK and asking me not to go near BBQs Etcetera and leaving. Before they drove off, one of them rolled down the window in the cruiser and said that whoever had changed the sign had caused at least one traffic accident, and that it wasn't funny.

I said I sure didn't think it was funny either.

I was glad for Jeannie covering for me. Sometimes she's good to me like that. She's overall the sort of woman you'd want to get married to, even if she does have a kid by somebody else. She's just mostly good all around.

She's thirty-seven. Three years older than me. She's got this kind of young and old thing going on for her at the same time. I think it makes her beautiful. Not beautiful like girls in makeup commercials beautiful, but still. Beautiful in the way strangers in the frozen food aisle at the grocery store can be beautiful. She's got these real live eyes with wrinkles right around them, tiny little wrinkles like she knows more than you about something you haven't thought about yet. And she's got a nice hard stomach, even though she's had a kid. Nice legs, too. I mean, Arton's five now, but I've seen women have a kid and then just go on and become a completely different shape. Jeannie, she looks the same. Looks about like I guess she always has. I didn't know her before she had Arton, but I've seen pictures.

She's got old knees, marks on both of them from playing hard when she was a kid. She's also got a long white angry-looking scar that runs down the inside of her left knee. It's from when they had

to operate to remove pieces of her kneecap after she fell off the ladder painting the porch. We were repainting the house ourselves to
save money. I was around back on the extension ladder doing shut-
ters, and she was up front on the little A-frame ladder painting the
porch ceiling. The ladder just got out from underneath her, as near
as we can tell, and she fell straight down onto the concrete slab. I
could hear it from where it was. The fall, that is. And shit like the
paint can hitting the ground. Jeannie didn't make any noise at all.
No bawling, no out loud crying. I came running around the front
and saw her just kind of laying up against the front wall of the
house, tears sliding down her jaw. She asked little questions all the
way to the emergency room, like would she have a cast, and did I
think she was hurt badly. Once we got there the doctors gave her
something to kill the pain right away, and then she was just plain
quiet. They said she'd been lucky not to break it clean in half, lucky
that she only had a couple of pieces floating around in there. That
all happened the year right after we got married. Now she's got
that scar and knows when it'll rain.

She still wears her hair in a ponytail. It's almost black. She doesn't
dye it or anything like that. Also she'll sometimes wear it in two
braids, one on each side. She knows I like it like that. Makes my
own knees ache a little.

We're good together, but we get into it every now and then, and
one of us will leave for a couple days. Seems normal enough. I guess
we maybe need more room than we thought, more room than we
got when we decided to move into her parents' old house. It's a
fine house, an upstairs and a downstairs, a damn big porch, nothing we'd have been able to afford on our own. Her parents got
their new place and just gave it to us. So we took it. Tough thing
to turn down.

So. We fight some. She'll take off to her parents, and she'll
usually take Arton with her. Sometimes I'll duck over to Don
Peterson's or Rub Malentine's or someone else's place for a night
or so. It's good to have friends who will put you up for a day or
two if you ask. Both Don and Rub have been married once each,

so they know how it can be. I'll call Rub, for instance, and he'll have a pitcher of frozen daiquiris going in the blender before I even get there. I'll come in the front door, he'll hand me a glass. Fucking goddamn, we'll say to each other later on, sitting on his sofa, watching ball games, getting drunk.

We always end up coming back home, though, Jeannie and me.

A day after I fixed the sign, I was in the paper. Well, the sign was, anyway. WE SELL SHIT made the paper, except that they had to have the photo editor do some fancy thing so the SHIT part of it was all fuzzed over so you couldn't read it. Can't have people seeing the word *shit* in the paper. Who knows what'll happen. I sat there in that big house all by myself that morning with the hot wind blowing in through the busted-out door and I read about myself. Sort of.

Mr. Albergotteson called the "culprit" a "real bandit with no regard for safety or business." That was me, I guess, the culprit. I didn't much like the word. Or the quote. I have regard for safety, for chrissakes. I kind of liked the bandit part, though. That or "bandito" would have appealed to me. I have a thing for those movies with the cowboys from Mexico. I like the capes and the big hats and all that.

I guess now I can say it was the thing being in the paper that got me started, gave me the idea for everything else. That and Jeannie not coming home. I missed her. I had to do something to get her to come back. I really fucking missed her, missed sitting up late to watch reruns of old shows. Not that we would have been able to do that with the TV in pieces in the back yard, but you can get at what I'm saying. I missed knowing she was in the house.

So, like I say, she didn't come home the next day. I decided I had to think of something to do to get her attention. And something to keep me busy. The days got long without rows and rows of charcoal bags to straighten up. I drank a few beers that afternoon and wandered around the house until I finally hit on the idea of going out to the big Baptist church out by her folks' house to rearrange that sign, too.

They've got a big damn light-up letter sign out in the front yard of the church out there, out by the parking lot. It's so they can display their big light-up God messages. HE IS COMING. ARE YOU READY TO MEET THE LORD. JESUS: FIRST IN FLIGHT. That kind of thing. Good for a laugh on your way by in the car. The first one had made the paper, the WE SELL SHIT sign, and I figured if I could get Jeannie a message in the paper, well, that would at least be better than a card or some flowers. Plus I liked how big it all felt, the light-up messages. You just get a feeling like people are going to read them. It's not what I planned when I first did the BBQs Etcetera sign, but that's how it turned out. So I figured another one was the way to go.

I waited a day and then went out to the church that Saturday night because I thought it would be good timing to have the sign redone in time for Sunday morning services. I should mention that I was a little drunk on Deep Seas. I'd been out with Rub, who was all for going out to get lit up once he found out about Jeannie leaving. They have this little bar down on the strip that sells these frozen margarita daiquiri rum runner concoctions out of huge round tubs on the wall that make the whole place look like a Laundromat for liquor. There are about forty flavors all spinning around in separate bins up on the wall, and you can buy drinks to go in these huge Styrofoam cups, and that's what Rub Malentine and I did for the better part of a couple hours. We each had two Deep Seas, maybe three, which is more than enough for anyone. Rub is almost always good to go out drinking with. We bought our Deep Seas to go, and then walked around down by the water with them, looking at all the high school girls dressed up like they were thirty years old. Goddamned sixteen-year-old girls looking for all the world like they were some other age entirely. It's enough to make you wish you don't know how old they are. Deep Seas are called that because of what color they are, this really dark green or blue, depending on which way you look at them. I don't know what's in there. Rum and colored sweet ice, I think.

All of this is just to say that Rub and I went out drinking, walked around down by the river and watched the barges go back and forth and the girls go back and forth, and then we went back to his house and watched a little baseball. We had a beer or two, and by that time I knew the sign thing was a perfectly good idea. Eventually I left Rub's house and lined up the front left tire of the truck with the double yellow line in the road and found my way out to the church without hitting any phone poles or police cars.

I got there, to the First Tabernacle of the Holy God Savannah River Baptist Church — that is its real name, apparently, because it says so in these very careful backlit raised plastic permanent letters at the top of the sign — and their goddamned sign was locked up. You would think a church would be trusting. It wasn't that bad a deal, since it only meant I had to break the lock with a screwdriver, but still. I felt like bandits probably shouldn't have to be forced to break locks with screwdrivers. It seemed crude.

I got the sign open without too much noise. It was dark and still pretty hot out. I was sweating some. A car drove by and didn't see me. The sign said:

SUNDAY'S SERMON
"SIGNPOSTS OF DAMNATION: AN ETERNAL
INTERNAL QUESTION"

I had no idea what that meant. It hit me that this was the problem with the changeable-letter signs. Any fucking idiot in charge could make up his own. Underneath all that, in smaller letters, it said:

DRIVE OUT THE DEVIL AND PRAISE THE LORD JESUS
FRIED CHICKEN PICNIC THIS SUNDAY
MONDAY BIBLE STUDY

That's when I realized I didn't have any extra letters. It hadn't occurred to me before. Right then, standing there, looking at that damn stupid sign with the lock I'd broken, I realized I was going to have to make do with the letters that were there. And I will say that it took me a damn long time to figure out what to do. I was a little woozy, and on top of that, how in the hell are you supposed to be able to make anything out of that, a little bit drunk or not? All I wanted to write was something like JEANNIE PLEASE COME BACK HOME, but the fucking letters were all wrong. I stood there a damn long time. More cars went by and didn't see me. I played with a couple ideas, but finally I settled on this:

SUNDAY'S SERMON:
PLEASE cOME hOmE lURrleNe
lOve IS GNAts toDAy
FRIED heArt
JESUS

It was like a game. Lucky for me, the small and big letters fit on the same row. I call Jeannie Lurlene sometimes. It's a pet name from back when we were dating. I can't even remember how it got started. I figured it was better I'd had to go for Lurlene, anyway, since if I'd spelled Jeannie the cops might have been able to put two and two together. I left the rest of the letters on the ground. I'm not a thief. I stood there and looked at my work a while, and then drove back home thinking I was a romantic fucking bandit. I sat on my porch and drank a beer for celebration. I got drunk. I missed my wife. I missed her damn kid. So I'd made a grand gesture. It seemed the thing to do. After a while I went in and slept on the downstairs sofa.

Later on, they called it the second sign in the paper, but really, that one was the first. That was the first time I meant to do anything.

"Jesus Christ, Lewis," Jeannie said on the phone. It was Sunday night.

"What?"

"You're gonna get yourself arrested, is what, you dumb shit. I should turn you in myself."

"Don't turn me in," I said. "Come home."

"Shut up," she said. "My folks think you're crazy."

"I'm not."

"Are you sure?"

"Yes," I said.

"Did you get a job yet?"

"It's the weekend," I said. "It's only been two days."

"Three," she said. "Three days."

"Why won't you come back home?" I said.

"Did you fix the door?"

"No."

"So it's just standing all broken wide open?"

"Yeah," I said. "I guess so."

"Fix the door, Lewis."

"OK," I said.

"Bye," she said, and hung up.

I moved up in the world. The church sign was on the evening news. It turned out the preacher had decided to leave the sign up, and he changed his sermon on the fly to address the evils of blasphemy. They interviewed him right there on the damn news, and that's what he said. That he'd changed his sermon. He was proud of his inventiveness. You could tell. The preacher also said he did not know who Lurlene was, and that he did not want to know.

I had bought a little black and white portable TV at the grocery store to replace the nice broken one in the yard. TVs at a grocery store. Cost me seventy-nine dollars on sale. The screen was tiny, but you could make out what was going on.

The Channel 6 ActionVan news guy, or whatever it is the news is called on Channel 6, even went so far as to interview a detective. The detective stood there in his suit and talked about the WE SELL SHIT and the COME HOME LURLENE sign at the same time, and he said he thought that someone was out there redoing people's signs, and he said that churches and businesses should consider hiring security guards if they didn't already have them. He also said that they hadn't been able to get a good set of fingerprints from either crime scene, but that they were still trying. The news guy asked him if he considered the acts crimes, and the detective allowed as how he did and he said it was a form of vandalism. He said there was obscenity to consider in the case of the BBQs Etcetera sign, and there might be secret obscenities in the church sign that they didn't know about yet. He said people should just exercise caution.

I hadn't even thought about fingerprints. The next day I went out and bought a pair of gloves. The cops did not call me or come back. I guess they were looking for someone else.

I first met Jeannie at a job fair out at the community college. They put one on every six months or so, and companies set up their little booths and you fill out applications, and you can pretty much choose a job if they're hiring and if they like you. We were both standing in line at some food service company and the girl they'd hired was doing presentations in groups, so we had to wait a damn long time. The girl called the next fifteen people in line for another presentation, and I was going to have to wait again, and I was cussing under my breath or something like that, and it made the woman in front of me laugh. That was Jeannie. She said she hated lines, too. She asked me if I wanted to go for nachos instead of waiting in line for a job neither of us really wanted. I'd never been asked out by a stranger before. So I said yes, and that's how it started.

We ended up at some fancy place neither of us could really afford, the kind of place that has blue and red chips along with the regular corn-colored ones, and neither of us cared for that too much. We also both wanted to order extra jalapeños. So we just sort of knew.

We dated a while, and I liked her. I started to like her kid, too. Arton. He was from her previous husband, a guy who had gone off to Alaska to work the fishing boats. He told her the heat didn't agree with him, and neither did being a daddy. Truth be known, I'm still a little unclear about the daddy part myself, but they're a package deal, so that's how it goes. I like Arton well enough, anyway. I've taught the kid to holler Touchdown! whenever Clemson scores. Or whoever we're cheering for that night. He asks me what color is good and what color is bad, and I tell him.

Jeannie was the first woman I ever knew who liked her steaks cooked the same way I did.

I did another sign. This was my plan: If I got on the news again, Jeannie would see the sign and she would decide to come back home because of the grand gestures and because I loved her enough to do all that. She likes all that romantic shit. It seemed like I should go a little bigger, so I did. I picked out a big sign marquee across a bookstore downtown.

I drove by Monday afternoon and scoped it out. It was up high, so I'd have to use a ladder. I was afraid you'd be able to see a ladder pretty easily, so I also planned to shoot out the street-light with my pellet gun. I wrote down what the sign said so I could plan what to do before I got there. I wanted the actual doing the sign part of things to go as fast as possible. I was learning. Getting better.

The sign said:

OUTSIDE OF A DOG A BOOK IS A MAN'S BEST FRIEND.
INSIDE OF A DOG IT IS TOO DARK TO READ. — GROUCHO MARX

Bookstore humor. Funny, I guess. The sign also said:

NOW SELLING NEW AND USED BOOKS

I took that home and planned everything out. Then later that night, I drove on back downtown, shot out the streetlight, set up the ladder and went to work. Everything was going perfectly. I felt like Colombo, but for criminals. I wore my gloves. I wrote:

LURLENE I'D SING NINE GOATS FOR WEEKS
MAKE MAN SAD KISS NOW

I was pretty proud of that for what I had to work with. I was leaving the rest of the letters in a little pile by the door and feeling proud and happy and thinking about a beer when this older guy came out of the store with a nightstick in his hand and a cheap plastic security guard uniform and started yelling at me. He wanted to know what I thought I was doing there. Said he'd called the police. I didn't really feel like giving him the whole answer, and I didn't know what else to do, and I guess I panicked a little, but I hit him with the ladder. I just swung it around and hit him in the head, and it layed him out flat on his back on the sidewalk. It happened in kind of a hurry. I looked at him a minute, and then I ran back to the truck and took off. I didn't know what to do. Fucking Christ, I thought, Fucking Christ. I didn't mean to do that. I thought that all the way home.

I got home and sat in the den a long time. Then I washed the dishes. I thought about calling Rub, seeing if he wanted to go out, but I didn't. Instead I just sat in the house. Drank can beers and stacked the cans up on each other. It didn't seem like there was much else I could do.

"Now you're mugging old people?" she asked me on the phone.
"What?"
"Did you hit that old man?"
"What old man?"
"They had to take him to the hospital, you know."
"Is he OK?" I asked.
"The paper says he is."
"He's fine?"
"They said he had a concussion. Read about it yourself. Your crazy shit is all over the paper. They said serial vandalizing. You're a serial vandal."
"I'm not a vandal."
"They say you are."
"I miss you."
"Shut up."
"I fixed the door," I said, even though it was a lie. In fact, I'd added a cat to the house. It had come in through the door, and now it was living in a closet.

"Even Arton knows about the signs. He's reading better every day, by the way. Whatever they do for him at kindergarten works. He wants to know why it's bad that people change the signs."

"It isn't bad."

"You hit a man, Lewis."

"Only because he'd called the police. I had to get away. I didn't hit him that hard."

"They're gonna put you in jail."

"They're not going to put me in jail."

"They might."

"I wear gloves."

"Why?"

"For the fingerprints."

"Oh." She was quiet a minute. "The paper says you hit him with a blunt instrument."

"It was a ladder."

"A ladder, Lewis? You hit that poor man with a ladder?"

"It was all I had," I said.

"I'm not coming home," she said.

"You have to," I said. "I love you."

"I'm not coming home with you like this," she said. "Did you get a job?"

"I've been busy," I said.

"Ask me how Arton is."

"How's Arton?"

"Well, his cut's not infected, if that's what you mean."

"Good," I said.

"Lewis?"

"Yes."

"What does 'love is gnats today' mean?"

"I don't know."

"What does 'sing nine goats' mean?"

"I don't know."

"If you're going to be running around like some deranged lunatic making messages on other people's signs, don't you think they should probably make sense?"

"I don't know."

"Mom says I should leave you. She says this should be my last straw. She says you're imbalanced."

"I'm not imbalanced."

"She says you'll never keep a job."

"I'll keep a job."

"That's what you said about the office thing. And the barbecue place."

"That was a crappy job. They both were."

"But it was a job, at least, right, Lewis?"

"I guess so."

"Are you eating OK?"

I'd had ravioli out of a can three nights in a row. "Yes."

"Goddamnit, Lewis, get a job. I'm hanging up now."

"I love you," I said.

"I know it," she said.

The longest Jeannie'd ever been gone before was a few days. It had been a week this time. I called over there the next day to talk, but I got her mother. She wouldn't let me talk to Jeannie. She said I should get help. I wanted to tell her to fuck the hell off, but I held back.

I fixed the door with a piece of plywood I bought at the hardware store. There was a HELP WANTED sign in the window, so while I was there I filled out an application. I was pretty sure it was fucked from the start, though, because on the part where they want you to list applicable skills, I wrote, "I know what nails are." So I figured I wouldn't get the job. Fucking forms. I mean, just interview me and see if I know how to stand up and point to lightbulbs and bolts. Find out if I can work in a goddamned hardware store. You don't need me writing things down.

Jeannie didn't call for two days in a row. I hung out afternoons down at Spoon's with Rub, shooting pool.

"It sucks," Rub said.

"Yeah," I said.

"She'll be back," Rub said.

"Yeah," I said.

"She'll get hungry for some dick," Rub said.

I told him if he talked like that about Jeannie much more I'd jam the cue up his ass thick end first. He said he was sorry. I didn't care if I believed him or not. We drank bad beer out of pitchers that didn't keep it nearly cold enough. I didn't tell him I was the one doing the signs.

I did one sign a night for four nights in a row. I admit the whole thing was getting a little out of hand. The whole thing was.

At the Gas n' Gulp I changed GAL. MILK HOT COFFEE OIL CHANGE CAR WASH to HI LRLN CHAFE ME WAIT GAL. I was proud of that one. I put the extra letters in through the mail slot in the door of the convenience store. That was the fourth one. It made the front page. The headline said "Guerrilla Poet Strikes Again." The sheriff said he was thinking about calling in the state police. Said it was a crime wave.

I am no kind of poet. This is for sure. Even though the paper said I was, I'm not. I don't know anything about poets. The paper said I was a poet because the signs had hidden meanings. It's not like I know anything fancy. I just made words out of what letters were there.

I did another church. The Methodist one out by the highway. Their sign said:

> THE LORD IS MY SHEPHERD, I SHALL NOT WANT.
> THE REV. SUSAN BRYNN MADDEN

My version:

> DAMNIT LURLY
> I NEED TREES
> WHY MAN LOST

I thought that was pretty damn good for what I had to work with. This shit is not easy, by the way. You're in a hurry and it's like the goddamned Jumble from the newspaper and you think every car is a cop.

The paper said the police suspected a Pagan group or maybe a Satanic cult. People wrote in letters to the paper that said whoever was doing it should burn in hell. "Church signs should be left alone," one letter said. "Whoever is doing this should burn in hell." I wanted to write my own letter back suggesting a few things he could do with his time instead of writing letters about me, but I didn't.

At 3:30 in the morning I hooked up one of those trailer signs out front of a furniture store to the back of the truck and drove it around back of the building. It said:

COUCHES
LOWEST PRICES IN TOWN

I spent some time on that one. I changed it and towed it back to its spot:

OUCH L SINEWS TOES

By then the paper had really gotten into the whole thing. Not a whole hell of a lot ever goes on around here, so the paper is all the time things like school board decisions. They were probably just excited for the change. They interviewed professors from Valdosta State and from Savannah State. One of them said the signs sounded like an "intimately realized poetic cry." That's what she said. I liked her. The other one called the signs "juvenile crap."

The last one I did was at Jimmy Carter High. The sign had said:

PTA MEETING THURSDAY
COUNTY TRACK MEET AT BURLSIDE MON.
GO LIONS GO

I at least know what I put on there was better than that. I put:

LENE I NEED YOUR MOLARS
BURNT PASTA
GOING DIE

"What the hell does that mean? Going die?"

"I ran out of letters. I wanted to write more about the pasta."

"I'm going to turn you in. I should divorce you and turn you in."

"Why?"

"Because you're insane, that's why," she said. "This is too much, Lewis. All this shit has to stop."

"Why?"

"For one thing, they'll catch you. Also it's stupid."

"It's not stupid."

"You'll be in jail."

"It was the pasta you like. With the cherry tomatoes from the yard."

"How the hell did you burn pasta?"

"I put in the skillet to get the tomatoes and the oil all through it, and then I got caught up watching the ballgame, and the oil just sort of caught on fire."

"Jesus, Lewis."

"Come back home, Jeannie. I got rid of the cat."

"What cat?"

"The cat that came in while the door was broken. I gave it to some girl down the street." I had decided not to keep it when it shat on the counter.

"Your security guard is OK," she said.

"How do you know?"

"I saw it on the news."

"Good."

"You haven't done anything else, have you? You haven't hit anyone else?"

"No."

"They're calling you a poet."

"Yeah. I'm not."

"They're saying you are."

"I'm thinking about going in with Rub, building a few decks," I said.

"What?"

"We've been talking about it. People pay like three thousand dollars for a deck. More."

"You've been talking about that?"

"Some," I said. We'd talked about it at the pool hall, we'd talked about it riding around some. It seemed like it could happen.

"You and Rub," she said.

"Yeah. He's got the tools and everything, and I've got a few tools myself, and he says he's maybe got enough money to get us started. Maybe print up some flyers and tape them to mailboxes."

"You think someone would hire the two of you to do something to their house?"

"I can fucking build a deck, can't I?"

"You know they're running a contest on Z-97 to find Lurlene," she said.

"Yeah?"

"I'm thinking I might go win that. It's a trip to Jamaica, I think."

"Don't do that."

"I think I just might go down there and say I know who she is. They'll put me on the radio."

"Don't."

"I think I'd like it if I was on the radio."

"Don't."

"I'm just saying I'm thinking about it, is all."

"Well," I said.

"You're really gonna build decks?"

"I said we were, didn't I?"

"I'm not coming home tonight," she said.

"Why not?"

"We're going to the movies. Me and Mom and Arton."

"Are you coming home soon?"

"You fixed the door?"

"I told you yes."

"Maybe we could buy a new TV," she said.

"Maybe," I said.

"One of those flat ones. If you and Rub really got going, we could buy one of those flat ones."

"Maybe," I said.

"Yeah," she said.

"I love you," I said.

"Goddamnit, Lewis."

"Call me when you get back from the movies."

"Maybe," she said.

"OK," I said, and hung up.

The hardware store never called. I can't say as I'm all that surprised. I would have ended up dropping an ax on some old lady's fucking foot, or putting the hex bolts in with the whatever else kind of bolts, and gotten into it with the manager, who would have been some pimple-faced kid and that would have been it anyway. So it's just as well.

I stopped doing the signs. Just like that. No big last gasp, no getting caught by the police, nothing. I just stopped. The BURNT MOLARS/GOING DIE was my last one. Plus it worked, anyway. Jeannie says she's coming home this week. The sign on the hardware store says NAILS BY THE POUND, SPECIAL ON PAINT. Maybe I would have liked it there. That's pretty simple, after all. The sign at BBQs Etcetera says GET FIRED UP. Idiots.

The newspaper can't quite let the whole thing go. In the local section every other day or so there's an update on where the police are in terms of finding the "Haiku Bandit." That's what they're calling me. I kind of like the name, but I don't really read the stories anymore. I'm a little bored of all of it.

Rub says he's got a big job lined up for us for next month, a big two-level deck with a hot tub. Says we might clear two grand each. I figure I can pay some bills and save up for Jeannie's TV. For now the little black and white one will have to do, I guess.

We were talking about the job the other night playing some pool. Rub wanted to know when the last time I built a deck was.

I told him a few years. I also told him he had better good and god-damned understand that I knew what I was doing and that we should have that straight right off the top. I told him I wouldn't need him on me all the time telling me what to do, telling me how to drive a nail or cut a fucking board. He said that was fine by him and we drank a few beers and kept right on shooting.

Jeannie says Arton got his stitches out. She says he won't have a scar. I was a little sad about that. A kid should have a scar, I say. It's good to have a little gash or something for when you're at the lunch table. So you can show off. "That's nothing," you can say. "Look at this fucker."

I don't know how much to say about all of it. Jeannie comes home soon. It's still hot as all hell and the paper says it's going to be that way a while. I've got the house pretty well cleaned up. I ordered a new door from some building supplier out by the interstate, and when that comes in, we'll take the plywood down. We're good together, me and Jeannie, I guess. We've got it figured out well enough.

I got fired from BBQs Etcetera two weeks ago. I did the signs, and then I stopped. Now I'm going to be building decks. That ought to last me a while.

Drew Perry's fiction has appeared in several magazines and journals, including *Alaska Quarterly Review, Black Warrior Review,* the *Nebraska Review,* and *South Carolina Review.* A graduate of the MFA program at UNC–Greensboro, he lives in Greensboro, North Carolina, with a half-wild pound dog and teaches in the undergraduate creative writing program at Elon University. He is at work on a novel, a collection of stories, and a semi-renovation of a very plain ranch house.

TITA RAMIREZ

I've long been very deeply in love with the fire-and-brimstone church signs so prevalent throughout the South—the ones that demand repentance or prayer or cash money, the ones advertising for a certain brand of Jesus—and I guess that part of this story had always been sort of rattling around in the spare room in my head. So when, one night in Atlanta, while visiting my family, we passed a barbeque supply store with a sign that had been changed along the lines of the one in the story, I figured I had something. I guess I should also say here that I'm the sort of person who reports to his friends egregious grammatical errors and misplaced possessives on gas station signs and volunteer fire department signs and the like. CHANGE YOU'RE SMOKE ALARM BATTERIES. That sort of thing.

I'm drawn to characters like Lewis. I'm interested in people who almost mean well, sort of. He tries hard in a lot of ways. Once I got his voice down, that was basically it—from there I just had to try to find out who he was married to, and why she'd be willing to stick around (or if she would). He really loves Jeannie. Past that, I'm not convinced he knows much of anything else for sure.

Michael Knight

FEELING LUCKY

(from *The Virginia Quarterly Review*)

Midnight, and Bruce Little was hunched against a pay phone under the awning of the Saint John Divine Hotel, shivering with cold and dialing collect to Mississippi. He called twice. No answer either time. This was February. This was Richmond. His daughter, Jane, was in the room asleep. His ex-wife, Barbara, was in Teaneck, New Jersey, with her new husband, worrying, he supposed, about Jane and hoping for good news from the police. He'd put eleven hours of road between them. Before that, he'd waited behind the hedge until they came out to build a snowman, then plucked Jane over the back fence when Barbara went inside to use the can. Now, he was impatient with fatigue. He counted the money in his wallet—nine one-dollar bills. He forced himself to smoke a cigarette to the filter before he dialed again. The operator cut in when the answering machine picked up.

The Saint John Divine was four stories, brownstone, maybe three dozen rooms. In another life, it had probably been a decent place, with a bellman in livery and an elevator boy, but now the old Otis was shot and the only other guests Bruce had seen were a pair of tipsy fags sneaking a white cat into their room. Bruce had a soft spot for places like this—local, half-dead, unashamed. He'd spent his share of nights in hotels since his divorce. This one, he'd found by accident. He was low on gas and he left the interstate at random, got snagged in a web of one-way streets. He had wanted to cover more ground, but Jane was fading fast and there was the hotel. Across the street was a church with the same name. He would ask directions back to the interstate in the morning. First, he needed Melinda to answer the phone. Melinda could wire him a little money. Nine dollars wouldn't get him home.

Bruce glared at the phone for a moment, like it was part of a conspiracy to prevent him from completing his call, then headed for the desk to make change. The night manager was perched on a stool behind the counter, watching a TV mounted eight feet above the floor. She was an older woman, pushing seventy, he thought, dyed-black hair in a bouffant cloud around her head. A metal screen separated her station from the lobby proper—matching chair and love seat, both done in plastic, and a coffee table littered with movie magazines. Bruce fingered three singles from his wallet, passed them through the screen. The night manager cashed them in, but didn't hand his quarters over right away.

"Is there something wrong with the phone in your room?" she said.

"Not that I'm aware of," Bruce said.

"If there's something wrong, you should let me know," she said.

"There's nothing wrong," he said.

"Because," she said, "how'm I gonna fix it if I don't know it's broke?"

"It's not broken," he said. "It's just my little girl isn't feeling very well. I didn't want to wake her up." This was true. Jane had started wilting halfway across Pennsylvania. By the time they hit Virginia, she was drifting in and out of sleep, her head wobbling on her neck, stirring just long enough to complain about how she felt— her stomach hurt, it was too cold in his car.

The night manager tipped her chin up, eyed him down the length of her nose, then rattled his change across the counter and returned her attention to the television. Bruce waded back into the cold. He slicked the quarters into the phone and dialed direct. When the machine answered, he said, "Hey, it's me." He let a few seconds of tape spool out. "I've got Jane with me and we've made it to Virginia." He paused, his breath misting on the air. "I told her all about you," he said. This was not true. He'd been afraid to mention Melinda to his daughter. "We're low on funds. I need you to Western Union us some cash, not too much, maybe a hundred bucks or so or whatever you can spare." He paused again, licked his lips. "Jane can't wait to meet you," he said. "The number at the hotel is—" His skin went prickly all over. "Well, shit," he said. He left the receiver dangling and hustled back to the office.

"What's the number here?" Bruce said.

He propped the door with his shoulder. A white cat darted outside between his legs. Without looking away from the TV, the night manager said, "You're letting the heat out."

Bruce stepped inside. The door inched shut on its hydraulic arm. The night manager laughed at something on TV.

"I need that number," Bruce said.

She held up her hand for quiet, waited a second for the commercial. Then, in a singsong voice, she recited the number and Bruce dashed back to the phone. The line was dead when he arrived. He pounded the receiver hard against the keypad until he felt his frustration waning. He hung up, rubbed his face with both hands. His breath came in ragged gasps. He repeated his daughter's name in his head—Jane, Jane, Jane, Jane—until he felt sufficiently composed. Then he walked back to the office, made certain the door was closed behind him, laid three bills on the desk and asked politely for more change.

The night manager sighed. "You have a perfectly good phone in your room," she said. "You stood there and told me so yourself. If you want to call long distance, all we ask is that you leave a ten-dollar deposit."

Bruce smiled and pushed his hands into his pockets and tried to look like somebody's father. "Please," he said. "My little girl."

"What if those nice young men in 9 were to come around hunting money for the snack machine, and I'd given you all my change? How would that be? I'm not made of quarters.

"This is the last time," Bruce said.

The old woman pursed her lips and shook her head. The screen made a net of shadows on her face. Bruce worried that she might refuse him, but, after a moment, she levered the register open, dredged up a handful of quarters and counted them one by one into his palm. When he reached the phone, Bruce pinned the receiver between his shoulder and his ear, pushed all twelve coins into the slot. To his surprise, Melinda answered on the second ring. "Thank God," he said, his legs going flimsy with relief. "I've called a hundred times. Where you been?"

In a quiet voice, Melinda said, "Here."

Bruce took a moment to digest her answer.

"There?" he said.

"I'm sorry," Melinda said.

"I don't get it," he said.

"This is a bad idea," she said. "I mean—we hardly know each other, Bruce. I can't mother somebody else's little girl."

"We talked about it," he said. "You were excited."

"Now I've had a chance to think," Melinda said.

"Melinda," Bruce said. "Don't—"

"I'm sorry," Melinda said again. "I'm hanging up."

Then she did hang up and Bruce listened to the dial tone for a minute before placing the receiver in its cradle. Sixteen dimes dropped into the coin return. The cold seeped into his bones. Bruce slouched off to check on Jane. He refused to look at the night manager as he passed, but he did stop at the snack machine to blow seven of his dimes on a cheese Danish wrapped in plastic.

Jane was sprawled atop the blankets when Bruce returned, all awkward knees and elbows, as if she had fallen into bed from a tremendous height. She was four years old. She was wearing red corduroy overalls, a white turtleneck and a blue quilted jacket. She was wearing sneakers and frilly socks. Until that morning, Bruce had never seen these clothes before. He cupped his hands and breathed into them to take the chill off. He palmed her brow. She was warm, a little clammy. She did not register his touch. Bruce tiptoed past and arranged himself on the second bed. He kicked his boots off and massaged the cold out of his feet. He emptied his pockets. Wallet, car keys, dimes. He had five cigarettes left in his pack. He had a small duffel in the bathroom. In it was a change of underwear, a pair of socks, a toothbrush, an electric razor, a stick of deodorant and an unloaded .38 revolver. He thought he could convince Melinda to change her mind, but, if worst absolutely came to worst, he would find a pawn shop in the morning and sell the gun.

Bruce took off his jacket and propped his back against the headboard and watched ESPN with the sound off for a while. He ate the Danish. It tasted like newspaper. He eyed his daughter. She looked exactly like her mother. After a few minutes, he got up and went into the bathroom to smoke a cigarette. He didn't like to smoke around Jane. There was a louvered window in the shower and he cranked it open and wedged a towel under the door to block the draft. The window overlooked the Dumpsters in the alley behind the motel. He saw the white cat nosing around back there. He clucked his tongue and the cat looked at him like it had seen everything in the world. A man smoking in the john was nothing special.

He closed his eyes and tried to remember how it had been with Jane before his marriage ended, before Barbara met another man, before the judge let Barbara and her new husband take Jane up to New Jersey. He hadn't seen Jane in sixteen months and he wondered what she remembered, too, wondered how Barbara had portrayed him. He doubted he came off too well. Then he tried to figure what had spooked Melinda. He blamed her change of heart on a lack of imagination. He'd been gone a week and she needed him around to paint the picture, to hold her in his arms and whisper the future in her ear. Bruce opened his eyes. The cat was gone. He dragged on his cigarette, exhaled out the window. He couldn't tell where the smoke ended and his breath began.

When he was finished, Bruce flushed the cigarette and stood in the doorway watching his daughter sleep, her lips parted, her chest rising and falling in slow motion. He thought maybe he should get her out of those clothes and under the covers. There hadn't been time to pack a bag and he wasn't sure which was better—undressed, no nightgown or fully-clothed in bed. He tried to think what he might have done when he was still in practice. He decided to split the difference. He would take off her shoes and her jacket and her overalls but leave the turtleneck and socks. He crouched at the foot of her bed, unlaced her right shoe. As he was slipping it over her heel, Jane blinked and stretched her arms over her head.

"Daddy?" she said.

She gazed at Bruce, then at the shoe in his hand. He felt like he'd been caught in the act of stealing it from her.

"It's me," he said. "Remember, baby?"

He got her out of her shoes and took the jacket off and unfastened the overalls and pulled them over her legs. Jane let him do with her as he pleased. He scooped her up, his forearm beneath her thighs, and she hooked her feet behind his back. With his free hand, he turned the blankets down. Jane hid her face against his neck.

"I'm cold," she said. "Let's go to Mamma's house."

"I'll tell you what. We'll go to Mississippi instead. It never gets cold in Mississippi."

As he was getting her situated in bed, fluffing her pillow, organizing the blanket beneath her chin, she reached up and touched his cheek, an affectionate gesture, like he had said or done something to deserve it. She ran her finger over his lips, his eyebrow, the bridge of his nose.

"Will Mamma be in Miss-ssippi?" she said.

"You never know about your mamma," he said. "Your mamma's hard to read. You never know where your mamma might turn up."

But Jane had already drifted back to sleep. Bruce could hear a faint, congested burble in her lungs. He tucked the covers in around her, then walked over and checked the heating unit, passed his hand over the vent. He thought maybe Jane was right. The room was too cold for little girls. He could feel lukewarm air breathing out against his palm. He tried to turn it up, but the knob had been removed. He covered Jane's brow with one hand, his brow with the other. He wondered what, if any, restorative measures he should take. The only thing that occurred to him was aspirin, but he didn't have aspirin or know where to buy aspirin at one o'clock in the morning in an unfamiliar city or have enough money to buy aspirin with if he had known where to find it. He wasn't even sure if aspirin was safe for little girls.

"Jane," he said. "Jane, baby."

She lifted up on her elbows, her eyes groggy and uncertain, and, immediately, Bruce regretted waking her. Probably, all she needed was a little rest and here he was keeping her from it to ease his own concerns.

"Daddy?" she said.

"It's me," he said. "I'm sorry, sweetie. Go on back to sleep."

He held her shoulders and she let him push her back against the pillow. He stroked her hair for a minute. Then he said, "I'm sorry, baby, but, listen, while you're up, how 'bout tell me how you feel?"

"I'm cold," she said.

"Do you feel sick?" he said. "Do you feel like you have a fever?"

"It's cold in here," she said.

Jane curled herself into a fetal ball, her knees drawn up, her fists beneath her chin. Bruce pulled the covers to her neck. He didn't know exactly how to read her answer. It might mean chills, but it might not mean a thing. She had, after all, complained about the temperature before. He didn't want to give in to paranoia. He hadn't been responsible for anybody in a long time and he recognized the possibility that he was overreacting. It was true that Jane was warm to touch, but there was nothing so warm as a sleeping child. He remembered that. He sat on the edge of the bed and searched her face. She had changed immeasurably since he had seen her last. She was taller and she had gained some weight, of course, and her hair was cut in a style suitable for little girls, but there was something else, something that he couldn't put his finger on, as if all the things that she had seen in his absence and all the things she had come to know were apparent in her features.

When he was sure Jane was sleeping soundly, Bruce jotted the Saint John Divine's phone number on the back of his hand, filled his pocket with the leftover dimes and walked outside to have another go at Melinda. The night manager didn't look away from the TV. It had started snowing while he was in the room. The flakes darted in the wind like schools of fish. He called collect, but Melinda didn't answer. Then he decided that collect was probably a bad idea—he needed to impress Melinda with his seriousness in this matter, with his paternal self-reliance—so he punched his last nine dimes into the slot. It rang twice before the operator interrupted to let him know he needed thirty-five cents to complete the call. Bruce hung up, listened to the rattle of his change. There were three quarters in the dispenser. He did the math, jiggled the tongue, no response. He stood there for a moment, the coins winking in his palm, his heart flopping in his chest, before starting for the office. He found the night manager exactly as he'd left her.

"I can't spare anymore change," she said at his approach.

"That's what I want to talk about," Bruce said. "Your pay phone took my money."

She shook her head. "That's not my problem. The phone is owned by an independent contractor."

"It's on the side of your hotel," he said.

"You have to write a letter," she said. "That's how they do the refunds. The address is on the phone."

"I don't have time for that," he said. "I need to make this call tonight."

She arched her eyebrows and drummed her fingers on the counter.

"Is there a phone in your room?"

She looked at him a moment longer, then swung her eyes back to the TV. Bruce was determined not to be bullied. It was important, he thought, to raise a protest of some kind.

"The heater," he said. "It's freezing in our room and my little girl is sick. The knob is broken on the heating unit."

The night manager said, "We keep the wall units at sixty-eight degrees. The policy was spelled out on your registration form."

Bruce opened his mouth, but closed it without speaking. His muscles shook beneath his skin. He smacked the wire screen with the heel of his hand and the night manager flinched, then composed herself and settled her eyes on him again. In a steady voice, she said, "You don't want me to get the police." She reached for her phone and held the receiver up. The dial tone bleated at him like a taunt.

"Do you have kids?" he said, but the night manager didn't answer. She propped her feet on the counter and cradled the phone against her breast. A laughtrack spilled from the TV.

Bruce walked outside without another word. He needed a minute to collect himself. He didn't want Jane to see him in this condition. Saint John's was dark, regal in its silence. It wasn't an unappealing scene if you took the time to look around. Everything was quiet and the snow sparkled like the world was made of broken glass.

Just then, a man wearing a kimono over his clothes turned the corner and headed up the sidewalk in Bruce's direction. He made kissing noises as he walked. He smiled at Bruce and rubbed his arms and did a friendly shiver. Bruce nodded in reply.

"Have you by any chance seen a cat out here?" the man said. "A white cat. Fu Manchu whiskers." He drew imaginary whiskers in the air around his mouth.

"I saw him in the alley," Bruce said.

The man made a sad face. "I just came from there," he said. He covered his brow with his right hand. "I told Jerry we should have left him in the car. He would've been fine in the car, don't you think? Jerry said it was too cold, but look what's happened now."

"I'm sorry," Bruce said.

The man gave Bruce a meaningful shrug and shuffled down the sidewalk. Bruce thought of Jane sleeping in the room. He felt suddenly alive and sure of himself, as if, after years of rotten luck, he had only to wait a short while longer before fortune smiled on him again. He hurried back inside and down the hall and worked his key into the lock. He opened the door to find his daughter's bed abandoned. He cast his gaze around the room in disbelief. His bed, her bed. The muted television. Her clothes still draped over a chair. The pillow held the imprint of her face. The toilet flushed and Jane emerged from the bathroom, looking pallid and exhausted.

"Dammit, Jane," he blurted. "You scared me half to death."

"I got sick," she said. "I'm sorry. I didn't mean—"

Her face contorted and she dissolved into blubbering. Bruce was disgusted with himself. He rushed over and picked her up and clutched her against his chest. Her body bucked with sobs.

"It's all right, Jane baby. Daddy didn't mean to yell."

He carried her into the bathroom, surveyed the toilet. There were traces of vomit on the rim. The air smelled like spoiled milk. He shut the door, walked her in a circle, bouncing her lightly in his arms.

"I'm sorry, sweetie," he said. "You didn't do anything wrong. You did good. You made it to the bathroom and everything. Half the time, when Daddy's sick, he winds up hosing down the room."

"Mamma takes me to the potty when I'm sick," she said.

"Your mamma's an old pro," he said. "The potty is the place to be."

Jane was calming some. Bruce could feel her breath against his throat, the heat of her skin against his chest.

"Do you feel better?" he said.

Jane wagged her head. He couldn't tell if that meant yes or no. He carried her to the bed and laid her down.

"What else does Mamma do when you get sick?" he said.

Jane said, "I can't remember what she does."

'That's all right," he said. "We'll get it sorted out."

He ducked into the bathroom and returned with a wet rag. He wiped her face and neck and around her ears.

"How's that?" he said. "Is that good? Is that something Mamma would do?"

Jane nodded and sniffled.

"It'll be all right," Bruce said.

He waited until she was asleep before he crept into the bathroom for a smoke. He opened the window and gazed out at the night. While he watched, the white cat appeared from nowhere, leapt onto a stack of flattened cardboard boxes and peered in his direction. It looked bored and wise and indifferent to the snow. He thought of the women in his life—Barbara in New Jersey and Melinda in Mississippi and his daughter in the next room. They had loved him for a while. One day, he imagined, when the police had caught up to him and Jane had been returned safely to her mother, she might remember this night fondly, might at least look back with a measure of affection on the lengths to which her father had gone for their reunion. It wasn't impossible. He had heard of stranger things. Bruce fished the gun out of his duffel. He wanted to go another round with that night manager, revisit the issue of the phone. He didn't have any bullets, but he was feeling lucky just the same.

Michael Knight is the author of a novel, *Divining Rod*, and two collections of short fiction, *Dogfight and Other Stories* and *Goodnight, Nobody*. His stories have appeared in *Esquire*, the *New Yorker, Paris Review*, and other places, including *New Stories from the South: The Year's Best, 1999* and *2003*. He lives in Knoxville, where he teaches creative writing at the University of Tennessee.

MARY BARNETT

From the get-go, I liked the basic premise here and the father/daughter relationship but this one didn't work until I wrote the scene with Bruce and the gay guy who's out in the snow looking for his cat. It's insignificant on its face, sort of peripheral, and I orginally put it in for pacing, but it makes the story bigger somehow. I think. I hope.

Elizabeth Seydel Morgan

SATURDAY AFTERNOON IN THE HOLOCAUST MUSEUM

(from *The Southern Review*)

I guess we're not going to talk about it?"

He poked his fried egg with his fork. "Tonight?"

She looked at her own plate. Almost empty. A scrap of sausage, a piece of biscuit. She wondered how she could have eaten at all — much less everything. She remembered a time twenty years ago she'd sat across from him in a booth like this and sneaked food off her plate into her napkin to hide the fact she couldn't eat at all. That was love.

This was worse.

And yet she could eat. The whole Number 4. She nodded. "Whatever you—?"

"I want to, just not now. OK?"

"Sure."

"There's not a whole lot more than I told you on the phone. The bone scan's Wednesday."

"Yeah. Well."

She forced the last of the dry biscuit down her throat with the cooled coffee. She misjudged the thick rim of the mug, dribbled drops of coffee down her chin. She wiped it with her napkin.

"Always a mess," she said with a small laugh. "Bad cup-lip co-ordination."

"Always has been."

"No, no. There was a long time. The time we weren't together? I was noted for my agility."

"Agile and coordinated."

"Graceful and dexterous."

"You were a juggler."

"All those years. In my late forties, I was a dancer."

"Oh, so only when I'm in your life . . ."

"And a tennis player. . ."

"I remember that part. You were playing a little tennis when we broke up. I think—"

"I started juggling right after that . . . but my partner dropped all the balls . . ."

They were good at banter. They smiled at each other, almost exactly like genuine smiling.

When they walked to the cashier, she felt heavy, each thing she'd eaten a separate weight, distinct masses under her breast.

He paid and went to the rest room. A woman was mopping the floor where they'd been sitting. Another woman was spraying and swiping the tables. The air was disinfectant. She realized there was no one else in the diner. It was odd. It had been full of people when they were ordering their brunch. She remembered the Asian family across from them. She'd seen black couples as they'd walked to the empty booth. Their waitress was a pale, gap-toothed country girl. He'd liked that, the mix of people. He tried to find places to eat in the South like this diner, or ethnic restaurants like the ones he took her to around Boston. He'd introduced her to places she'd never been in her own hometown.

"Are you closing?" she asked the lady with big hair who was clearing the cash register.

The lady looked at her with a scowl, but then gave her a big, lip-sticky smile. "Winter? We close at two on Saturdays."

When she mentioned it to him, walking to the car, he said it was a law.

"Huh? What are you talking about?" She couldn't remember what she'd just told him.

"The law—closing at two on Saturdays."

"What law?"

"In Virginia you can only have public diversity half a day."

"Oh, James," she said with a quick laugh, pulling up the hood of her jacket. Usually she would have played the game with him, batting something back like "Only Confederates in the afternoon," but today she couldn't think.

He took the wheel of her car. She shivered, turned the heat blower to high even though its air was still cold. They were going to Old Dominion Camera Store for something he needed for his camera. It was the last of the serious camera stores in Richmond, down to half its size since one-hour development. He was an amateur photographer who loved black-and-white pictures—gritty, disturbing urban pictures, natural light. He loved the work of . . . of somebody else she couldn't remember. He'd taken her to the man's show in Boston; he'd given her the catalog. She knew nothing about the subject. She hated some of the pictures and their invasion of people's lives. She thought of being poor, or sick, or in emotional chaos—and having some stranger stick a camera in your face.

Though she was a visual artist, photography was not an interest they had in common—books were. They loaded each other with books, book reviews, book news. He seemed to read everything in the media on literary matters and e-mailed her copies he thought she'd like. He watched C-SPAN2 and taped it in case she was watching *The Simpsons;* she called him Alan Bookspan.

Now she was forcing herself to do it, but it was natural for her to bring up a book.

"So I finished *Sophie's Choice.*"

"After twenty years?"

"Oh, James," she said. "For the thing honoring Styron at—"

"What'd you think?"

"I don't know," she said.

"That's all?"

"Yeah. Oh, turn here. Roseneath will get us to Carytown."

The camera store was in Carytown, an old part of Richmond. It was closed. Closed at one o'clock on Saturdays, said the sign on the door. They got back in her car. He didn't make a joke about Saturday closings down South, but she knew he was thinking it.

"Where now?" he said.

She tried to think of something to do. If only it wasn't so cold—the park near here would be beige and leafless, a cutting wind off Byrd Lake. And James didn't like to walk so much as he used to. Both secondhand bookstores would be closed by the time they got across town. What she'd really like to do is go sit in a dark bar like old times, before he quit. Drink and talk, in the dark.

"A movie?" she asked.

"I don't think so . . ." He turned to her for the first time today. He didn't start the engine. Then he spoke gravely: "Do you think anyone survived the Holocaust?"

"What?" She was confused. What had they been talking about that prompted this? "What do you mean?"

"I think . . . I don't know. I don't know what I mean."

"You don't know? I've never known you not to . . ."

"To what?"

"Have an opinion?"

"You've never known me not to have . . . an opinion?"

"Well, about books, politics . . . stuff . . ."

"You haven't really known me—yet," he said, starting the car.

She looked at him, shocked. But his tone of voice, his face in profile, was genial. It was no accusation. It was his calm statement of fact. She knew it was true—there'd been too much time between their young love and their reunion. The move to Boston, AA.

She waited. But now he turned away to back out of the parking space and didn't continue. She was not used to his silence.

She glanced at the clock on the dashboard. The afternoon had hours left in it, hours before tonight when he said they'd talk.

"There's a Holocaust museum here in Richmond."

For the first time since he flew in last night, she thought, he was paying attention. He came to a full stop in the alley.

"Here? What's it like?"

"I don't know."

"How do you know—?"

"I've read about it in the paper, seen the signs."

"What signs?"

"Well, like—state tourist signs, or one, anyway—it points to where it is. It's at a local synagogue on Roseneath."

"You want to go?"

"Go to the Holocaust museum on Saturday afternoon?"

"Why not?"

"Well, isn't that their day of worship? Or something? I mean, I don't . . ."

"Which way? Wasn't Roseneath the way we came?"

"You really . . . ? It's just a local thing, you know. . . ."

"It'd be interesting. After we both saw that exhibit in Boston—and you just read Styron." He was still stopped in the alley. He turned to her. "The Holocaust. It's been on my mind. Hasn't it been on yours?"

"Not lately," she muttered, giving away her irritation. Couldn't he understand how her mind didn't have room? How could his? Unless he was trying anything to avoid talking to her about his news. She looked at him hard. He looked so normal—but something had returned. Something was inside his shoulder now, and he was to have a complete bone scan in Boston on Wednesday. That's all he'd said so far.

"Let's do it," she said. "You're the only person I know who will ever want to." She passed that sign three times a week on her way to teach her drawing class. She'd begun noticing it when school started. She'd never given a thought to going where the sign pointed.

"Tell me where it is on Roseneath," he said, taking her hand after he turned out of the alley.

• • •

It was just a few blocks around the corner. A smaller sign pointed to a plain two-story building behind the synagogue. He turned into the parking lot, empty but for a single car.

"I thought there'd be a lot of people, that they'd be coming for services."

"I guess I did, too," he said. "Must be in the evening."

"I bet the museum's closed on Saturday afternoon."

"It looks like it." They sat for a moment with the motor running; then he switched it off. "I'll go check."

She watched him in his old winter jacket, his Basque beret, walk toward the nondescript building where the small sign on Rose-neath had pointed VIRGINIA HOLOCAUST MUSEUM. He tried a door on the side, then walked back. He walked with a tilt she remembered from when they'd been lovers in their thirties. He walked the same at sixty, but now it was a little more like a limp. They had both been alive during the Holocaust, during the war. They had both been little children, safe in America.

"It's open," he mouthed as he walked back to the car, gesturing for her to come on.

Her heart sank. Instead of talking about what was happening to him, to them, they were going to visit this empty building that claimed to be a museum.

He pushed open the heavy metal door where a small, hand-written sign said ENTRANCE TO MUSEUM. Inside, the walls were beige cinderblock and tile. There was a long hall, a staircase with round metal banisters. It looked like an elementary school. It must, in fact, have been a school. It was empty now, and silent. Another written sign was taped to the walls by the stair: MUSEUM with a crayoned arrow pointing up. She wanted to turn around and leave. This place was like the dreams she'd been having, dreams of hall-ways, old schools, cold corridors where she was late for a strange exam in an unnumbered room upstairs.

"Hey, wait," she called.

But he had already headed up the steps. She followed him.

At the top was a glass display case, on its surface a jar of dollars, a stack of brochures, and a guestbook. Beyond it were two man-nequins—a man and a woman—dressed in uniforms she couldn't identify. A hallway led off to the left. An office was to their right, its door opened. A man was talking on a phone, but when he saw them standing there, he hung up and came toward them.

"Here to see the museum, folks? Good! It's been a slow day. We mostly have school groups, you know. But more and more, we get the out-of-towners. Ever since the signs went up. I'm Jonas Latman, and I'll show you how to tour our museum with these Walkmen. It's what we call our 'self-guided' tour. We have actual guides, too. But not on Saturday. It's the young ones need the guides."

"But not us old ones," she said, taking her sweetheart's hand.

Mr. Latman gave her an appreciative grin and glanced at the man he would assume was her husband. "I'd say the three of us were about the same place—at the self-guided stage," he said. Though he had a slight foreign accent, he pronounced the word "about" like an old Richmonder, almost like "aboot." Then he reached be-hind the display case and retrieved two cassette players and ear-phones.

She noticed the yarmulke on his bald head as he bent to show them how to fasten the players around their waists like seatbelts, how to pause, rewind. And where to go.

"Back downstairs," he pointed, "then walk to the end of the long hall and start your tape at the foot of the other stairway. You'll come back up and be directed through a series of rooms. They'll be dark, but don't worry, a light will come on when you enter. Motion sensor—saves money, you know. Oh, and there's a room where you crawl through a tunnel in the dark. You don't have to. You can go around it if you'd rather. You'll see. Well, I think I've covered it. You'll end up here." He pointed to the two uniformed mannequins. "The liberators. If you have questions after, I'll be right there in my office."

"Thank you," they said in unison.

They walked back downstairs and found the starting point at the foot of the other staircase.

They were both fiddling around with their earphones and players. "Let's hit the 'start' button at the same time," he said.

"OK. Now?"

"Now."

They pressed down on the buttons together.

The preamble began. A deep, male voice gave some facts and
told them to walk upstairs onto a landing where the display was
devoted to Kristallnacht. They looked at each other and nodded,
pointing upstairs to confirm they were hearing the same thing.
Then she saw his face take on the look of someone who's looking
at you but listening to another voice. He had looked that way
all day.

On the landing, on a low shelf, there were sculptures featuring
shards of glass and a desecrated Torah, a few artifacts including a
Jewish storefront sign from Berlin and a couple of old envelopes
with glass fragments arranged around them. There were several
black-and-white photographs of smug vandals and shattered store
windows. There was not really much to regard, but the voice on
the tape was eloquent as it described the night in 1938 when throughout Germany every Jewish building was trashed and looted — the
crystal proclamation of what was to come. But it wasn't a proclamation, she thought; no one knew then what was to come.

Then they were told to proceed up a few more steps and push
open a picketed iron gate that blocked the second-floor hallway.
The wrought German words across its top were translated by the
unemotional narrator in their ears: WORK WILL MAKE YOU FREE.

She pushed open the gate first, but then stood uncertainly at
what she was facing: an opened doorway into total dark. James
went on ahead of her, disappearing for long seconds before he trig-
gered the motion sensor and light flooded the room. Then she followed.

They were confused, both turning to the left to look at the displays while the voice was describing things unrelated. It took them
a while to understand the whole room was about one family's fate
in Lithuania. A large Jewish family rounded up in the town of Kovno

by invading Nazis, marched into the barbed-wire ghetto seen in the photographs on the wall, crammed into the room and outhouse depicted in constructions at the end of the room. As the narrator went into detail about the conditions in the Kovno ghetto, she was staring at an eight-by-ten photograph of Nazi police shooting the fallen, bloated bodies of Jews on a street while bystanders watched. The bodies were bloated, said the typed caption, because water had been forced in their mouths and "other orifices" with firehoses. It was an authentic photograph. The swollen bodies were clearly discernible, as were individual faces in the curious crowd watching the shootings. Some were smiling.

She pointed to the "stop" button, took off her earphones.

"He's not talking about what we're looking at."

He shook his head.

"James, what *are* these pictures?"

She walked on past the unbearable to the other images on the wall—the ghetto entrance, people lined up to be checked in and out; the last picture was an oddly pleasant photo of two smiling men and a young boy and a motorcycle.

"We made a wrong turn," he said, pushing his earphones off his ears. "Let's start over."

"He hasn't gotten to these pictures yet . . ."

"Uh-uh . . . He's talking about a 'tableau'—rooms where his family lived—"

"Over there, built into the corner. Are you rewinding?"

"Hmm." He punched more buttons. "Can't get it to the beginning of this room."

She tried, too, winding too far back, too far ahead.

They stood there in the middle of the room with its hand-painted walls depicting the roofs and spires of Kovno, Lithuania, its amateur sets of scenes from the ghetto, its one wall of black-framed photographs captioned in Courier typed on a faded ribbon.

"He has a good voice," she said. "So deep—and is that accent Yiddish? Mixed with Southern?"

"It's him," he said.

"Who?"

"The man who greeted us—Jonas, was it?"

"You think so?"

"I'm sure. Did you catch his last name?"

"No," she said. "I think I'll give up on timing the tape to this room, just look around."

"OK," he said, still pushing "rewind" and "forward." "I'll cue you when we step back out in the hallway."

She examined the mock-up of a ghetto room, a small table where the tiny plastic bags of bread and beans and rice were labeled as the measured weekly food rations for a large ghetto family.

She turned to see James standing by the entrance. He was looking again at the photograph of the killers with their rifles pointed down at the prostrate, water-bloated Jews. She came up behind him, looking over his shoulder. *Sneaking a peek,* she thought, feeling guilty, as if she were spying on him as he gazed at pornography. She was ashamed she was interested herself, though so sickened by the subject.

Then her eyes lowered an inch. She was staring straight at his right shoulder. It looked slanted, weakened. What was in there? What evil thing was growing inside? She turned her face toward the door and took his left arm.

They went out to the hallway and returned to their tapes and the guided tour by the man whose name they couldn't remember. They were led to the next room, where they learned what happened to the narrator's family. He had been a seven-year-old boy, one of the children of forced laborers in the ghetto. His mother had been made to load coal cars. One morning the Jews had to line up in the street for "selection" conducted by a Nazi sergeant named Helmut Rauca. Somehow this little museum had dressed out a tall mannequin in the full Nazi uniform that Sergeant Rauca would have been wearing. The model of Rauca loomed with his riding crop as he had over the masses at dawn, as the narrator, a boy pressed between his parents, must have seen him. At roll call, whole families were chosen to be sent out of the ghetto to a concentration camp "to work." Sergeant Helmut Rauca, said the narrator, "decided with a flick of a riding crop who would live or die" as he pointed families to the left or right. It soon became clear to the narrator's father, a lawyer, that families led by professionals, writers, and intellectuals never returned. One morning the father was asked to step forward. Sergeant Rauca asked his profession. The narrator paused. "My father told Rauca he was an auto mechanic. Rauca pointed to the right. We all followed Father to the right, back into the ghetto."

She knew they were at the same place on the tape when she saw James smile at this. Their eyes met. They were hearing it together, the son's pride in his wily father.

The narrator went on to tell of his father's disastrous attempts at working as a mechanic on a Nazi truck— and of their family's escape from the ghetto in the dark under the barbed wire and into a hay wagon to flee to the Lithuanian countryside.

As they left this room, going back into the hallway, they heard sounds ahead of them: a chuffing train, a dog barking. Recordings, sound effects. And yet she thought she heard actual voices as well, high-pitched voices. He, too, looked puzzled, sliding his earphone back.

"Are there other people in here? Ahead of us?" she asked.

"Didn't seem like it."

"We've been alone in here," she said. "I know that—"

"It doesn't feel like there's anyone else in the building."

"It's sound effects?"

"Must be," he said.

They entered a chuffing, train-whistling boxcar fashioned from a section of the hallway and then were told to "exit" its side door into the next room. Here the barks of the dog became louder. And in this room was the entrance to the dark tunnel they had been told of. At the end of a row of photographs and artifacts, it was a low opening in the wall at the back of the room.

The barking stopped. She listened to the narrator tell of the farmer who let them hide under his potato field, of the tunnel his father and uncles dug, the excavation it led to where they would exist underground for almost a year. She looked closely at the pictures of the good Christian farmer who risked his life, of the patch of his flat potato field that covered nine people. She stared a long time at the sepia photograph of a young man; his dark liquid eyes seemed to look into hers. He was a cousin, who one night had lifted the lid of the hiding place and sneaked across the fields to a village to get food. He had been captured, made to dig his own grave, and shot.

When she turned, she saw her lover on his hands and knees at the mouth of the tunnel. He was crawling in. She remembered the narrator's name. The man who'd said you didn't have to go in the tunnel if you chose not to. His name was Latman.

The recorded Mr. Latman was telling about what it was like to live in a hole in the earth. She looked around her—a statue of a dog stood on a platform depicting the potato field. In the nights when Mr. Latman's father had stealthily dug their hiding place, he had befriended the farmer's dog. When they went underground, the dog had stood faithful guard over them every night. The recorded barking began again. She was alone in the room. She shivered, and felt a sudden panic.

There was nothing to do but get down on her knees and crawl into the darkness.

She'd crawled a few feet and felt she was in something round, a big pipe. She could see nothing ahead of her. She wanted to find James. How far ahead was he in the dark? Her fear seemed to expand the way she felt her body was filling the pipe. *What was he thinking now?* she wondered. He didn't want to talk about it. Not yet. She called his name, but there was no reply. She kept going.

Suddenly there was noise behind her in the dark. Little children's voices. Laughing.

"Hey, there's somebody in here!" squealed a young voice.

"Ooh, this is scair-ree," another child said. Giggles came from further back.

"Ben? Who's in here? Is somebody up ahead?"

"Who's there?" came a voice almost in her ear.

"ME!" she roared, turning her head like a dog barking backward.

She could feel a scampering retreat behind her, heard receding giggles.

Her minute of panic dissipated with the children's laughter. She crawled around a curve to find a barely visible earthen cave, where mannequins depicted the Latman family huddled around a lantern. She paused there, letting her eyes adjust. She discerned the model of a child curled under a blanket at the feet of the adults. The sound of laughing children still in her ears, she thought, *I was five that year, the year these people, that boy, lived in this hole. I was playing hide-and-seek with my brother and sister on warm summer nights.*

She wanted to get out of this tunnel, stand up, get back to James.

She emerged into the main room. It seemed blazing with light.

He was there, talking to Jonas Latman. Around the two men danced three beautiful children—two little boys with wide mischievous grins and sparkling eyes and a smaller girl with blonde ringlets. They were darting out of Mr. Latman's reach as he tried to talk and grab one of them at the same time.

She walked toward them, blinking in the brightness.

"I'm sorry to disturb you," he said as she approached. "They got away from me. I've told them and told them . . ."

It was strange to hear the voice of the tape recording coming from him. Strange, too, to hear its taped neutrality sound so stressed and human.

"Here is Mr. Latman, darling. It's just what we thought—he is the boy—this is his story."

"Children! Go back to my office. Right now!"

They quieted, but didn't obey.

"Grampa?" said the golden-haired girl, taking his hand with both of hers. "Can we play in the cave? Pleeeze?"

"Forgive me," he said, holding up the palm of his free hand, "I'm babysitting today."

They both smiled at him, murmuring, "No problem." She mentioned something about knowing how kids . . .

"Go!" he said to the children sternly. But immediately relented: "After the guests have finished with the tour . . . now, scat. Back to my office. *Right now.*"

The little girl and the youngest boy hugged his legs, and they all ran out. Into the "boxcar," she thought, and out its other end.

"Play in the cave!" scoffed Mr. Latman. "Can you imagine? It's a game to them. The place my father saved us . . . the way we survived."

"You must be very proud of such a father," she said.

"A great man, yes. And my mother, too, still with us in 2000. Heroes together to us all. Your husband was just asking about him. I was telling him my father survived to live a long and productive life. He helped plan this museum. He gave the history." Mr. Latman's eyes were moist. "He gave the facts. You know what? On his deathbed he told me how he shored up our hiding place with wood. Walls and a roof. Without any nails."

"And you re-created it," James said, "the whole . . . ah . . ."

". . . experience," she finished. "You let us see it."

"Lots of help, lots of help," he shrugged. "But my grandchildren? Can you believe it? They use it for games, for hide-and-go-seek."

But she saw that Mr. Latman was smiling, his face illuminated, his eyes now full of mischief like the little boys'.

In the parking lot they walked past the only other car. Above the Civic's license plate a sticker read VISIT THE VA HOLOCAUST MUSEUM. It was Jonas Latman's, of course. There had been no other visitors this gray Saturday afternoon.

"The odd thing was—did you notice?"

"What?" she said, suddenly reaching to him, holding his shoulders with both hands.

"How he felt? About the children playing in the tunnel? His father's—"

She pulled him to her. "He seemed happy. He seemed happy with us, too."

"Us, too," James said.

Elizabeth Seydel Morgan adapted her previous story in this anthology, "Economics" (1992), as a screenplay. Retitled *Queen Esther*, it won the Virginia Film Festival's First Prize for screen-writing. Her fourth collection of poems from Louisiana State University Press will be *Without a Philosophy.* Her work has appeared in *Five Points, Iowa Review, Georgia Review, Shenandoah, Virginia Quarterly Review, Poetry,* and *Blackbird,* among other periodicals and online journals. Morgan—and her children and grandchildren—live in Richmond, Virginia. But she divides her time (a phrase worth a poem) between Richmond and Long Mountain in the Blue Ridge.

SUSAN FRENCH

I call myself a poet, but I needed prose to narrate the experience of going through a local Holocaust museum. Like a poem, the story unfolded its meaning as I wrote it. It suggested that terror or mortal illness can be ameliorated by experiencing vicariously the terror of other mortals. The woman, who thought she had no link to the Holocaust, is led to make connections with both human horror and the tenacity of the human spirit.

Annette Sanford

ONE SUMMER

(from *New Orleans Review*)

When Granny came that summer, she brought along her parakeet, a small, mostly green bird with too-knowing eyes and a monotonous way of repeating dull phrases: *Better watch out! Sing to me, sweetie. You precious baby.*

Until she got that bird, I was her precious baby. Manners were big with her, but she let that bird walk around on the table while we ate. Let him poo-poo on the table. She scolded him, but I could tell she thought it was a cute thing he'd done. She apologized when he flew up and pooped on my shoulder. She said, "Tell Nancy you're sorry," and then she made a noise with her lips that brought him swooping down to shower her with kisses.

"He better not ever kiss me," I told Granny.

My mother and father (Granny's only son) tried to start conversations about people in the neighborhood that Granny knew and things that happened at the store and down at the church. They tried not to notice Jackie sitting on the bread plate or drinking out of a glass.

I hoped he would drown when he lit on my glass. I hoped my cat Poncho would spring up and eat him, but after Jackie came, Mama said Poncho couldn't come in the house.

"It's his house," I told my mother.

"Granny is our guest," she said, even though Granny had come to stay all summer. To live with us until school started. "Jackie is good for Granny," Mama said. "He gives her something to think about."

"She can think about us." I was nine maybe. Or maybe ten, the month Jackie reigned.

One good thing. He went to bed early. Granny put his cage on a table in my room and kissed him good night. Sometimes after the fancy cover she had made was arranged over the cage, Jackie went on boring us: *Rain!* he squawked. *Hear the rain?* Only he called it *grain* because he couldn't pronounce words starting with *r. Gradio. Gred.* His only imperfection, Granny told us.

The first night we sat on the front porch after Jackie retired, my parents in rockers and Granny in a straight chair because she preferred it on account of her back. Rheumatism, she said. I sat on the steps so I could run out in the yard to catch lightning bugs.

I brought one back, crawling over my hand. I showed it to Granny. "Tomorrow," she said, "you'll have Jackie to sit on your finger."

My father said, "I want you to come down to the store in the morning, Mother. (His grocery store she owned half interest in.) We have business to see to. About your river property."

"Harold," my mother said. "Granny won't sleep if you get into that tonight."

"What do you mean *see to?*" Granny asked.

"We'll talk about it down there. I'm just mentioning it so you and Jackie won't make other plans."

"We're going to visit Cora Nell in the morning. I've already called her."

"You have all summer to visit Cora Nell."

"I have all summer *to see to some business* about my river property!" Granny had a sweet, kind voice but when she felt shoved against a wall, she sat up as straight as the back of her chair and sounded like a hammer clanging on flint rock. "I'll be down to your office next week, Harold. Or the week after that."

"Suit yourself," be said. He stayed steady when he talked to his mother. "But the sooner the better. There's money involved."

"Harold," my mother said.

"Money?" said Granny.

"We'll discuss it tomorrow."

"I want to know now."

Daddy got up and kissed her. "I'm going to bed."

"You throw out a bomb like that," my mother said, "and then you walk off to bed! In five minutes," she said to Granny, "he'll be asleep."

"Ella Mae," said Granny, "what is this about?"

My daddy was already way down the hall.

"I know so little about it, Granny, I really can't say."

"You're married to Harold."

"For fifteen years," I put in. "On the fourth of August it'll be sixteen and we might have a party. Beer and everything."

Ordinarily my mother would have sent *me* to bed for mentioning beer to my teetotalling grandmother, but Granny had Mama cornered, and she needed me with her.

"You're bound to be in on this, Ella Mae."

I said helpfully, "It's about the dam."

"What dam?" said Granny, her eyes a little bit like Jackie's eyes.

"The one they're going to build where the river is."

"Is that true, Ella Mae?"

My mother's voice when she's pushed against a wall comes out shaky. "I'm not up on the facts."

"The pecan bottom," I said, "is going under water."

Granny made a sound like Jackie squawking.

"I'm sorry, Granny," my mother said.

"Nobody is going to build a dam on my property! Or even put up a fence unless I say so."

"I'm sure not," said Mama. "Anyway, it's not anywhere near settled. It's a possibility, that's all."

"The land around here is flat as an ironing board. Dams are built in valleys between hills."

"A lot of people don't like it," I put in.

"Nancy Jane," Mama said, "this business is between your daddy and Granny. The thing for you to do is go put on your pajamas. You're on the sleeping porch, remember. And I want evidence that you've brushed your teeth."

She'd wormed out of me that sometimes I just wet the toothbrush, so now I had to report back smelling like Pepsodent to kiss her good night. (In my family we did a lot of kissing. Birds and all.)

I always gave up my room when Granny came. This was the first time I'd minded. I loved my Granny, but I didn't love Jackie, do-doing on things belonging to me. I liked regular birds that flew around in the yard, but there was no comparison between them and that parakeet. Something about his bill curving down to his mouth where his round tongue rolled out made me think of sick people in rooms with the shades down and medicine bottles on the table.

Actually, though, our house belonged to Granny. She lent it to us after I was born, and moved away to Jacksonville where her sister lived. When I was younger and she came to visit, I would beg her to stay longer, falling down on the floor, crying to convince her. She played cards with me and made angel food cakes. She bought me fancier dresses than my mother approved of, and took me to the picture show whenever the feature changed.

Stretched out on the sleeping porch after the Pepsodent check, I looked out at the elms, black against the sky, and wanted them not to build the dam where Granny's pecan bottom was. In the spring we went there and picked dewberries out of the weeds, and grassburrs off our socks. In the fall, all the pecans I picked up I sold for Christmas money. During flood times we stood on the county bridge and marveled at the water rising in the bottom. I finally went to sleep, thinking about dam water covering the highest branches, the tree trunks drowning, gasping for breath until they crashed down and motor boats ran over them.

In the morning Granny didn't get up as early as she should have. Other summers she rose before day and made the coffee and rattled around until she woke us all up.

"Peep in there, Nancy, and see if she's still asleep."

"What if she's dead?"

"Hush!" said Mama.

"Well, she could be. She's ninety."

"She's seventy-four."

I'd been dying to know, but Granny never would tell me. She said children had no business asking adults rude questions.

I tiptoed down the hall and right away I heard Jackie cooing, it sounded like, and Granny talking low to him. I knocked on the door and Granny said, "Come in quietly. Jackie and I are having our devotional."

My Granny was religious. Pious, my daddy said, as if it was a word that tasted like mineral oil. Instead of a pillow, Granny slept on a Bible. "Jacob," she once told me, "used a stone for a pillow."

"When he rassled that angel that crippled his foot?"

She seemed surprised that I knew who Jacob was, but she wasn't quite pleased. "There's more to the story than a crippled foot, Nancy Jane. Jacob wrested a blessing from the angel."

Rested? I thought, but I didn't go into it. I didn't mention it now either, looking at her bird nibbling at her nightgown. I said, "Is Jackie pious?"

She looked over her glasses. "He is very attentive to the scriptures."

I was interested in that. "Do you think you can convert him?"

She didn't hesitate to tell me that God's creatures in the animal world didn't need converting. They were as innocent as babes, incapable of sin.

I thought of the mess he'd left on my shoulder. "Do you take him to church?"

"Not at present. I may later."

"I hope I'm there when you do."

She closed her devotional book and waved her hand at Jackie, who flew over to the dresser and pecked at himself in the mirror.

"I thought about that dam all night," she said tiredly.

"Me, too," I offered as consolation. "They need to put it some place else where there's no pecans."

She closed her eyes and pinched the bridge of her nose. "Change," she said.

I thought she meant nickels and dimes that she'd put some place to give me, and I waited expectantly to receive them.

"You'll know when you're my age, Nancy, the inevitability of change. Eventually one loses everything one loves."

"It's probably in your purse," I said. "Do you want me to look for it?"

She opened her eyes and fixed a stare on me. "You're old enough now to give serious thought to what's happening around you."

I knew what was happening: Daddy was in the bathroom shaving his face. Mama was in the kitchen wondering where we were. And Jackie, Granny's bird, was on top of my head.

"Get off !" I said in a near shriek.

"He doesn't respond, Nancy Jane, to that tone of voice."

I knocked him off, bringing forth a screech and a lop-sided swoop into Granny's lap.

"At this moment," she said, "I regret to acknowledge that you are my granddaughter!"

"I'm sorry." I saw nickels and dimes flying out of the picture. "He was fixing to do you-know-what in my hair."

Mama came in. "Ladies," she said, "breakfast is ready."

"Good morning, Ella Mae."

"Good morning, Granny."

"Ella Mae, how would you like to call me Trilby?"

"Oh," said my mother. "Well, I don't know."

"Trilby!" I laughed.

"Trilby is a revered Southern name, and it happens to be mine." Granny turned back to my mother. "After fifteen years, I believe we have attained the closeness of sisters."

Mother's eyes darted around. "The thing is, I've always called you Granny. Or Mother Lewis."

"You're getting older yourself," Granny said crisply. "In a few more years *you* could be a granny. How would you like people to forget that your name is Ella Mae?"

"I'd be glad if they did. I'd rather be called Agnes."

"That's neither here nor there. I'm asking you to consider my request. You will make me very happy if you agree." My grandmother looked at me. "You, of course, will continue to call me Granny." She rose from the bed. "I'll dress now for breakfast."

My mother and I hurried out, not noticing Jackie hurrying with us until my mother opened the back screen to call my father out of the garden, and Poncho ran in and Jackie flew out.

"Oh, my lord!" My mother grabbed her throat.

"I'll run tell Trilby!"

She snatched me down the steps. "Get the butterfly net! Harold!" She ran screaming to the garden. "Jackie is loose!"

I came running back. "He's in the peach tree!"

My father approached slowly. "Sit on the steps, Nancy. See if he'll come to you."

He didn't come.

"Go inside and get the cage."

Mother exclaimed, "Granny will know!"

"She's going to know anyway if we don't catch him."

Fortunately for me, she was gargling in the bathroom. I tore out with the cage. My father set it on an elm stump.

"Come away from it, Harold!"

"When Jackie flies in, I'm going to shut the door."

Jackie did, and he did, and we all went trembling back into the house.

"Are we going to tell her?" my mother whispered.

"Not if we don't have to."

I got the cage back in the room while the bath water was gurgling out of the tub.

My father was at the table reading the newspaper when Granny came in, all fresh and smiling, and took the chair beside him.

"Is there anything in the paper about the dam, Harold?"

He looked up, startled.

"Nancy explained it to me." She shook out her napkin. "The sooner we let these people know that dam water will not be flooding my pecan bottom, the easier it will be for everyone concerned."

"We'll discuss it at the store," my father said. "I'd like you to be there by ten." He poured her a cup of coffee. "Olan Barnes is stopping in."

"Lawyer Barnes?" Her chin jutted out. "Is it a social call?"

"He said he'd like to see you."

Granny's hand shook a little when she picked up the cup. "Your father and I sacrificed, Harold, to buy that bottom land."

"I know you did, Mother, and we all love it, but times change."

I caught on then, about change. I saw how bad it scared Granny to think about it. Everything she loved, she had lost to change. Grampa Lewis and no telling what else.

I got up from the table. "I'll bring Jackie in here so he can sit in the sun."

While Granny got ready, Mama washed the dishes and I dried. "Why does she want you to call her Trilby?"

"I think she wants an ally, instead of a daughter-in-law." Mama explained. "She wants me on her side if she has to fight Dad."

"Fight Dad?"

"In a battle of wills. If it comes to that."

"You mean Dad wants the dam and she doesn't?"

"No, he doesn't want it either, but the government does. We'll have to go along eventually, he says, and it's better to agree now than to wear ourselves out hanging on for two or three years when in the end they'll condemn Granny's land and take it anyway."

"Steal it?" I was horrified.

"Oh no. They'll pay for it."

"But Granny wants the pecan bottom. She doesn't want money."

Mama wiped off the counter. "That's it exactly."

Granny asked me to walk downtown with her. Two blocks to Dad's grocery store. "Afterward," she said, "we'll go to the drugstore and have a soda."

"I'd rather have an ice cream cone."

"Fine," she said.

"A cone will cost less and then I can have something else." She didn't reply. "Like bubble gum. Or a movie magazine?"

"Yes," she said, so I knew she wasn't listening.

"I'll go on and wait for you down there."

She took my hand. "I want you to go with me. To the meeting," she said.

Me. A child. A little pitcher with big ears. "What for?" I said.

"It won't take but a minute, and then we'll go treat ourselves."

It took an hour and a half. I had to go out twice and bring in cokes. I had to sit there and listen to Mr. Barnes droning on in his sweet potato voice. (He yammered, my father said, until you wanted to choke him.) I think I went to sleep at some point because I dreamed something nice but when I came to again Granny was saying *no* for the jillionth time and Daddy was saying, *You don't have to decide today.*

When it was over, Granny took my hand and walked out of the store like her petticoat was on fire. She turned toward our house, and I said, "Aren't we going to the drugstore?"

"Not today."

"You said we were."

She didn't answer. At the house she walked straight down the hall without speaking to Mama and went in my room and closed the door.

"Poor thing," Mama said. "It must have been awful for her."

"It was awful for Daddy and Mr. Barnes. She said no to everything."

My mother stared. "She took you in there?"

"I heard it all." But of course I didn't. I didn't hear anything except an exchange of voices more monotonous than Jackie's. "Can I have an advance on my allowance for an ice cream cone?"

"It's almost lunch time. Set the table."

That's the way it went the whole rest of the month. Meetings with Mr. Barnes and Daddy, though I never went again. It wrung out Granny. The only thing that comforted her was Jackie, his silly sayings and his twitter that never stopped. She took him with her when she went to Cora Nell's, and then she didn't go again because Jackie, she said, was not well received.

On the Fourth of July, Granny produced a man friend. We didn't know she had one. She telephoned him the night before, and then she told us he was coming for the Lion's Club picnic and fireworks afterward, so he would probably spend the night.

"I'll sleep with you on the sleeping porch," she said to me.

We were all struck dumb. Grandfather Lewis had been dead longer than I'd been alive. She'd had only lady friends in all that time. At least that's what we thought because it never occurred to us to think anything else.

"We'll be happy to have him," my father finally said. "Mr. Walker?"

"Yes."

"A widower?"

"Divorced."

"Children?" my mother said.

"Grown and gone."

"What does he do to make money?" I asked.

"He doesn't do anything. He is retired."

"From what?" Dad said.

Granny smiled sweetly. "Ask him, Harold."

Mr. Weatherford Walker was a retired attorney-at-law. He stayed the next day, too, and went to church with us and then on Monday morning he and Granny went to see Mr. Barnes without Daddy.

"It's all right," Daddy said after they left to eat breakfast together downtown and prepare for their meeting. "She'll be more satisfied if her own lawyer is in on this."

"Do you like him?" I asked.

"It doesn't matter if I do or I don't."

"What if they marry?"

"Marry!" my mother said.

"She's only seventy-four."

They sent me to the library on my bicycle with a big plastic bag to bring books for everybody. "Even Mr. Walker?"

"Yes, certainly," Dad said. "We want him to have something to do when he gets tired of talking."

"He talks more than Jackie."

Dad gave me a kiss and a pat on the head.

The first terrible thing was that Mr. Walker died that morning in Mr. Olan Barnes's office. The second awful thing was that while he and Granny were there, I went out in the backyard and opened Jackie's cage and shooed him out.

When the siren went off (it lets us know when there's a fire or an accident), I was sitting on the back steps with a library book acting like I had no idea Jackie was loose in the trees.

Then Mama came out, white-faced and speechless.

"What's the matter?" I said from a dried-up mouth, my breakfast on its way up, my heart pounding.

Mama gasped, "Mr. Walker's had a spell!"

Saved! I thought. And blood filled my head. "What kind of spell?"

"It must have been his heart." Mama was holding herself together with her hands around her neck. "They've taken him to the hospital. I'm going there now."

I scrambled up. "I'll go with you!"

"You stay here and answer the telephone."

I went anyway, and she seemed not to notice, she was walking so fast. I stayed a little behind her and saw for the first time she was a tiny bit pigeon-toed. *Was I?* I wondered. And how could I find out without having to ask?

Daddy and Granny were coming down the steps at the hospital when we came up, Daddy holding onto Granny who looked more ninety than seventy-four.

"What . . . ?" said my mother.

"He died," said Dad.

"Oh, Granny . . ." Mama took her arm and they led her to our car and put her in.

Granny was breathing through her mouth and wiping her face.

I got in beside her. "Are you all right, Granny?"

"Weatherford died," she said.

"What happened to him?"

"Nancy Jane!" From the front seat.

"He seemed fine this morning, Granny."

She took my hand. "He was. He was perfectly fine. Then he made a noise as if he were socked in the stomach and fell out of Lawyer Barnes's leather chair." Her eyes closed. "For the rest of my life I'll hear him hitting the floor."

"You need to lie down, Granny," Mama said when we had her in the house. "Here, I'll turn down the bed for you."

"Jackie?" she said.

I had forgot about Jackie.

Granny sat up. "Where is my Jackie?"

"I'll run get him," I said. "I hung his cage in the peach tree and then we left . . ."

"Ella Mae, bring me some water."

I raced outside. "Jackie! Sweetie! Come on down here! Come get in your cage!" I made his little love coos and ran from tree to tree. "Your Granny wants you!" But there was no sign of him, only his toys in his cage and half a cup of seed.

I began to cry, loud boo-hooing noises that brought on hiccups and brought Mama rushing out.

"Jackie's gone!" I wailed. I fell down on the grass and covered my head.

Mother said, aghast, "His cage is open!"

"I didn't do it!"

"Of course you didn't do it." She ran around as I had, searching the trees. "He'll come back in a minute. Run get your father and don't let Granny know."

Luckily for us, Granny had fallen asleep from the tranquilizer they gave her at the hospital.

We called and called for I don't know how long. My father whistled a little tune Jackie liked to sing. Mama made kissing noises.

A black feeling came over me. The wages of sin. I was underneath a rock, maybe Jacob's pillow, but no angel could rest me. I was halfway to hell.

"Nancy Jane," said Mama. "Take the cage and go around the neighborhood. Get some of the children to help you look."

I felt a leap of hope. There were trees everywhere he could be sitting in! I rounded up three friends. I told them the first one who found him and got him back in the cage could make up stuff for me to do for the next week, and I would do it.

"Will you jump in the Guadalupe?" Naming our river.

"I will if you want me to." Though I couldn't swim.

We didn't find Jackie. Not even one green feather.

Granny took it hard. "On top of Weatherford dying, my precious bird is dead!"

I tried to help. "I don't think he's dead, Granny."

"Then he'll starve to death somewhere."

"Maybe somebody will find him who loves birds."

"He's gone!" she said. "He's gone forever!" She wept for a long time and we couldn't comfort her.

We all went to Jacksonville for the funeral of Mr. Weatherford Walker, and then we brought Granny back to finish out her visit, but she wouldn't stay. She spent one night and then asked to be taken home.

"Mother," my dad said, "I know you don't want to think about it, but we ought to decide something about the river bottom."

"The dam," said my grandmother. "I don't give a damn about the dam."

My father opened his mouth and shut it again.

"When you get the papers ready, send them and I'll sign them. I've learned in the last few days, change is not to be reckoned with."

"If you'd like to think about it a while longer . . ."

"I intend never to think of it again. When the money comes, put it in the bank for Nancy Jane."

I cried inordinately.

Even Granny grew concerned. "Jackie was a dear little bird, but we'll get over losing him. The tragedy is . . ." Her face crumpled. "Unlike my Weatherford, Jackie had no soul." She held me tightly. "That poor little creature had only a gizzard."

My Granny lived for another seven years, but we went to see her, she never came to us, she never visited us again.

Jackie's cage Daddy hung in the storeroom.

No one ever said to me, how did Jackie get out? No one offered the explanations I had thought up: a child must have come along and wanted to play with him, the latch was faulty, the wind blew the door open.

They all knew what happened. But they couldn't speak of it. Acknowledging my act with words would require admitting that their precious child, like Jackie, had no soul, only a gray gizzard and no chance at all of getting into heaven.

In a writing career spanning thirty-plus years, Annette Sanford has published more than forty short stories in magazines and journals; two short story collections, *Lasting Attachments* and *Crossing Shattuck Bridge*; and most recently a novel, *Eleanor and Abel*. Her work has appeared in numerous anthologies, including *New Stories from the South* and *Best American Short Stories*. Sanford has twice been awarded NEA Fellowships. In 1976 she gave up a long career teaching high school English to write full time, supplementing her income for a number of years by writing paperback romances under five pseudonyms. She lives in Ganado, Texas.

*M*any years ago I gave my mother-in-law a green parakeet I won in a grocery store drawing. She named it Lu-Net in honor of my husband, Lucius, and me and gave it free range of the dinner table and the tops of our heads and everything else. Lukey and I were not at all sorry when Lu-Net escaped through an open door, but it grieved my mother-in-law to such an extent that one day her neighbor, sick and tired of it all, reminded her: "It only had a gizzard, Essie, not a soul!" Recently remembering with pleasure that remark, I put together bits and pieces of other memories and "One Summer" took shape.

Jill McCorkle

INTERVENTION

(from *Ploughshares*)

The intervention is not Marilyn's idea, but it might as well be. She is the one who has talked too much. And she has agreed to go along with it, nodding and murmuring an all right into the receiver while Sid dozes in front of the evening news. They love watching the news. Things are so horrible all over the world that it makes them feel lucky just to be alive. Sid is sixty-five. He is retired. He is disappearing before her very eyes.

"Okay, Mom?" She jumps with her daughter's voice, once again filled with the noise at the other end of the phone—a house full of children, a television blasting, whines about homework—all those noises you complain about for years only to wake one day and realize you would sell your soul to go back for another chance to do it right.

"Yes, yes," she says.

"Is he drinking right now?"

Marilyn has never heard the term "intervention" before her daughter, Sally, introduces it and showers her with a pile of literature. Sally's husband has a master's in social work and considers himself an expert on this topic, as well as many others. Most of Sally's sentences begin with "Rusty says," to the point that Sid long ago made up a little spoof about "Rusty says," turning it into a game like Simon Says. "Rusty says put your hands on your head," Sid said the first time, once the newly married couple was out of earshot. "Rusty says put your head up your ass." Marilyn howled with laughter, just as she always did and always has. Sid can always make her laugh. Usually she laughs longer and harder. A stranger would have assumed that she was the one slinging back the vodka. Twenty years earlier, and the stranger would have been right.

Sally and Rusty have now been married for a dozen years— three kids and two Volvos and several major vacations (that were so educational they couldn't have been any fun) behind them— and still, Marilyn and Sid cannot look each other in the eye while Rusty is talking without breaking into giggles like a couple of junior high school students. And Marilyn knows junior high behavior; she taught language arts for many years. She is not shocked when a boy wears the crotch of his pants down around his knees, and she knows that Sean Combs has gone from that perfectly normal name to Sean Puffy Combs to Puff Daddy to P. Diddy. She knows that the kids make a big circle at dances so that the ones in the center can do their grinding without getting in trouble, and she has learned that there are many perfectly good words that you cannot use in front of humans who are being powered by hormonal surges. She once asked her class: How will you ever get ahead? only to have them all— even the most pristine honor roll girls— collapse in hysterics. Just last year— her final one— she had learned never to ask if they had hooked up with so-and-so, learning quickly that this no longer meant locating a person but having sex. She could not hear the term now without laughing. She told Sid it reminded her of the time two dogs got stuck in the act just outside her classroom window. The children were out of control, especially when the assistant principal stepped out there armed with a garden hose, which didn't faze the lust-crazed dogs in the slightest. When the female— a scrawny shepherd mix— finally took off running, the male— who was quite a bit smaller— was stuck and forced to hop along behind her like a jackrabbit. "His thang is stuck," one of the girls yelled and broke out in a dance, prompting others to do the same.

"Sounds like me," Sid said that night when they were lying there in the dark. "I'll follow you anywhere."

Now, as Sid dozes, she goes and pulls out the envelope of information about "family intervention." She never should have told Sally that she had concerns, never should have mentioned that there were times when she watched Sid pull out of the driveway only to catch herself imagining that this could be the last time she ever saw him.

"Why do you think that?" Sally asked, suddenly attentive and leaning forward in her chair. Up until that minute, Marilyn had felt invisible while Sally rattled on and on about drapes and chairs and her book group and Rusty's accolades. "Was he visibly drunk? Why do you let him drive when he's that way?"

"He's never visibly drunk," Marilyn said then, knowing that she had made a terrible mistake. They were at the mall, one of those forced outings that Sally had read was important. Probably an article Rusty read first called something like "Spend time with your parents so you won't feel guilty when you slap them in a urine-smelling old-folks' home." Rusty's parents are already in such a place; they share a room and eat three meals on room trays while they watch television all day. Rusty says they're ecstatic. They have so much to tell that they are living for the next time Rusty and Sally and the kids come to visit.

"I pray to God I never have to rely on such," Sid said when she relayed this bit of conversation. She didn't tell him the other parts of the conversation at the mall, how even when she tried to turn the topic to shoes and how it seemed to her that either shoes had gotten smaller or girls had gotten bigger (nine was the average size for most of her willowy eighth-grade girls), Sally bit into the subject like a pit bull.

"How much does he drink in a day?" Sally asked. "You must

know. I mean, *you* are the one who takes out the garbage and does the shopping."

"He helps me."

"A fifth?"

"Sid loves to go to the Food Lion. They have a book section and everything."

"Rusty has seen this coming for years." Sally leaned forward and gripped Marilyn's arm. Sally's hands were perfectly manicured with pale pink nails and a great big diamond. "He asked me if Dad had a problem before we ever got married." She gripped tighter. "Do you know that? That's a dozen years."

"I wonder if the Oriental folks have caused this change in the shoe sizes?" Marilyn pulled away and glanced over at Lady's Foot Locker as if to make a point. She knows that "Oriental" is not the thing to say. "She knows to say "Asian," and though Sally thinks that she and Rusty are the ones who teach her all of these things, the truth is that she learned it all from her students. She knew to say Hispanic and then Latino, probably before Rusty did, because she sometimes watches the MTV channel so that she's up on what is happening in the world and thus in the lives of children at the junior high. Shocking things, yes, but also important. Sid has always believed that it is better to be educated even if what is true makes you uncomfortable or depressed. Truth is, she can understand why some of these youngsters want to say motherfucker this and that all the time. Where *are* their mommas, after all; and where are their daddies? Rusty needs to watch MTV. He needs to watch that and *Survivor* and all the other reality shows. He's got children, and unless he completely rubs off on them they will be normal enough to want to know what's happening out there in the world.

"Asian," Sally whispered. "You really need to just throw out that word Oriental unless you're talking about lamps and carpets. I know what you're doing, too."

"What about queer? I hear that word is okay again."

"You have to deal with Dad's problem," Sally said.

"I hear that even the Homo sapiens use that word, but it might be the kind of thing that only one who is a member can use, kind of like—"

"Will you stop it?" Sally interrupted and banged her hand on the table.

"Like the 'n' word," Marilyn said. "The black children in my class used it, but it would have been terrible for somebody else to."

Sally didn't even enunciate African American the way she usually does. "This doesn't work anymore!" Sally's face reddened, her voice a harsh whisper. "So cut the Gracie Allen routine."

"I loved Gracie. So did Sid. What a woman." Marilyn rummaged her purse for a tissue or a stick of gum, anything so as not to have to look at Sally. Sally looks so much like Sid they could be in a genetics textbook: those pouty lips and hard blue eyes, prominent cheekbones and dark curly hair. Sid always told people his mother was a Cherokee and his father a Jew, that if he was a dog, like a cockapoo, he'd be a Cherojew, which Marilyn said sounded like TheraFlu, which they both like even when they don't have colds, so he went with Jewokee instead. Marilyn's ancestors were all Irish, so she and Sid called their children the Jewokirish. Sid said that the only thing that could save the world would be when everybody was so mixed up with this blood and that that nobody could pronounce the resulting tribe name. It would have to be a symbol—like the name of the artist formerly known as Prince, which was something she had just learned and had to explain to Sid. She doubts that Sally and Rusty even know who Prince is, or Nelly, for that matter. Nelly is the reason all the kids are wearing Band-Aids on their faces, which is great for those just learning to shave.

"Remember that whole routine Dad and I made up about ancestry?" Marilyn asked. She was able to look up now, Sally's hands squeezing her own, Rusty's hands on her shoulders. If she had had an ounce of energy left in her body, she would have run into Lord & Taylor's and gotten lost in the mirrored cosmetics section.

"The fact that you brought all this up is a cry for help whether you admit it or not," Sally said. "And we are here, Mother. We are here for you."

She wanted to ask why Mother—what happened to Mom and Mama and Mommy?—but she couldn't say a word.

There are some nights when Sid is dozing there that she feels frightened. She puts her hand on his chest to feel his heart. She puts her cheek close to his mouth to feel the breath. She did the same to Sally and Tom when they were children, especially with Tom, who came first. She was up and down all night long in those first weeks, making sure that he was breathing, still amazed that this perfect little creature belonged to them. Sometimes Sid would wake and do it for her, even though his work as a grocery distributor in those days caused him to get up at five A.M. The times he went to check, he would return to their tiny bedroom and lunge toward her with a perfect Dr. Frankenstein imitation: "He's alive!" followed by maniacal laughter. In those days she joined him for a drink just as the sun was setting. It was their favorite time of day, and they both always resisted the need to flip on a light and return to life. The ritual continued for years and does to this day. When the children were older they would make jokes about their parents, who were always "in the dark," and yet those pauses, the punctuation marks of a marriage, could tell their whole history spoken and unspoken.

The literature says that an intervention is the most loving and powerful thing a loved one can do. That some members might be apprehensive. Tom was apprehensive at first, but he always has been; Tom is the noncombative child. He's an orthopedist living in Denver. Skiing is great for his health and his business. And his love life. He met the new wife when she fractured her ankle. Her marriage was already fractured, his broken, much to the disappointment of Marilyn and Sid, who found the first wife to be the most loving and open-minded of the whole bunch. The new wife, Sid says, is too young to have any opinions you give a damn about. In private they call her Snow Bunny.

Tom was apprehensive until the night he called after the hour she had told everyone was acceptable. "Don't call after nine unless it's an emergency," she had told them. "We like to watch our shows without interruption." But that night, while Sid dozed and the made-for-TV movie she had looked forward to ended up (as her students would say) sucking, she went to run a deep hot bath, and that's where she was, incapable of getting to the phone fast enough.

"Let the machine get it, honey," she called as she dashed with just a towel wrapped around her dripping body, but she wasn't fast enough. She could hear the slur in Sid's speech. He could not say slalom to save his soul, and instead of letting the moment pass, he kept trying and trying—What the shit is wrong with my tongue, Tom? Did I have a goddamn stroke? Sllllmmmm—sla, sla.

Marilyn ran and picked up the extension. "Honey, Daddy has taken some decongestants, bless his heart, full of a terrible cold. Go on back to sleep now, Sid, I've got it."

"I haven't got a goddamned cold. Your mother's a kook!" He laughed and waved to where she stood in the kitchen, a puddle of suds and water at her feet. "She's a good-looking naked kook. I see her bony ass right now."

"Hang up, Tommy," she said. "I'll call you right back from the other phone. Daddy is right in the middle of his program."

"Yeah, right," Tom said.

By the time she got Sid settled down, dried herself off, and put on her robe, Tom's line was busy, and she knew before even dialing Sally that hers would be busy, too. It was a full hour later, Sid fast asleep in the bed they had owned for thirty-five years, when she finally got through, and then it was to a more serious Tom than she had heard in years. Not since he left the first wife and signed off on the lives of her grandchildren in a way that prevented Marilyn from seeing them more than once a year if she was lucky. She could get mad at him for *that*. So could Sid.

"We're not talking about my life right now," he said. "I've given Dad the benefit of the doubt for years, but Sally and Rusty are right."

"Rusty! You're the one who said he was full of it," she screamed. "And now you're on his side?"

"I'm on your side, Mom, your side."

She let her end fall silent and concentrated on Sid's breath. He's alive, only to be interrupted by a squeaky girly voice on Tom's end—Snow Bunny.

Sid likes to drive, and Marilyn has always felt secure with him there behind the wheel. Every family vacation, every weekend gathering. He was always voted the best driver of the bunch, even when a whole group had gathered down at the beach for a summer cookout where both men and women drank too much. Sid mostly drank beer in those days; he kept an old Pepsi-Cola cooler he once won throwing baseballs at tin cans at the county fair, iced down with Falstaff and Schlitz. They still have that cooler. It's out in the garage on the top shelf, long ago replaced with little red and white Playmates. Tom gave Sid his first Playmate, which has remained a family joke until this day. And Marilyn drank then. She liked the taste of beer but not the bloat. She loved to water ski, and they took turns behind a friend's powerboat. The men made jokes when the women dove in to cool off. They claimed that warm spots emerged wherever the women had been and that if they couldn't hold their beer any better than that, they should switch to girl drinks. And so they did. A little wine or a mai tai, vodka martinis. Sid had a book that told him how to make everything, and Marilyn enjoyed buying little colored toothpicks and umbrellas to dress things up when it was their turn to host. She loved rubbing her body with baby oil and iodine and letting the warmth of the sun and salty air soak in while the radio played and the other women talked. They all smoked cigarettes then. They all had little leather cases with fancy lighters tucked inside.

Whenever Marilyn sees the Pepsi cooler she is reminded of those days. Just married. No worries about skin cancer or lung cancer. No one had varicose veins. No one talked about cholesterol. None of their friends were addicted to anything other than the sun and the desire to get up on one ski—to slalom. The summer she was pregnant with Tom (compliments of a few too many mai tais, Sid told the group), she sat on the dock and sipped her ginger ale. The motion of the boat made her queasy, as did anything that had to do with poultry. *It ain't the size of the ship but the motion of the ocean,* Sid was fond of saying in those days, and she laughed every time. Every time he said it, she complimented his liner and the power of his steam. They batted words like *throttle* and *wake* back and forth like a birdie until finally, at the end of the afternoon, she'd go over and whisper, "Ready to dock?"

Her love for Sid then was overwhelming. His hair was thick, and he tanned a deep smooth olive without any coaxing. He was everything she had ever wanted, and she told him this those summer days as they sat through the twilight time. She didn't tell him how sometimes she craved the vodka tonics she had missed. Even though many of her friends continued drinking and smoking through their pregnancies, she would allow herself only one glass of wine with dinner. When she bragged about this during Sally's first pregnancy, instead of being congratulated on her modest intake, Sally was horrified. "My God, Mother," she said. "Tom is lucky there's not something wrong with him!"

Tom set the date for the intervention. As hard as it was for Rusty to relinquish his power even for a minute, it made perfect sense, given that Tom had to take time off from his practice and fly all the way from Denver. The Snow Bunny was coming, too, even though she really didn't know Sid at all. Sometimes over the past five years, Marilyn had called up the first wife just to hear her voice or, even better, the voice of one or more of her grandchildren on the answering machine. Now there was a man's name included in the list of who wasn't home. She and Sid would hold the receiver between them, both with watering eyes, when they heard the voices they barely recognized. They didn't know about *69 until a few months ago when Margot, the oldest child, named for Sid's mother, called back. "Who is this?" she asked. She was growing up in Minnesota and now was further alienated by an accent Marilyn only knew from Betty White's character on *The Golden Girls*.

"Your grandmother, honey. Grandma Marilyn in South Carolina."

There was a long silence, and then the child began to speak rapidly, filling them in on all that was going on in her life. "Mom says you used to teach junior high," Margot said, and she and Sid both grinned, somehow having always trusted that their daughter-in-law would not have turned on them as Tom had led them to believe.

Then Susan got on the phone, and as soon as she did, Marilyn burst into tears. "Oh, Susie, forgive me," she said. "You know how much we love you and the kids."

"I know," she said. "And if Tom doesn't bring the kids to you, I will. I promise." Marilyn and Sid still believe her. They fantasize during the twilight hour that she will drive up one day and there they'll all be. Then, lo and behold, here will come Tom. "He'll see what a goddamned fool he's been," Sid says. "They'll hug and kiss and send Snow Bunny packing."

"And we'll all live happily ever after," Marilyn says.

"You can take that to the bank, baby," he says, and she hugs him close, whispers that he has to eat dinner before they can go anywhere.

"You know I'm a very good driver," she says, and he just shakes his head back and forth; he can list every ticket and fender-bender she has had in her life.

The intervention day is next week. Tom and Bunny plan to stay with Sally and Rusty an hour away so that Sid won't get suspicious. Already it is unbearable to her—this secret. There has only been one time in their whole marriage when she had a secret, and it was a disaster.

"What's wrong with you?" Sid keeps asking. "So quiet." His eyes have that somber look she catches once in a while; it's a look of hurt, a look of disillusionment. It is the look that nearly killed them thirty-odd years ago.

• • •

There have been many phone calls late at night. Rusty knows how to set up conference calls, and there they all are, Tom and Sally and Rusty, talking nonstop. If he resists, we do this. If he gets angry, we do that. All the while, Sid dozes. Sometimes the car is parked crooked in the drive, a way that he never would have parked even two years ago, and she goes out in her housecoat and bedroom slippers to straighten it up so the neighbors won't think anything is wrong. She has repositioned the mailbox many times, touched up paint on the car and the garage that Sid didn't even notice. Sometimes he is too tired to move or undress, and she spreads a blanket over him in the chair. Recently she found a stash of empty bottles in the bottom of his golf bag. Empty bottles in the Pepsi cooler, the trunk of his car.

"I suspect he lies to you about how much he has," Rusty says. "We are taught not to ask an alcoholic how much he drinks, but to phrase it in a way that accepts a lot of intake, such as 'How many fifths do you go through in a weekend?'"

"Sid doesn't lie to me."

"This is as much for you," Rusty says, and she can hear the impatience in his voice. "You are what we call an enabler."

She doesn't respond. She reaches and takes Sid's warm limp hand in her own.

"If you really love him," he pauses, gathering volume and force in his words, "you have to go through with this."

"It was really your idea, Mom," Sally says. "We all suspected as much, but you're the one who really blew the whistle." Marilyn remains quiet, a picture of herself like some kind of Nazi woman blowing a shrill whistle, dogs barking, flesh tearing. She can't answer; her head is swimming. "Admit it. He almost killed you when he went off the road. It's your side that would have smashed into the pole. You were lucky."

"I was driving," she says now, whispering so as not to wake him. "I almost killed him!"

"Nobody believed you, Marilyn," Rusty says, and she is reminded of the one and only student she has hated in her career, a smart-assed boy who spoke to her as if he were the adult and she were the child. Even though she knew better, knew that he was a little jerk, it had still bothered her.

"You're lucky Mr. Randolph was the officer on duty, Mom," Tom says. "He's not going to look the other way next time. He told me as much."

"And what about how you told me you have to hide his keys sometimes?" Sally asks. "What about that?"

"Where are the children?" Marilyn asks. "Are they hearing all of this?"

"No," Rusty says. "We won't tell this sort of thing until they're older and can learn from it."

"We didn't," she whispers and then ignores their questions. Didn't what? Didn't what?

"The literature says that there should be a professional involved," she says and, for a brief anxious moment, relishes their silence.

"Rusty is a professional," Sally says. "This is what he does for a living."

Sid lives for a living, she wants to say, but she lets it all go. They are coming, come hell or high water. She can't stop what she has put into motion, a rush of betrayal and shame pushing her back to a dark place she has not seen in years. Sid stirs and brings her hand up to his cheek.

Sid never told the children anything. He never brought up anything once it had passed, unlike Marilyn, who sometimes gets stuck in a groove, spinning and spinning, deeper and deeper. Whenever anything in life—the approach of spring, the smell of gin, pine sap thawing and coming back to life—prompts her memory, she cringes and feels the urge to crawl into a dark hole. She doesn't recognize that woman. That woman was sick. A sick, foolish woman, a woman who had no idea that the best of life was in her hand. It was late spring, and they went with a group to the lake. They hired babysitters round the clock so the men could fish and the women could sun and shop and nobody had to be concerned for all the needs of the youngsters. The days began with coffee and bloody marys and ended with sloppy kisses on the sleeping brows of their babies. Sid was worried then. He was bucking for promotions right and left, taking extra shifts. He wanted to run the whole delivery service in their part of the state and knew that he could do it if he ever got the chance to prove himself. Then he would have normal hours, good benefits.

Marilyn had never even noticed Paula Edwards's husband before that week. She spoke to him, yes; she thought it was Paula's good fortune to have married someone who had been so successful so young. ("Easy when it's a family business and handed to you," Sid said, the only negative thing she ever heard him say about the man.) But there he was, not terribly attractive but very attentive. Paula was pregnant with twins and forced to a lot of bed rest. Even now, the words of the situation, playing through Marilyn's mind, shock her.

"You needed attention," Sid said when it all exploded in her face. "I'm sorry I wasn't there."

"Who are you—Jesus Christ?" she screamed. "Don't you hate me? Paula hates me!"

"I'm not Paula. And I'm not Jesus." He went to the cabinet and mixed a big bourbon and water. He had never had a drink that early in the day. "I'm a man who is very upset."

"At me!"

"At both of us."

She wanted him to hate her right then. She wanted him to make her suffer, make her pay. She had wanted him even at the time it was Paula's husband meeting her in the weeks following in dark, out-of-the-way parking lots—rest areas out on the interstate, run-down motels no one with any self-esteem would venture into. And yet there she had been. She bought the new underwear the way women so often do, as if that thin bit of silk could prolong the masquerade. Then later, she had burned all the new garments in a huge puddle of gasoline, a flame so high the fire department came, only to find her stretched out on the grass of her front yard, sobbing.

Her children, ages four and two, were there beside her, wide-eyed and frightened. "Mommy? Are you sick?" She felt those tiny hands pulling and pulling. "Mommy? Are you sad?" Paula's husband wanted sex. She could have been anyone those times he twisted his hands in her thick long hair, grown the way Sid liked it, and pulled her head down. He wanted her to scream out and tear at him. He liked it that way. Paula wasn't that kind of girl, but he knew that she was.

"But you're not," Sid told her in the many years to follow, the times when self-loathing overtook her body and reduced her to an anguished heap on the floor. "You're not that kind."

People knew. They had to know, but out of respect for Sid, they never said a word. Paula had twin girls, and they moved to California, and to this day, they send a Christmas card with a brag letter much like the one that Sally and Rusty have begun sending. Something like: We are brilliant, and we are rich. Our lives are perfect, don't you wish yours was as good? If Sid gets the mail, he tears it up and never says a word. He did the same with the letter that Paula wrote to him when she figured out what was going on. Marilyn never saw what the letter said. She only heard Sid sobbing from the other side of a closed door, the children vigilant as they waited for him to come out. When his days of silence ended and she tried to talk, he simply put a finger up to her lips, his eyes dark and shadowed in a way that frightened her. He mixed himself a drink and offered her one as they sat and listened with relief to the giggles of the children playing outside. Sid had bought a sandbox and put it over the burned spot right there in the front yard. He said that in the fall when it was cooler, he'd cover it with sod. He gave up on advancing to the top, and settled in instead with a budget and all the investments he could make to ensure college educations and decent retirement.

Her feelings each and every year when spring came had nothing to do with any lingering feelings she might have had about the affair—she had none. Rather, her feelings were about the disgust

she felt for herself, and the more disgusted she felt, the more she
needed some form of self-medication. For her, alcohol was the
symptom of the greater problem, and she shudders with recall of
all the nights Sid had to scoop her up from the floor and carry her
to bed. The times she left pots burning on the stove, the time Tom
as a five-year-old sopped towels where she lay sick on the bathroom
floor. "Mommy is sick," he told Sid, who stripped and bathed her,
cool sheets around her body, cool cloth to her head. It was the vision of her children standing there and staring at her, their eyes as
somber and vacuous as Sid's had been that day he got Paula's letter, that woke her up.

"I'm through," she said. "I need help."

Sid backed her just as he always had. Rusty would have called
him her enabler. He nursed her and loved her. He forgave her and
forgave her. I'm a bad chemistry experiment, she told Sid. Without him she would not have survived.

On the day of intervention, the kids come in meaning business,
but then can't help but lapse into discussion about their own families and how great they all are. Snow Bunny wants a baby, which
makes Sid laugh, even though Marilyn can tell he suspects something is amiss. Rusty has been promoted. He is thinking about
going back to school to get his degree in psychology. They gather
in the living room, Sid in his chair, a coffee cup on the table beside
him. She knows there is bourbon in his cup but would never say
a word. She doesn't have to. Sally sweeps by, grabs the cup, and
then is in the kitchen sniffing its content. Rusty gives the nod of a
man in charge. Sid is staring at her, all the questions easily read:
Why are they here? Did you know they were coming? Why did you
keep this from me? And she has to look away. She never should
have let this happen. She should have found a way to bring Sid
around to his own decision, the way he had led her.

Now she wants to scream at the children that she did this to Sid.
She wants to pull out the picture box and say: This is me back

when I was fucking my friend's husband while you were asleep in your beds. And this is me when I drank myself sick so that I could forget what a horrible woman and wife and mother I was. Here is where I passed out on the floor with a pan of hot grease on the stove, and here is where I became so hysterical in the front yard that I almost burned the house down. I ruined the lawn your father worked so hard to grow. I ruined your father. I did this, and he never told you about how horrible I was. He protected me. He saved me.

"Well, Sid," Rusty begins, "we have come together to be with you because we're concerned about you."

"We love you, Daddy, and we're worried."

"Mom is worried," Tom says, and as Sid turns to her, Marilyn has to look down. "Your drinking has become a problem, and we've come to get help for you."

I'm the drunk, she wants to say. I was here first.

"You're worried, honey?" Sid asks. "Why haven't you told me?"

She looks up now, first at Sid and then at Sally and Tom. If you live long enough, your children learn to love you from afar, their lives are front and center and elsewhere. Your life is only what they can conjure from bits and pieces. They don't know how it all fits together. They don't know all the sacrifices that have been made.

"We're here as what is called an intervention," Rusty says.

"Marilyn?" He is gripping the arms of his chair. "You knew this?"

"No," she says. "No, I didn't. I have nothing to do with this."

"Marilyn." Rusty rises from his chair. Sally right beside him. It's like the room has split in two and she is given a clear choice—the choice she wishes she had made years ago, and then maybe none of this would have ever happened.

"We can take care of this on our own," she says. "We've taken care of far worse."

"Such as?" Tom asks. She has always wanted to ask him what he remembers from those horrible days. Does he remember finding her there on the floor? Does he remember her wishing to be dead?

"Water under the bridge," Sid says. "Water under the bridge." Sid stands, shoulders thrown back. He is still the tallest man in the room. He is the most powerful man. "You kids are great," he says. "You're great, and you're right." He goes into the kitchen and ceremoniously pours what's left of a fifth of bourbon down the sink. He breaks out another fifth still wrapped with a Christmas ribbon and pours it down the sink. "Your mother tends to over-react and exaggerate from time to time, but I do love her." He doesn't look at her, just keeps pouring. "She doesn't drink, so I won't drink."

"She has never had a problem," Sally says, and for a brief second Marilyn feels Tom's eyes on her.

"I used to," Marilyn says.

"Yeah, she'd sip a little wine on holidays. Made her feel sick, didn't it, honey?" Sid is opening and closing cabinets. He puts on the teakettle. "Mother likes tea in the late afternoon like the British. As a matter of fact," he continues, still not looking at her, "sometimes we pretend we are British."

She nods and watches him pour out some cheap Scotch he always offers to cheap friends. He keeps the good stuff way up high behind her mother's silver service. "And we've been writing our own little holiday letter, Mother and I, and we're going to tell every single thing that has gone on this past year like Sally and Rusty do. Like I'm going to tell that Mother has a spastic colon and often feels 'sqwitty,' as the British might say, and that I had an abscessed tooth that kept draining into my throat, leaving me no choice but to hock and spit throughout the day. But all that aside, kids, the real reason I can't formally go somewhere to dry out for you right now is, one, I have already booked a hotel over in Myrtle Beach for our anniversary, and, two, there is nothing about me to dry."

By the end of the night everyone is talking about "one more chance." Sid has easily turned the conversation to Rusty and where

he plans to apply to school and to Snow Bunny and her hopes of
having a "little Tommy" a year from now. They say things like that
they are proud of Sid for his effort but not to be hard on himself
if he can't do it on his own. He needs to realize he might have a
problem. He needs to be able to say: I have a problem.

"So. Wonder what stirred all that up?" he asks as they watch the
children finally drive away. She has yet to make eye contact with
him. "I have to say I'm glad to see them leave." He turns now and
waits for her to say something.

"I say adios, motherfuckers." She cocks her hands this way and
that like the rappers do, which makes him laugh. She notices his
hand shaking and reaches to hold it in her own. She waits, and then
she offers to fix him a small drink to calm his nerves. "I don't have
to have it, you know," he says.

"Oh, I know that," she says. "I also know you saved the good
stuff.

She mixes a weak one and goes into the living room, where he
has turned off all but the small electric candle on the piano.

"Here's to the last drink," he says as she sits down beside him.
He breathes a deep sigh that fills the room. He doesn't ask again
if she had anything to do with what happened. He never questions
her a second time; he never has. And in the middle of the night
when she reaches her hand over the cool sheets, she will find him
there, and when spring comes and the sticky heat disgusts her with
pangs of all the failures in her life, he will be there, and when it is
time to get in the car and drive to Myrtle Beach or to see the kids,
perhaps even to drive all the way to Minnesota to see their grandchildren, she will get in and close the door to the passenger side
without a word. She will turn and look at the house that the two
of them worked so hard to maintain, and she will note as she always does the perfect green grass of the front yard and how Sid
fixed it so that there is not a trace of the mess she made. It is their
house. It is their life. She will fasten her seat belt and not say a
word.

Born and raised in Lumberton, North Carolina, Jill McCorkle has taught creative writing at The University of North Carolina, Bennington College, Tufts University, and Harvard. Five of her eight books of fiction—five novels and three collections of stories—have been named *New York Times* Notables. Winner of the New England Book Award, the Dos Passos Award for Literature, and the North Carolina Award for Literature, she lives near Boston with her husband and their two children.

DEBI MILLIGAN

*U*sually *my stories begin with a line of dialogue or the idea of a particular character and then take shape along the way. With "Intervention," my idea was the ending; I imagined a person getting into a car with someone she knew should not be driving. I imagined that she was knowingly committing a kind of sacrificial suicide, if not on that particular ride then the next one or the next. For a year I kept toying with that idea, thinking of reasons a person would do such a thing. This is her spouse; she is devoted. But why to this extent? I began writing about the intervention about to take place within this family and before I knew it, I was in Marilyn's past and viewing the history of a marriage where Sid's loyalty and faithfulness and forgiveness had held it all together for years. I began to see and understand how he had evolved into this man who now has a drinking problem, and I was surprised to find how I sided with him, and how Marilyn's act of getting into the car became something I admired and was in fact symbolic of her own redemption and a marriage bond that because of all it weathered is now indestructible.*

Bret Anthony Johnston

THE WIDOW

(from *New England Review*)

Her husband kissing her cheek, then stepping outside and scooping the dog into his arms. How tenderly he lowered him to the truck seat, how nonchalantly he set the pistol on the floorboard before driving away into the night. The dog was a miniature black poodle named Peppy, and Richard had owned him before they were married. Peppy's muzzle was silver, like his paws. He had cataracts and he hadn't eaten in a week.

She lay in bed when her husband returned. She heard him wash with the garden hose, then enter the house and creep into their bedroom to unload his pockets onto the dresser.

"Where's your shirt?" she asked, then before he could answer, "Oh."

He sat on the bed, pulled off his boots. She touched his back.

"Where," she said."

"A field off Yorktown. A cornfield that's just been plowed."

"Did he—"

"Minnie."

"How much would a vet have cost?"

"Oh, I think the old boy deserved better than that."

He'd said this for a week, though she knew he also wanted to save money. Overtime had been slim lately, and they were seven months pregnant. In bed, she could smell the dark field on him, a mealy scent that promised he would handle such things. She whispered, "Are you okay?"

He stayed so quiet she thought he was weeping, or about to. He who never wept, he who always calmed her when she fell to pieces. She wanted his tears, though, wanted to drink and absorb them.

"Honey?"

He said, "My ears are still ringing."

Minnie Marshall didn't sleep the night before arranging her funeral. She stayed up in the den, smoking and watching television and applying a mud mask. Her foot kept time with the ceiling fan; September in south Texas. She thought of when they buried Richard, of course, thought of the long line of mourners, the poem Lee had read. She hadn't known he would read anything—hadn't known he even wrote poetry. Would he write one for her?

Before he returned home to care for her, Lee—thirty-three, unmarried, renting the bottom floor of a house in St. Louis, and writing his dissertation on, what, migrant labor?—had taught high school history. She had liked telling people this. Yet, lately, she often thought of him as the boy who'd run screaming from butterflies, as the infant who some nights would only quiet when Richard shredded rags beside the crib; the ripping noise awed him. Or she thought of the year he'd been stricken with rheumatoid arthritis, when they spent days watching cartoons and soap operas, or if his knee felt strong, going to the pond and tossing crumbs to ducks. The ducks had always cheered him. She had known him best then. High school and college seemed waves that knocked him away from her. After his father died, he'd visited more, but he remained distant, a guest who spoke only when spoken to. She'd learned not to pry on those short stays, but imagined that extended time together would foster conversations, wear thin his reticence. Now, home for a year, he seemed never to have unpacked his bags; he seemed to have layered himself in silence like winter clothes.

Some mornings she allowed herself to make a racket to rouse Lee sooner, to clang pots or drop spoons into the sink, but today she let him sleep. She felt croupy and beleaguered. She brewed coffee and thumbed through the paper. When Lee had lived in Missouri, she'd sent him articles and she still sought out stories to interest him. Always she saved the obituaries for last. None of today's names was familiar, neither from the cancer center nor life before. The sunrise was opening the kitchen. She mixed batter for waffles, beat eggs, fried sausage. Normally Lee ate cold cereal, but she hoped a solid breakfast might start the morning right. The cooking took an hour and she had just sat down when he began stirring. Her heart quickened. She took her ashtray from the table. Smoke bothered him while he ate.

He said, "You can stay."

"Get 'em while they're hot," she said. Slowly, she brought a heaping plate to him. If she rushed, or forgot to pause after standing, she found herself light-headed and reeling, then on the floor, hearing Lee's frantic voice rushing to her. She fell often, far more often than he knew.

"Did you sleep well?" he asked.

She sipped her coffee. "Wonderfully. How about you, sweetheart?"

"I thought I heard you walking around last night."

"I wanted some chocolate," she said. "I drifted off watching a show about France."

He nodded and resumed eating. As in his youth, he still cut food with his fork rather than a knife. He mixed ketchup into his eggs, stirred sugar into his coffee. He sopped syrup and sausage grease with his toast. She loved watching him eat.

"There's more of everything," she said.

He shook his head, still chewing, and rose to rinse his dishes. He returned the ashtray. "How do you feel?"

"Full of energy," she said brightly. She lit a cigarette. "I thought we'd go to the pond after the appointment. We can get sandwiches for a picnic."

He smiled, even laughed a little, and looked at her as if she'd suggested sprinting to Houston. Probably he'd expected her to complain. "Have you taken your medicine?"

She held smoke in her lungs, then blew it over her shoulder, away from Lee. Sometimes she lied about taking her pills and spent the day worried he'd catch her, but this morning she was on her best behavior. "All done," she said. Then after a moment, "More cars are broken into at funerals and weddings than anywhere else. People forget to lock their doors because they're too emotional."

He set a ceramic bell on the table. The bells were all over the house. She would ring one if she fell, or felt pain or had trouble breathing, or if whatever was coming for her came and she couldn't bear to face it alone. The bells comforted Lee and shamed her.

She yawned.

"You should nap before we go. Or I can reschedule."

She waved her hand dismissively. After a moment, she asked, "Do you know what the French used to call the guillotine?"

"A little early for a beheading, isn't it?"

"The widow."

He swept crumbs into the sink. A jolt of guilt for not washing the breakfast pans stung her; she could almost remember washing them. In Lee's presence, she was acutely aware of tasks she'd not completed. She said, "Daddy spent some time in France before I met him."

He braced himself. No one else would have seen his inward tensing—a quick, panicky inhalation as if she were about to drag him under water—but she noticed. The water was talk of his father. She doubted that Lee avoided the discussions because they depressed him; rather he thought they grieved her. And they did. What she couldn't explain was how she loved talking about Richard, adored hearing his name. She felt happiest in those unforeseen moments when she turned and for an instant, thought she'd seen him; when she woke still believing he lay beside her.

She said, "My traveling days are over."

"Mama . . ."

"I wasn't going to say that." She snuffed out her cigarette then tried lighting another, but her lighter wouldn't immediately spark. She said, "Traveling just seems such a hassle now."

"You'd like France," Lee said. "When a person lights a cigarette, he offers everybody one."

Linda "Minnie" Marshall was fifty-five when the doctor said cancer. Her boys were both gone. Richard—husband and engineer, taker of early retirement package, reader of mysteries and griller of lobster—had died six years before; Lee had lived in Missouri since college. She worked as an accountant, owned a late model Oldsmobile and lived in the three-bedroom house the life insurance had paid off. She had seen the doctor because she'd been more tired than usual—her potassium was low again, she'd guessed. The exhaustion could have been a blessing; her body could have finally been adjusting to a life alone, settling into a routine without the boys, and if she honored the change, her days might bring her happiness again. If not happiness, at least less sorrow. But the doctor had sat heavily on the rolling stool, removed his glasses, and outlined options for treatment. Because he gave her a fair chance for recovery, she knew she would die.

She had considered not telling Lee of the disease, had considered letting it run its course untreated. He would be cowed by the diagnosis—she knew this as surely as she knew his name—and he would not understand how it could come as a relief. For years he'd beseeched her to move beyond his father's death, and now, finally, she would. Then, unexpectedly, she was mortified and needed him home. She needed his company in the chemo ward, needed to see him when the oncologist pressed the stethoscope to her back or pointed to X rays where the tumor in her lung glowed like a star. She needed him to interpret what the doctors said; she did not want him to censor the information, but he lied and she knew it. When she asked him about the flashes of color in her peripheral vision, pinwheels and splotches and starbursts, he blamed the sun or tricks of light. When she asked about her ruined handwriting, he claimed to see no difference. When she asked how long she would live, he said you couldn't trust doctors.

Dressing for the appointment took over an hour. Breakfast had drained her, and now she was winded doing her makeup, weak legged slipping into her skirt. Every button was a chore. How perfectly easy it would have been to stretch out and shut her eyes, but she pressed on because she'd already cancelled the meeting twice. She thought to take a nerve pill, but decided against it; she was bleary enough. For years she'd rushed to dress for work and get Lee to school, and now she wondered how she'd ever managed. A wave of pride rolled inside her. The doctors had said her memory would fail, and often she'd forgotten what she tried to remember, but the unbidden past returned vividly. The musky scent of Richard's hair gel; the sequined fabric she'd sewn for one of Lee's Halloween costumes; years later, the noise of him and his girlfriend in the shower, thinking she should be angry, but really feeling pleased; the mower still idling on the afternoon she found Richard in the half-cut yard; the thought thirty minutes before, *I bet he's thirsty;* the grass clippings on the glass of water she'd brought him. The memories assailed her, asleep or awake. She wore them like pearls.

Lee drove because she no longer could. She swerved and veered, sped and stalled. Twice she'd gotten lost a mile from home. Both of them blamed her medication, but she knew the pills were not the problem. Now she rode in the passenger seat, checking herself in the mirror. Half-circles hung under her eyes, her face gaunt and pale. Her makeup looked rushed. Her hair, though, was fullbodied and healthy. After the treatments, it had grown back thick and dark and lovely, another woman's hair.

"I feel like we're going to a museum," she said. "We're all dressed up."

Despite the sun and humidity, she wore heels and a long-sleeved satin blouse. The sleeves hid the bruises that dappled her arms; the softest bump scarred her. Also, she was always so cold now.

Lee said, "Too spiffy for ducks. I vote for lunch and a matinee."

"We can change clothes. I'll want to sit in the sun after this."

Then a thought occurred: "But don't dress me like this, okay? Just jeans and a T-shirt. Sneakers. No makeup."

"Okay, Mama."

"And no jewelry. The morticians steal it."

Lee adjusted the rearview mirror. As with talk of his father, he refused to discuss her dying. Yet she needed him to know these things. Because she'd botched the past year of his life, she strove to spare him her burial. The dementia would set in soon. No one had said that outright, but she saw it coming. Poor Lee. Listening to her babble and watching her body falter, feeding her soup and waiting, waiting, *waiting* for her last breath would be torment enough without fretting over her jewelry and car, her house and clothes and last wishes. In the recliner at night, she devised ways to slip information into conversations, but the ideas evaporated with the sunrise. Her ideas were dew and mists.

"The last time I wore this, Daddy took me to *The Nutcracker*," she said, though suddenly the memory seemed slippery, possibly completely wrong. "Nothing like that had ever come to Corpus. He bought tickets for Christmas. Your father looked so handsome in a suit."

"And you look fabulous in red," he said, glancing at her blouse. "You should wear it more often."

That she would never again wear the outfit was palpable in the car, and she waited for the feeling to disperse. They passed a corner where people sometimes sold puppies from truck beds, but none were out. She hated the dogs being sold that way, but their absence always disappointed her.

"Here's a test," she said. "What was in Dad's car when I met him?"

Lee shook his head. Richard had strolled into the office where she worked as a receptionist. He wore a tweed jacket, a full beard. She had said *Just a minute,* had said it in an abrupt, frenzied tone that made him chuckle, and he'd started calling her "Minute." By the time he left, he only called her Minnie and it had become her name.

"A poodle," she said. "A little black poodle I could see through the window. Isn't that something?"

He smiled at her.

They rode beside the bay, light glimmering on the marbled water. She said, "Isn't the weather gorgeous? We can walk a trail at the pond."

"You *are* feeling good."

She wanted to say *Fit as a fiddle,* but suspected the words might wound him, so she checked herself. And now that he'd acknowledged her energy, she was momentarily relieved of the charade. She was an actress between scenes, out of breath and nervous. Her heart raced. Outside, the blurred horizon seemed close enough to touch. She remembered going to the pond during chemo, Lee's hand on her elbow as she stepped over the exposed roots of live oaks. Now, he turned a corner and the sun blinded them. He lowered both visors, but she pushed hers back up. The heat felt glorious on her battered arms.

"Daddy used to fix pancakes for his poodle on Saturday mornings," she said, lighting a cigarette. "His name was Peppy. He died before you were born."

The minister beginning the last prayer of the service, Minnie regretting Richard being on a diet when he died. She wished she'd been able to cook for him that last month, to prepare one of her recipes he loved. What it would've been, she had no idea. Just as she had no idea how she would survive life without him.

Lee folded the sheet of paper with his poem on it and slid it into his pocket; she heard the paper crease.

Richard would have said she'd spent too much on his funeral—as he'd always accused about Christmas presents—and they would've argued over the receipts at the kitchen table. He'd always meant to plan his funeral, to save her the trouble and prevent her from spending what she'd just spent. He was fifty-eight, and the wet grass had kept bogging the mower. He'd said he would come right in; they were going to a movie that night. She hadn't cried during any of this, not in front of anyone, not even Lee. She was proud of that. Maybe Richard would have been proud, too.

"Amen," the minister said, raising his head and opening his eyes. Shrimp, she thought. He might have wanted my fried shrimp.

In the funeral home, she wanted a nerve pill more than ever. The high ceilings and tall windows and Spanish tile floors made her anxious. She sat on a plush couch while Lee registered with an old woman behind the reception desk. How the woman stood it, Minnie couldn't imagine; how the water trickling in the stone fountain didn't drive her mad. Behind her, heavy oak doors opened into the chapel, and down the hall were viewing rooms, the re-frigerated floral displays. All of it nauseated her; she fought off a shiver. A slow, tinny music whispered in the speakers. Among the headstones, you could hear and smell the ocean less than a mile away, but inside there was only the incessant gurgle of the foun-tain, the smell of frozen flowers.

"Won't be long," Lee said.

"That's a lousy thing to say."

His eyes shut, a short exhale. "You know what I mean."

She rocked forward and straightened his shirt, something she'd done all her life; just then it seemed she could list every in-stance. She said, "Look at your collar. We can go shopping after our picnic."

He leaned back, his standard response. "How do you feel?"

"Tense," she said. "They'll try screwing us into every little thing."

"Let's hear what they say."

"They'll say, 'The more you spend, the more you care.'"

She heard shoes clacking on the tile, but only connected the sounds with the approaching man when he loomed over her. She began levering herself from the couch, cringing and struggling in the cushions until finally Lee supported her elbow. Her head swam in dizziness and she worried she'd already exposed some vulnera-bility, forfeited an advantage. When she recovered, she flashed Lee and the man a smile. Their eyes were waiting for her to fall.

She said, "Haven't keeled over yet."

Lee adjusted his sleeves; the man chuckled politely. In a voice like a doctor's, he said, "Mrs. Marshall, I'm Rudy Guerrero."

At first, she liked him calling her Mrs. Marshall, but walking to his office, she suspected the formality was a tactic to flatter widows, a calculated plea to trust his wet eyes and dark, expensive suit. She steeled herself. A large mahogany desk crowded the room, and she caught Lee admiring it. The Windberg painting on the wall was the same as in her oncologist's office, but she still liked it very much: a deer drinking from a creek, gauzy morning light shafting through vines. She was staring at the painting when Guerrero unbuttoned his jacket and sat in the deep leather chair. He opened an embossed folder, patted a handkerchief to his brow.

"Does a person absolutely have to be embalmed?" she asked.

Guerrero folded his hands together, glanced at Lee. "Well," he said, chuckling again. "State law doesn't require—"

"Perfect. Let's skip that."

Lee exhaled. Guerrero twisted the ballpoint of a heavy silver pen into place. Nodding, he said, "A tough customer, I like it." Minnie heard the pen skimming across the desk. She glanced at Lee but he averted his eyes. Somehow, she'd expected him to be pleased.

She arranged to draft monthly payments from her checking account, then if necessary, her life insurance would cover the rest. More than anything, she wanted to pay off the funeral. She and Richard had never discussed this, but there seemed a tacit agreement that whoever lived longer would sacrifice for Lee. Her last duty was to be thrifty with her dying. The practicality buoyed her. But as she deliberated between grave vaults and cement casing, between a church funeral and a graveside service, Lee voted against her. She wanted a plaque where he wanted a monument. He sighed and shifted in his seat. She suggested compromises when she could, but nothing satisfied him. Maybe a mother's funeral could never satisfy her son.

Then, so swiftly that she worried he'd overlooked something, Guerrero closed his folder and ushered them from his office. In the hall, she tried to touch Lee's cheek— a gesture to say, *We're doing fine, Good job, It's almost over*—but lifting her arm nearly toppled her and he had to grab her waist. Guerrero opened a door past the floral displays and stepped demurely aside. He said, "I'll check back shortly."

The chilled air smelled of oak and lilacs, and it almost buckled her knees. She felt dizzy, tasted bile in her throat; her stomach dropped. Three coffins—two open, one closed—rested on pedestals in the middle of the room. Sections of others, their hulls and sides, were affixed to the walls and illuminated by individual brass lamps. She had spent an afternoon in the showroom when Richard died, but had insisted Lee stay home. Now, he looked stunned, lost. She turned away to gather herself, feeling as though they'd happened upon a car accident. She imagined sitting beside the pond, heard herself telling Lee, "At least that's behind us." If they could only survive this, if she could hold it together, she thought Lee would reward her among the mesquite trees that hemmed the water; she plied herself with ideas of him shedding his layers of silence and talking with her in the sun.

She got her legs back slowly, the vertigo subsided. She made her way around the displays, fighting off the fearful reverence the room demanded. The poplar and maple and tucked satin seemed such a waste. The champagne-colored velvet and taffeta interiors were expensive and worthless. And the pillows! She'd forgotten coffins came with those. Who needed a pillow? Her heels clicked on the floor, like hammering in a church. When she moved into the steel displays—20 gauge, 18 gauge, stainless, what did it all mean? what did it matter?—she saw herself reflected on the gleaming surfaces. She winked at Lee in her reflection, but his eyes darted away. She touched the firm, stitched padding; he clasped his hands behind his back.

"Now it feels like we *are* at a museum," she said. "We take a step and stop, then step and stop."

"It's a regular Smithsonian."

She laughed, though he gave her a cross look and she realized he'd not meant to amuse her at all.

"Did I tell you what the French call guillotines?"

He nodded, inching back toward the oaks.

"The guillotines turned wives into widows," she said. He leaned to study a cherrywood casket. She said, "I like this one. It looks comfortable."

Basic steel, the shade of blush. Small gardenias, the same cream color as the satin lining, trimming the lid. A thin chrome bar along its side. She couldn't have cared less for it.

Lee said, "It's the cheapest."

"And the prettiest."

"What about this one? You love pine."

"Oh, it's beautiful, but you could fit three of me in there." She wanted him to laugh or at least smile—please, please—but he just paced forward, arms still behind his back. She said, "You look like a security guard."

Maybe she'd glimpsed a small grin forming, but he squelched it and slid his hands into his pockets. If he were a child, she could have aped silly faces or ripped rags to cheer him, but now he was gone.

"Daddy's poodle used to bark at waves. At the beach, we'd—"

"The price doesn't matter, Mama."

"I know, honey. I just love this one, really. The gardenias are precious."

"You bought Dad a nice one."

She almost blurted *He deserved a nice one,* but refrained. She crossed the room and pretended to consider the more expensive caskets. Lee said nothing. He'd turned callous and unreachable. She tried to remember which model she'd bought Richard, but couldn't. It had brass bars like saloon banisters, but none with bars looked familiar. Maybe the style was discontinued, but she felt certain the failing was hers. If she ruined everything else, shouldn't a widow at least remember her husband's casket? So much about her would disappoint him, her fear and depression, the burden she'd become for Lee, and the slow, sorry withering that now defined her life. Perhaps she was getting exactly what she deserved.

"Hello?" Guerrero stepped inside, hesitantly. "How are we?"

Minnie looked at Lee, then back at the man.

"Never better," she said. "I'll take this one."

Lee wanted to rest before their picnic. Her choices had disheartened him, and though Minnie thought it better to eat lunch and get their minds off everything, she conceded. At home he retired to his room and left her to stew. Maybe he wanted to spare her his anger, but his silence was more punishing. And more exhausting. She had meant only to relax briefly then start washing laundry, but in the recliner, the waking world receded. A patchwork of images—Guerrero's meaty hands and the painting behind his desk; Lee dropping her at various entrances to save her energy, then parking the car alone; Richard at the beach, holding a conch, saying *Hey, would you look at this;* a cakewalk from her youth, the music stopping precisely when she stepped onto the winning star—then she slept. In her dream, Richard appeared as a stranger, but she nonetheless recognized him as the man whose absence choked her heart, and his voice poured like water. Sleep felled her and when she woke, the windows were black.

"Someone was tired," Lee said.

The light in the kitchen burned her eyes. She pulled a chair out from the table, and the legs scraping across the tile rankled her. Her lighter would not fire. She tried for what seemed minutes, then just as she resigned herself to getting a light from the stove, smoke filled her lungs. She exhaled with her eyes closed. Her mouth tasted clammy, sour. Lee was leering at her, she felt him. She hung the cigarette on her lips and went to the refrigerator for a Coke. He smiled as she crossed the kitchen, but she concentrated on not stumbling. Her head was clouded, her body more drained than before, sapped specifically of patience.

She held the bottle toward him: "I can't open this."

He twisted the cap, and the ease of the action seemed accusatory. In the garage, the washing machine buzzer sounded. She winced.

"Headache?" he asked.

"We missed the ducks."

"Maybe tomorrow. Maybe you'll feel better."

"I felt fine today," she said. "Besides, I have things to do tomorrow."

She half-hoped he would call her bluff and argue (an unfamiliar, yet powerful feeling), but he just went to change the laundry. Her legs were restless, small spasms jerking and knotting in her calves. Her stomach ached from not eating. All other nerves felt exposed, stung by the light and air.

"Why didn't you wake me?" she asked when he returned. "I wanted to talk over lunch."

"We'll have a nice supper. We can talk now."

She dragged on her cigarette and stabbed the butt in the ashtray. In the window, her reflection appeared even more diminished than it had that morning.

"You just didn't want to go," she said, trying to light another cigarette.

"You needed rest." His tone was stoic and confident, meaning he thought he was right. Before it had always comforted her; tonight it grated. He said, "How does cream of chicken sound?"

"What would have been so terrible about a picnic? The money? How much would we have spent? Twenty dollars? Can't we afford that on a day like today?"

"I'm not the one so concerned with money."

"A bronze grave vault is a bit excessive, Leiland."

He pinched the bridge of his nose, shut his eyes. "Is this the kind of night we're going to have?"

Maybe, she thought. She felt destitute of courtesy and tact, suddenly unconcerned with doing the right thing. Nothing had panned out as she'd wanted, nothing. She'd pinned her hopes on talking beside the pond, believing it would restore them, but now everything was dashed. She wanted to strike out, to be cruel, and nothing was worse than feeling this way toward him. Usually when he wanted to argue, she yielded. Yet before she knew she would say it, when she only knew she felt compelled to say something, she said, "I want to be cremated."

He put his hands on the window frame and gazed into the back-yard. Or maybe his eyes were closed, maybe he was taking deep breaths, counting to ten. He said, "You need a nerve pill."

"No, Lee, I don't. You can't just dope me up all the time."

"Me? *Me* dope you up?"

"I can't talk to you. I can't even talk to my own son."

"What, Mother? What do you want to say?"

What did she want to say? Suddenly, nothing. Before there seemed so much, but now, everything had vanished. She said, "Sell the house, don't rent it."

"Oh, Jesus," he said, something she'd never heard him say.

"Sell the car. Take my jewelry to a jeweler. Not a pawn shop."

"Mother."

"Donate my wigs and clothes. That's what I want."

"Mother."

"I don't want you to be sappy. I want you to invest the money. If I want to be cremated, that's my choice. And if I want to have a picnic at the goddamned pond, the least—"

"Mother!" His voice rattled the windows, filled the room. Then silence filled it. When he spoke again, his tone had softened, as if in apology: "The pond is gone."

She shook out another cigarette. Her fingers trembled. "That's absurd."

"It's been gone for two years, maybe three. It's a car wash now. You sent me the newspaper clipping."

She shrugged. She flicked her lighter, and shook it, but it wouldn't catch. She tried and tried, but got nowhere. She tossed the ciga-rette and lighter onto the table and held her face in her hands. Lee sulked into the hall. Her throat tightened; wet pressure welled be-hind her eyes. Hadn't they gone to the pond during treatment? She understood none of it, neither her son nor herself, their silences, their arguments. She no longer knew his role or hers, what was re-quired of her and what would handle itself. She didn't understand how to die. Lee ran water in the bathroom. She wanted to chase after him, to scream for help or ring her bell. She wanted to beg him not to shut himself in his room, wanted to dispense with the lie that today, or any day in the last year, was normal. Before, the charade seemed necessary for him, but now she realized she had depended upon it more than he ever had. He would survive this, rebuild a life that she would never see: a life, simply, without her. And shouldn't this please rather than terrify her? She wanted to admit she was terrified, terrified to sleep or be awake, and she wished she'd lived a life different in every way except for him and his father; she wished she still had a chance. She wished she could bear to buy a beautiful coffin. She wished Richard was still alive, so Lee wouldn't have to drive her to the funeral home and watch her come undone. She wished, for all of their sakes, that she would've died first.

He returned to the kitchen and said, "Just wait a minute. I'm going to the store."

She was trying the dead lighter again. He patted his pockets for his keys and wallet. She hated him driving to the store because undoubtedly he thought if she didn't need lighters and cigarettes, she wouldn't be dying. He resembled his father, his light hair and sloped shoulders and even his reticence, and as he checked the cupboards, the likeness was too much. All of it was too much, too much. As the tears came, she wondered what else she'd forgotten or would forget, what else he was withholding. She wondered where the ducks had flown after the pond, if he remembered how much he'd enjoyed them as a child. She wondered if he would ever have children, who would be their mother and what they would know of their grandmother. She wondered if they would get any of her features. The only trait that seemed worth passing on was her new lovely hair, which, really, wasn't hers at all.

In a month the den would become a sickroom. A hospital bed would be delivered, tubes from the oxygen machine would snake over and behind her furniture; her furniture would be buried under hospice charts, hospital gowns, packages of diapers. Nurses came and went. She held guarded conversations with them—as she had with Rudy Guererro—but soon pockets of forgotten information devoured her speech. She would forget Lee's name. Though never who he was. Through that long, slow fade there always remained a silky, durable cord of memory that connected them, a child and his mother.

She woke in the recliner with the television on and Lee reading on the couch. Her mouth tasted dry. A new lighter, a pack of cigarettes and a chocolate bar lay beside the bell on the end table. She did not remember Lee settling her down or helping her into the recliner before going to the store. She remembered the fighting, and hoped it was over.

She said, "Good morning, sunshine."

He leaned forward, smiling in the lamplight. "It's almost midnight. I'll warm your soup."

She smoked as her eyes adjusted. Her body felt less fragmented, her thoughts less scattered. She was satisfied with the funeral arrangements and relieved to have them behind her. *A tough customer,* Guererro had called her. After a few minutes, it occurred to her that she felt marvelous.

Lee returned with juice and soup and her nighttime medication, eight pills she had to swallow two at a time. He kissed her forehead, a gesture she adored but never admitted for fear he would stop. He lay on the couch and hooked his arm over his eyes, crossed his ankles. As she ate—when had he learned to make such delicious soup, soup so good it made her hungrier to eat?—she noticed he wore socks she'd bought from a catalog. Sometimes just seeing him mystified her. Every night, he stayed awake long enough to make sure she wouldn't get sick. Every night she dreaded the moment he went to bed.

She relit her cigarette, drank more juice. She said, "Are you awake?"

"Okay," he said, startled. He raised his head, then lay back. "Yes, I am."

"Do you know what the French call—"

"The widow." He lifted his arm from his eyes and winked at her, smirking. Briefly she felt ashamed for repeating it—how many times had she told him? — then she let herself off the hook, because he had.

She said, "You're right about the pond."

He nodded, his elbow over his eyes again.

"And I don't want to be cremated."

"I know."

Four pills still waited beside the ashtray, though she recognized none of them. Lately, she remembered only the shapes of her muscle relaxers and nerve pills, the tablets she reached for most often. They bathed her in a perfectly warm, perfectly weightless oblivion, and as she melted, she wondered if the cottony nothingness enveloping her was how it would finally feel. She hoped so. In her darkest moods, she'd considered emptying the bottles and chasing the pills with vodka, but that would cancel her insurance. If Lee had to act as her nurse, she could at least pay for his trouble.

"Let's see if the ocean's still there," he said, suddenly.

She flinched. She thought he'd drifted to sleep. Then she heard the words as if in an echo, and her heart lurched.

"Dad used to come in my room and say that. I remembered it today."

Her skin tingled. How many times had she heard Richard say that, either to her or Lee? The words lifted her, sent her memory reeling, as if in a second's time she'd gotten delightfully drunk.

"You'd still be in bed," he said. "We rarely went to the water, though. Usually, he'd find some road to get lost on."

"Sounds familiar," she said. Maybe it sounded familiar, maybe not.

"So we were probably lost, but one morning he showed me where he'd buried Peppy."

She drew on her cigarette. A wave swelled beneath her. The tingling on her skin was replaced with a trembling in each nerve, an expectant hush.

"He said he'd convinced the vet to let him do it."

"What a thing to remember."

He uncrossed his ankles, then crossed them again. "I'd never seen him cry before. I must have been six or seven. I didn't know what to do."

She cleared her throat, quietly. "And?"

"I just waited," he said. "Eventually he quieted down and started the truck."

He was lying, of course, just as he had to explain the splotches in her peripheral vision, her illegible signature. Or he was exaggerating, suddenly committed to calming her. Perhaps now he couldn't ignore what was imminent, inevitable. Perhaps because she could no longer keep anything from him, he longed to resurrect and recast what he could for her. Probably he'd contrived his father's tears that afternoon or as she slept, but maybe he'd not imagined them until now. And what was he saying? That he was sorry? Or that he too would weep privately but eventually recover? None of it mattered; he was exalting her, filling her every cell with breath. She listened as she would to an opera, hearing not language but just his voice and its lament of time and love and doomed hopefulness. Oh, the surprise and absolute mystery of a child.

He said, "We'd go all over, those Saturday mornings."

It was as if he'd just returned from a long absence, or was a skittish animal finally coaxed into approaching. She turned to him, slowly, careful not to scare him away.

"Tell me," she said, putting out her cigarette. "Tell me where you've been."

———

Bret Anthony Johnston's first collection of stories, *Corpus Christi*, is forthcoming from Random House. His fiction has been widely published in places such as the *Paris Review*, *Open City*, and *New Stories from the South: The Year's Best, 2003*. A graduate of the Iowa Writers' Workshop, he teaches creative writing at California State University.

DIANI

*T*he Widow" is the second of three stories in the collection about Minnie. It came from an image I couldn't get out of my head: Minnie sitting in her recliner, her foot keeping time with the ceiling fan. At first, I thought she was awaiting MRI results, but as the utterly disappointing early drafts prove, she obviously wasn't. Likewise, the sorry middle drafts show she wasn't waiting for her son to return home. She wasn't scared or nervous or worried, not exactly. I would have been all of the above, and accepting that she wasn't, took me half a year. Usually I get a handle on characters by understanding their desires and losses, but Minnie continued to stump me until I realized that what she wants and what she's lost are one in the same: her son. Once I knew that, which in turn revealed what had kept her foot tapping—a uniquely maternal mix of apprehension and excitement about planning her funeral—the story took shape.

I'm indebted to Ethan Canin for his generosity and enthusiasm toward the story, to Jodee Rubins and Stephen Donadio for giving it such a fine New England home, and of course to Shannon and Kathy for making it feel so welcome in the South. Finally, I'm grateful to Jennifer Marek, who, after reading the published story, drove by the duck pond to see if it was still there.

R. T. Smith

DOCENT

(from *The Missouri Review*)

Good afternoon, ladies and gentlemen from hither and yon, and welcome to the Lee Chapel on the campus of historic Washington and Lee University. My name is Sybil Mildred Clemm Legrand Pascal, and I will be your guide and compass on this dull, dark and soundless day, as the poet says, in the autumn of the year. You can call me Miss Sibby, and in case you are wondering about my hooped dress of ebony, my web-like hairnet and calf-leather shoes, they are authentic to the period just following the War Between the States, and I will be happy to discuss the cut and fabric of my mourning clothing with any of you fashion-conscious ladies at the end of the tour—which by the way will be concluded in the passageway between the crypt and the museum proper. If anyone should need to avail themselves of the running-water facilities, I will indicate their location before you enter the basement displays; and please, all you gentlemen, remove your caps in the chapel, and also, ladies, kindly ask your little darlings to keep a hush on their voices as they would at any shrine. No camera flashes, please, in the General Lee alcove. No smoking, of course—a habit I deplore.

Now, I am sure you know a lot already, and I may cover ground you have heard before, but please respect those who enter this tour with an open heart, and I will periodically pause to entertain questions, though I do not personally see any reason why they would arise.

The Lee Chapel, before you, was completed with intricately milled brick in 1868 on a Victorian design during the General's tenure, but it wore no green gown of ivy to begin with; I myself adore the ivy and do not care for the decision to trim it back. At this time of the afternoon it turns the light attractively spectral, wouldn't you agree? And I do not believe ivy could rip the building down. The chapel itself, which has never been officially consecrated by a legitimate denomination, should not be confused with the Robert E. Lee Episcopal Church, which you can see, with the steeple facing Washington Street, at the end of the paved walk. I am told there are two Episcopal churches in the world which are not named for saints, but that is not one of them—which is told locally as a joke, if you think such things are funny.

If you look directly above to the bell tower, you will see the black face and white numbers of the timepiece, which with its chimes duplicates the Westminster Clock in London and is dedicated to the memory of Livingston Waddell Houston, a student drowned in the North River, though I do not recall when nor deem it important. The pendulum, of course, is invisible, as in all the best devices. The numerals, you will notice, are not normal American ones with curves and circles but the I's and X's and V's of Latin numbers, a language which was taught here to the young men from the beginning—and still is to some few, especially those who wish to stand for the bar. Did you know that the "Lex" in "Lexington" is Latin for "law"? I have heard, however, that the young ladies who have matriculated—let's see, it's been some dozen years now since that infliction—do not enroll in dead languages. They are here, no doubt, for progress, and do not have time for such niceties. If such a perspective keeps them provided for and protected, they truly have my envy. In just ten minutes the hour will strike, and we will hear the tintinnabulation of the bells. I love that sound and will not abide random chatter once it begins.

As we proceed through the front portals, you will see on either

side caracole staircases with bentwood banisters, and we will file to
the left, but mind you do not cross the velvet ropes to climb the
steps because insurance issues must guide our path. We are entering a National Historic Landmark that is also a museum and a
tomb, and especially in these troubled modern times, we must
show the greatest respect. Perhaps we could say that the very existence of this edifice—which is, as I say, a National Historic Landmark—is one of the rare benefits of that old and storied war, but
watch your step: we do not want to add you to the already la-
mentable casualty count.

As we enter the vestibule, please do us the kindness of signing
our guest register, which bears the autographs of presidents and
princes, as well as luminaries from Reynolds Price to Burt Reynolds,
from Maya Linn, the memorial designer, to Rosalynn Carter,
Woodrow Wilson, Bing Crosby, Vincent Price, and the Dalai Lama.
Fifty thousand visitors annually, I believe, many of them repeaters,
from far and away, devotees of Lee, people who love the Stars and
Bars or have a morbid curiosity, I suppose, about the Fall of the
South. If you have a morbid curiosity about the Fall of the South—
which is not the same as a healthy historical interest—please save
your comments for your own diaries and private conversations.
One of my cardinal epigrams, a compilation of which I will pen
myself someday under the title *Miss Sibby Says,* is this: "History is
not gossip; opinion is seldom truth."

I am sure many of you all know as much about General Lee as
I do, but it may be that some of the information you know is false,
so I will highlight only selected facts as we file through the an-
techamber and into what one is tempted to call "the sanctuary" but
is actually only a multipurpose auditorium, though a splendid and
clean one. You could eat off the floor. When the General, who was
indeed a legend but hardly a myth, agreed to come here as president, right after the sorrows and fury of the war that rent our land
in half and wasted a gallant generation, he did so because, as he
said, Virginia now needs all her sons—though there were fewer
than forty students enrolled at the time. This chamber will seat six

hundred, so we know he had a vision. He was a military man with many projects and plans—"strategies" they call them—and I was once betrothed to just such a disciplined and tactical gentleman myself, but fate has denied me that marriage, among other joys. If you have been denied a significant portion of life's joys and your own prospects, you will indeed understand.

The school, of course, was then called Washington College and had been spared from Yankee fire in the end by that revered influence and the statue of dear George atop the cupola of the main building on the colonnade (which always sounds too much like "cannonade" to suit my ear). We all wish that our dear Virginia Military Academy had been similarly spared, but alas, invaders have their own designs. Many people, such as foragers and raiders, can come into a place as easily as into a person's life and leave matters far more damaged than they found them, for they have their own designs.

And please do not hesitate to touch the pews or try them out. If you'll kindly look at the wall to your left, you will see the engraved plaque testifying that the General, whom some students wanted to call President Lee—which you must admit has a nice ring to it— sat here during services, though he often napped, accustomed as he was to catching a few winks on campaign. A man who has marched and fought as a steady diet for years will find civilian life a difficult fit, and General Lee was no exception, though it was in his ancient blood, as genealogical experts have proved that he was descended from Robert the Bruce through the Spottiswoods, though far more honorable than one Spottiswood descendant, whom I knew all too well but whom discretion prevents me from calling by his sullied name.

I daresay some of you have served your states and countries and may have posed for portraits like the two flanking the memorial gate. On the left you see the Father of our country depicted on the grounds of Mount Vernon, and you will no doubt note that the Virginia militia uniform he wears so handsomely looks English, complete with gorget and musket, for he fought for the German

Hanover English kings against French and Indian savagery, though he would later alter his opinion of the French. You can see he is a young man, confident and noble, even a touch haughty, with marching orders in his pocket, and the sky behind him is overcast, as with both today's sky and the current political climate, but there is a ray of light unsuppressed, and we can all hope to witness that ourselves someday. This is not to say that every officer who encamps, lays siege, then suddenly debouches is acting on official orders, for some are not to be trusted.

Before we ascend the steps and cross the stage to examine the second but primary portrait, the image of the most trustworthy man imaginable, I should inform you that this chapel has been renovated and expanded on several occasions and was almost razed in 1919 by no less fifth-column a foe than its own president-of-the-moment, who claimed it was a firetrap with a perilous heating system and a roof that leaked like a war-worn tent—though despite today's threatening weather, you should not be alarmed. He had designs of his own and wished to replace it with a huge Georgian structure, and his name was Smith, supposedly, but the Mary Custis Chapter of the United Daughters of the Confederacy, in which I am still proud to claim emerita membership, entered the fray, along with the Colonial Dames and the DAR, until the renovation party was vanquished, the field secured and the site declared a shrine. My own relations were in the vanguard of this action, which may bring to your mind the question of my personal role as docent, which used to mean "professor," though I am surely not one of those types. A docent is a hostess, a volunteer, like so many of our martyred sons. I like to think of my function as an older sister who opens the door to hidden history. "Decent" is only one letter removed, and decency is what I strive for daily, despite personal disappointments. My own fiancé never felt such hospitality was a function an unattached lady should perform, but since his furtive departure, I have done what I please and have risen through the ranks of a somewhat special and discreet society called the Keepers of the Magnolia, who are dedicated to preservation of the past. In

France the magnolia flowers are called *les fleurs du mal,* and we Keepers have appointed ourselves sentries against the invasion of evil revisionist history and the casting of shadows over past glories. The battalions of blasphemers come into my dreams, whenever I can manage to sleep—the unholy reunderstanders and conde-scenders, and they may wear the masks of scholars but are no bet-ter than carrion rats, their tails scratching the hardwood till I wake up mouthing a silent scream.

This space is now employed by the university for a variety of pro-grams and gatherings, since as I said it is not an actual church, and the atmosphere of holiness depends entirely upon who is present. And now you and I are here and can add our reverence to the gen-eral fund. In the past few months we have hosted six weddings (all of which I have attended in my docent attire), one tipsy Irish poet, our own famous alumnus Tom Wolfe the Younger dressed in a French vanilla ice cream suit and spats while speaking of the death of art. We have heard the angry opinions of Mr. Spike Lee (no re-lation, of course), tapped our feet to the Armenian guitar band right after a forum on cultural diversity. We have been entertained by near-president Al Gore, and just yesterday the community wit-nessed the famous celebrity Dr. Maya Angelou in a headdress like a parrot and with a mighty voice, but you no doubt are eager to get back to the more historical highlights of our tour.

Yes, Theodore Pine's portrait here is the original, and the family said it was lifelike and true to their father's features, perhaps around the time of the Wilderness, though it was painted thirty years after his death on that chilling and killing October day from what some say was a stroke, and if he was in fact the victim of foul play, as I myself have sometimes suspected, *no evidence has surfaced* in all this time, but he was a strong man and a good one, younger than I am now—not old enough to easily succumb to the natural shocks that flesh is heir to. He used no spirits or nicotine and had always dis-played a flirtatious vigor, though Mary Chesnut's diaries remark that he was "so cold and quiet and grand" as a young man. No doubt he felt already the inconvenient weight of destiny, and she, as I remember, was blind to some species of charm. Yet if he was in fact the subject of knavery, *no verifiable evidence has ever surfaced,* though there was no official investigation—which should itself arouse our suspicions. We know the Northern press reviled him, and more than once public sentiment in the victorious states was roused toward trying him for treason and marching him straight to the gallows. So great a man cannot but beget enemies. I am certain you have known of plots yourself to undo the virtuous and lay waste to their peace of mind. Some men smile and smile and are villains, as the poet says. When the General breathed his last, the rain came down in torrents for days in a loud, tumultuous shouting sound, and flash floods were widespread and ruinous.

Few people are aware that the General's birthday, January 19, coincides with that of Edgar Allan Poe, who represents the dark side of our Virginia psyche. Fewer still realize that the General's extended family's loveliest estate was not Arlington, which was his wife's Custis dowry, but Ravensworth. If that connection is not enough to lend this chamber a chill, I ask you to imagine that perhaps Mr. Poe's "Annabel Lee" in fact concerns a young lady from family the poet could only aspire to. The cosmic inequities of romance abound. A sad prospect, but we may only ponder it and move on.

Above the wrought iron gate is the Lee family crest, with its Latin motto, *Ne incautus futuri,* which means not without regard for the future, a valuable reminder to those who would dance lighthearted till dawn rather than consider the demands of the morrow. My favorite detail is the squirrel rampant and feeding above the argent helm, which reminds us of those animals' foraging and storage, their self-sufficient happy chatter and industry, though Lee himself in no way resembled vermin. He was five feet eleven and every inch a king.

The centerpiece, of course, here under the various regimental Stars and Bars, is this recumbent statue carved from a single block of Vermont marble by Edward Valentine—truly his name, according to sources, but deceit abounds. He was said to be from Richmond (where I came out as a debutante further back than any of you can possibly remember), and I believe it is the rival of any statuary in Italy, where I have always hoped someday to visit, though I was long ago disappointed in my best opportunity. And strong as the temptation may be, please do not touch the statue, for any mortal contact would mar the surface of the stone, which is like the magnolia blossom itself. Have you ever touched a petal and watched it rust before your eyes? Precious things are the most vulnerable, for the slightest blemish can destroy. Could that be why we are most devoted to what must perish? He looks, in this muted light, serene at last.

I would like to direct your attention to the texture Mr. Valentine's chisel has given the General's campaign blanket, the soft-leather look of his boots, the elegant beard, but please, I repeat, do not touch the statue, for the living hand with its native oils will soil this chiseled stone. Our touch could not now warm him, and see how at peace he appears, in complete repose? He is and is not at once a "touchstone," but if you bend your ear closely, you can almost hear the beating of his hidden heart.

Mrs. Lee instructed that her beloved be depicted napping before an engagement, sword at his side, gauntlets nearby. He is not to be considered dead, but only resting, and there are some who claim that he might yet rise, might return when the Commonwealth most needs him, though his actual remains are located in the crypt beneath the stairs. Doesn't that word "crypt" remind you of the writings of Mr. Poe? It means a secret code. This chapel is, as you may have surmised, a structure with its own secrets.

Do you recall Mr. Disney's charming film *Snow White?* Since first I saw the princess in her trance I have thought of the General as someone under an enchantment, awaiting the right deliverer, but perhaps it is the trumpet of the Second Coming for which he waits. And no, I do not for a moment believe, as one rude visitor from Florida implied, that his effigy resembles a large salt lick which animals might tongue down to nothing. The very suggestion disgusts me. He could never under any circumstances be nothing and was present even when not in attendance. Mrs. Lee was herself chair-

bound and grew accustomed to his absence. She endured for three
sad years of widow-weeping after his untimely passing but at last
found the peace of oblivion. It is perhaps a peace we should not
ourselves underestimate.

As you know, General Lee could never sleep in a bed after Ap-
pomattox, for he was haunted by the many gallant men he had led
to the grave. In fact, who is to say that he ever truly left the war,
as he wore his gray coat and campaign hat with a military cord until
that October day when he succumbed. Considering his stern cor-
rectness and the martial bearing that he never abandoned, it would
not surprise me if he did not sometimes see the students as his
troopers and Lexington as beleaguered Richmond in miniature.
He wore the dignity of conflict to the end. His last words were,
"Strike the tent."

Now be careful as you descend the staircase. You will pass the
vault itself, which is carved into the bowels of the earth like a dun-
geon, with its many Lees walled in, from the rogue Lighthorse
Harry to his sons and grandsons, and you can see the diagram of
his family tree with its fabled roots deep in the richest Virginia soil.
Mrs. Lee herself is there behind the bricks, and so outspoken was
her love of cats, one can only speculate as to whether some feline
remains might be found there as well. Other relatives have been
unearthed from the cemeteries where they were first interred and
transported here in high ceremony, which is enough to make a
mere mortal's skin crawl, but you will appreciate how important it
was that they all come home.

Before I leave you to wander through the gallery with its pis-
tols and portraits, documents and costumes, and his office as he
left it, with maps and papers, his veteran Bible and the massive but
eloquent correspondence that he sustained like a man still issuing
orders, I would like—well, yes, I must remember to direct you to
the restrooms yonder and the gift shop where you might purchase
post cards, key chains, paperweights, bracelet charms, videos, and
other keepsakes. You will no doubt desire a souvenir of this visit.
As you pass his desk, I suggest you speculate on what momentous

documents hide there before our very eyes, in plain sight. It was there he wrote the college honor code and there he penned his personal motto: "Misfortune nobly borne is fortune," a code I always strive to honor.

And please do not forget to express your generosity in the contribution box, for though there is no charge for admission, the chapel does not sustain and clean itself like some haunted mansion but rather requires our vigilant assistance. So long as we can generate donations, this shrine is one cause that will not be lost.

There is time, here on the threshold, for one last morsel of history from Miss Sibby—the story of Traveller, the noble steed who is finally interred outside the lower exit. What an astonishing narrative his story is. He was born in 1857 and named Jeff Davis, then purchased in 1862 by the General, who renamed his mount after Washington's favorite stallion. He carried his master through the entire war and then to Lexington, where they were close companions, often making the jaunt to the mineral waters of Rockbridge Baths. Some evenings the General could think of nothing but the mud and gunfire, the broken bodies of young men, the twisted faces of the wounded and weevils in the meal, and on those occasions he would excuse himself from table and walk out to Traveller's stable, run his burdened hands down the muzzle and brushed mane of his boon companion, then step out to the garden to relieve himself in starlight, listening for ghosts, looking heavenward and weeping. "It is all my fault," he repeated after the bloodbath of Gettysburg, for he was not one to dodge responsibility, unlike some I might name.

Traveller marched solemnly at the funeral with boots reversed in his stirrups and lived until 1871, at which time he stepped on a rusty nail and died of lockjaw. (Does that strike you also as a little bit difficult to believe?) He was himself a symbol of the South's pride and beauty, and therefore had many enemies. Death loves a shining mark, and he was buried unceremoniously in a ravine cut by Woods Creek, but his amazing journey had just begun. Raised from the grave in 1875 by the Daughters, his bones were sent away for preservation, but an inexplicable red hue had infused them, and there was no turning them white. In 1907 the skeleton was returned and mounted in the museum, where the students who had earlier plucked souvenir strands from his tail—well, not those students, obviously, but later ones of the same ilk—circulated the word that academic success was insured by carving one's initials upon the bones, like sailors making scrimshaw. In a less harmful jest, a buck goat's bones were once smuggled into the museum, assembled beside the General's steed and accompanied by the label "Traveller as a colt." You cannot ever guess what boys will think of next, even after they rise to manhood and begin to sow promises like seeds, or pebbles that resemble seeds but yield no issue.

Beside the door you will see Traveller's memorial stone, which is even in this cold time of the year decorated by visitors with coins and candy, apples and miniature battle flags. It is a place for wishing and the site I linger at when my day here is finished and I am waiting for evening to embrace me.

If you should care to pose any questions about the General and his highborn kinsmen, his four maiden daughters or his influence on the liberal curriculum, I would be delighted to address them now, though I have decided it no longer prudent for me to speculate on what the General would have thought about the admission of females to the college or what his ghost might have to tell us about his sudden decline after the war or what he thought of the works of the scandalous and ill-fated Mr. Poe, who also attended West Point, but was more bête noir than noblesse oblige.

Now I must leave you, for the security guard on duty there with the evil-looking eye has taken it upon himself to restrict my tours to the chapel proper, which is why I at once savor and regret the fact that it has never been consecrated as a church. If you do not choose to rendezvous at the monument to equestrian fidelity, I thank you for your interest and kind attention to our sepulchral treasure as well as your indulgence of an old woman's eccentric ways. I bid you, now, at this charmed threshold, a fond and wistful adieu.

R. T. Smith's recent stories have appeared in the
Southern Review, the *Missouri Review,* the
Virginia Quarterly Review, and *New Stories from
the South: The Year's Best, 2002,* all from a new
story collection called *Jesus Wept.* His most recent
books are both collections of poetry: *The Hollow
Log Lounge* and *Brightwood.* Smith is the recipient
of a 2004 Fiction Fellowship from the Virginia
Commission for the Arts and edits *Shenandoah:
The Washington and Lee University Review.*

SARAH KENNEDY

*W*hen I was champing at the bit of adolescence, my paternal grand-
father (think Boss Priest in The Reivers*) presented me with his
embossed leather set of the Pulitzer editions of Douglas Southall Freeman's
hagiography of Lee because he saw that I was already an avid student of the
general's much-admired character and career. Over the years, the Lee shelf in
my bookcase has filled up with the more measured assessments of Marse
Robert, and I have begun to balance my old iconography with a salty
iconoclasm. Since coming to work for Washington and Lee University, where
the cult of Lee is not so rampant as one might imagine, I have found both my
reverence and my reservations escalating.*

    *Add to this my encounters with nearly demented museum docents in
Georgia and Alabama, and I began wondering (despite the taste and reserve
that govern the stewardship of the Lee Chapel on campus), "What if this
shrine I see almost daily utilized doting and wounded docents of the sort I
have seen elsewhere? Suppose one was teetering on the brink, half rogue
docent, half ghost? What would she sound like?"*

    *My own longtime lazy investigations of Lee and my notion of a deranged
docent converged as some sort of prayer on a small prop plane from Atlanta to
Montgomery one stormy morning, and I scribbled notes as fast as my jittery
hands could manage. It was pure fury at first, an aria in my head all week,
but when I returned home, the melody had cooled, and research was required.
This imagined voice crying in the wilderness is the result, and by the way,
most of the evidently "counterfeit" information that fuels the story is, actually,
real information. Honest.*

APPENDIX

A list of the magazines currently consulted for *New Stories from the South: The Year's Best, 2004,* with addresses, subscription rates, and editors.

The Antioch Review
P.O. Box 148
Yellow Springs, OH 45387-0148
Quarterly, $35
Robert S. Fogarty

Apalachee Review
P.O. Box 10469
Tallahassee, FL 32302
Semiannually, $15
Laura Newton

Appalachian Heritage
CPO 2166
Berea, KY 40404
Quarterly, $18
George Brosi

Arkansas Review
P.O. Box 1890
Arkansas State University
State University, AR 72467
Triannually, $20
Tom Williams

Arts & Letters
Campus Box 89
Georgia College & State University
Milledgeville, GA 31061-0490
Semiannually, $15
Martin Lammon

Atlanta
1330 W. Peachtree St.
Suite 450
Atlanta, GA 30309
Monthly, $14.95
Rebecca Burns

The Atlantic Monthly
77 N. Washington St.
Boston, MA 02114
Monthly, $39.95
C. Michael Curtis

The Baffler
P.O. Box 378293
Chicago, IL 60637
Annually, $24
Solveig Nelson

Bayou
Department of English
University of New Orleans
Lakefront
New Orleans, LA 70148
Semiannually, $10

Black Warrior Review
University of Alabama
P.O. Box 862936
Tuscaloosa, AL 35486-0027
Semiannually, $14
Fiction Editor

Boulevard
6614 Clayton Road, PMB 325
Richmond Heights, MO 63117
Triannually, $15
Richard Burgin

The Carolina Quarterly
Greenlaw Hall CB# 3520
University of North Carolina
Chapel Hill, NC 27599-3520
Triannually, $12
Fiction Editor

The Chariton Review
Truman State University
Kirksville, MO 63501
Semiannually, $9
Jim Barnes

The Chattahoochee Review
Georgia Perimeter College
2101 Womack Road
Dunwoody, GA 30338-4497
Quarterly, $16
Lawrence Hetrick

Chicago Quarterly Review
517 Sherman Ave.
Evanston, IL 60202
Quarterly
S. Afzal Haider

Cimarron Review
205 Morrill Hall
Oklahoma State University
Stillwater, OK 74078-0135
Quarterly, $24
E. P. Walkiewicz

Columbia
415 Dodge Hall
2960 Broadway
Columbia University
New York, NY 10027-6902

Semiannually, $15
Fiction Editor

Confrontation
English Department
C.W. Post of L.I.U.
Brookville, NY 11548
Semiannually, $10
Martin Tucker

Conjunctions
21 East 10th Street
New York, NY 10003
Semiannually, $18
Bradford Morrow

Crazyhorse
Department of English
College of Charleston
66 George St.
Charleston, SC 29424
Semiannually, $15
Bret Lott

Crucible
Barton College
P.O. Box 5000
Wilson, NC 27893-7000
Annually, $7
Terrence L. Grimes

Denver Quarterly
University of Denver
Denver, CO 80208
Quarterly, $20
Bin Ramke

The Distillery
Motlow State Comm. College
P.O. Box 8500
Lynchburg, TN 37352-8500
Semiannually, $15
Dawn Copeland

Epoch
251 Goldwin Smith Hall
Cornell University
Ithaca, NY 14853-3201
Triannually, $11
Michael Koch

Esquire
250 West 55th Street
New York, NY 10019
Monthly, $15.94

Fiction
c/o English Department
City College of New York
New York, NY 10031
Quarterly, $38
Mark J. Mirsky

Five Points
Georgia State University
MSC 8R0318
33 Gilmer St. SE, Unit 8
Atlanta, GA 30303-3083
Triannually, $20
Megan Sexton

The Florida Review
Department of English
University of Central Florida
Orlando, FL 32816
Semiannually, $10
Pat Rushin

Gargoyle
P.O. Box 6216
Arlington, VA 22206-0216
Annually, $20
Richard Peabody

The Georgia Review
University of Georgia
Athens, GA 30602-9009
Quarterly, $24
T. R. Hummer

The Gettysburg Review
Gettysburg College
Gettysburg, PA 17325-1491
Quarterly, $24
Peter Stitt

Glimmer Train Stories
710 SW Madison St., #504
Portland, OR 97205
Quarterly, $32
Susan Burmeister-Brown
      and Linda B. Swanson-Davies

Granta
1755 Broadway
5th Floor
New York, NY 10019-3780
Quarterly, $37
Ian Jack

The Greensboro Review
English Department
134 McIver Bldg.
University of North Carolina
P.O. Box 26170
Greensboro, NC 27412
Semiannually, $10
Jim Clark

Harper's Magazine
666 Broadway, 11th Floor
New York, NY 10012
Monthly, $21
Ben Metcalf

Hobart
9251 Densmore Ave. N.
Seattle, WA 98103
Biannually, $7
Aaron Burch

The Idaho Review
Boise State University
Department of English
1910 University Drive

Boise, ID 83725
Annually, $9.95
Mitch Wieland

Image
3307 Third Ave., W.
Center for Religious Humanism
Seattle, WA 98119
Quarterly, $36
Gregory Wolfe

Indiana Review
465 Ballantine Ave.
Indiana University
Bloomington, IN 47405
Semiannually, $12
Laura McCoid

The Iowa Review
308 EPB
University of Iowa
Iowa City, IA 52242-1492
Triannually, $20
David Hamilton

The Journal
Ohio State University
Department of English
164 W. 17th Avenue
Columbus, OH 43210
Semiannually, $12
Kathy Fagan and Michelle Herman

Kalliope
Florida Community College–
   Jacksonville
South Campus
11901 Beach Blvd.
Jacksonville, FL 32246
Triannually, $16
Mary Sue Koeppel

The Kenyon Review
Kenyon College
Gambier, OH 43022

Triannually, $25
David H. Lynn

The Literary Review
Fairleigh Dickinson University
285 Madison Avenue
Madison, NJ 07940
Quarterly, $18
René Steinke

Louisiana Literature
SLU-10792
Southeastern Louisiana
   University
Hammond, LA 70402
Semiannually, $12
Jack Bedell

The Louisville Review
Spalding University
851 South 4th Street
Louisville, KY 40203
Semiannually, $14
Sena Jeter Naslund

Lynx Eye
c/o ScribbleFest Literary Group
542 Mitchell Drive
Los Osos, CA 93402
Quarterly, $25
Pam McCully, Kathryn Morrison

Meridian
University of Virginia
P.O. Box 400145
Charlottesville, VA 22904-4145
Semiannually, $10
Jett McAlister

Mid-American Review
Department of English
Bowling Green State University
Bowling Green, OH 43403
Semiannually, $12
Michael Czyzniejewski

Mississippi Review
University of Southern
   Mississippi
Box 5144
Hattiesburg, MS 39406-5144
Semiannually, $15
Frederick Barthelme

The Missouri Review
1507 Hillcrest Hall
University of Missouri
Columbia, MO 65211
Triannually, $22
Speer Morgan

The Nebraska Review
Writers Workshop
Fine Arts Building 212
University of Nebraska at Omaha
Omaha, NE 68182-0324
Semiannually, $15
James Reed

New England Review
Middlebury College
Middlebury, VT 05753
Quarterly, $25
Stephen Donadio

New Millennium Writings
P.O. Box 2463
Knoxville, TN 37901
Annually, $12.95
Don Williams

New Orleans Review
P.O. Box 195
Loyola University
New Orleans, LA 70118
Semiannually, $12
Christopher Chambers, Editor

The New Yorker
4 Times Square
New York, NY 10036
Weekly, $44.95
Deborah Treisman, Fiction
   Editor

Nimrod International Journal
University of Tulsa
600 South College
Tulsa, OK 74104-3189
Semiannually, $17.50
Francine Ringold

The North American Review
University of Northern Iowa
1222 W. 27th Street
Cedar Falls, IA 50614-0516
Six times a year, $22
Grant Tracey

North Carolina Literary Review
English Department
2201 Bate Building
East Carolina University
Greenville, NC 27858-4353
Annually, $10
Margaret Bauer

Northwest Review
369 PLC
University of Oregon
Eugene, OR 97403
Triannually, $22
John Witte

Ontario Review
9 Honey Brook Drive
Princeton, NJ 08540
Semiannually, $16
Raymond J. Smith

Other Voices
University of Illinois at Chicago
Department of English (M/C 162)
601 S. Morgan Street
Chicago, IL 60607-7120
Semiannually, $12
Lois Hauselman

The Oxford American
(check the *Oxford American* Web
   site for updates on the magazine's
   current address and subscription
   rates: OxfordAmericanmag.com)

318   APPENDIX

The Paris Review
541 E. 72nd Street
New York, NY 10021
Quarterly, $40
Fiction Editor

Parting Gifts
March Street Press
3413 Wilshire Drive
Greensboro, NC 27408
Semiannually, $12
Robert Bixby

Pembroke Magazine
UNC-P, Box 1510
Pembroke, NC 28372-1510
Annually, $8
Shelby Stephenson

PEN America
PEN American Center
568 Broadway, Suite 401
New York, NY 10012
Semiannually, $20
M. Mark

Ploughshares
Emerson College
120 Boylston St.
Boston, MA 02116-4624
Triannually, $24
Don Lee

PMS
Univ. of Alabama at Birmingham
Department of English
HB 217, 900 S. 13th Street
1530 3rd Ave., S.
Birmingham, AL 35294-1260
Annually, $7
Linda Frost

Post Road Magazine
853 Broadway, Suite 1516
Box 85
New York, NY 10003

Semiannually, $16
Rebecca Boyd

Potomac Review
51 Mannakee Street
Rockville, MD 20850
Semiannually, $18
Eli Flam

Prairie Schooner
201 Andrews Hall
University of Nebraska
Lincoln, NE 68588-0334
Quarterly, $26
Hilda Raz

Puerto del Sol
Box 30001, Department 3E
New Mexico State University
Las Cruces, NM 88003-9984
Semiannually, $10
Kevin McIlvoy

River City
Department of English
University of Memphis
Memphis, TN 38152-6176
Semiannually, $12
Mary Leader

River Styx
634 North Grand Blvd.
12th Floor
St. Louis, MO 63103
Triannually, $20
Richard Newman

Roanoke Review
221 College Lane
Salem, VA 24153
Annually, $8
Melanie Almeder

Rockhurst Review
Department of English
Rockhurst University

1100 Rockhurst Rd.
Kansas City, MO 64110
Annually, $5
Patricia Cleary Miller

Santa Monica Review
Santa Monica College
1900 Pico Boulevard
Santa Monica, CA 90405
Semiannually, $12
Andrew Tonkovich

Shenandoah
Washington and Lee University
Mattingly House
Lexington, VA 24450
Quarterly, $22
R. T. Smith

The South Carolina Review
Center for Electronic and Digital
    Publishing
Clemson University
Strode Tower, Box 340522
Clemson, SC 29634
Semiannually, $20
Wayne Chapman

South Dakota Review
Box 111
University Exchange
University of South Dakota
Vermillion, SD 57069
Quarterly, $30
John R. Milton

Southern Exposure
P.O. Box 531
Durham, NC 27702
Quarterly, $24
Chris Kromm

Southern Humanities Review
9088 Haley Center
Auburn University

Auburn, AL 36849
Quarterly, $15
Dan R. Latimer and Virginia M.
    Kouidis

The Southern Review
43 Allen Hall
Louisiana State University
Baton Rouge, LA 70803-5005
Quarterly, $25
James Olney

Southwest Review
307 Fondren Library West
Box 750374
Southern Methodist University
Dallas, TX 75275
Quarterly, $24
Willard Spiegelman

Sou'wester
Department of English
Southern Illinois University at
    Edwardsville
Edwardsville, IL 62026-1438
Semiannually, $12
Allison Funk and Geoff Schmidt

StoryQuarterly
online submissions only:
www.storyquarterly.com
Annually, $10
M.M.M. Hayes

Tampa Review
University of Tampa
401 W. Kennedy Boulevard
Tampa, FL 33606-1490
Semiannually, $15
Richard Mathews

Texas Review
English Department Box 2146
Sam Houston State University
Huntsville, TX 77341-2146

Semiannually, $20
Paul Ruffin

The Threepenny Review
P.O. Box 9131
Berkeley, CA 94709
Quarterly, $25
Wendy Lesser

Timber Creek Review
8969 UNC-G Station
Greensboro, NC 27413
Quarterly, $16
John M. Freiermuth

Tin House
P.O. Box 10500
Portland, OR 97296-0500
Quarterly, $29.90
Rob Spillman

TriQuarterly
Northwestern University
629 Noyes St.
Evanston, IL 60208
Triannually, $24
Susan Firestone Hahn

The Virginia Quarterly Review
One West Range
P.O. Box 400223
Charlottesville, VA 22904-4223
Quarterly, $18
Ted Genoways

West Branch
Bucknell Hall
Bucknell University
Lewisburg, PA 17837
Semiannually, $7
Robert Love Taylor

Wind Magazine
P.O. Box 24548
Lexington, KY 40524
Triannually, $15
Chris Green

The Yalobusha Review
Department of English
University of Mississippi
P.O. Box 1848
University, MS 38677
Annually, $10
Joy Wilson

Yemassee
Department of English
University of South Carolina
Columbia, SC 29208
Semiannually, $15
Fiction Editor

Zoetrope: All-Story
The Sentinel Building
916 Kearny Street
San Francisco, CA 94133
Quarterly, $19.95
Tamara Straus

ZYZZYVA
P.O. Box 590069
San Francisco, CA 94159-0069
Triannually, varies
Howard Junker

PREVIOUS VOLUMES

Copies of previous volumes of *New Stories from the South* can be ordered through your local bookstore or by calling the Sales Department at Algonquin Books of Chapel Hill. Multiple copies for classroom adoptions are available at a special discount. For information, please call 919-967-0108.

NEW STORIES FROM THE SOUTH: THE YEAR'S BEST, 1986

Max Apple, BRIDGING

Madison Smartt Bell, TRIPTYCH 2

Mary Ward Brown, TONGUES OF FLAME

Suzanne Brown, COMMUNION

James Lee Burke, THE CONVICT

Ron Carlson, AIR

Doug Crowell, SAYS VELMA

Leon V. Driskell, MARTHA JEAN

Elizabeth Harris, THE WORLD RECORD HOLDER

Mary Hood, SOMETHING GOOD FOR GINNIE

David Huddle, SUMMER OF THE MAGIC SHOW

Gloria Norris, HOLDING ON

Kurt Rheinheimer, UMPIRE

W. A. Smith, DELIVERY

Wallace Whatley, SOMETHING TO LOSE

Luke Whisnant, WALLWORK

Sylvia Wilkinson, CHICKEN SIMON

New Stories from the South: The Year's Best, 1987

James Gordon Bennett, DEPENDENTS

Robert Boswell, EDWARD AND JILL

Rosanne Caggeshall, PETER THE ROCK

John William Corrington, HEROIC MEASURES/VITAL SIGNS

Vicki Covington, MAGNOLIA

Andre Dubus, DRESSED LIKE SUMMER LEAVES

Mary Hood, AFTER MOORE

Trudy Lewis, VINCRISTINE

Lewis Nordan, SUGAR, THE EUNUCHS, AND BIG G. B.

Peggy Payne, THE PURE IN HEART

Bob Shacochis, WHERE PELHAM FELL

Lee Smith, LIFE ON THE MOON

Marly Swick, HEART

Robert Love Taylor, LADY OF SPAIN

Luke Whisnant, ACROSS FROM THE MOTOHEADS

New Stories from the South: The Year's Best, 1988

Ellen Akins, GEORGE BAILEY FISHING

Rick Bass, THE WATCH

Richard Bausch, THE MAN WHO KNEW BELLE STAR

Larry Brown, FACING THE MUSIC

Pam Durban, BELONGING

John Rolfe Gardiner, GAME FARM

Jim Hall, GAS

Charlotte Holmes, METROPOLITAN

Nanci Kincaid, LIKE THE OLD WOLF IN ALL THOSE WOLF STORIES

Barbara Kingsolver, ROSE-JOHNNY

Trudy Lewis, HALF MEASURES

Jill McCorkle, FIRST UNION BLUES

Mark Richard, HAPPINESS OF THE GARDEN VARIETY

Sunny Rogers, THE CRUMB

Annette Sanford, LIMITED ACCESS

Eve Shelnutt, VOICE

NEW STORIES FROM THE SOUTH: THE YEAR'S BEST, 1989

Rick Bass, WILD HORSES

Madison Smartt Bell, CUSTOMS OF THE COUNTRY

James Gordon Bennett, PACIFIC THEATER

Larry Brown, SAMARITANS

Mary Ward Brown, IT WASN'T ALL DANCING

Kelly Cherry, WHERE SHE WAS

David Huddle, PLAYING

Sandy Huss, COUPON FOR BLOOD

Frank Manley, THE RAIN OF TERROR

Bobbie Ann Mason, WISH

Lewis Nordan, A HANK OF HAIR, A PIECE OF BONE

Kurt Rheinheimer, HOMES

Mark Richard, STRAYS

Annette Sanford, SIX WHITE HORSES

Paula Sharp, HOT SPRINGS

New Stories from the South: The Year's Best, 1990

New Stories from the South: The Year's Best, 1991

Nanci Kincaid, THIS IS NOT THE PICTURE SHOW

Bobbie Ann Mason, WITH JAZZ

Jill McCorkle, WAITING FOR HARD TIMES TO END

Robert Morgan, POINSETT'S BRIDGE

Reynolds Price, HIS FINAL MOTHER

Mark Richard, THE BIRDS FOR CHRISTMAS

Susan Starr Richards, THE SCREENED PORCH

Lee Smith, INTENSIVE CARE

Peter Taylor, COUSIN AUBREY

NEW STORIES FROM THE SOUTH: THE YEAR'S BEST, 1992

Alison Baker, CLEARWATER AND LATISSIMUS

Larry Brown, A ROADSIDE RESURRECTION

Mary Ward Brown, A NEW LIFE

James Lee Burke, TEXAS CITY, 1947

Robert Olen Butler, A GOOD SCENT FROM A STRANGE MOUNTAIN

Nanci Kincaid, A STURDY PAIR OF SHOES THAT FIT GOOD

Patricia Lear, AFTER MEMPHIS

Dan Leone, YOU HAVE CHOSEN CAKE

Reginald McKnight, QUITTING SMOKING

Karen Minton, LIKE HANDS ON A CAVE WALL

Elizabeth Seydel Morgan, ECONOMICS

Robert Morgan, DEATH CROWN

Susan Perabo, EXPLAINING DEATH TO THE DOG

Padgett Powell, THE WINNOWING OF MRS. SCHUPING

Lee Smith, THE BUBBA STORIES

Kathleen Cushman, LUXURY

Tony Earley, THE PROPHET FROM JUPITER

Pamela Erbe, SWEET TOOTH

Barry Hannah, NICODEMUS BLUFF

Nanci Kincaid, PRETENDING THE BED WAS A RAFT

Nancy Krusoe, LANDSCAPE AND DREAM

Robert Morgan, DARK CORNER

Reynolds Price, DEEDS OF LIGHT

Leon Rooke, THE HEART MUST FROM ITS BREAKING

John Sayles, PEELING

George Singleton, OUTLAW HEAD & TAIL

Melanie Sumner, MY OTHER LIFE

Robert Love Taylor, MY MOTHER'S SHOES

NEW STORIES FROM THE SOUTH: THE YEAR'S BEST, 1995

R. Sebastian Bennett, RIDING WITH THE DOCTOR

Wendy Brenner, I AM THE BEAR

James Lee Burke, WATER PEOPLE

Robert Olen Butler, BOY BORN WITH TATTOO OF ELVIS

Ken Craven, PAYING ATTENTION

Tim Gautreaux, THE BUG MAN

Ellen Gilchrist, THE STUCCO HOUSE

Scott Gould, BASES

Barry Hannah, DRUMMER DOWN

MMM Hayes, FIXING LU

Hillary Hebert, LADIES OF THE MARBLE HEARTH

Jesse Lee Kercheval, GRAVITY

NEW STORIES FROM THE SOUTH: THE YEAR'S BEST, 1996

NEW STORIES FROM THE SOUTH: THE YEAR'S BEST, 1997

NEW STORIES FROM THE SOUTH: THE YEAR'S BEST, 1998

New Stories from the South: The Year's Best, 1999

William Gay, THOSE DEEP ELM BROWN'S FERRY BLUES

Mary Gordon, STORYTELLING

Ingrid Hill, PAGAN BABIES

Michael Knight, BIRDLAND

Kurt Rheinheimer, NEIGHBORHOOD

Richard Schmitt, LEAVING VENICE, FLORIDA

Heather Sellers, FLA. BOYS

George Singleton, CAULK

NEW STORIES FROM THE SOUTH: THE YEAR'S BEST, 2000

PREFACE *by Ellen Douglas*

A. Manette Ansay, BOX

Wendy Brenner, MR. PUNIVERSE

D. Winston Brown, IN THE DOORWAY OF RHEE'S JAZZ JOINT

Robert Olen Butler, HEAVY METAL

Cathy Day, THE CIRCUS HOUSE

R.H.W. Dillard, FORGETTING THE END OF THE WORLD

Tony Earley, JUST MARRIED

Clyde Edgerton, DEBRA'S FLAP AND SNAP

Tim Gautreaux, DANCING WITH THE ONE-ARMED GAL

William Gay, MY HAND IS JUST FINE WHERE IT IS

Allan Gurganus, HE'S AT THE OFFICE

John Holman, WAVE

Romulus Linney, THE WIDOW

Thomas McNeely, SHEEP

Christopher Miner, RHONDA AND HER CHILDREN

Chris Offutt, THE BEST FRIEND

Margo Rabb, HOW TO TELL A STORY

Karen Sagstetter, THE THING WITH WILLIE

Mary Helen Stefaniak, A NOTE TO BIOGRAPHERS REGARDING FAMOUS
   AUTHOR FLANNERY O'CONNOR

Melanie Sumner, GOOD-HEARTED WOMAN

NEW STORIES FROM THE SOUTH: THE YEAR'S BEST, 2001

PREFACE *by Lee Smith*

John Barth, THE REST OF YOUR LIFE

Madison Smartt Bell, TWO LIVES

Marshall Boswell, IN BETWEEN THINGS

Carrie Brown, FATHER JUDGE RUN

Stephen Coyne, HUNTING COUNTRY

Moira Crone, WHERE WHAT GETS INTO PEOPLE COMES FROM

William Gay, THE PAPERHANGER

Jim Grimsley, JESUS IS SENDING YOU THIS MESSAGE

Ingrid Hill, JOLIE-GRAY

Christie Hodgen, THE HERO OF LONELINESS

Nicola Mason, THE WHIMSIED WORLD

Edith Pearlman, SKIN DEEP

Kurt Rheinheimer, SHOES

Jane R. Shippen, I AM NOT LIKE NUÑEZ

George Singleton, PUBLIC RELATIONS

Robert Love Taylor, PINK MIRACLE IN EAST TENNESSEE

James Ellis Thomas, THE SATURDAY MORNING CAR WASH CLUB

Elizabeth Tippens, MAKE A WISH

Linda Wendling, INAPPROPRIATE BABIES

Brock Clarke, FOR THOSE OF US WHO NEED SUCH THINGS

Lucy Corin, RICH PEOPLE

John Dufresne, JOHNNY TOO BAD

Donald Hays, DYING LIGHT

Ingrid Hill, THE BALLAD OF RAPPY VALCOUR

Bret Anthony Johnston, CORPUS

Michael Knight, ELLEN'S BOOK

Patricia Lear, NIRVANA

Peter Meinke, UNHEARD MUSIC

Chris Offutt, INSIDE OUT

ZZ Packer, EVERY TONGUE SHALL CONFESS

Michael Parker, OFF ISLAND

Paul Prather, THE FAITHFUL

Brad Vice, REPORT FROM JUNCTION

Latha Viswanathan, COOL WEDDING

Mark Winegardner, KEEGAN'S LOAD